The Paris Wife

BOOKS BY MEGHAN MASTERSON

The Queen's Dressmaker

MEGHAN MASTERSON

The
Paris
Wife

bookouture

Published by Bookouture in 2021

An imprint of Storyfire Ltd.
Carmelite House
50 Victoria Embankment
London EC4Y 0DZ

www.bookouture.com

ISBN: 978-1-80019-690-2
eBook ISBN: 978-1-80019-689-6

For Scott, who made the bad times better

CHAPTER ONE

Paris, August 1856

*Belladonna, or deadly nightshade, is also called atropine,
a Latin derivative of the name of Atropos, one of the three
Fates of Greek mythology. Atropos chose the death of mortals
and cut the thread of their lives from her loom.*
— Excerpt from Livia Valenti's book of herbal studies

Caterina has forgotten her tarot cards on the low side table in front of the window. The bright colors of the deck stand out against the gray sky and silver spatter of rain on the glass, drawing my gaze. I run my finger over the stiff edges of the cards, and a few of them slide free of the stack. I don't believe in predicting the future through tarot, but I pick up the new top card anyway, idly glancing at the scene painted upon it. The artwork is quite fine. I can understand why Caterina likes to look at them so often.

"Which one is it?" she asks, coming into the room.

I replace the card and straighten the deck, turning away from it. "The Two of Swords."

"Reversed?"

"No, it was upright."

"It makes sense," Caterina says. "The Two of Swords tends to come up in a stalemate situation, when a person is facing a choice but imagines that if they ignore it long enough, it'll go away. It could mean you're in a state of indecision, feeling weighted down and uncertain of how to proceed. You want to protect yourself but are afraid to make the wrong decision."

I suppress the urge to roll my eyes. Caterina doesn't deserve my scorn. Although I don't share her interest in divination—I prefer facts—she doesn't mean any harm by it. "I'd need two swords for protection, then? What's the blindfold for?" I ask, referring to the woman painted on the card. Dressed in a white gown, she holds two swords crossed over her breast, which might be a good defense except for the fact she's also blindfolded by a white ribbon, while a dangerously rock-studded sea churns behind her.

Caterina smiles, knowing I'm humoring her. "It means you can't see past your indecision, past the situations you've found yourself in."

I scoop up the deck of cards and pass them to her. "How unfortunate for me." Bitterness winds through my voice, and I immediately feel a pang of regret. It isn't Caterina's fault that my first tarot reading promised a drastically different future than the one that fell around me like a net, proving it's all nonsense. It isn't Caterina's fault that I'm not happy. "I'm sorry, Caterina. You know I'm a skeptic."

She tucks the cards into the pocket of her skirt. "Don't apologize. I just think they're rather fun, that's all."

Crossing to the other window framing the front of the room, where I keep a pot of mint on the matching side table, I gaze at the wet street below. "It never seems to rain long in Paris, but I wish it would stop now. I'd like some fresh air."

"I know you're longing to get out into the garden," says Caterina. "If we were staying here for more than a few months, you'd be planting herbs every day, wouldn't you, Livia?" She glances at me with affection, knowing the mention of herbs always sparks my interest. Growing up with my doctor father and his medical knowledge, I know dozens of uses for nearly every kind of plant.

"I might begin anyway. There's not much else to do." My husband, Niccolo, rented this house in Paris only a fortnight after our marriage. Having to leave the bronzed beauty of my beloved Turin left a bruise against my already wounded spirits, but there wasn't any choice. Niccolo works for Conte Camillo Cavour, the prime minister of Piedmont-Sardinia. Conte Cavour is a fervent believer in a unified Italy, and he sent his scandalously beautiful cousin, the contessa di Castiglione, to Paris to sway the emperor, Napoleon III, to his cause. To achieve his vision of a united Italy, he'd need the assistance of the French ruler—and his troops—to throw off the Austrian rule in the north. As far as I can surmise, though no one has told me anything, La Castiglione's mission is not proceeding with enough speed, or she's else not sending back enough information, since Niccolo is obliged to be here as another diplomatic set of eyes and ears for Cavour.

We live in a large, elegant house on avenue Joséphine, which I'm told is a very fashionable street, located on the right bank of the Seine and not too far from the Bois de Boulogne, but relocating to Paris only a fortnight after our hasty wedding only added to my feeling of rootlessness. I'm curious to meet the contessa, but we've been here for two weeks already with no word from her at all.

"If you can't go outside, you could always sew more swaddling blankets."

Caterina smiles at the way my lip curls at her teasing suggestion. My fingers already ache from the extra time I've devoted to that task over the last week, driven by the reason that the blankets will be needed soon enough.

I stretch my hand toward the pot of mint, brushing my fingertips across the jagged edge of a leaf. The movement stirs its clean, cool scent into the air, and a spark of purpose clears my mind and straightens my spine. I retreat from the window and fetch my shoes. I didn't choose the circumstances that brought me here, but I won't let them control my life going forward.

"I'll be outside." This house has a small garden, but it's been neglected and most of the plants are useless flowers, although they're quite pretty, even now at the end of summer. "You don't have to come with me—I know you don't like the rain."

Caterina and I always speak with companionable bluntness while in the privacy of my room, although we try to be more careful if Niccolo is within earshot. Ostensibly my maid, Caterina is also my dearest friend, and came with me to my married household in Turin, following us to France. She isn't a very good maid, as the shawls and dresses scattered across the bed can attest, but she is an excellent confidante.

"I'll tidy up in here instead." Caterina waves airily toward the disarray of the room. "Or I could finish sewing the red gown you started. It won't take long, there's hardly any fabric." This is true, since it's a tiny garment for an infant.

My palm sweeps reflexively over my belly, only slightly rounded so far. "Thank you, Caterina. I meant to finish it earlier but my back ached too much."

"All the more reason to stretch your legs now," she says kindly.

Downstairs, I hurry past the parlor, seeing Niccolo's fawn-colored hound, Luce, sprawled in the doorway. He follows Niccolo everywhere, so his presence is a certain signal that my husband is sitting in the parlor, and I don't particularly want to make small talk with him at the moment.

Once I've slipped through the back door into the verdant space of the garden, the misty raindrops feel fresh and invigorating against my cheeks. The damp smell of earth and greenery lifts my spirits. The spears of day lily leaves and the dark purple of violets look decorative, but as I pace around, I imagine where I would plant more useful herbs. There isn't much space, so I'd need to concentrate on the most common medicines. Calendula, which is good for skin conditions, would grow well in the corner, laden with sunshine on a clear day, and their jaunty orange shade would look pretty against the stone color of the house. I've mentally plotted the layout a dozen times already, and yet haven't started transforming the garden at all. Though it might give me pleasure while we're here, it seems a possible waste of time when we're meant to return to Turin within the next year.

Back inside, I don't manage to avoid Niccolo again. He must have heard the door, for he lingers in the hallway near the parlor, watching for me. It's the first time I've seen him today. I took breakfast alone in my room, using pregnancy nausea as an excuse, although I feel well enough today.

"How are you this morning, Livia?" His voice sounds calm and steady. I've never seen Niccolo ruffled. His expression does flicker slightly as he notices the streak of mud decorating the hem of my skirt, but his tone remains pleasant. "It must be quite wet in the garden. I hope you aren't chilled."

"I'm fine, thank you." My reply comes out more briskly than I meant, but Niccolo's tendency to constant solicitude makes me feel like an invalid, or a soft, spoiled lady who doesn't know how to fluff her own pillows. I daresay he'd be shocked to hear the details of some of the tasks I helped my father with, including stitching up wounds and once cauterizing an amputated arm. A little rain certainly won't hurt me.

"I'm happy to hear it." He clears his throat to cover the silence falling between us. "We've been invited to visit Virginia Oldoini, the contessa di Castiglione, this afternoon."

"It isn't much notice." I'm caught off guard.

"I'm sorry for that. I have some news from home to pass along to her, and I know she's curious to meet you, but if you aren't feeling well enough, I can make excuses."

"No, I'd like to go. It just caught me by surprise, that's all." My cheeks warm as I think of the mud carelessly spattered on my gown, my hair in a loose braid, how my disarrayed appearance would contrast with the contessa's worldly sophistication. "What time? I must dress more properly for the occasion."

"Not until three o'clock. You have time." He lifts his hand as if to brush the stray curl of hair away from my cheek, but checks the motion. "I think you look very well." His gold lashes fan across his cheekbones as his gaze shifts down, away from mine, and his voice drops to an awkward rumble. "Radiant, even."

"It's the rain," I say, dumbfounded, and awkwardly feeling as though I must make an explanation. Niccolo isn't usually one for compliments. "Also, I mixed a new skin cream last week. I suppose it must be effective." I made it to alleviate a fit of pure boredom, being accustomed to helping my father dispense medicines and treatments, and now having almost nothing to do during the day. "I'll go and get changed," I say, hastily heading for the stairs.

Caterina clicks her tongue in annoyance at the sight of the mud on my skirt.

"It doesn't matter," I say. "This is an old dress. I'll just wear it outside again tomorrow, no sense cleaning it yet." My wardrobe has improved since my marriage, though I sometimes take comfort in wearing my old favorite gowns at home. As I go to the wardrobe and sift through the soft linens and silks, I'm grateful for Niccolo's generosity since I'll be able to wear something appropriate for meeting a countess.

Caterina helps me choose a dress in a delicate dove-gray shade, fastening a necklace with a single pearl as a pendant around my throat. Since I'd removed it before going out to the garden, I slip on my wedding ring too, admiring the garnet stone as it manages to glint even in the dull light drizzling through the lacy curtains of my bedroom. I'm still wearing my bracelet—I never take it off.

Niccolo says nothing about my appearance but helps me into the carriage with a polite smile and a reassuring squeeze of my hand. I would have preferred to walk—everyone knows where La Castiglione lives on avenue Montaigne, and it's a short distance from our house—but the sky darkens anew, slivers of rain darting relentlessly through the air.

"Here we are," says Niccolo, as we alight from the closed carriage a short while later. If I thought our Parisian residence was stylish, I see now it's snug compared to the almost daunting sumptuousness of La Castiglione's house. A requirement for the mistress of the emperor, I suppose, for he must visit her home on occasion.

After we're admitted by a footman in a formal velvet frock coat, I can't help staring in awe at the interior. The high ceiling and wide windows let in airy beams of light—or they would, on a sunnier day. In its absence today, the lamps are all lit, reflecting golden light off the marble-tiled floor, and the furniture gleams with polish. Its scent of lemons hovers in the air, a crisper undertone to the heavier, floral aroma of the enormous roses heaped into a vase near the doorway of the drawing room.

"The contessa will be with your shortly," says the footman. "You may wait for her in the salon."

I perch on the edge of a green velvet couch, while Niccolo stands in front of an unlit fireplace, hands clasped behind his back. Though he tilts his head as if studying the lavish painting of a gauze-draped, rosy-skinned nymph, his fingers tap together with impatience. He turns away all at once, the jerkiness of his motion and the faint redness creeping along his collar making me think that perhaps he wasn't really seeing the painting at all—until he realized it might seem strange to stare at a large portrait of a scantily clad nymph in front of his wife.

"The painting is well done," I say, to reassure him. It doesn't bother me if he admires it. "The apple in her hand is particularly lifelike."

He opens his mouth to reply, and then from somewhere else in the house, a door slams closed, and two male voices drift through the corridor: the footman and a man who has evidently just arrived at the house.

Niccolo's attention swerves toward the sound. His feet already move toward the doorway as he glances back over his shoulder at me. "I'm so sorry—you must excuse me for a moment. I'll return quickly."

Before I can speak, he disappears down the hallway, leaving me alone in La Castiglione's salon. Without him, the opulence of the room feels cold, its lavish decorations impersonal. The nymph looks insufferable, her rosebud mouth twisted into a smug little smile. I'd be very surprised if the contessa uses this room often. It has the feel of a space kept mostly empty.

After a moment or two, I feel as stiff as the overstuffed sofa cushion, as out of place as the sheet of paper lying crookedly on the otherwise spotless table across the room. I rise and let my curiosity lead me toward it.

The paper turns out to be a photograph, one of the finest I've ever seen, the image clear and vivid. I don't touch it—I haven't seen many photographs this close before—but after only a casual glance, the portrait captures my attention fully. The woman in the picture stares out of the frame, right at the viewer, her expression aloof yet somehow enticing. Her dress, a lavish and voluminous affair of black tulle, spills down to her feet, but leaves her shoulders scandalously bare to show the drapery of pearls at her throat, only a little paler than the exposed swathe of her flawless skin. I've never seen such sultry confidence, and though I can't imagine wearing such a frivolous, beautiful gown, I admire the intricate style of her hair, braided into a diadem.

"I see you're admiring my portrait. I'm quite fond of that one; I posed for it only a few months after I arrived in Paris."

Startled by the sound of a woman's voice, I straighten and turn to see the newcomer so quickly that my head spins. The cascade of her golden hair and the narrow waist of her glimmering scarlet gown can only belong to La Castiglione. As I take a step forward to greet her, hoping it hasn't seemed like I was snooping through her salon, my belly lurches, twisting into a knot that tickles my throat. I freeze, grabbing at the back of a chair, and pray I don't vomit.

"Are you well, Livia?" Dimly, I register she knows who I am. She must have run into Niccolo in the hall. She reaches my side in an instant, seizing my elbow to offer support. My heartbeat drums in my ears while dark spots dance in front of my vision and my head spins. I take a deep breath, and the feeling slowly ebbs, leaving only an irritating trace of nausea. And a healthy dose of embarrassment. From the scalding heat of them, I'm sure my cheeks must be crimson.

"My apologies, signora," I say breathlessly. "I get moments of dizziness sometimes. It has passed now."

"You must eat something," she announces. "I get lightheaded when I'm hungry, too. I often have a bite to eat at this time of day myself, but I haven't called for anything yet." The contessa grips my arm between her slender, strong fingers. The scent of lilies clouds around her, and for a moment I think my dizziness will return, but it passes as she steers me toward the kitchen. "Won't they be surprised?" Delight turns her voice as musical and dainty as wind chimes, and her blue eyes gleam. "I almost never venture into the kitchen. I daresay it'll give poor Marco a fit of nerves. I hired an Italian cook recently, you know. I lasted the first six months with a French one, but in the end I missed *cantuccini* too much. Those little almond biscuits always make me feel warm somehow."

"I understand that feeling," I say. "I'm a bit homesick myself."

"Don't worry. It passes." She pushes the door open. "Paris is a remarkable city. And now you must tell me what you want to eat."

The bustle of the kitchen nearly overwhelms my senses, with the clang of pots and the smell of garlic and fish and smoke.

Though the oven stands at the far end from me, I feel the dry caress of its heat curling through the bread-scented air. A tidy bunch of sage lies on the table, ready for chopping, and a stray parchment of garlic skin floats across the floor in the wake of the apprentice's steps as he carries spices.

"I don't want to intrude on your hospitality." My voice sounds as timid and tentative as I feel. "It's very kind of you, of course, to offer—"

"Don't be absurd. Choose something. I'm rather fond of berries, myself. Perhaps you'd like to eat some of those? Or maybe the *cantuccini*?"

The cook, Marco, lays his paring knife amid ribbons of lemon peel, and smiles. Though his gaze skates over me with cursory politeness, his attention focuses on the contessa, gravitating toward her the way a flower follows a beam of afternoon sunshine.

"Signora contessa, I can put together a plate of *cantuccini*, as well as fresh *baci di dama*, or perhaps some berries. We have some nice, ripe currants, or the bread is freshly baked." He gestures toward a selection of food piled to the side of the counter, clearly in preparation for the contessa to request her afternoon food preferences.

I slide my gaze over a basket of small, fist-sized rolls of white bread, next to a plate of golden *cantuccini*, dusted with fine white sugar, and the *baci di dama*, crisp hazelnut biscuits pressed together with chocolate filling. The cluster of rosy grapes and a white bowl of dark berries, probably the currants he mentioned, hold more appeal than I expected. My gaze turns longing as I stare at the luscious, dark berries and my mouth waters at the memory of the sharp-sweet flavor of currants. A hunger pang shakes my insides as if the baby is leaching everything from me, down to the marrow of my bones.

"The currants," says the contessa gaily. "I might have made the same choice. Go on—help yourself."

Marco slides the bowl across the counter toward me, still watching the contessa. As I reach for the dish of currants, my eyes narrow. About half of the berries are larger and blacker than most of the currants. Not many would notice, especially since they're well-mingled, but I'm not a doctor's daughter for nothing. A pang runs through my body that makes my blood feel slow and thick in my veins.

Those are deadly nightshade berries. I would swear it.

CHAPTER TWO

Paris, August 1856

Thornapple is too bitter to eat, but the seeds could be made into a tea or sprinkled over bread. Signs of thornapple poisoning include dilated pupils, delirium, and drowsiness.
— Excerpt from Livia Valenti's book of herbal studies

Marco sees me staring at the berries, and I catch a flash of his grin as he reaches for an apple, twirling his knife. "They look tasty, don't they?"

"I'm not sure they're currants." I hate the uncertain tone of my voice but can't quite erase the cautious note.

He glances at them again, his gaze sweeping and quick. "Forgive me, signora, but perhaps you would prefer to eat something else if the berries are not to your liking." His knife snicks cleanly through the apple, and he proffers half of it. "An apple?" His courteous smile feels grating, as if he humors me like a child.

Beside me, La Castiglione fidgets, sweeping her finger through a splash of flour on the counter, and then wiping it against the gauzy shawl draped carelessly over her shoulders. "Please, choose anything you like, and then we'll go back upstairs." Her charming smile lights up her face, making her eyes seem almost violet, but I catch a brittle edge to her tone. She shifts closer toward the door, calling a command to one of the maids hurrying through the hallway.

I examine the berries again. It would be easy for an amateur to pick deadly nightshade berries, completely oblivious to their danger, and I almost doubt my instincts. Surely such carelessness wouldn't happen in such a prestigious kitchen as this? But as I inspect them, my certainty only grows. Dread spikes along my skin and my heart beats faster. These berries look luscious and tempting, but they're sickness and death wrapped in juicy purple ripeness.

My warning freezes in my throat as I look up, and neither the cook nor the contessa are paying the slightest attention to me. I can't think how to tell them without sounding paranoid or foolish. After Marco's dismissal, I don't think they'll believe me. Caterina's tarot card, the Two of Swords upright, flits into my mind unbidden, and I remember her description that it means being trapped in stasis, avoiding choices and responsibility. Resentment burns under my skin; I've been helpless and indecisive for too long. I can't be that way any longer.

Acting out of pure, visceral instinct, I knock the bowl from the table. It takes only a small nudge, and neither Marco nor La Castiglione notice the movement. It clatters to the floor, breaking into three triangular pieces. The berries scatter, pooling amid the broken glass and rolling under the table. I can't risk anyone thriftily scooping them up and rinsing them off, so with an exclamation of dismay, I crouch as if to clean up the mess, making sure to shuffle my feet and crush many of them. The purple juice ruins my fine white shoes, but I don't care.

Marco rushes to my side. "Signora, let me!"

"I'm sorry. My hand slipped as I picked up the dish."

He clucks soothingly. "It's no matter. It will be easy to clean up." He glances toward the contessa, making sure she sees his helpfulness. He reminds me of a puppy eager for praise. It unfurls a shadow of regret for the mess, but at least I know no one will ingest the berries now. That shadow darkens to suspicion when I realize Marco himself could have procured the berries. Or perhaps they were picked accidentally, which would not be an unheard-of error, though a tragic one. Filled with confusion, and cheeks scalding from the acute glare the countess levels in my direction, I can hardly steady my voice as I ask if there are any more berries.

Apparently assuming I wanted to eat them, Marco shakes his head with regret. "I'm afraid not, signora. Please, take this plate of *cantuccini* instead. I will send up something to drink shortly."

"Perhaps you ought to sit down." The contessa herds me through the door with a regal sweep of her arm. I don't dare resist. "I hope you won't suffer so much dizziness for the entirety of your pregnancy."

I glance at her in surprise. My belly doesn't show yet, at least not under the loose sweep of my skirt, with my special maternity corset holding my waist just above its swell, and I haven't spoken of it to anyone outside the household. It's difficult to imagine serious, reserved Niccolo announcing it, but now I wonder if he has.

Her mercurial smile flashes again, unexpectedly kind. "I'm right, am I not? I have a young son of my own; I recognize the signs in another woman."

"You are. And I hope so, too. The illness is mostly sporadic."

"Good. Of course, you must know how to treat it. I'm told your father is doctor to my cousin Camillo's household." In spite of the return of her friendly tone, I feel as though I'm trailing after her down the hall, always one step behind her elegant, hip-swaying steps, her long, slender neck half turned to address me as she hurries back to the salon.

"Yes," I confirm, glancing around the room. Niccolo is still absent.

"If you're like me, the nausea and dizziness will be all over after the first three months. And then the next three—they can be quite diverting." Her smile takes on a wicked edge, and laughter rolls from her throat, rich and sweet as burnt sugar. "I never expected that a child in the womb would give me such desire, even for my husband."

A sliver of heat burns along my cheekbones, and I hope she doesn't notice me blushing. Her free-spirited worldliness makes me dread appearing shy and prudish by contrast. "Er, is he in Paris with you?" I ask.

"Yes, but after a few months I insisted on my own residence. It was too awkward having him hanging about the house during the emperor's visits." His title falls from her lips as if gilded, the words ringing with a possessive kind of pride. "We're separated now. I can't say I miss Francesco, particularly. Ours was not a love match, though it was a good marriage. It's because of him I can call myself Contessa di Castiglione. My father was a marchese, of course, but Francesco was appointed aide-de-camp to the king back in Piedmont, so he's quite well connected." She proffers the plate of *cantuccini*, and I take one obediently. "And you? Are you fond of your husband?"

The almond biscuit feels dry and rock-hard between my fingertips. "We are so recently married, it is too soon to say." I regret my candor almost at once. "That is, he's good to me and I'm trying to settle in here, in Paris."

She nods sympathetically, her lips pursed. She sits on the sofa as if she'll be photographed or painted any moment, her arm bent, chin resting on her hand, head somehow still tilted at a graceful angle so her golden hair falls over her shoulder like a waterfall. With her place at court and the emperor's side, I imagine she must be accustomed to being watched constantly. Life must be a performance to her, and I can't believe I confessed anything of my disappointments in marriage.

"I hope you'll let me help you settle in," she says. "We must be friends, of course. It's such a comfort to have another Italian woman to converse with. I can introduce you to the best dress-makers, take you around to the most fashionable places. Are you interested in photography? I'm quite fascinated with it. You saw my portrait on the table over there, but I have a few others. I met the most interesting photographer, Monsieur Pierre-Louis Pierson." She slips into flawless French pronunciation when uttering his name. "His work is favored by the court, which is how I heard of him, but I've posed for several photographs at his studio, including the one you saw. I love photography as an art form. To capture a moment in time and preserve it forever is almost a miracle, don't you think? I have many ideas for more photographs, and I'm sure I'll be at Pierson's studio many days to come."

Sometime during her enthusiastic description of Pierson's studio, a maid creeps in with a tray of tea and more food to nibble on. I scan the plate with wary eyes, noting the rosy grapes, soft white rolls of bread, and some kind of tart with a pale, creamy filling. No berries, and each item looks expensive and delectable, not dangerous at all.

"Are you still hungry? Please, help yourself to anything." Generosity floats through her tone, but the glance she flicks to the forgotten almond biscuit in my hand carries a distinct amount of reproach.

I exhale slowly to keep my voice from shaking. I'm still confused by the incident in the kitchen, and combined with La Castiglione's scrutiny, it adds up to nervousness that makes my hands tremble.

"I must tell you something, signora. I should have spoken sooner, only I wasn't quite sure how to bring it up. I don't want to frighten you."

She was listening with a careless half-smile curling around her lips, her hands draped in her lap, but at my last sentence, she grows tense. Though her posture doesn't change, still reclining against the back of the sofa, alertness narrows her gaze and sharpens each line of her body, surrounding her like an aura. "Go on." Her voice becomes clipped and hard.

"The berries… I did not spill them by accident. I didn't want you—or anyone—to eat them." I lick my lips, which feel dry as paper. "I think some nightshade berries were mixed into the bowl. I've studied some poisons, you see."

Her brows arch slightly, the corners of her lips pinching. I squeeze my fingers together until the knuckles whiten, bracing myself for her insistence that I was mistaken. I don't expect her to believe me, and now that we're sitting in the elegant parlor with fresh tea in bone china cups and sweet, golden-brown biscuits resting on a silver-trimmed plate, I almost distrust my own earlier certainty. It seems too incongruous to be real.

She speaks slowly. "I'm sure it must have been a mistake."

Thinking she means my mistake, I smooth a wrinkle in my pale gray skirt, forming an apology in my mind. When I look up, she stares back at me with wide, frightened eyes, and I realize she does believe me, after all.

"Yes, most likely. It isn't easy to tell the dangerous ones from the good ones. I wish I hadn't smashed them all now. I almost doubt my own certainty… I think I panicked."

Her mouth quirks. "You certainly were zealous in your destruction of the berries. Your shoes are ruined. I can see the purple stains on them from here."

A tremulous laugh rips from my throat, taking my nervousness with it. "It doesn't matter. They pinched my toes anyway."

La Castiglione rises from her seat across from mine, and sits beside me. She bends her face close, as if we share secrets. "I have enemies, no doubt. Anyone close to the emperor surely must, for a connection to him grants power, and power is what all people desire. However, I confess it's difficult to imagine I could have an enemy so ferocious as to send poisonous berries to my household."

"It could have been an accident. On my part, recognizing them in error, or on the part of the person who picked and sold them."

"I will question Marco to find out where they were obtained."

"I'm sure you'll find it was a mistake." I try to sound soothing, and I must succeed because she reaches for my hand, squeezing it once. Her enormous emerald ring digs into my skin.

"I pray you're right." She releases my hand, leaning back, but her gaze fixes intently on my face, those blue irises peering as if she'd stare into my soul. "I think I ought to keep you close, Livia. A countrywoman, as well as a woman knowledgeable about medicines… I'm glad you've come to Paris. Thank you for telling me about the berries."

"I should have at once. I had to do something, and I feared you would not believe me."

"So you smashed the bowl. A bit drastic, but effective." Her smile flashes, luminous as moonlight. "I was quite irritated with you in the moment, you know. And the whole time you were probably saving my life."

"I know it was drastic." Her warm gratitude, the way she leans toward me as if we're sharing secrets, makes me speak freely. "I kept thinking of my friend Caterina's wretched tarot card that she pulled for me this morning, telling me to take action, and I couldn't hold back from doing something decisive." I fumble over the description, realizing too late this is far too specific for the contessa, but my nerves are still ragged.

To my surprise, La Castiglione tilts her head, eyes brightening with interest. "Tarot? Does this Caterina do readings upon request? I've always had a fascination with the occult, but it's been years since I gained any knowledge of my future. I could use it now."

Her enthusiasm deters me from sharing my own thoughts on the fallibility of the cards, so I nod. "Caterina is my maid, and also my friend." It's easy to reply with perfect truth that Caterina would likely be delighted to discuss the cards with the contessa. I can hardly wait to see the expression on her face when she hears of the contessa's interest.

"You must call upon me again, then, and bring Caterina with you. Perhaps we can also discuss other matters of your medical knowledge. I've been longing for a new skin cream." Her fingertips caress her cheek. "My whole reputation is built upon the foundation of my beauty, you know. I must preserve it." She speaks matter-of-factly, her beauty so widely and consistently acknowledged that she seems to possess no modesty or humbleness about it at all.

"Of course," I say, grateful Niccolo warned me she might ask for this. The topic is fresh in my mind, and I've thought of a few possible suggestions for her. "I could create something exclusive to you, prepared for your specifications."

"It must have a pleasant smell," she says. "The emperor likes to rest his chin just here—" Tilting her head to the side, she slides her fingers across the delicate line of her throat, over her collarbone, and I can imagine the emperor tucking his chin there, his pomaded mustache brushing her skin as he breathes in the scent of her hair, his cheek pressed close to hers.

It makes me wonder if she's in love with him. There's a certain softness accentuating the beauty of her features as she poses, but what do I know of love?

"Of course." My mood lifts. I like the idea of creating some beauty creams for the contessa. It will be a distraction from my memories of love's dangerous, empty promises, and may help to ease some of my homesickness. I cannot help my father with his medicines any longer, but I can put my knowledge to use at least.

La Castiglione sips her tea, then shoves the teacup and saucer away with a careless clatter. "Livia, you must tell me how to recognize the deadly nightshade berries." Her teeth score her rouged lower lip. "Just in case."

"I think it was a mistake," I say firmly. "No one wants to harm you." She looks as though she needs the reassurance, and though I stand by my decision to assume the worst and not risk her eating the berries, I regret I've given her cause for worry. I describe the berries to her, explaining the appealing dark purple, nearly black, gloss of them. "If you peel the skin back, the inside of the berry has a texture almost like blackcurrant jam. The berries themselves look like blackcurrants, which I believe is how they came to be mixed in with the berries today. The juice is fairly thin, and each berry has about a dozen seeds. They tend to be a bit larger than currants, closer to a cherry in size." I've recorded this description in my personal notebook, where I write down everything I've learned about different herbs, many of them poisons, and the properties of nightshade berries spring to my mind almost as if the page lies open in front of me.

She listens intently, hardly blinking as she watches me. "I shall remember." Her tone carries the serious weight of a decree. "I don't suppose I'll eat berries for quite some time. I've lost my enthusiasm for them."

To assuage her fears, I also give her some advice about tasting berries, suggesting she only eat one, and wait a little while to monitor its effects before proceeding to ingest any more, but her mouth twists up in a little pout of disgust, and then she laughs, throwing up her hands.

"No, no—I shall avoid them entirely."

"Perhaps that's for the best, signora, if it gives you the most comfort."

She tosses her golden hair over her shoulder, straightening. "After today, how can there be so much ceremony between us, Livia? You must call me Elisabetta—all my closest friends and family do."

Flattered by her friendliness, a glow of delight warms my heart. I was so anxious about meeting the infamous La Castiglione, and while I wouldn't quite say I feel entirely at ease with her, I never expected us to be on such familiar terms already. We're about the same age, but I imagined our circumstances would create a gulf between us, and I'm pleased to be wrong. Having another friend will make Paris seem less cold and unfamiliar.

"Thank you." I pause. "I expected you to go by Virginia. Niccolo said it was your name."

"Oh, it is. I have more names than I know what to do with. My parents must have been as indecisive as I am when it comes to choosing a ball gown." She rises and sweeps her arms out in a theatrical gesture. Her eyes brighten with amusement, gleaming just like the blue lapis or sapphire—I'm not sure which—serving as the eye on the gold snake bracelet wound around her wrist. "Virginia Elisabetta Luisa Carlotta Antonietta Teresa Maria Oldoini, pleased to meet you." Her laughter chimes delicately. "I prefer Elisabetta of all those names. And yours? Is it a fond nickname for Olivia?"

I shake my head. "No. It was the name of a classical Roman empress. I think my father took a fancy to it."

"Yes, I remember now," she says, although I'm not sure she tells the truth. She speaks with a touch too much insouciance. "It's a pretty name, and it suits you."

"Thank you."

"Livia," she repeats. "Didn't she have a reputation as a poisoner?" Her lips curve in a faint, dry smile.

Apparently she does remember. "Yes. Although it was centuries ago; who knows if it was true." I try to sound bland, but I'm all too aware of the connection between Empress Livia's reputation and my own knowledge.

She dips her chin in a small nod. "Well, rumored or not, it seems the name goes hand in hand with expertise in poisons—and their avoidance. It was quite fortunate for me today." As we rise, she links her arm with mine. "What a pair we make! Like day and night, with my golden hair and bright blue eyes, and your raven locks and tawny-brown eyes. And people think my head's in the clouds, all because I care for beautiful things, but with your knowledge of poisons, you must be quite clever. Perhaps we'll be good for each other."

"I hope so." Her praise overwhelms me, but I find myself beaming, eager to please her. I wonder what she'd think if she knew the reason for my dark hair and lightly bronzed skin. My maternal great-grandmother came from Saint-Domingue, one of the French colonies, but my family never openly mentions her. This is less to do with the fact that she was a slave, and more to do with her scandalous actions: she murdered a foreman on a sugar plantation, stabbing him in his bedroom, and was quickly hanged for it. My grandmother, only a girl of thirteen at the time, escaped to France and then Italy, where she eventually gave birth to my mother. Like me, she has dark hair and eyes, and we are usually presumed to have Greek or Spanish heritage. My mother never corrects this assumption. No one wants to admit to having slave ancestry, although I think it can't really be too uncommon. Even here in Paris, the famed novelist Alexandre Dumas is the son of a black general who was born in Saint-Domingue. I always remember it because it's the same place my great-grandmother was from. And I like his books, too.

Niccolo hovers in the doorway just then, waiting for Elisabetta to notice and invite him into the salon.

"There you are," she says. "I thought you'd wandered out to a casino."

A shadow of annoyance flickers over his expression, but he schools it back to polite deference almost at once. "No, signora." His gaze fastens on me, contrite and soft. His eyes look gray as the rain. "My apologies for leaving you alone, Livia."

Elisabetta's impatient voice interrupts him. "She was fine. In fact, we've become quite well acquainted now, haven't we?" With her wide eyes, her expression shifts to beseeching as she turns to me.

"Yes, we are."

"Excellent," says Niccolo. "My discourteous absence may have been more beneficial than not, then." He glances back toward me. "I didn't expect my brother to be here, and yet I heard his voice in the hall. You'll understand I needed to speak to him."

"Yes, of course." I've never met Niccolo's brother, who wasn't present in Turin for our hasty wedding, though I know from Niccolo's references that he's younger, and considered to be a bit of a scatterbrain by the rest of the family.

"Don't sound so impatient, Niccolo." Elisabetta rolls her eyes, lounging on the sofa with her arm stretched along the back. "He only arrived here today. I would have sent you a note, but you were already planning to call at my house this afternoon."

"I did not mean to imply you're responsible for his movements," says Niccolo, but the stiffness of his tone matches the tense set of his shoulders, and the appeasement falls flat.

"Take him home and feed him," says Elisabetta. "He's already raided my kitchen, and attempted to drink the expensive brandy I keep just for the emperor." She speaks with affectionate amusement, though, and I can tell she isn't really irritated.

"Of course." Niccolo's flat tone doesn't ease the tension between them.

I cast about for a way to slice through the uncomfortable pause. "Will he be staying with us, Niccolo?"

"Probably, though for how long, who can say? He'll be with us for supper tonight."

"I look forward to meeting him," I say, with perfect truth. Clearly there's more to his presence in Paris than a happy family reunion, and the contessa seems to know him rather well if he'd visit her before his own brother.

If I found Paris daunting at first, with its cosmopolitan atmosphere and unfamiliar streets, that now pales in comparison to the questions rising in my mind about my marital family, and my new acquaintance with the sophisticated contessa, to say nothing of the nightshade berries. My head spins. I draw in a deep breath in a futile attempt to stave off a wave of being utterly overwhelmed. Home has never felt so far away.

CHAPTER THREE

Paris, August 1856

There's an old wives' tale that putting a question about love in an empty poppy seed pod and placing it under one's pillow will bring the answer in a dream. Poppy will indeed bring dreams and drifting, but they aren't to be trusted.
— Excerpt from Livia Valenti's book of herbal studies

Back at the house on avenue Joséphine, I go to the privacy of my bedroom, kicking off my shoes and reaching for my hairbrush. Much as I'd like to sprawl on the bed and let my thoughts swirl over the strange incident of the berries, I don't have much time before I'll be expected back downstairs for supper.

"What in heaven's name happened to these?"

Caterina's voice snaps me out of my dark reverie, and I turn away from the window.

I didn't hear her come in, but she holds my white leather slippers aloft, pinched gingerly between two fingers, as though the shoes might give her a rash if she touches them too much. Dark purplish stains of berry juice streak across the toes, and a half-crushed berry clings to one like a wart.

"I'm sorry. I ruined them."

"I don't know how, when there's no proper garden for you to dig through here." An affectionate smile crosses her face.

"You won't believe the story," I say, beckoning for her to come to my side.

She drops the slippers carelessly on the floor, and tosses her long chestnut braid over her shoulder. "I'm looking forward to the tale. Tell it dramatically, won't you?" She must think it's an amusing story of me having a clumsy moment, but her exaggerated enthusiasm fades into genuine shock as I relate my discovery of the poisonous berries in the kitchen.

"Are you sure?" Eyes wide, she starts to gnaw on her already ragged thumbnail before catching herself and grabbing my wrist instead. "They were nightshade berries, beyond a doubt?"

Her fingers dig into me, and I shake her off. "Reasonably certain. I've gone over it in my mind, and I keep concluding the berries resembled nightshade more than anything else."

"Well, if anyone would know, it would be you," says Caterina.

"Good thing no one else can hear us. Your words make me sound like a murderess." It isn't a word I'd use lightly to anyone else. Caterina knows of my family's dark secret. She also knows just how much I've studied poisons.

"An expert," Caterina corrects, helping me button my dark blue dinner gown. My father studied poisons, purely for academic interests. He liked speculating if the sudden deaths of historical figures could have been caused by poison, but soon he turned to me for my opinion. I studied poisons because they were fascinating, but my interest ran deep. I spent more time than he did reading about different symptoms and cures. Together, though, we compiled a fair amount of knowledge of antidotes and healing treatments. I maintain a book of herbal studies, within which I note the properties of various poisons for my own interest, as well as keeping record of some of my father's more conventional knowledge and recipes. Since I'm no doctor, I sometimes think it's a frivolous thing to spend so much time on, but now I'm glad of it.

Caterina taps her fingers gently on my wrist, a signal I've been fidgeting with my bracelet, as I often do when I'm worried. It isn't a typical bracelet, being threaded with a small lancet instead of a pendant. It's an odd choice for an ornament of jewelry, but I didn't choose it for decorative purposes. Most doctors carry one for blood-letting. Mine is quite small and very sharp. With a flick of my nail, it could neatly pierce a person's skin. I'm careful not to release the clasp, though. I don't want to touch the lancet's small blade. Besides being honed to needle sharpness, I've also taken care to coat it with a mixture of oil and hot pepper essence. It's not a deadly weapon, and yet I don't feel safe without it close to my tense fingers.

"Will you tell Niccolo?" she asks.

My breath slides out in a long, hesitant sigh. "No... not yet. I just can't imagine it."

Caterina nods in understanding. My new husband and I are still practically strangers to each other, and his air of solemn reserve doesn't invite confidences.

"Anyway, the contessa knows, and she thought it was most likely an accident. There's not much to tell Niccolo, really." I glance at the clock hanging above the green chair next to the window. "I'd better get downstairs."

"I'll help you with your hair." Caterina takes the brush from me. "I wish you'd leave it down—I'd cheerfully trade my soul for curls like yours."

"No, you wouldn't," I reply, accustomed to her overstatements. "And that wouldn't be appropriate at all for supper. Besides, your hair is lighter, and that's considered more beautiful." Elisabetta's golden locks are a prime example of classical beauty.

She waves off my words, almost hitting my elbow with the brush. "Yes, but it's so thin and straight. Your curls are luxurious."

I snort with derision, but remain unmoved. "Nevertheless, you know I won't leave it down." I never do, not anymore.

"I do," she says sadly, already replaiting it and deftly twisting it up with pins.

I drape a gauzy dark blue shawl around my shoulders, both for modesty and for decoration, and straighten my spine, trying to imagine I possess even an ounce of the contessa's supreme confidence as I sway down the long staircase.

Niccolo rises when I enter the dining room. He always does, and while I cannot fault his impeccable manners, sometimes the formality of this habit makes me feel there's an impassable gulf between us, that we'll never be at ease with each other.

"Good evening, Livia." His voice sounds light and pleasant. It doesn't match the spark of his eyes as he glares at his younger brother, Bernardo, lounging at the far end of the massive table with a wine glass in his hand.

From every reference I've heard of Bernardo, I've gained the impression he treats every aspect of his life with careless benevolence, and I don't mind that he doesn't bother to stand up when I enter the room. Niccolo does, though.

Catching his brother's stern eye, Bernardo rises slowly, holding out his arms to bow with exaggerated nonchalance. The wine sloshes perilously close to the rim of the glass. "Good evening, signora."

Though the grand gesture and the tone of his voice could be construed as mocking, the charming grin that accompanies them sets me at ease. Closer to my own age, several years younger than Niccolo, he doesn't seem to take anything seriously, and it makes it easy for me to follow suit.

I greet them both, and take a seat in the chair Niccolo helpfully pulls away from the table for me. His hand hovers near my elbow, but since I don't ask for any assistance, he doesn't actually touch me. Sometimes I wonder if he thinks my pregnancy has rendered me utterly helpless, on the verge of fainting every moment. While it's true I have occasional, brief spells of nausea or dizziness, for the most part I feel quite well and have been trying to stay active around the house.

"It's good to meet you at last," I say to Bernardo, playing the part of wife and hostess. I'd hardly spared any thought for him until today, distracted by the upheaval of my marriage and being uprooted from Turin to Paris. I'm curious now, though. "I must admit I would have expected our first meeting to be in Piedmont, not France."

"My presence in Paris seems to be a surprise for everyone," Bernardo says.

"Not an unpleasant one." It's almost a relief to have another person at the supper table. Niccolo mostly dines out in the evenings, meeting with diplomats and politicians to further Conte Cavour's agenda of Italian unification, but on the few times he has been home, our conversations leap stiffly from mundane topics like the weather to the household staff. His attentive way of listening always gives me the impression he waits for me to choose the topic of conversation, and I fall short of his expectation every time, flailing for subjects that might interest both of us.

Bernardo favors me with a slow-burning smile. "I'm glad of it. I'm happy to meet you, as well. I should have been at the wedding. I hardly imagined Niccolo marrying again, never mind so suddenly."

Niccolo's previous marriage isn't unknown to me, but from the way he shifts in his chair, fingertips straightening the butter knife in front of him, I can tell he doesn't want us to talk about it. I don't know much about her, only that her name was Carlotta, they had no children, and she died of consumption after two years of marriage. I don't know if he loved her.

"Perhaps he wouldn't have, until he met me." Even as I speak, letting a smile curl around my lips to channel some of La Castiglione's playful audacity, my bold response startles me. I've never teased Niccolo in such a way—how could I, when our feelings and interactions are muted and transactional? But when Niccolo straightens, shoulders back, his gaze darting gratefully toward me, I'm glad I defended him against the faint judgment in Bernardo's tone.

"No doubt," Bernardo replies. "Now that I've had the chance to meet you, I understand perfectly." Despite his careless posture, slouching in his chair as he lazily swirls the last mouthful of wine in his glass, he manages to deliver this with the air of a grand compliment. "Welcome to the family."

"Thank you, Bernardo."

"Please, call me Bellino. It's a family nickname. I loathe being called Bernardo. It reminds me of my grandfather, and he was extremely dull and pious." He smiles, a little wickedly, daring anyone to comment on the contrast between the elder Bernardo's reputation and his own outlook on life.

The smile serves to highlight the reason for his nickname; he does possess a certain masculine beauty, with bright sky-blue eyes, hair glinting with hints of gold, and features that wouldn't be amiss on a classical statue. Next to him, Niccolo is like the blurred copy, as if one of them was made by the sculptor and the other by his apprentice. The blue of Niccolo's eyes is flattened by a dash of gray, and his hair is sandy brown instead of golden. I think his smile would alter his features, lighting him up, but he does it so rarely, I can't be sure.

Niccolo doesn't smile now as he answers his brother. "Our grandfather was a respectable man. We shouldn't speak ill of him."

"Oh, I know. Don't speak ill of the dead." Bellino reaches for the wine bottle, freshening his glass. "The most interesting topics are never suitable for the supper table, but in this case I'd have to agree we aren't missing much by not speaking of him." He turns to me. "Our illustriously respectable grandfather died before I was born, but I've never heard a story about him worth repeating, unless one is looking for a record for most prayers said in a day."

"It's lucky," I tell him. "Family stories that are good for telling usually aren't happy ones." I should know, after all.

Niccolo looks like he wants to argue with Bellino, but the arrival of our meal stops him. Swept with relief, I accept his insistence I be served first. Though I ate a bit of bread and cheese after returning from Elisabetta's, hunger makes my stomach ache again already. The pregnancy has my appetite all twisted up. I'm hungry at odd, frequent times, but sometimes I feel full after only a few bites.

As I dip my spoon into the rich sauce of the beef stew, a fluttering sensation swoops through my belly. I freeze in surprise, for it's the first time I've felt the baby quicken.

"Is everything all right?" Niccolo asks, his attentive gaze raking over me.

"Yes, it's only—" I swallow the rest of my sentence. I'd been about to tell Niccolo I felt the baby move for the first time, but it feels like an intimate thing to say in this setting, with the emptiness of the large table, seating only the three of us, and the high ceilings where our voices echo around the crown molding. Bellino's curious glance also forestalls me. "I'm fine, thank you."

No one chatters much through the meal. At first, I hardly notice, poised in anticipation for that airy bubble of movement again. When my thoughts stray back to the nightshade berries and La Castiglione, I glance suspiciously down at my stew. I've already eaten half of it, and encountered no unexpected bitter or sweet flavors. Not that I expect them here at home, but a mistake could so easily happen anywhere. A thrifty shopkeeper might pick some unknown, wild mushrooms and sell them. An inexperienced cook might dig monkshood root instead of horseradish. As I muse, I notice Niccolo glancing at me frequently, his expression anxious. Assuming he wants me to fulfill my role as the lady of the house, to fill the silence as a hostess, I search for a suitable topic of conversation. It's difficult; all I can think of is poison.

"Will you be staying in Paris long?" I ask Bellino, the simplest question that pops to my mind.

He tosses a strand of hair away from his forehead. "I don't know yet. I'm rather at a loose end at the moment. I thought Niccolo might need some assistance here; God knows Camillo Cavour isn't an easy man to please. He's always got a dozen plots hatching at once. It's nice to see Elisabetta again too, of course."

"You're welcome to stay as long as you like," says Niccolo. "There likely won't be much to do with the political negotiations. It's only a matter of persuading the emperor to meet with Conte Cavour. I believe the emperor may be sympathetic to the cause of Italy's unity. He was involved with the Carbonari as a young man, when he spent time in northern Italy, after all."

I listen with interest. I'm vaguely familiar with the Carbonari, a secretive revolutionary society fighting to overthrow Austria's rule in northern Italy, because of their occasional bouts of patriotism back home, but hearing Napoleon III spent time as a member surprises me.

Niccolo glances down at the linen tablecloth, voice lowering. "Elisabetta has his ear, too, so I hope an alliance against Austria is only a matter of time."

Bellino shoves his wine glass away. "His ear? That's not all she has." His bawdy laugh grates after the soft cadence of Niccolo's voice. "Resorting to sending her to the bed of an emperor, like a common courtesan—it should be a shameful tactic, if it wasn't so damned effective. Then again, maybe it's not, since Cavour sent you here, brother. Sometimes I wonder why he doesn't travel to Paris himself. Surely the emperor would be forced to meet with him then. Cavour's as headstrong as Elisabetta, just as accustomed to getting his own way." He turns to me, flicking the lid of his pocket watch open and shut, its restless clicks punctuating the air. "The two of them are cousins, you know."

He seems to expect a response from me, and I do have a theory. I push aside my shyness and force myself to speak. "Perhaps he believes the emperor must come to believe unification is his own idea, for it to be most effective. Or Conte Cavour is more interested in what Elisabetta has to report back to him, not what she has to say to the emperor. Her intimate knowledge may help him develop his own negotiation strategy." I can't quell a trace of impatience at Bellino's apparent failure to see the complexity of the issue. I envied Elisabetta almost at once, not for her beauty, but for her self-assurance. She appears to have control of her own situation, and Bellino doesn't seem to be crediting her with that. A hint of sharpness creeps into my voice. Niccolo's glance skates to mine, telling me he heard it, but I can't tell from his expression if he agrees.

"Either that or he's playing with loaded dice, making sure he's got every strategy covered." Bellino's careless response shows he missed my tone, at least, which is probably for the best. "Well, perhaps not every strategy. There are some politicians who favor more drastic measures."

"Not Cavour," says Niccolo.

Bellino ignores him, talking to me. "The extremists who fiercely support Italian independence have occasionally suggested the emperor's assassination would benefit Italy. It would throw France and Austria into chaos, leaving Austria unprepared to hold on to its Italian territory."

Niccolo clears his throat roughly. "This isn't a suitable dinner conversation. Livia will think you're a savage, Bellino."

Annoyance flickers across Bellino's expression, but then he smiles at me. "Oh, I am. I'm the reckless one, the less cultured brother. But I always mean well, even if I don't know when to hold my tongue. I hope I haven't offended you, Livia."

"Not at all." In fact, I'm fascinated and horrified—what if the nightshade berries weren't meant for Elisabetta, after all? I wonder if the emperor ever dines at her house.

Niccolo seizes the chance to steer the conversation away from politics. "I'm glad you and Elisabetta seemed to get along so quickly, Livia. I felt guilty about leaving you alone."

"My fault," says Bellino. "I'd dropped in to see Elisabetta before coming here. I surprised everyone with my arrival in Paris."

"She was very friendly to me," I tell Niccolo. "She's very knowledgeable and passionate about photography. I found it very interesting."

"Perhaps you'd like your portrait taken someday," he suggests.

I nearly decline, but my memory drifts back to the hypnotic portrait of La Castiglione in her black tulle dress, and the idea gains temptation. I'd like to wear something beautiful and be photographed, although of course it's a vanity I'm not worthy of. I'm a doctor's daughter, not a contessa or the mistress to an emperor.

"Perhaps someday." All at once, my appetite vanishes and the smell of the food cloys at the back of my throat. I lay my spoon down and lean back in my chair. "I'm feeling rather fatigued. I hope you won't mind if I retire for the night."

Niccolo rises in one smooth, quick motion and comes to my side. "Not at all."

I stand from my chair before he can assist me, a bit annoyed by his fussing and hovering. "Good night, then."

He follows me to the door of the dining room. "Shall I escort you?"

"No, thank you. You needn't take the trouble; I know the way by now." My smile feels crooked.

"Are you sure you're well?" He stares into my face, and the sharpness of his question feels like an interrogation.

"Quite well." I glance at Bellino, but he doesn't appear to be listening, sitting at the far end of the table and fidgeting with his pocket watch again. "I felt the baby quicken earlier tonight, that's all."

"That's all?" he echoes. "On the contrary, I think it's momentous news." A smile ghosts around his lips.

"Are you happy?" I ask, astonished by the sight. I wish he'd smile more; he wouldn't seem so intimidating then.

The smile fades. "I will always be happy to hear of your good health," he says stiffly. Just as he does every night, he reaches for my hand, lifting it to his lips. His fingertips hold mine gently, but nevertheless, it's impossible for me to snatch them away. Usually this gesture is quick and formal, with his mouth scarcely touching my skin, but tonight his lips press softly against the back of my hand, and I feel the warm graze of his breath. "Good night, Livia," he whispers.

Instead of reading before bed, as is my habit, I lie awake for a long time, my thoughts swirling. The possibility of intentional poisoning still seems slim—the event seems surreal, and I could have been mistaken—but La Castiglione or the emperor could have been the target. Perhaps I can ask her how often he visits. It's a good thing Elisabetta wants to be friends. Knowing her better, and keeping an eye on her health, may help ease my suspicious mind.

As I drift closer to sleep, my thoughts unexpectedly skip to Niccolo, and the look on his face as he kissed my hand tonight. Tenderness softened the shape of his mouth, making it less stern, and his eyes glowed, turning them almost silver instead of blue-gray. It reminds me of our first meeting, months ago, when I still harbored hopes of love in my future.

*

Turin, Italy, April 1856 (four months earlier)

As I strolled along the tree-lined avenue, the intensity of someone's gaze nudged at my back, an almost tangible feeling. I didn't turn at once, though it cracked my sense of peace. The botanical garden of the Castello del Valentino wasn't a private place, though it seemed empty when I arrived, the only sounds the whisper of the breeze through the hedges and a couple of birds calling to each other. I'd been loitering, soaking up the atmosphere, since the garden was my favorite place in the world. My father had sent me to take cuttings from a few herbs, which I had permission to do since he, as a doctor, enjoyed the patronage of Count Camillo Cavour, who'd been appointed prime minister of Piedmont-Sardinia four years before, quite a favorable turn for our family's fortune.

I finished taking a cutting of silver-gray sage, enjoying its sharp scent and the velvety feel of the leaves, before lifting my basket from the cobbled path. I headed toward the back of the garden, angling toward one of the four rounded towers of the *castello*. I still needed to gather soapwort from where it grew in the corner, between a gnarled yellow rosebush and a chipped statue of a rearing horse.

Though the Castello del Valentino was a royal house, I didn't think any of the king's family were currently in residence. Just in case, as I passed near the only other person in the garden, the one whose gaze I'd felt, I looked toward him, checking if I'd need to make a gesture of obeisance, or quietly retreat altogether.

The man standing across the garden was a stranger, though. Sandy-gold hair peeked out from under his dark hat, and his clothing was of fine quality. As he raised his hand to swat a bee, the slanting ray of sunlight caught a ruby ring on his finger, scattering a spark of red light. Since he appeared well-off, and could possibly be a lesser noble like a *cavaliere*—although a wealthy merchant was just as likely—I ducked my head respectfully, and judging the distance between us too great for more than that, continued toward the *Saponaria*, also called soapwort, because it is good for making soap.

As I cut some stalks, the sweet fragrance of the pink flowers hovered in the heavy evening air. The mix of floral and herbal smells was one of the reasons I often volunteered in the garden, and I breathed deeply. It was easy and relaxing to pick soapwort, as well. It had properties that helped make soap foamy, but was otherwise safe, though it was grown away from the ponds and slightly apart from the other plants because it could be invasive. Not all the plants I gathered were as pleasant.

The stranger had disappeared by the time I strolled toward the entrance of the garden, realizing it had grown late. My family would be waiting, so I tucked the basket more firmly over my arm and quickened my step.

And nearly collided with the stranger as I rounded the corner of a bed of lilies.

He crouched low, one knee resting on a flagstone, staring intently at the ground.

I lurched back, almost tripping over the hem of my dress.

He rose at the same time, reaching his hand for my arm to steady my balance.

"I must apologize, signore. I did not see you," I said.

Releasing his grip on my arm, he offered me a small smile. "Well, no. How could you, when I was kneeling on the ground? I'm not a madman, I promise; it's only there was a small frog on the path, and I thought to move it back to that pool of water just ahead."

I glanced down. Sure enough, a smooth green frog, its back dotted with a constellation of black speckles, sat beside his feet. I looked back up, straight into the man's blue-gray eyes. He seemed to be peering at me rather hopefully, as if he sought to reassure me he hadn't intended anything awkward, that he hadn't been lurking in the garden.

"The path is a dangerous place for a creature as tiny as this frog," he said. "But I must confess, I hesitated to pick it up. Some frogs are poisonous, aren't they?"

"This one isn't. These frogs are quite common in the garden. They like the moss around the pond. It might be easiest to move it with a leaf, though." Rummaging through my basket, I tugged one of the large, oblong leaves of mullein free. Good for coughs and skin conditions, but I could spare one leaf for the rescue of a frog. "Allow me." I sank to the ground and nudged the frog with the edge of the leaf. The man knelt as well, which made me feel awkward, since I didn't know if he outranked me, but then it occurred to me that it would be worse if I knelt at his feet while he stood, and I appreciated his gesture.

The frog hopped onto the leaf with a little coaxing, and I folded the edges up to keep it contained. "Now to take it to the water," I said.

"I'm fortunate you were here," the man said, as we hurried toward the small pool of water bracketed by flat rocks.

"It's only a frog. I'm sure you would have managed." I placed the mullein leaf down on a mossy patch, and the frog jumped free with a disgruntled chirp.

"What's your name? I'm Niccolo Valenti. Though I live here in Turin, I've never come to this garden before now, and it's clear I should have." He rested his hand against the trunk of the olive tree close to the decorative pool, and I noticed the top of his index finger was missing at the big knuckle. I stared a moment too long, admiring the clean way it had healed, before I realized how rude it must seem.

I answered too quickly, gaze skirting back to his kind face. "Livia Cavallo. My father is the doctor for Conte Cavour's household."

"I'm well acquainted with Conte Cavour; I work for him myself." He glanced at my basket. "Is that why you've picked different kinds of herbs? For salves and things? You must know the medicinal use of most of the plants in this garden." A curious note crept into his calm, deep voice.

"I do." I tried to sound modest, but I was proud of my knowledge. Ever since I could walk, I liked to follow my mother while she brewed the tinctures my father required, until I mostly took that task over myself. I loved listening to Father's lessons on the properties of medicine, and he was the only other person I knew who'd happily talk about the advancement of using ether for tooth extractions, and what it could eventually mean for other surgeries.

"Which one is your favorite plant?" Niccolo asked.

His question surprised me, and I tilted my head a bit to better see his face. He regarded me steadily, his expression serious and interested, not mocking.

"It's difficult to choose, but I always admire borage."

His eyebrows rose, dark gold and smooth. "It's in salads sometimes, isn't it?"

I smiled. He clearly didn't know which plant I referred to. "I'll show you." Walking half a step behind, he followed me across the garden. We paused in front of the borage patch.

"This one?" He reached forward and touched one of the fuzzy, drooping leaves.

I had to admit borage wasn't the most aesthetically pleasing plant, with its messy leaves and sprawling shape, but I still liked it. I showed him the first-blossoming, blue star-shaped flowers. "The flowers are nice, but I like them best because the bees do." Even now, several bees burrowed industriously among the flower petals. "Honey made by bees with access to borage is always good, and the plant has useful properties as well. Pliny wrote that it could be added to wine to help melancholy, and even though that was many centuries ago, I think it still has merit today if brewed into a tea." Belatedly, I realized he probably wouldn't be familiar with the details of Pliny's medical texts. Most people didn't read classic or modern medical books as much as I did. I was constantly raiding my father's library.

He didn't seem to mind. "I understand," he said, nodding. His mouth curled at the corners just slightly, but he seemed good-humored, and that made me brave.

"I'll show you my last reason why this is my favorite spot in the garden," I said on impulse. "Stand here." I gestured to the correct stone on the path. I'd scratched it with a faint cross once. "Now breathe in slowly."

Borage's fresh scent, reminiscent of cucumber, rose into the air, mingling with the heavier, dusky smell of the lily of the valley planted a short way down the path, and just the faintest sharp, piney edge of rosemary. The combination was the most interesting and alluring scent I'd ever found. I tried to make perfume of it once, but it hadn't worked very well, so I made sure to enjoy it in the garden whenever I could.

He blinked in surprise, gaze flickering to mine. "The air smells very pleasant here." A shy smile bloomed across his face. It brightened his face so much that my heart stumbled a little. "I didn't expect it."

"Neither did I, the first time I discovered it." I explained the combination to him. "I've never told anyone about it before." As I spoke, a bee bumbled into my hair, tangling in the long black wave of it that fell over my shoulder—I'd only tied it back for the garden trip, instead of pinning it up, as I probably should have.

Quickly and lightly, he reached forward and tugged the bee free, letting it fly away. Somehow, neither of us got stung.

"I'm glad you shared it with me."

I liked the soft roughness of his voice. Just as I wondered if I should show him the corner of the garden where odd scents somehow combined—lavender and garlic—the clatter of footsteps and voices interrupted the moment.

"There you are, Niccolo," called one of the two approaching men, wearing a burgundy jacket buttoned tightly across his barrel chest. "We've been looking for you."

"Good evening," said the other man to me, whom I recognized as an important clerk within the household of the *castello*.

Niccolo turned toward the men. "I sought some fresh air before supper."

Belatedly, I realized he must be visiting not only the gardens, but the Castello del Valentino, maybe even having a meeting with Conte Cavour himself. Though the prime minister didn't live in the *castello*, it made sense that he would conduct business from its large rooms.

"I've discovered an appreciation for the gardens here," Niccolo said, nodding to me. "I was lucky to have an expert to show me around."

"Indeed, she is very knowledgeable," agreed the clerk.

I smiled and thanked them, hiding the spark of uncomfortable surprise darting through me. I knew Niccolo must be well-to-do, by his clothes and manners, but I'd been conversing with him very casually, traipsing around the garden, and now it seemed he was more important than I realized. Not just a clerk for the prime minister's office, but someone who met with him in person. He had probably just been humoring me while I chattered about Pliny and borage. My cheeks burned.

"Being charmed by the gardens myself, I'm sorry to have to rush you back to the *castello*," the clerk said apologetically to Niccolo. "Conte Cavour adjusted the schedule, and we'll be dining earlier than originally planned."

"I'm glad I was able to enjoy the gardens for a short time, anyway." Niccolo gave me a courteous smile. Some of the warmth seemed to have disappeared from his face, making him reserved and distant again.

"I must ask to be excused as well," I said. "I must get these herbs home." The basket weighed heavily on my arm.

"Of course. Perhaps we'll see you here again soon," said the clerk.

"Thank you," Niccolo said politely.

I paused at the gate of the garden, adjusting the basket over my arm, and couldn't resist glancing back. The clerk and the man in the burgundy jacket strolled toward the *castello*, laughing, but Niccolo hung back, lingering in the garden. He turned to me, and our eyes met across the distance. The connection of it made my heart skip a beat. I lifted my hand for a brief wave of farewell. He didn't return the gesture at once, so I turned back toward the road. Feeling foolish, I hoisted the basket higher and hurried home.

*

Present

As the baby flutters in my belly, prompting me to shift against the pillows, I wonder if Niccolo and I will ever have an easy relationship. I'm tired of faltering around him, always nervous and awkward. Sometimes I think he only cares about the child, and hardly thinks of me at all. At least my baby will have a proud father, if not parents who love each other as mine do. That still counts for something.

CHAPTER FOUR

Paris, August 1856

Meadow saffron is highly toxic, and closely resembles wild saffron, which is safe to eat. Meadow saffron causes abdominal pain and distress, but new symptoms may continue to appear even days after consumption, escalating to respiratory paralysis.

— Excerpt from Livia Valenti's book of herbal studies

Several days later, La Castiglione invites us for a small supper party, and includes a note for me to extend the invitation to Caterina, and that she should bring her tarot cards.

On the afternoon of the event, my room turns into a whirlwind of pastel dresses and satin ribbons, of floral silks and dainty shoes. Caterina and I begin by sorting calmly through the broad oak wardrobe, but end with everything scattered over the bed, mixing sashes with different gowns and deciding which necklaces to wear. Caterina has plenty of dresses of her own, but it's exciting to dress up for a visit with the glamorous countess, so we decide she'll borrow one of mine, silk decorated with pale pink and yellow flowers. I choose a dark gold gown with beading around the bodice and leaves and vines embroidered all down the skirt.

"You should wear this, too." I hold up a necklace with a moonstone pendant on a gold chain, draping it over the dress she's chosen. "It will give you a mysterious air, perfect for reading the cards."

She runs her fingertip over the stone's iridescent gleam. "You don't mind? Isn't this one you received after your wedding?"

Just before we left Turin for Paris, Niccolo gave me a few pieces of jewelry that had belonged to his late mother.

"They're very beautiful," I said, glancing at each piece in turn. "I'm not sure I'll dare wear family heirlooms like these."

"I hope you do. You're part of the family now, and they belong to you." His voice was warm and smooth as hot chocolate, and I expected he might touch me, perhaps slide his arm around my waist or plant a kiss on my cheek. He did not, and as the tension eased from my shoulders with relief, I thanked him for the gift.

"Yes, but I don't mind lending it to you today," I tell Caterina. It's mine now, after all. I wore it once shortly after Niccolo gave it to me, and when he didn't comment, I concluded I'd attributed too much pressure to the gift and began to feel more comfortable about wearing the jewelry.

"I have a pair of jet earrings that will complement it. I'll be right back. They're in my room."

The room seems messier after Caterina's departure. I hang some of the discarded dresses back in the wardrobe, and tidy the shoes into a row. As I straighten, my gaze falls on Caterina's tarot cards, forgotten again but ready to be tucked into her pocket for our visit.

I fan them across the coverlet, wondering which ones La Castiglione secretly hopes to see. The Lovers, perhaps, or the Wheel of Fortune, a card that could indicate success and prosperity in her affair with the emperor.

The Knight of Cups slides under my fingertips as I spread the cards out, and I pause, staring at the familiar depiction of an armored knight astride a pure white horse, clutching a gold cup in his hands. I was happy to see this card when Caterina first read for me.

She smiled slyly, eyes gleaming with teasing humor. "It signifies romance. And it's upright, not upside down—it means you might meet someone soon." A black streak marred the armored chest of the knight, and she brushed it away. "Just a bit of thread. Perhaps it means he'll have a scar," she joked.

"I doubt a painted card, no matter how pretty, can tell if I'm going to fall in love," I said, but under the practical tone of my words, my heart leapt. Of course I wanted to fall in love. I was nineteen, with no suitors yet, and the idea that a tarot card turned up under my hand because love was in my future made me dream of a romance worthy of a fairy tale.

I wanted my knight in shining armor.

It isn't what I got, though.

I scan the cards for the other one I remember from that reading with Caterina, searching for the Empress. She sits on a red-draped throne, a scepter raised high, a crown adorning her proudly lifted head. A thick forest serves as her backdrop.

"This card signals abundance and beauty," Caterina said. "Often, it's in the form of femininity and fertility."

A faint bubble of movement uncurls deep in my belly, the sensation still unfamiliar. As if I need the Empress to remind me of fertility. I flick my nail against her scepter, and scoop the cards back into a stack, perhaps a bit more briskly than necessary.

Caterina returns just after I put them back, the earrings dangling from her fingertips. I'm grateful she didn't catch me poring resentfully over the cards this time.

"Are you nearly ready?" I ask.

"In terms of being dressed, yes. I'm a bit nervous, though."

"Don't be," I console her, although I can't deny a twinge of nerves myself. Even though Elisabetta was kind and welcoming when we met, she's still a bit daunting. "We'll be together."

We walk to her house, past the Pont de l'Alma and the broad swathe of the Seine, its waters tinged with bronze in the sunset-glazed light. Bellino walks ahead with Caterina, making her laugh loudly a couple of times. Niccolo and I keep a more sedate pace, but we don't speak much, only remarking on some of the landmarks of Paris. He looks sophisticated in his long coat and dark blue, double-breasted waistcoat, but also aloof, and it makes me tongue-tied.

La Castiglione keeps us waiting again, though not for as long as my first visit, and this time we've been shown into a more intimate parlor than the formal salon of before. This room has more of Elisabetta's touch, with soft velvet throw pillows on the sofas and intriguing masks hanging upon the walls.

"Livia, I'm so glad you're here. And this must be Caterina?" She sweeps into the room with all the presence of a queen, but a warm smile for each of us. Today she wears a silver-blue satin gown with ruched white ribbon trim. Combined with the silver and sapphire necklace wound about her throat, the colors remind me of the sea, especially with the way the neckline swoops below her bare shoulders and the swathe of the wide skirt swings with each step. If anyone can successfully dress as if inspired by a classical sea goddess, it's La Castiglione.

She offers her hand to Niccolo and Bellino in turn. Niccolo makes a slight, perfectly correct bow, his expression impassive as usual. In contrast, Bellino's greeting seems clipped, though still courteous, and his blue eyes burn bright like the center of a candle flame.

"Why don't we send the gentlemen to play billiards while we chat?" Elisabetta suggests, steering the brothers toward the door. "The billiard room is just down the hall. Davide, my footman, will show you."

Niccolo glances to me as he departs, one eyebrow raised, as if to confirm I'll be able to manage without him. I give him a quick nod before shifting my attention back to Elisabetta, who turns toward Caterina and me, her voice lilting with happiness.

"It's good of you to come early. I've been so curious to see your tarot cards, Caterina. I adore mysterious, occult things." She flicks a curious look to me. "Have you ever had anything come true from one of these sessions, Livia?"

"Never in the way I anticipated," I admit.

"It sounds as if that only adds to the mystery." She looks pleased.

As Caterina starts shuffling her cards, chatting with Elisabetta in a low voice, I stroll a short distance away from them, inspecting the stack of books perched on the edge of the mantelpiece. I'm not too interested in hearing Elisabetta's card reading—it feels like an intimate thing to witness, and I don't want to intrude—so I switch my curiosity over to the books. La Castiglione doesn't strike me as a voracious reader, but she has an interesting mix here, including a couple of tomes about photography, a collection of classical mythology, and a novel by Alexandre Dumas, *The Queen's Necklace*. I make a mental note to ask her if I might borrow it. It's about Marie Antoinette and a scandal involving a fabulously expensive diamond necklace, and seems a fitting thing to read now that I'm in Paris.

On the other side of the mantel, another of Elisabetta's photographs stands in a black frame. In this one, she poses with her arm delicately bent, her elbow, plump and soft as a peach, resting on the frame of a floor-to-ceiling window, or perhaps a French window. Her eyes gaze upward, looking outside and beyond, dreaming of something else, and the heavy black cape swathed about her shoulders and hanging almost to her feet gives her a funereal air. She looks mournful and yearning and impatient all at once, somehow older than she does in real life. I steal glances across the room at her, reconciling the vivacious golden beauty in the salon with the somber black and white figure of the photograph.

Caterina's voice drifts across the room. "The Ace of Swords upright. I'm not surprised. It represents power and victory, so it makes sense it would come up for you."

Elisabetta sounds amused. "I can't deny being mistress to the emperor has perks, including a certain amount of power. I hope victory means the success of my cousin's dreams of a united Italy."

"Do you dream of it, too?" Caterina sounds tentative.

I turn away from the photograph, interested to hear the answer. I think it would be better for Italy to serve its own interests, instead of being under the thumb of Austria, but sometimes I find it difficult to imagine how it would affect my daily life, if it would at all. Most day-to-day things have little to do with politics, I think.

"Of course." Elisabetta shrugs carelessly. "I wouldn't be here if I did not, would I? I'd like to see Italy regain the glory it held during the Renaissance." She picks up the card, waving it like a fan, and her voice lowers to a soft note as she looks to me. "I drop hints to the emperor—of course I do. But he is not a man to be told what to do. He needs to think it's his own idea. So mostly, I listen, and when the time is right, I nudge. I report all this back to Camillo, my cousin, but it seems he's growing impatient if he sent Niccolo."

"He hasn't spoken to me about it very much," I say.

"Perhaps you can ask him."

"He isn't a forthcoming man."

She seems to remember she's holding the Ace of Swords, and thrusts it back into Caterina's hand. "My dear, you just need to pick the right time. Or the right place. The tangle of bedsheets tends to be both." She winks one long-lashed eye at me.

I try to smile back in a knowing, blasé manner, but my cheeks burn with heat.

"Have I embarrassed you?" Elisabetta rises and takes both my hands between her cold ones. "I'm sorry. I didn't mean to, darling. Sometimes I just speak without thinking. I didn't think you'd be shy, not when you're already expecting."

"It's all right. I don't mind. It's just warm in here."

"I often felt overly warm during my pregnancy, too," she says comfortingly, rummaging through a cupboard for a fan and passing it to me. "When are you due? April, I'd guess. You can't be very far along yet."

I consider lying to her, but I know it will be useless when the baby comes early. People would speculate and whisper, no matter what I say now. It's better to be honest. I breathe against the knot pushing under my ribs. "January."

Elisabetta blinks in surprise, and a wicked smile lurks around the corners of her mouth. "Livia, you surprise me. I never would have guessed that you and Niccolo were lovers before marrying. You both seem so proper. I don't mean any offense by that, I hope you understand." She grins. "I think I like you even better, now. Women shouldn't fear a whiff of scandal about them. It only means they're free of some of life's dull conventions."

"I suppose that's true." I struggle to make my voice light. I don't feel free at all.

"This explains the way Niccolo looks at you," continues Elisabetta. "Absolutely besotted. It's not many men who marry their mistresses. Most of them are relieved to get what they wanted with no further obligations." Her smile loses a touch of its luminous charm. "Now, back to the tarot. Caterina, I think we were on the Tower, reversed."

"Thankfully," says Caterina. "Upright means certain disaster, but reversed is the avoidance of it."

As Caterina explains the nuances of the rest of the contessa's cards, I turn my attention back to the enigmatic photograph of her. I begin to think it captures some of the complexities of her character that she protects under the bright, bold veneer of beauty and charm.

After the card reading, Elisabetta tugs at my wrist, an impulsive gesture that's saved from being intrusive by the warm smile she casts to me and Caterina. "Come upstairs with me. We still have some time before the rest of the guests arrive, and I have the perfect necklace to match your dress, Livia. Will you borrow it?"

"It's not necessary." Even as I reply, sounding as shy as I feel, I follow her up the wide staircase, trailing behind the shimmering swathe of her skirt.

"Necessary." She pauses on the landing, rolling her eyes. "No, but it's pleasant to share things and make lovely fashion combinations. Don't worry—there's no obligation, not among friends."

As we enter the opulent privacy of Elisabetta's rooms, I judge we're safe from being overheard, and broach the subject of the nightshade berries.

"No more trouble with berries, I hope?"

"No, nothing at all. Did I tell you I questioned Marco quite thoroughly? The poor man was terrified he'd lose his place in my household." Her smile takes on a sharp edge. "I'm certain he told the truth when he insisted he'd purchased the berries from a local vendor, whose children often pick some of the berries, and apparently included some poisonous ones by accident. Gruesome, isn't it?" She clasps her hands together as if bound, lifting her head dramatically. "Death dances so close to us, one can feel its cold touch at the wrists."

"I'm glad that mystery is solved. So many poisons appear harmless, and that only makes them more dangerous. It's a relief to hear it was only a mistake." I pause. "I'd wondered, later, if the emperor ever dines at your house."

"Oh no, he rarely eats anything at my house, and certainly not a plain dish like berries. It was always far more likely to be a mistake than an attempt by enemies, and that's how it turned out. I suppose I hardly have any enemies," she says, with a touch too much levity, considering the fact she mentioned them herself when it first happened. "Plenty of people quiver with envy about anyone close to the emperor, but I have many more petitioners. I certainly get enough pleading letters."

"Pleading?"

"Oh yes. For favors, for recommendations, for money, for introductions to the emperor's ministers—as if I'm even well acquainted with them. They aren't present in the emperor's bedchamber." Her lashes flick downward, making shadows across her cheeks. "Or mine, I should say. He always comes to me." She clears her throat. "What do you think of this necklace to complement your gown?"

The necklace, a delicate gold affair with a fragile pendant shaped like a leaf, and dotted with a green stone, does match my gown perfectly. I plan to demur on wearing it for the evening, but as soon as she fastens it around my throat, I stare in surprise at my reflection in the mirror. Though I let Caterina help herself to Niccolo's heirloom jewelry, I didn't pick anything for myself, leaving my throat bare. Elisabetta's necklace somehow pulls the shape of my gown into something delicate, highlighting the hint of my collarbones above the fabric, and the stone catches a gleam of bronze in my eyes. I feel pretty.

"See?" She pats my hand briefly. "You must borrow it. It looks divine, as if it was meant to be." She drops her voice to a confiding tone. "Anyway, darling, you can't be seen bare-throated around the peacocks of the court, a few of whom will be here tonight. They'd notice, and whisper."

I blanch. "But—that's so trivial."

Elisabetta nods, almost gaily. "I know. And that's why they care. It's important to them, it's all they have. They don't have their plants or their books, like you do. They'll love you, though, all the more for not being able to understand you. You're my enigma."

"I must admit, I'm nervous now."

"Don't be. It's only a supper party, and I'll make sure you're well taken care of. And you look perfect, Livia. Image can be strategic, you know. It can be a shield, if it makes you feel less nervous to think of this dress as your armor. Take another good look in the mirror, and remember this moment, before your first fancy Parisian supper party."

"I won't ever be able to forget it." Next to Elisabetta, with her borrowed jewels, I look almost as regal as she does, my eyes amber and mysterious next to her sparkling blue ones as our gazes meet within the glass, and she smiles.

"Good. Some memories are so vivid it's as if they're burned into your mind—perhaps this shall be one for both of us. I like those rare gems of memories. They capture a moment in time, rather like a photograph."

Perhaps this is why she loves photographs so much. "I hope so." Though my nerves have eased as my confidence in my appearance rises, I still don't quite want to leave the friendly intimacy of her chambers, with only Elisabetta and Caterina, for the bustle of a formal dining room with a dozen strangers. "Do you have a favorite vivid memory?" I ask Elisabetta. "One you'd like to capture in a photograph but cannot?"

She thinks for a moment, her painted lips pursing together. "I do. I remember the night that Louis first laid eyes on me. I could hardly fathom that I'd come to call him by his first name—in that moment, I could only think of him as the emperor. A title, a goal, the very reason for my presence at the ball."

I listen quietly. Elisabetta has scarcely referred to her relationship with the emperor as a political goal, but I know it's true since the prime minister sent her to Paris with the intent that she seduce the ruler. How strange it must have felt.

Elisabetta continued, lifting her head dramatically, her voice throaty with telling the story. "It was midnight, and I stood on the staircase, posed like a trophy. My gown clung, laced so tight to my waist that I could hardly sit down, but I didn't need to. I waited on the stairs while he approached me, gaze flicking, like everyone's, to the skin displayed above the low neckline of my dress, decorated with an edge of sheer white cloth to make it seem even lower." She smirks a little, as if it was all a clever game she excelled at playing.

"Did you greet him?" I ask.

"No. I waited for him to speak first. 'It's a pity you're arriving to the ball so late,' he said. I just looked at him for a minute." Her voice loses a bit of the narrative cadence, and drops to a lower, confiding tone. "It was the first time I'd seen him up close. His hair, combed neatly to the side, didn't hide the rising expanse of his forehead. He had forty-seven years to my nineteen, and they were beginning to show in the thickening at his waist, the crows-feet dragging at his eyes. I didn't mind those, in fact; his eyes twinkled as he gave me a small, rueful smile, and it helped me to smile at him." She turns back to the mirror, making a small, coquettish smile that surely echoes the one she first bestowed upon the emperor. "'No, sire,' I told him. 'It is you who's leaving early.'"

Caterina and I grin at each other, thrilled by her audacity.

"What did he say next?" asks Caterina.

"I gave him no time to say anything. I made my way down the stairs, moving as if I couldn't resist the allure of the music. He watched me the whole time—I could feel his stare brushing over my hair, the bared skin of my shoulders. My gown was no shield that night, but an invitation. I'm used to being watched—sometimes I believe people would rather look at me than listen to me—but I courted every gaze that night." Her brows draw together, pensively, and she doesn't look at either of us. "And as I walked away from the most powerful man in France, maybe all of Europe, I imagined the world shifting around me, and I thought perhaps beauty could be a useful currency after all."

We fall silent for a moment. I reflect that beauty can be a danger, too, but I fear the attention it brings more than Elisabetta does.

"You didn't see it that way before?" Caterina sounds tentative.

"I came to Paris under Camillo's orders," says Elisabetta. "But once I was here, once I'd met the emperor, I saw how his favor could make my life interesting after all."

Changing the subject, she offers Caterina an ornament for her hair, even though she'll be dining with Beatrice, Elisabetta's maid, and I appreciate her kindness to my best friend. I'm left with the feeling that Elisabetta has taken me under her wing, but that it's more of a stage than a shelter.

At supper, Elisabetta is a model hostess, introducing us to her few other guests—it's a small, intimate party—in such a way that conversation flows easily right from the start. I'm slightly acquainted with two of her guests already. Roberto Rossi, one of Niccolo's friends, is also here. He's a writer from Florence, living off a generous inheritance from his grandfather. He came to Paris of his own accord, and as far as I can tell, spends most of his time penning political essays about the plight of Italy. Over soup, he complains of how the independent kingdom of Piedmont in the north is surrounded by Austrian-controlled provinces, like Lombardy-Venetia. "Austria has no place there, and must be expelled," he says.

His wife, Angelica, a short, slender woman whose brown hair and eyes make me think of a kind little sparrow, called upon me once at the house on avenue Joséphine, shortly after our arrival in Paris. I appreciated her friendly overture, but we sat in awkward semi-silence, sewing in between bouts of her seizing upon stories of her two young children to tell me. It was the only topic of conversation we seemed to have in common.

Elisabetta assigns me the chair beside her, around the corner from her spot at the head of the table, inexplicably treating me almost like a guest of honor.

"You're too kind," I say to her in an undertone, when she leans close to me. "I have a better seat at the table than the *baronessa*."

The *baronessa*, one of La Castiglione's French court acquaintances, swanned into the room in a beautiful purple silk gown, and if the way she stares down her nose at me is any indication, she expected to hold my seat. Part of me likes the burst of victory uncurling inside me, but I'm also very aware she outranks me.

"My dear, as far as I'm concerned you saved my life." She pats my hand. "Have a bit more polenta—it tastes like home—and simply enjoy yourself."

After the meal, when the plates have been cleared and everyone begins to mingle, wine or coffee in hand, I duck outside, eager for a few minutes of quiet. After the clatter of cutlery on porcelain, the shrill laughter and layered noise of several simultaneous conversations, the quiet of La Castiglione's small garden feels heavy and soothing in my ears. I lift my face to the sky, searching for stars, as the cool air refreshes my skin. A sliver of moonlight pierces the thin drapery of clouds, but without the hazy glow of a nearby gaslight standing along the street like a sentry, I wouldn't be able to see much at all. The haunting melody of a nightingale drifts though the sky, and that whisper of a song washes the rest of the tension from my shoulders. I breathe deep as the baby flutters inside me.

Through the silhouettes of a couple of manicured bushes, I notice a man walking down the street, his steps slow and steady. His head cranes to the side as he peers toward the house. Fairly sure I can't be seen in the shadow beneath a linden tree, I shuffle back into the darkest part anyway, musing people must often be curious about the famous La Castiglione. I wouldn't like that notoriety, myself.

As the man pauses, the yellowish beam of the gaslight falls over his face, and I suck in a shaky breath. The shape of his cheekbones, the stubborn angle of his jaw, the proud set of his shoulders all pierce me with a sharp ache of memory. I remember the cadence of his voice rumbling near my ear, the feel of his fingers sliding through my hair.

He turns, and if not for the dark safety of the shadows cloaking me, I'd swear his eyes meet mine across the distance. I turn to a statue. Not breathing. Not blinking. Even when he turns away, I'm seized with shock.

Corbara wouldn't be here in Paris. Would he? I last saw him in Turin. It's a trick of the light, a deception of my thoughts. My pulse thrums against my throat, but I take a deep breath, softening the reaction to my mistake. The stranger continues down the road, and vanishes out of sight.

It shouldn't matter. Corbara's in my past; I'm married now. Our paths should never cross again.

I won't let them.

Trembling, I turn away from the street, reaching the steps to return to the golden warmth of La Castiglione's party, just as Niccolo slips through the doorway.

"Are you all right?"

"Yes, of course." I sound calm again, to my relief, but I'm icy inside.

"I noticed you disappeared and wanted to make sure you were well."

"I just needed fresh air."

He moves closer to my side, enough that the warmth of his body grazes mine, and I fight the brief temptation to lean into the comfort of it. "It's peaceful out here. I can see why you sought the garden for a few moments."

The way he glances around tells me he'd be willing to linger, but I march toward the steps. "We'd better get back inside."

"Anything you wish," he says. "If you're tired, if you want to go home, just tell me."

"I don't mind staying a while longer."

As I cross the threshold of the doorway, the whisper of the nightingale's song skims over my skin, leaving a shiver in its wake. I resolve not to think of Corbara. I probably imagined his resemblance upon a stranger. He ought to be far away, after all, still in Turin, while I'm in Paris, enjoying a luxurious dinner party with a new friend. He needn't fill my thoughts.

CHAPTER FIVE

Paris, August 1856

Rhubarb is a good example of a plant with mixed properties. The red stalks are edible, even tasty, but the broad leaves can cause weakness, nausea, burning in the mouth, and other symptoms in as little as an hour after consumption.
— Excerpt from Livia Valenti's book of herbal studies

Sleep tantalizes me after Elisabetta's dinner party. It's like a trickster, weighing the corners of my eyes, loosening my limbs, and yet whirling my thoughts into such a tempest that I can get no rest.

I don't want to think of Corbara. That part of my life is over. But thanks to that illusion of shadow and lamplight, though, he won't depart from my mind. The memories feel as bright as his smile, as harsh as the burn that brought him into my life in the first place.

*

Turin, Italy, April 1856 (four months earlier)

I walked slowly, letting the breeze lift the curls away from my cheeks, turning my face toward the glimmer of sunshine peeking through the clouds. I'd volunteered to fetch more valerian root, although Father's store of it was only a little low. I mostly just wanted to be outside. Idly, I wondered if Niccolo Valenti might be in the garden again. It had only been a few days since I met him.

I paused along the Po river, taking a moment to admire the graceful flight of a pair of birds swooping over the glistening stretch of water. As I turned away from the water, back toward the street, I noticed two men passing down the quiet road, muttering to each other. One of them had reddish hair and the ruddy skin to match, and walked with a pronounced limp. The other, with tanned skin and a very ragged jacket, cradled his arm close to his chest. His face looked tight with pain, pinched around his eyes and mouth. Even so, the discomfort of his expression didn't hide the fact that he was handsome. It almost added to it, making him look like the tormented hero in a painting of a classical story.

I peered at his arm, trying to judge the cause of his discomfort. His shoulders looked broad and firm, not deformed, so dislocation seemed unlikely. His arm bent normally at the elbow, and he clutched the back of his hand, pressing it to his chest, which ruled out his wrist as well. As the torn sleeve of his jacket flapped in the wind, I caught a flash of red skin. A burn, perhaps? Or possibly a large scrape.

"Let the air on your arm," said the coppery-haired man to his companion. "It will cool it down."

A burn, then. Still watching, I waited for the wind to move the loose fabric of his jacket again, so I could see better. He hissed as the wind skated across the tender flesh, his dark hair falling across his forehead.

"It doesn't feel like it's helping," he said.

They seemed to notice me around the same time, staring back. I felt my skin flush at being caught in such rudeness.

The one with the limp scowled at me, but said nothing.

"Do you need help?" asked the one with the burned patch on his arm. He straightened his shoulders and offered me a tentative smile.

I shook my head, edging down the road to continue home. As I passed closer to them, the scarlet of his arm caught my attention again. The white bubble of blisters made a destructive topography along his skin. "The air won't help." It wasn't my business, and they were strangers, but I had to speak, even though the glare of the red-haired one made me feel I was interfering. "You need a fine linen cloth, soaked in cool water or milk. A burn ointment would be even better. My father is a doctor, and I've seen him treat burns before."

He smiled again. "Would he consent to treat two travelers, do you think? We aren't as disrespectable as we presently appear, I promise. It's been a rough journey for us these last few days. Adventures take a toll, as it turns out."

The other remained quiet, but some of the suspicion faded from his gaze.

"Probably he would," I said.

"If not, then perhaps you could help us instead. You seem very knowledgeable. I'm sure we'd be in good hands." His smile, just a little crooked, had a roguish quality that affected me more than I wanted to admit. I felt my pulse flutter. I told myself it was the compliment of believing a woman could do a doctor's work, nothing more. I knew it was true, and so did my father, but not many others.

I didn't hesitate long before answering. "Come with me, then."

"Thank you. What is your name? I'm Vittorio Corbara." He jerked his chin in the direction of his russet-haired friend. "That's Pietro Ferrero."

After I introduced myself, he thanked me. "I daresay meeting you today is the best fortune we've had all week."

I tucked a curl of hair behind my ear. "You might not say that later—not many people like visiting doctors."

"I'm sure you have healing hands."

I glanced at him to see if he meant any kind of double entendre with his words, but Signor Corbara's face looked serious and calm. A little drawn again, in fact. His burn must have pained him more than he wanted to admit.

It took longer to walk home with the two ragged adventurers in tow, for Pietro Ferrero's limp slowed him down. They encouraged each other with good-natured jabs.

"Hurry up, Ferrero. You're slower than an old mule."

"Quiet, Corbara. Your tongue wasn't burned, that's certain."

At the house, both of them sank into chairs with evident relief. Once Father laid eyes on them, I hardly needed to explain the circumstances of our meeting. It was clear they needed medical care.

"Likely a bad sprain," he said of Ferrero's ankle. "I'll need to examine it." He turned to me. "You know what to do for a burn. Pomatum number sixty-four will do nicely for an ointment, I think."

"What's that?" Corbara asked me in a low voice, as Father fussed over Ferrero's leg and I went to the cupboard for ingredients.

"Just a salve made with egg, sweet oil, beeswax and calendula. We keep track of our recipes by number."

"I knew I was in good hands," Corbara said with satisfaction. While I mixed the ointment, using calendula and honey and a fresh egg, he removed that wretched jacket. He made no sound, but the tension in his jaw betrayed that his teeth were clenched as he shimmied the cloth cautiously away from his arm. The sleeve of his shirt had been hacked short, but he carefully rolled up the ragged ends.

I laid one gauzy square of linen in the bowl of ointment, letting it soak up the thin salve, and dipped another in a shallow dish of milk. I inspected Corbara's arm before touching it. Quite a large patch of his forearm was burned, the flesh bright red and swollen. The blisters puckered, but looked white, without the sickly yellow tinge of infected pus. It could have been worse, as burns went.

"This might hurt." Gently, I laid the milky linen across his raw skin.

Corbara's body tensed, and his arm twitched once. His eyes had squeezed shut, but he opened them and gave me a sheepish look. "It wasn't as bad as I expected. Maybe you shouldn't have warned me." His exhale sounded shaky. "In fact, it feels a lot better now. That first touch stung, but now it feels cool. God, it's such a relief." His eyes met mine, bright with fervency. I'd never met anyone with leaf-green eyes before. One of them had a small crescent of russet brown. It lent him a mysterious appearance. I surmised the coloring was related to the scar running through his eyebrow, and wondered what accident might have caused it.

Realizing I'd been staring into his eyes for far longer than was proper, I cast my gaze back down to his arm. "You're lucky the burn isn't too deep. It hasn't reached the muscles. If that happened, you'd lose sensation, and be at greater risk for infection."

"Will it leave a scar?"

"Probably."

"I don't mind. I have lots of others. Aren't you going to ask how I sustained this grievous injury?"

"You may tell me if you wish."

He sighed through his nose. As I'd just adjusted the cloth, I suspected it was partly out of disappointment, partly to hide the twinge of pain. "Hmph. It's more flattering when asked, but very well, I shall divulge this secret to you. It was a fire."

I clasped my hand to my heart, feigning dramatic surprise. "Really? My goodness, how shocking."

His laughter rumbled like a cat's purr. "All right. The fire part was obvious, given the burn. It was a house fire. We were passing by shortly after it ignited, and I heard a child crying inside. I dashed inside to carry him out. The fire hadn't spread very far yet." His mouth curled self-deprecatingly. "I thought I could do it. Fire spreads faster than one expects, though. As I careened through the smoky doorway, child slung over my shoulder, a burning chunk of rafter fell, scraping past my arm. My sleeve caught fire. I didn't realize at first, but Ferrero tackled me as soon as I put down the child."

"You're lucky to have escaped with such minimal injuries." The second linen gauze had been soaking in the mixture of Pomatum No. 64 for our whole conversation, and I judged it had soaked up enough of the ointment. "Hold still, Signor Corbara." I peeled the first linen sheet away from his arm, and replaced it with the fresh one and its coating of salve.

He sighed as the new cloth settled into place, draped over his forearm. When he leaned his head back, his hair fell away from his closed eyes. He opened them and gave me a sideways look. "Aren't you going to congratulate me on saving the child?" Amusement lurked around the corner of his mouth. "Lord knows no one else did; there was too much panic, and the little boy just cried. My only recognition will have to come from you, Livia."

"Hold still." It took effort not to let a smile burst across my face in response to the roguish curl of his lips, the irreverence of his words.

His voice lowered to a serious note. "I will." He turned to a statue.

I made sure the linen covered the entirety of his burn, and that there were no dry spots to pinch at his tender skin. He did not move the entire time.

"Livia, could you please hand me the boneknit salve?" My father looked up from Ferrero's swollen ankle.

"Of course." I straightened, leaning away from Corbara.

"I thought his ankle was only sprained," he said. "What's boneknit salve?"

"We use it for breaks sometimes, but it's also good for bruising." I turned away, heading for the counter. A fresh batch of the boneknit salve stood on the bottom shelf, wrapped in a cloth to keep it dark and cool. I'd helped make it a few days ago, extracting the goodness from the comfrey leaves and mixing it with sweet oil. I paused, and glanced back at Corbara, chin on shoulder. "I'm glad you saved the child."

He grinned lazily. "I knew you would be." The way his eyes gleamed belied his casual tone, though. I smiled back, and went to help with the sprained ankle.

Due to my father's strict instructions, Pietro Ferrero needed to avoid walking on his ankle for at least a week, and since he worried Corbara's burn would develop an infection, Father and I went to treat them daily at the inn they stayed at not far from our house. Corbara often met us outside, pacing restlessly along the street, his gaze sweeping skyward.

"I can't sit still," he said. "It's a good thing I didn't hurt my leg. I'd be going mad cooped up inside, but I think Ferrero is handling it quite well. He likes to be idle, really."

Ferrero heard him through the open window, and his muffled curse rose through the air.

"Walk with me," said Corbara, after I'd applied a fresh dressing of the burn salve to his arm. The blisters were shriveling, and his skin peeled in patches. The redness had also faded, and I judged the risk of infection to be fairly small now. He tilted his head persuasively. "I'll tell you how I got the scar in my eye—I know you've been wondering about it."

"I have," I confessed. "I've never seen an excess of pigmentation in someone's eye before, although I read of it once."

"Excess of pigmentation?" His brow arched. "I didn't know it was called that."

"That's why the spot is darker," I explained. "Why it's brown instead of green, like the rest of your eyes."

His teeth flashed white as he grinned, lighting up his whole face. "Why, Livia. You noticed my eyes are green. I think you must like me."

I ignored this, although I felt heat surging in my cheeks. I'd come to realize he was an incorrigible flirt, and tried not to ascribe too much of it to myself, personally. I wasn't always successful. He was one of the handsomest men I'd met, and it was easy to banter with him. "Some people are born with it. I don't know why. In rare cases, it can be caused by trauma, as well." I paused. "In your case, I surmise you sustained an injury in a brawl or even a duel, probably over a lady. Perhaps your scandalous manners provoked her husband into attacking you."

Corbara laughed. "I do sometimes tell the story that way. Of course, I'm always the hero of the tale, and her husband a drunken lout who beats her." He bent close enough to me that the velvet softness of his breath skimmed across my neck, tickling my ear. "The truth is, I was kicked by a horse when I was eight years old."

Seized with interest, I peered into his face. "And your sight is still good?"

"Yes, perfect."

"How surprising."

He gnawed on his lower lip. "I cannot lie to you, Livia. Not after you've been the best healer I could hope to have." He paused and clasped his hands dramatically in front of his chest. "It was not a horse." His voice dropped to a murmur. "It was a goat."

I put my hands on my hips. "Are you sure? A goose might have done it. I think a goose beak could've made that scar through your eyebrow."

"Geese are terrifying creatures," he said severely. "If it was a goose, I would have told you right from the start. If the street were suddenly to be engulfed by flames, I'd save you, even though I now know how much a burn will hurt. I'd carry you to safety even as smoke clogged my lungs and my steps faltered. But the sudden advance of a flock of ill-tempered geese—you'd be on your own. Unless you had a club with which to defend yourself, you'd have to hope to run as fast as me. Cross my heart, it was a goat that scarred my eye."

My laughter rang through the air, raising my spirits with it. Corbara's smile carried a hint of pride, but more delight.

*

Present
Paris, August 1856

Shortly after rising—I slept in a little, letting the gray morning keep me drowsy—I dress in a gown of soft blue and hunt for a sturdy pair of shoes with the thought of going in search of an apothecary. I want to make a tea of chamomile and valerian tonight, to help me sleep, but I don't have any valerian root. I must find an apothecary where I can purchase it, or a garden where I may pick it. I hope the apothecary will stock some of the more obscure herbs as well. I know where to procure them all at home in Turin, but Paris is still so foreign to me.

The memory of Corbara's distinctive profile, stark against the angled light of the street lamp, slams into my mind's eye. Panic surges in the back of my throat. It takes several ragged breaths to calm myself again.

I sink to the edge of the bed. Corbara shouldn't be in Paris, and yet I saw him. It's hard to believe he would have followed me here, but at the moment, I can't think of another explanation. It's the last thing I want—I never want to see him again. I'm afraid he'll never let me go, I'm terrified he'll haunt me forever, and I don't know where the poison grows in Paris.

The thought scalds my conscience, and I dismiss it as an impulse. I'm not like my great-grandmother. I feel cornered, but there's no murder in my heart. It's only natural that I'd think of poison in a moment of fear: it's my expertise. It's only a bolstering, vicious daydream to imagine how, if Corbara crashes back into my life, I'd know how to slip him thornapple, which causes hallucinations and blurred vision, its sweet-tasting seeds easily sprinkled into a gruel or over biscuits. Or hemlock, its lacy leaves easily mistaken for parsley, but which initiates a paralysis of limbs and progresses to the lungs, ending in death rather than freshened breath.

No, valerian root is all I need, and any apothecary should have that.

I'm about to reach for my dark green wool coat, when Niccolo knocks at my door. Still weighted by grim thoughts, I blink at him, not quite managing to hide my surprise. I never see him this early in the day. Sometimes our paths don't cross until the evening meal.

"I thought we might have breakfast together." Although he doesn't smile, exactly, there's something friendly and nervous in the curl of his lips, the hopeful glint in his blue-gray eyes.

It's impossible to decline. "Certainly." I break the awkward pause. "Shall we go to the dining room?"

A little crease forms over his eyebrows. "It's so formal and cold there. I thought perhaps the salon would be more comfortable."

"Of course. Please, lead the way."

Though it's a pleasant room with muted green striped wallpaper, a bookcase, several sofas and chairs, and a blue patterned rug, I've never lingered in the salon. It feels too much like intruding into Niccolo's space, since he tends to write correspondence and read in that room, so I avoid it. Besides, my own bedroom is large, with a sitting area, and it's plenty of space for me.

As we enter the salon, I see breakfast has already been laid on the table between two upholstered chairs. A gleaming silver coffee pot perches between two small china cups, next to a plate heaped with fresh rolls and a little dish of honey. Relief skips over me that I didn't turn down his breakfast invitation. He's clearly been looking forward to it.

Niccolo catches my sideways glance. "I wanted us to have some time to talk. As you can see, I hoped you'd be amenable to breakfast."

I perch on the edge of the nearest chair. "Thank you. I'm quite hungry, in fact." The sight of the golden crusted rolls sends a spasm of hunger through me.

"If you'd prefer chocolate instead of coffee…" Niccolo trails off, sounding uncharacteristically uncertain.

"No, this is fine."

The clink of his spoon against the side of the cup seems loud in the ensuing silence. When he lifts the coffee to his mouth, the position of his hand makes his maimed finger more noticeable, and my eyes skate over it. I often forget he has this scar, and I'm rather curious to know how it happened. I wonder if he'd mind telling me.

"Do you have everything you need?" he asks. "I hope you're starting to feel at home here."

"Yes, thank you."

"And are you finding enough to occupy your time?"

"Yes. I wanted to procure some herbs for making a lotion for Elisabetta today." I don't mention my own sleeping tonic. He'll just worry if I'm not resting.

I can't read his expression in the momentary silence. "There's a storeroom near the kitchen that no one is using. It might be convenient for you to use for your medicines," he says at last. "I will have it cleaned today, and then you may begin using it."

"Thank you." I cringe at my repetition, trying to think of something else to say. His quiet intensity always knocks me out of ease for some reason. "And are you meeting with any diplomats today?"

"Perhaps. Nothing that can't be rescheduled. Do you need help with your errand?"

"No." I wonder if the too-quick response made it sharp, because his gaze flickers down, but I don't think I could stand more of this stilted conversation while he follows me around the apothecary shop. If there was ever any magic in our first meeting back in the garden of the Castello del Valentino, it's dried up now, ground to dust and scattered. "I shall manage, but it's kind of you to offer," I say, trying to sweeten my refusal.

He clears his throat. "I believe you said earlier you wanted more books. Please make a list. I'd like to have them added to our shelves here for you."

"Thank you." My cheeks burn and I want to swallow back the words, replace them with something that sounds more heartfelt, not yet another repetition. "Truly, I do appreciate it."

"It's nothing." His voice sounds gruff, almost impatient.

I finish the last sip of coffee and replace the cup on the table, noticing he seems to be finished as well. "I'd like to get outside before the shop becomes too busy."

"Good idea." He remains in the chair, cup resting on his knee. The arrow of sunlight piercing through the window glints off his ring, and his eyes look sad.

I feel it too, disappointment clinging like wet sand. As I walk toward the door, I resolve to think of some interesting things to talk about with him next time, even if it means making a pathetic secret list of topics and begging Caterina for ideas. It isn't Niccolo's fault we're not at ease with each other, and he deserves better. I pause in the doorway. "Niccolo?"

His head lifts, gaze piercing mine.

"Thanks." This time the word rings with true gratitude, not obligatory manners. "We should have breakfast together more often."

The corners of his lips curl in a shadow of a smile. "I'd like that."

CHAPTER SIX

Paris, September 1856

*The black trombetta dei morti mushroom appears deadly and
macabre, as its name implies, but is safe for consumption.
— Excerpt from Livia Valenti's book of herbal studies*

I work in the storeroom near the kitchen most of the morning,
which has been swept and dusted with surprising speed. Niccolo
must have ordered it as a priority. A beam of sunshine warms the
room, and I find myself humming softly as I arrange the items
Caterina and I purchased after a prolonged visit to the apothecary,
stocking up on some of the ingredients for the most common
household remedies. Today might be one of the happiest days
I've had so far in Paris.

Although I suppose it isn't necessary for me to maintain a
store of medicines, it fills me with a pure contentment to feel
the soft crumble of marshmallow root, to breathe in the sweet
grassy tang of chamomile flowers. When I survey the tidy row of
shining glass jars filled with herbs, I feel more satisfaction than I
have yet in this household. Even though I'm not a doctor myself,
and my father isn't here for me to assist, it seems like a good idea
to keep a supply of the basics here. If anyone in the household
comes down with a sore throat or stomach complaint, I can help
them. I might need to make a few things for myself, even. My

father often recommended raspberry leaf tea for pregnant women as they neared their labor, and an ointment of calendula and lavender would soothe the skin over my belly, which is starting to stretch and tighten.

By the time I've finished packing everything away, my back aches more than it should. I suppose that's another factor of my pregnancy. I press my knuckles into the muscles above my hips, sighing with relief, then turn to go back upstairs to my room, opening the chest at the foot of my bed in search of seeds. I brought a few packets of them from home, given to me by my mother the day before we left Turin.

"If you plant them, they'll make you feel more at home," she'd said. "As they grow roots, so will you."

I'd taken them, though I scoffed internally, too bitter about the hastiness of my marriage and the subsequent departure to France. Now that my resentment has tempered to determination to make the best of things, I'm glad to have them. I'll plant them after lunch.

My fingers brush over the small ebony box concealed in the bottom of the chest. It has a secret catch, and isn't easily opened unless one knows the trick of it. It's a unique trinket, but I've never had anything important enough to keep within its concealed compartment.

I open the drawstring of my small silk purse, fishing past the few coins and finding the tightly wrapped packet I purchased at the apothecary. Caterina didn't see this purchase; she was distracted, sifting through piles of rose petals, exclaiming she wanted to make scented sachets for her wardrobe.

"Belladonna," the shopkeeper said to me. Maybe I imagined the knowing glint in his eye, the shadow creeping through his tone. "Yes, I have it. Some doctors use it to treat tetanus, or mix it with a little opium for nervous disorders."

"I don't need any opium," I said. "Just the belladonna, for its use in dilating the pupils of an eye. It can be good for eye issues, too, you know."

He shrugged, either not caring about my excuse, or dismissing my knowledge. I wasn't a real doctor, after all.

I tip the contents of the packet into the ebony box. The few dried leaves and crumbled root of deadly nightshade look innocuous in that space, like bits from a forest floor, so delicate that they'd disintegrate under a light touch, or dissolve into liquid, rendered forever invisible. I marvel at the strange, dark wonder of a plant that can be so fragile and harmless, yet so dangerous. My lancet bracelet swings against my wrist as I ease the ebony box closed again.

Deep inside me, the baby flutters, heralding a lurch of nausea. My fingers clench tightly around the box as I breathe through the flip of my stomach, the tingle of my cheeks. When it passes, I loosen my grip and stare at the box, balanced on my palm, now crisscrossed with the imprint of its corners. It was a defensive whim that led me to buy it, and now I'll tuck it safe into my trunk, stuffed into the toe of an old slipper. Perhaps it will comfort me to know it's there, though I shouldn't ever need it.

Someone raps loudly on the door. The staccato sound jolts me to my feet, the box clutched again in my fist. "Who is it?"

Lorenzo, Niccolo's manservant, calls through the door. "Signora, you have a visitor."

I wasn't expecting anyone. Taken by surprise, I stuff the box into the bodice of my dress—thankfully, I've got a high collar today—and open the door.

"The contessa di Castiglione is here to see you," Lorenzo says.

In my current state, La Castiglione is the last person I want to see. My hair straggles at my neck, and my nails are dusty from crumbled mullein flowers and their fuzzy leaves, which are good for chest colds when brewed into a tea with ginger or mint. Not to mention, I've just been staring at a box of nightshade, tendrils of shadow clutching at my mind and my heart.

At least my dress is clean since I wore an apron in the storeroom. "I suppose I'd better go down."

"I know it's unexpected, but I'm not sure I can send her away." Lorenzo looks abashed.

"It's all right. I'll see her. Is Niccolo here?"

He shakes his head. "He went out an hour ago."

Elisabetta rises from her armchair as I enter the salon. "Livia, I hope I'm not inconveniencing you too much. I wanted to talk to you, and when my lunch plans were cancelled, I thought I'd drop in."

"It's no trouble at all," I say, surreptitiously swiping my fingertips over my nails. "Is everything all right?" Her casual words don't match the crease of worry between her eyebrows, or the way she fidgets with the enormous ring on her finger.

"Yes, well enough. No more poisoned berries—you needn't fear of that."

While pleased she doesn't seem to be suffering any anxiety over the berries, I'm uncomfortably aware of the nightshade currently concealed on my own person. Even though I don't intend to use it, I like to know it's available, like a protective weapon. My skin prickles with guilt.

"I suppose I'm in a bit of a restless mood," says Elisabetta. "I'm meant to send a letter to Camillo, and I haven't even started. Do you know he insists I use a secret code for my correspondence with him? At first it gave me a thrill every time I sat down to write to him, but that luster has faded."

I blink in surprise. "I suppose it must be tedious, to cross-reference every word against the cipher."

She flicks a curl away from her cheek. "It's etched into my memory by now—once fluent in the code, it's like reading and writing in any other language. Even easier than English, dare I

say. It's the subject matter of the letters that grows wearisome…
'I attended another ball last week. The emperor danced with me,
and later called upon me at home. He was not inclined to speak of
politics, if you understand my meaning.' Or, 'At a picnic outing
full of judgmental court ladies, I fell and twisted my wrist. It was
humiliating, and I tore the hem of my expensive dress besides. It
isn't cheap dressing to impress an emperor, as Francesco reminds
me often.' Camillo doesn't much care for these truthful updates,
and they seem too trivial for the pretentious gravitas of the code."

"Is your wrist all right?" I ask with concern.

"That was months ago, before you arrived in Paris. It was only
lightly sprained." She sips her tea. "It's a relief to share this with
you, Livia. None of my court acquaintances would understand,
nor the pressure of the situation back home that requires me to
write so often to Camillo in the first place."

"If you have no update, must you write?"

Elisabetta's lip curves upward in a wry smile, acknowledging
the sympathy in my tone. "You'd think not, but Camillo insists.
Evidently, he can't imagine that Louis isn't obsessed with Austrian occupation of Italian land. I suppose it's partly from sheer
optimism, and perhaps knowing that Louis was a member of the
Carbonari in his youth."

"Surely that must be an influence?" I ask. "If he cared enough
to join a resistance group dedicated to overthrowing Austrian rule
in Italy then, why doesn't he now?" I'm curious to hear more about
the emperor's mysterious past, and the Carbonari itself. Since
coming to Paris and living adjacent to Niccolo's diplomatic tasks,
I've heard rumors of the group's elaborate initiation ceremonies,
and that it operates in small groups of people so if any police
infiltration were to occur, they would learn only a few names,
at best.

"Bitterness," says Elisabetta simply. "He grew up in Switzerland
and spent time in his twenties in Italy—back then, the Bonapartes

were still in exile, and it certainly wasn't a guarantee any of them would become emperor of France." She looks to me to check I'm following. "His older brother joined the Carbonari first, and he was passionate about the cause. But from what Louis has told me, the Carbonari used them to lure more recruits. They thought the Bonaparte name might draw soldiers, adding French support to Italy's cause."

I nod, enjoying the clarity of Elisabetta's explanations. Her political astuteness is just as impressive as her dramatic visions for photographs. And I can see that Camillo is following the Carbonari's tactics now, using Elisabetta to persuade the emperor to order troops.

"But French troops never came. And so they asked the brothers to leave the army. Even now, some twenty-five years later, Louis is angry when he remembers. It was humiliating for them, fleeing like vagabonds, wanted by the Austrian police, even sneaking out of Italy with false papers. It's really a miracle he became emperor at all," Elisabetta adds pensively. "His brother died in Pesaro, before they escaped, making Louis the heir, and a man with resentment in his heart."

"It's a sad story. Does your cousin know?"

Elisabetta hesitates. "Much of this was told to me in confidence, in moments of intimacy. Camillo knows the history, yes. But I don't think he understands the bitterness. It makes little difference; he'd ask me to continue in any case. I do believe I provided some comfort to Louis, when he told me. Perhaps it will help."

I think of Elisabetta listening to the emperor speak of his brother's death, and find it difficult to imagine that tender intimacy. Would she have stroked his hair? Would his voice have cracked?

"Do you like him?" I ask.

I realize at once it was the wrong question. Too personal, too sentimental. Elisabetta would have laughed and spilled secrets if

I asked her if he snored, or if he was impatient in bed. Instead, her mouth pinches and she reaches for a biscuit, snapping it in half, heedless of the crumbs dusting her skirt. "Certainly, I like him. I like the attention, I like the gifts." She clips her words, making them short and bristly.

Unsure what to say, I only nod, trying to look serene even though I worry I've offended her somehow. It makes me realize how much I've come to rely on her bright presence in my days here in Paris.

"Did Bellino ask you to put forth the question?" she says at last. Her eyes look narrow and dark, gleaming like faint moonlight on midnight water.

I'd expected a jagged response from her, but not this. "Bellino?" My voice sounds as blank as my expression must be as I stare at her in bafflement. "No. It was merely an idle question. I didn't mean to intrude, it's only that I've never met anyone so close to an emperor, and I'm curious."

She cuts my excuses short with a sigh. "It's all right, Livia. You didn't deserve prickliness from me, and I can see by your astonishment that Bellino hasn't spoken to you of the emperor at all."

"Of any subject. We aren't well acquainted yet. He's hardly home at all."

Her lips twitch into a small curve of amusement, and her tone sounds wry. "Well, I know him very well—he still visits me quite often. We used to spend summers together back in Italy."

"Niccolo, too?" I'm spiked with sudden curiosity.

"No, he wasn't there much. Your husband has always been serious and hard-working." It doesn't quite sound like a compliment when she says it, the implication being that he's boring. A prickle of unexpected protectiveness runs over my skin. "Being six years older, he was often with his father, who was some kind of politician, a financial minister or something, learning to follow in his footsteps. He and my cousin Camillo spent some time together; it's no surprise he works for him now. Anyway, Bellino tends to be a bit... protective. And he means well, but he can be a dreadful busybody. If he has any thought of prying into my relationship with the emperor, I'd tell him plainly it's none of his affair."

"Of course." I nod seriously, trying not to show how fascinated I am by her stories of their youth, in case it seems unsophisticated. I wish she'd known Niccolo better. I'm seized with fresh curiosity to know more about him.

Elisabetta pauses, seems to remember she holds two broken shards of almond biscuit. "The emperor is often restless," she says after a moment, in a confiding tone. "It makes me tense too, and sometimes it's difficult to sleep after his visits." She nibbles on the *cantuccino*.

"That's easily enough remedied." Relieved this is something I can assist with, I lean forward. The hard lump of my belly stops my motion partway. "I'll send you home with a packet of chamomile and valerian tea."

She smiles. "That would be lovely. And don't think I've forgotten about those lotions—I'm quite excited to use them."

"I found all the ingredients this morning. I can make them soon."

She beams with delight. "Wonderful. Livia, I meant to ask, have you ever been to the opera here in Paris?"

"No." It's a tempting prospect, though. When I first arrived in Paris, I would have dismissed the idea in favor of draping a blanket over my feet—which are always cold, now that I'm pregnant—and reading. The city is beginning to feel less daunting, and I'm brave enough to start exploring. Maybe that's Elisabetta's influence.

"My dear, you mustn't deprive yourself any longer. It's great fun, and we'd be out so late. I always love traipsing home at the crest of dawn, and sleeping away the morning, don't you? It feels so wonderfully decadent."

I can't truthfully admit I feel the same. I'm used to rising early. At home, we'd get up at first light, or soon after at the very least, and my mother and I would help prepare medicines or undertake other household tasks while my father visited patients. It's true that sleeping all morning feels decadent, because people who work don't get to do it. I smile at Elisabetta, thinking perhaps it might be nice to try it. My life is different now, after all, and why shouldn't I have some fun?

For a long time that has felt out of reach, but now I smile at the prospect of an enjoyable outing with Elisabetta.

"You must ask Niccolo to rent us a box," Elisabetta continues. "I had one, but it seems Francesco hasn't paid for it for the rest of the season. That man clutches his purse strings so tightly you'd need to cut them, not untie them."

"I assumed the emperor would have a box for you."

She makes a little moue of disappointment. "Sometimes, but not always. His wife…" She lets the sentence hang, but I understand. If Empress Eugénie dislikes public displays of favor for her husband's mistresses, I can't blame her. "Persuade Niccolo for some night soon, won't you? Perhaps the four of us can go."

"Four? You mean to bring Francesco?"

"Heavens, no. I meant Bellino. He's much more entertaining than my husband, and I'm sure Niccolo would prefer his company. Your husband can be a bit grim, can't he? But he gets along with his own brother, and then you and I can remark upon everyone's dresses between acts and giggle in peace."

"If he's so grim, how am I supposed to persuade him to pay for the box?" I already know I'll try to talk to him, though. She's painted such a carefree, glamorous portrait of the event that I find myself longing to experience it.

"You're carrying his child. He wouldn't dare deny you anything."

During the rest of the visit, she tells me of her latest photography plans. She intends to pose as a nun for her next portrait, wearing a structured and voluminous white gown, with a long white wimple framing her face and mostly covering her hair.

"I'll cross my arms protectively over my waist," she explains. "And stare straight into the camera, daring anyone to judge me. But only God may judge a nun."

"I didn't expect that costume," I admit.

"No one will," she says. "That's why I'm so drawn to the idea. What a perfect opportunity for a dichotomy. I can't resist it. Especially in contrast to the rumors about me."

"Rumors?"

She waves a hand, but the gesture is somehow too airy. "It's just envious court whispers." Her tone shifts to a harder note. "They say I spent my last night in Italy in the bed of King Vittorio Emanuele. It was a test, they say, drunk on the scandal of their own musings. To make sure La Castiglione was enticing enough for the emperor, she had to pass a test by spending the night with the king of Piedmont-Sardinia. She satisfied that notoriously lecherous monarch, so she must be wanton enough to please our own lascivious emperor."

"You've shown them by keeping his interest for nearly a year," I say. "He clearly cares for you, truly."

She leans back against the sofa, turning her face toward the window so the daylight makes her skin glow, pale and smooth. "And what does the circumstance matter, for their stories? I could have been walking in the gardens of Florence, admiring the roses and birdsong, when the king cornered me, and everyone else who'd been in the garden became suddenly and conspicuously absent. Or I could have been discreetly invited to his bedchamber, sent in at midnight, costumed in a sheer nightdress, my hair hanging loose and scented with jasmine, a siren sent to tempt a man who hardly needed urging to sow his oats.

"It doesn't matter. The possibility that any of the scenarios might be true is enough to fan the fervor of gossip. None of them want to know the real details, because it might turn out not to be true at all."

I'm silent for a moment. "Cruel whispers can't pierce your skin. Malicious gossip can't bruise your flesh."

She gives me a genuine smile. "Trust a doctor's daughter to relate it back to physical wounds. But you're quite right, Livia. Anyway, my body isn't mine, just as the rumors say. Right now it belongs to the emperor, and that ought to be the toughest armor a woman can possess."

After Elisabetta departs in a flurry of silk and a trail of lily perfume, I head outside to the garden. I know I ought to go straight upstairs and hide the ebony box again, but the lingering trace of Elisabetta's perfume triggers a wave of threatening nausea, and I'm desperate for fresh air. I'll be glad when the baby is born and these unpredictable symptoms are over.

Near the stairs to the kitchen, I nearly collide with Bellino.

His hand grabs my elbow, steadying me as I stumble back. Laughter rumbles in his throat. "I'm sorry, Livia. Did I scare you? Your eyes are as round as the moon."

I shake him off. "Momentarily startled only. I didn't expect to see you down here. Raiding the kitchen, were you?"

He grins. "You guessed? I suppose I'm not as stealthy as I thought. Although there's no need to sneak; the cook here is kind enough to give me something before I even ask. I'm almost starting to believe he keeps a bowl of sugared almonds prepared for my inevitable visits." He pauses. "Were you on your way somewhere? Am I interrupting?"

"Not at all. I'd just been checking the supply of medicines." This is mostly true, anyway, but the ebony box feels heavy against my ribs. "I was walking to the garden now. If you're headed that way, perhaps we may stroll together."

He falls into step beside me. "My brother did tell me your father was a doctor."

"I learned much from him. I used to help him quite a lot. Niccolo was kind enough to let me use the empty room, down near the kitchen, to make salves and tinctures for the household."

Bellino smiles lazily as we step through the door into the small garden. When he turns to me, the sunshine makes his eyes gleam with flecks of light blue, like a pool of clear water. He looks utterly guileless. "I may have to call for your aid, then, next time I've overindulged in wine, although I'm not sure I'll dare. Niccolo wouldn't want you to strain yourself on my account. He'd rather see you brew remedies to care for your own health."

"I'm healthy. There's no reason the child shouldn't be." I cup my hands around the swelling of my belly. The hardness of it surprises me still, sometimes.

"It isn't only that." Bellino stretches his finger toward a butterfly perched on a scarlet poppy petal. "He worries you aren't happy here."

The butterfly drifts aloft, passing close to my face. The whisper of its wings brushes my skin like a friendly caress. I know I oughtn't to speak so bluntly, but I remember the awkward distance between Niccolo and me at breakfast and a surge of resentment spurs my words. "You're kind to say so, but I'm not sure he thinks of me often at all. And I can't imagine him making such a remark to you."

"He doesn't need to—I've known him my whole life. My earliest memory is of Niccolo—we were running along the lane with his new hound pup frolicking beside us. You forget I've also seen Niccolo married before, and he wasn't the same with Carlotta."

The mention of Niccolo's late wife snaps my attention to something sharp. He has so rarely mentioned her that I've been afraid to as well, but I can't help being curious. Elisabetta's comment that Bellino can be a bit of a busybody echoes in my mind, and I hope he'll prove her right in this case. I want to hear more. "How so?"

"Oh, he treated her well enough, but I never caught him staring at her." Bellino picks a sprig of honeysuckle and steps toward me. "I never saw him turn to a doe-eyed statue when she walked by." He bops the flowers against the tip of my nose, laughing, and then presses the stem into my hand.

I can't help smiling a little. His playful spirits lift my own, and relax some of my usual reserve. The honeysuckle's perfume drifts through the air, as sweet as Bellino's smile.

"Niccolo's probably just shy now, since everything happened so suddenly," he continues. "He's always been a bit shy, in fact. I confess to being surprised he seduced you back in Turin."

"He told you?" Taken aback, I blurt the question before I can think of a more dignified response. I suppose it makes sense he would address it. I've already come to terms with the truth that people can count on their fingers easily enough, and when my baby is born in a little more than three months, they'll know without a doubt my child was conceived before my marriage in late July. Bellino knows already, likely; living in the household, he can see my belly is too swollen for my marriage date. I just don't know him well enough to feel at ease discussing the topic with him. But if he's my brother-in-law now, I need to reconcile myself to speaking frankly with him. I decide I'm glad Niccolo said something first. Hiding the truth only gives gossipy whispers more strength.

Bellino nods. "Don't be embarrassed. There's nothing shameful in having children. Niccolo must have been ecstatic when you conceived so quickly, even if it meant a hasty marriage. I think he's always wanted a child, but his late wife never showed the slightest sign of pregnancy. When she first fell ill, he hoped perhaps her weariness was a sign she was finally expecting, but then the coughing began. And didn't stop."

The Paris Wife   89

"Am I much like her?" I ask, unable to keep the wisp of insecurity out of my voice. Back in Turin, in the brief space of time after the wedding, but before our arrival in Paris, I found a portrait of her covered with a sheet and tucked behind a bookcase in the library. Her brown eyes stared haughtily through the paint, and her curtain of rich chestnut hair sheltered a long swan-like neck draped with pearls. Even in still life she exuded an aura of nobility, a cool sense of self-assurance. I turned away, scowling. She looked like she'd flit gracefully from one important person to another at a ball, the perfect accompaniment to Niccolo's diplomatic tasks in Paris. She looked like she'd always know the right thing to say, and not be seen as somewhat of a curiosity because of her knowledge of illness and medicine.

Bellino snorts. "Not at all."

"She was very beautiful," I say.

"I didn't mean you aren't, Livia. Her personality was very different. Sometimes she laughed and bantered and her charm was infectious. But she was also easily bored and could be spiteful—often to amuse herself." He shrugs. "There I go, speaking ill of the dead again. Good thing Niccolo isn't here to scold me." He shakes his head self-deprecatingly, and a golden curl drapes itself over his forehead. I like that he's friendly and free with his opinions.

It feels good to be forthright with him. I believe we can be friends. "Sometimes I've felt like a bit of an imposter here, as if perhaps I'm a poor replacement for Carlotta."

"Certainly not." He crosses his arms. "I'm sure no one believes any such thing."

"Thank you for the reassurance."

Ever restless, he kicks a stone off the path. "I don't need thanks for telling the truth. You'll settle in." He gives me an encouraging smile. "Maybe you should try to spend more time with Niccolo. He's been fussing over politics lately, and it makes him too glum.

I don't blame him—Camillo makes him write reports nearly every day, I swear. I think focusing on family would likely cheer him up."

I nod, considering. "I'm glad we had this talk, Bellino. We know each other better now."

"I'm glad of it too." Craning his neck, he scans the sky. "Do you suppose it's too early for wine?"

"Is it ever too early, as far as you're concerned?"

"On rare occasions, I maintain some semblance of propriety," says Bellino. "Did you see Elisabetta earlier? I meant to have a word with her, but she left quickly."

"Yes, it was only a brief visit, but she's been quite friendly to me."

"It seems she's taken you under her wing," he says. "How do you like her?" He doesn't look at me as he asks, fussing over the cluster of small white flowers on a tangled sprig of wild carrot, sometimes called Queen Anne's lace.

I notice the careful way he avoids my gaze, and remember Elisabetta's description of their past summers, growing up together. I think of the way he went to her house first, upon arriving in Paris, rather than to see Niccolo. That there's a connection or history of some kind between them is as obvious as the thorns on the rose bush growing just beside a bright forest of slender poppies. I should have noticed it earlier.

"She's the most interesting person I've ever met, I think."

Bellino's lip curls with a puff of dry laughter. "You aren't exaggerating there."

"She talked to me about some of her photographs. She's planning to pose as a nun in the next one."

He straightens slowly, his brow arched. "As a joke? How bizarre, when everyone knows of her status in the emperor's bed."

"I suppose so." The roughness of his tone makes everything click into place. It should have been obvious from the start, but I've only realized now that he and Elisabetta must have been lovers during some of those summers they spent together. Pity stirs in my heart, for he's clearly jealous of her new relationship, and there's nothing he can do about it. I wonder if Elisabetta cares as much for him.

If she does, she hides it well.

"Elisabetta has always liked her dramatics," he says, his voice still carrying that hard cadence.

"I like her photographs." Loyalty to Elisabetta spurs me to defend her, but it's also true. "I've never seen anything like them."

"At first, I thought they were a vanity." Bellino clicks the lid of his pocket watch open and shut, fidgeting with it. "Maybe they're not. It's nice of you to be supportive of her hobby. Didn't I say you were a good person, Livia? Kinder than the rest of us, I think. No wonder Elisabetta likes you so much."

I blush under his compliment. "I think her opinion of me was rather influenced by our first meeting. She believes I saved her life, but at least she doesn't think I'm crazy." I confide the whole tale of the nightshade berries to him. Even now, I sometimes wonder if I was too paranoid, but in my memory, the berries still look just as dangerous.

Bellino pales at the story. "Good God. It's never occurred to me before that my food might be poisoned. I thought that sort of thing only happened to tyrants or blackmailers, or in novels. But to hear it can happen by accident—I'll be hellishly afraid to eat from now on."

"Don't be. It's quite rare for poisonous plants to be ingested by mistake. Most of them aren't really considered food—nightshade berries and mushrooms are some exceptions. No one would want to satisfy their hunger with roots or leaves."

He laughs in surprise. "You've reassured me, and I hope you'll tell more stories of strange medical cases you've seen, poison or not. I've just realized it's a morbidly fascinating topic."

"Of course." Knowing I have a deadly dose of nightshade leaves on my person right now makes me feel sly, like a liar. I don't like the feeling. It burns along the nape of my neck. "Another time, though. I'll have to remember the best ones."

He sobers again. "I am glad no one ate those berries. What a scare."

"It was," I agree, straightening so the corner of the ebony box doesn't dig into me.

As I go back up to my room, my thoughts keep spinning back to Niccolo. I don't know if I believe Bellino's assertion of Niccolo's smitten feelings. More importantly, even if Niccolo does care for me, I don't know if I can love him back.

The edge of the ebony box feels sharp against my skin, pressing close to my heart.

CHAPTER SEVEN

Paris, September 1856

Oleander flowers are beautiful, and deadly. The sap can cause blistering, and if ingested, the plant brings abdominal distress, hallucinations, and erratic heart rate until death. Livestock avoids it, and the plant is sometimes used as a lovely hedge in place of a fence.
— Excerpt from Livia Valenti's book of herbal studies

In the two months since our marriage and arrival in Paris, I've never visited Niccolo's bedroom. Our habit is to bid each other goodnight in the parlor, or the dining room. He always kisses my hand, politely wishes me a good evening, and then I don't see him again until breakfast, sometimes not even until later in the day.

I linger in the hallway outside his room now, soaking up the comforting glow of the candles flickering in decorative wall sconces, dallying to inspect a painting of a draft horse with elegantly feathered feet and a long mane. At the doorway, nervousness ricochets my pulse to a staccato pace. I twist my fingers in the edge of my long wool shawl, draped around me to distract from the fact that I'm wearing my heavy linen nightgown. As I lift my hand to knock, my courage almost fails me, and only my promise to Elisabetta to ask Niccolo if we can go to the opera keeps my feet in place. No, if I'm truly honest with myself, Bellino's frank conversation keeps me here just as strongly. If he tells the truth, if Niccolo cares for me underneath that aloof exterior, I think I want to know.

The door must not be shut tight, for as my knuckles collide with the wood paneling, it slowly pushes open, and golden light spills through. Niccolo sits at a table near the window, head bent over the silver gleam of the dagger he's polishing. I expected him to be writing, and the contrast makes me hesitate in the doorway.

Niccolo's lips part with surprise, but he recovers quickly and rises to his feet. "Livia, is everything all right?" He strides to my side, gaze flicking to the curve of my belly before settling with worry on my face. His fawn-colored hound, Luce, trails at his heels, and pushes his muzzle into my hand.

"Yes." I lick my dry lips. The intensity of Niccolo's stare disconcerts me. "I just thought perhaps we ought to talk."

In the brief, crushing silence before he replies, I contemplate feigning nausea and making my escape back to my own bed. I stroke the hound's silky ears and take a steadying breath. The trepidation I feel around Niccolo frustrates me. I must spend the rest of my life with him, so it has to stop.

"Of course." The courtesy of his tone doesn't quite hide his lingering surprise, but he doesn't sound displeased. "Would you like to sit down? There's some wine in the decanter, but I can call for something else, if you like."

I let him guide me to the chair beside the table, but decline anything to drink. "I hope I didn't interrupt." I glance at the dagger.

"Not at all. I was just sharpening it." He pauses. "It used to be my father's."

"I'm sure he'd be pleased you take such good care of it. What happened to him?" I hope he doesn't mind the question, but neither of Niccolo's parents were at our wedding. Bellino wasn't either, for that matter, but he was in Florence and unable to arrive in time for our hasty nuptials. Their parents had passed away, I knew, but not how long ago.

"He became ill after my mother's death of pneumonia, five years ago." Niccolo says. "The doctor said it was his heart."

"A weak heart?" I struggle to picture an older version of Niccolo with a florid complexion and a paunch. It isn't uncommon for older men who eat many rich foods to have weak hearts.

"I suppose it could be considered weak, by some. I've always believed he just couldn't go on without her." He clears his throat. "What did you want to talk about, Livia?"

For some reason this annoys me. I know our habitual formality means my visit to him tonight breaks the tradition, but shouldn't I be able to talk to my husband without a prescribed subject in advance? That I actually did come here with a purpose only irrationally adds to my frustration. I don't like this state we're in. My irritation makes me bold, and instead of mentioning Elisabetta's request about the opera, I try to broach the subject in a broader way, to show I'd like to talk about more than just the weather or who might be visiting us for supper. Luce rests his chin on my lap, and the silent comfort of his presence steels me to proceed. "I want to talk to you about our purpose in Paris, about the unification."

Niccolo's brows arch. "You do?"

Exasperation winds through my voice. "Yes. I'm not completely unaware of what goes on in the household, and I have opinions."

The tips of his ears redden. "Forgive me. I meant no offense. The topic was merely unexpected."

I fold my hands in my lap, sitting up straight and trying to be as regal as possible. Maybe if I appear to suit the role of a clever and confident lady of the house, we'll both believe it. And now that I've brought it up, I do want to discuss it. I want to know when I can return home to Turin, though I know it will be at least a few months after the birth. "Is there no way for us to speed along the negotiations with the emperor?"

"I'm not able to command the emperor," Niccolo says gently. "Much as I wish to, he hasn't been interested in arranging a meeting, even with Elisabetta's urging." He sounds faintly doubtful on the last; perhaps he wonders if she's really trying to persuade the emperor at all.

"Is there anything else we can do to satisfy Conte Cavour?" Aware I sound churlish, but unable to help it, I shift in my chair. The baby kicks, just as restless as me. I'm tired of hiding; I want to be involved in the household and all its issues now. With a strange pang, I realize I've slowly started to think of Niccolo and Bellino as my family, and I don't want to be at arm's length anymore.

Niccolo's mouth softens with sympathy. "I'll be happy to return home to Turin too, Livia. In the meantime, we must be patient." He pauses. "If anyone can persuade the emperor, it's Elisabetta."

"She's trying. She tells me so. I don't understand why you must be here supervising, when she seems to be handling everything herself. Neither does she."

"Livia, are you so unhappy in Paris? I've tried to make the house comfortable, but if something displeases you, I want you to tell me."

The serenity of his answers is starting to grate against my desire for decisiveness. "It's not that. The house is very nice." But it isn't home, and I don't feel comfortable telling him that. "I suppose I have little patience with politics."

"I know what it's like to be homesick, and I'm sorry if you feel isolated here. I'd hoped…" He clears his throat. "I hope Caterina is some comfort, at least."

I open my mouth to assure him I'd be lost without her, to thank him again for paying her a handsome salary, but he forestalls me, leaning forward and speaking just a shade louder. "I will write again to the emperor. I can promise that much. But don't let your hopes rise too high for his quick response. He's never responded to any of my letters before, and rarely to Cavour. He doesn't seem ready to commit to anything." His voice softens again. "There's only so much I can do, but I will try."

His kindness should ease my spirits, but instead I find myself unable to quell a tide of impatience and frustration. I wish he'd stop talking to me in the tone one would use to lure a skittish puppy. I hate that we're strangers trapped in a life together. My skirt of my nightgown swirls around my ankles as I storm out of the chair and move toward the window. Outside, the wind lifts the tree branches into restless banners, and rain catches the moonlight and turns it to silver.

Niccolo walks up behind me. I feel the faint heat of his body, though he does not touch me. "What else is bothering you?" At last, an edge of emotion scrapes through his voice.

I turn to face him, the words spilling from me in a thoughtless rush. "We don't even know each other. I hardly know anything about you. I don't know how you lost your finger, or what color you like best. And you don't know me—you don't know I've made a study of different types of poisons, or that I've no patience with Caterina's fascination with tarot cards, or my great-grandmother murdered a foreman on a slave plantation in Saint-Domingue. I don't know how we can live together as strangers."

To my horror, my voice cracks on the last word. I mustn't cry. I suck in a slow, calming breath, inwardly cursing the occasional volatile effect the pregnancy has on my emotions. Perhaps I shouldn't have told him so many secrets.

Niccolo reaches toward my cheek, but lets his hand fall before he touches my skin. His eyes look bluer than usual, the golden light of the room washing away the gray. "I lost my finger when I was ten years old and it got caught in the pulley of a well." He holds up his hand, revealing the shortened index finger. "It snapped off so quickly I hardly noticed until a moment or two later, when the pain began."

I brush my fingertip over the neatly healed scar. "Does it pain you still? I've heard, sometimes, that people with lost limbs feel them aching for years afterward."

He shakes his head. "No, but sometimes I imagine I feel things with it." He leans down and pats his dog's head. "I'd swear I can feel his fur with my absent fingertip." His hand stretches toward my hair, but he doesn't touch the braid hanging over my shoulder. "I imagine I'd feel the softness of your hair, just the same as my other fingers would." His voice softens to a rasp. "I'm partial to red. And I do know about your family. Your father told me the bare details, when our marriage was arranged. I didn't know you're an expert on poisons, but it doesn't surprise me. You're one of the most knowledgeable people I've ever met, especially where plants are concerned. And I can't say I have much faith in tarot cards, either."

"Does it bother you?" I lift my chin. "That my great-grand-mother was a murderess?"

Niccolo's eyes pin to mine, and he slides one step closer. "No. She isn't you. Do you remember when we met, in the garden at the Castello del Valentino? First, I was struck by your beauty. In the late sunshine, your skin looked dipped in gold and you moved with such grace and confidence I almost thought you didn't touch the ground. Then you were kind to me, as I clumsily tried to rescue a frog, and clever too, knowing more about it than I did. There's nothing in your history, or your family's, that could erase those precious first impressions from my mind."

I stare back into his earnest gaze, surprised and moved. I can't think of anything to say; my lips part, but no words come to express how much his speech—the longest and most intimate I've heard him make—has touched my heart. His chest feels warm, inches from my own, and my breath quickens. If I rocked forward, the swell of my belly would press against his hips. When I blink, dizziness threatens to wash through me, sweet and intoxicating as too much wine.

"Livia." He turns my name to something luxuriant, soft as velvet. "Do you want me to kiss you?" He bends his face closer to mine, and the whisper of his voice caresses my lips.

My breath shortens. Anticipation freezes my bones. My heartbeat hammers through my veins and I can almost imagine myself leaning into his embrace, turning my mouth up to his for ravishment. Would he be gentle, or would he clutch at my body, drowning me under his own desires? Uncertainty turns me to stone.

Niccolo rocks back, taking two steps away. "I promised on our wedding night I wouldn't touch you again until you asked. I meant it." He draws in a ragged breath. "You have nothing to fear from me, I swear it."

A wave of cool air cascades over me as he steps back, rolling across my throat, down my arms. My throat feels tight, and I don't know if it's due to relief or disappointment.

Niccolo sits at the table, carefully sheathing the dagger and then resting his chin in his hands. "You're right we don't know each other well enough. It's a strain on us. I hate the silences, the awkwardness between us. I thought the breakfast would help, but it didn't."

We haven't had one of those breakfasts again since, in spite of saying we would. The disappointment holds us back. "So do I." My lips curl at the corners at the realization that both of us, not just me, have been struggling to think of something to say, and failing completely. It's too bittersweet to be funny, but it does remove some of the pressure I feel about it.

"Perhaps breakfast is too formal. Perhaps we should meet every night before bed for shared conversation, like this. It can be as long or short as you wish, so long as we each learn one new thing about each other."

I like his suggestion, and give him another fact to show my approval. "My favorite color is a particular shade of orange. The warm, cheerful color of calendula flower petals."

His eyes glimmer, the distance between us making them almost silver now. "I don't know what calendula flowers look like, but if you show me, I'll make sure they're planted all around the gardens at home."

The sweetness of his response chips away at the ice around my heart. Impulsively, I cross the room to his side. "Don't move." He obligingly stills as I bend my face close to his. His hair smells like rosemary soap, sharp and clean, and feels soft against my lips when I press a kiss to his temple. Niccolo remains motionless, though I sense from the tension in his body that he holds his breath. I can't name the emotion that swamps me as I draw away from that chaste kiss and remember his words about our first meeting, his promises to write to the emperor, and to plant flowers. His vow that my history doesn't matter to him. It's hard to believe in the latter, but at least he said it… Resting my fingertips gently on his jaw, the other hand on his shoulder, I press another kiss to his cheekbone and then withdraw, feeling absurdly grateful. I've been frightened of him at times, resentful of our hasty marriage, but perhaps Niccolo is a better husband than I dreamed. Than I deserve, even. I'm glad I left the nightshade box in the trunk again.

"Good night." I cast the words over my shoulder as I stride away, dazed by the confidence of my actions. My nerves burn with shock and I feel hot, cheeks tingling. I want to press my face into the dark coolness of my pillows, and for the first time, I wish I didn't have to retire to such a lonely bed. My feet hesitate in the doorway, as if I might turn and call Niccolo to my side, but then I march back down the hallway alone.

In the morning, I belatedly remember to ask Niccolo about the opera, and since Bellino sits beside me, sipping coffee in desperate way that makes me think he's suffering from an over-indulgence in wine, it's easy to make the suggestion.

Bellino leaps on the plan at once. "I think that's a grand idea. It's about time you two took advantage of some of Paris's cultural delights. The Théâtre Impérial de l'Opéra shouldn't be missed."

"What do you know of cultural delights?" Niccolo teases his brother, good-naturedly catching the croissant his brother hurls at him in response.

My teacup probably hides my shocked delight. I've never seen the two of them grin at each other like this, or ever witnessed Niccolo not use cutlery with practically surgical precision. Now he's holding baked goods in his hand, plate forgotten on the table, and grinning. If the prospect of a night at the opera makes everyone this cheerful, I wish we could go every day.

CHAPTER EIGHT

Paris, September 1856

Foxglove, also known as 'dead man's bells,' is toxic in every form, from the roots to the flowers and seeds. Signs of foxglove poisoning may include irregular heartbeat and convulsions.

— Excerpt from Livia Valenti's book of herbal studies

"I hope you'll find the photography studio just as fascinating as I do," Elisabetta says, as her carriage clatters along the street. "Paris boasts about one hundred and fifty portrait studios, proving how fashionable photography has become, but this one is my favorite."

"I'm a little nervous," I admit. "I've never been photographed before."

"It's nothing to fear. Perhaps you're imagining all eyes upon you, but in truth, it shall only be myself and Monsieur Pierson. I'll be at your side." She pauses. "Unless you'd rather pose alone, of course."

I shake my head. "No. I think it will be lovely to have my first photograph as one that commemorates our friendship, and our time in Paris."

"It's a relief to be out of the house for a while," Elisabetta confides. "Beatrice has a terrible cough. She was ill a few weeks ago, just a cold. Only the cough won't go away. It's not her fault, but it grates on my nerves terribly."

"I'll make up something to help her. Probably lingering congestion in her chest." A salve to rub on her chest would help, I think, my mind turning to my father's recipes for such things.

"I knew my complaints were falling on the right ears," teases Elisabetta.

As we step inside the studio of Messieurs Mayer and Pierson, my breath catches in awe at the reception area with its tiled floors, lavish wall paneling, and elegantly carved furniture. The waiting area opens into a high-ceilinged gallery, flooded with light.

"When I first stepped into this room, I felt like a bird slipping through its cage door into the freedom of the open space beyond," Elisabetta murmurs to me.

It feels like a theatre to me, as I gaze upon the backdrops of serene landscapes and gardens, which could cleverly slide on rails, and can't resist trailing my fingers over the surprising lightness of a row of balustrades, which turn out to be made of papier-mâché.

Monsieur Pierson's long black coat and dark mustache lend him an air of conventional seriousness that doesn't match the way his eyes flicker with interest when Elisabetta mentions she's thinking of posing with her face in profile.

"Indeed? Most people prefer to face the camera. We can try a few different poses." He's clearly had practice guiding his clients into flattering postures, and helping them choose the right background. I do not argue as he selects a backdrop of a stone-lined courtyard for Elisabetta and me. It reminds me of Turin, in fact, and I applaud his choice.

He purses his lips as he tells us different ways to stand, his brow creased critically. "Madame Valenti, your hands look too stiff." He flexes his own fingers open and shut a few times, encouraging me to do the same.

I do, but it feels like my bones vibrate with even more tension. I can't stop thinking about how to hold my hands, pressing them flat against the mass of my dark green skirt.

"Perhaps I ought to hold something." I sound a little helpless, until I spot a bucket filled with tall stalks of foxglove, blooming with pastel purple. "One of those flowers?"

"That would make a nice touch," agrees Monsieur Pierson.

"We should each hold one." Elisabetta plucks two spears of flowers from the bucket, handing one to me. "We're both wearing green, and the purple will offset it nicely. You'll do that, won't you, monsieur?"

"Of course, madame." To me, he adds, "My studio is famous for painted photographs, adding color and the prestige of a painting, but with the thrill of modern technology."

"I've seen some of your work," I say. "The *comtesse* has shown me some of her portraits. They're quite remarkable."

"And this portrait shall be, too," he promises.

While he arranges his equipment, Elisabetta talks to me in a low voice. "Francesco came to see me last night." Displeasure laces through her words; clearly, she prefers living apart from her husband. "He just settled my account here—and now I shall begin it again. He complains about paying it, although I mostly maintain my own household expenses. Camillo sends me money when I pester him enough."

"As he should," I reply. "How can you expect to entertain the emperor if your husband sits in the parlor downstairs?"

She nods. "Francesco has begun wearing his facial hair in the same manner as the emperor, with a narrow beard and the ends of his mustache shaped into thin points. I've pondered what it means. Is it symbolism, such as I employ in my portraits? Does he want me to see him standing in the parlor, just a few feet to the left of where the emperor stood a night earlier, and notice their similarities? Perhaps he wants me to be reminded of him when seeing the emperor—or even the other way around."

"It's very strange. Did you ask him?" Sometimes I don't feel worldly enough for Elisabetta's situations.

"I told him I don't like it, and he denied changing his beard at all." She rolls her eyes. "He thinks I want to return to Italy with him, but I have no intention of leaving Paris. Ah, it looks like Monsieur Pierson is ready for us to pose."

We stand in the center of the backdrop, heads bent close together. Pierson suggested it, perhaps inspired by our earlier whispering. I'm sure it looks like we're sharing secrets. I face the camera, holding the foxglove delicately in front of me. It feels much more natural to have greenery in my hand, and the faint floral scent calms me. Elisabetta turns her head toward me, her foxglove falling down by her side.

She poses for a second photograph in solitude. I don't mind. Being photographed once is enough for me, but enthusiasm shines from her, lighting up her skin and making her eyes gleam like a summer sky. It's interesting to watch her work with Pierson, without being involved myself. She clearly knows what she wants, but is willing to take his suggestion. It will take time for the photograph to develop, but I imagine it will be lovely. The bold pattern of her checked dress and its thin vertical flowered stripes highlight the narrow swoop of her waist, emphasized further by the belling sleeves and high, white lace collar. Pierson says it adds interesting structure. Her expression, face in profile, appears natural and curious, looking around at the world and finding delight in it.

In the carriage ride home, I tell her how striking the image was, and she smiles.

"I can't wait to see it. It felt right, as I posed. I felt like we captured something close enough to my true self to be authentic, but also created a new veneer of allure. I liked the way it felt."

"It will be marvelous," I assure her.

"Our portrait together shall be, too. I think your eyes will stand out—staring straight from the photograph and into the viewer's soul."

I laugh. "That doesn't sound pleasant."

"I don't mean it's how you are. Just the image." She leans back against the velvet upholstered carriage seat, contented. "Posing for photographs reminds me of a masquerade ball. Behind a mask, a person can be anyone she wishes. I believe photographs contain the same power."

An interesting idea, and one that makes me further curious to see our finished photograph. I wonder if Niccolo will like it, too. "Thank you for taking me, Elisabetta."

"My dear, we'll have you well-versed in the delights of Paris before long," she promises.

I spend part of the afternoon mixing up a strong salve of peppermint for Beatrice's cough, and, since the sky is clear, streaked with sunset orange, the air crisp and refreshing, I decide to walk to Elisabetta's to deliver it.

Her footman, Davide, ushers me inside her house. "The *comtesse* is in her sitting room. I shall let her know you've arrived."

"I need to see Beatrice first." I hold up the jar of salve.

"Thank you, madame. She'll be happy to have that," he says, with obvious relief. I suppose her lingering cough has been worrying everyone, not just Elisabetta.

After explaining to Beatrice how frequently to use the salve, and also suggesting she try breathing over a bowl of hot water to loosen some of the phlegm in her lungs, I make my way down to the sitting room. Davide has disappeared, but I know my way around Elisabetta's house well enough by now, and she ought to be expecting me.

I hesitate in the doorway, hearing Bellino's voice. I hadn't known he was here. He fusses over Elisabetta's young son, Giorgio, the two of them on the floor in front of the fireplace. Giorgio has fallen asleep, his mouth half-open, the toy soldiers they must have been playing with scattered on the blue and white rug around them. The glaze of the fire burnishes their golden hair to mellow copper, and the ungainly sprawl of Bellino's legs makes long shadows in the dim light. It might be an interesting photograph, which makes me smile. I've clearly been influenced by Elisabetta's obsession with them.

"He's an engaging little fellow." Bellino rises and crosses the room to where Elisabetta sits at a desk, pen and paper lying in front of her as she gazes idly into the flames. He wraps his fingers around hers and pulls her to her feet, the gesture so intimate I feel awkward interrupting, frozen in the hall near the door.

"Golden hair and blue eyes, just like yours and mine... Sometimes I like to imagine he's my son," Bellino murmurs, lifting their clasped hands to his heart.

Elisabetta stiffens. "He's not."

"I know, I know. He was born in wedlock, recognized by your husband. But it's possible, isn't it?"

I slide further away from the door, into the shadow of the darkened evening hall, relieved they haven't seen me, but unsure how to proceed. How can I interrupt now? Perhaps I should go back down the hall, come back in a few minutes, but Elisabetta's voice carries through the room again, keeping me rooted to the spot. I can still see them through the half-open door.

"No, it's not."

"We stopped being lovers after you married, but not immediately after."

"Only once, and it wasn't the right time."

Bellino's hand slides down her arm, lingering near her waist, and his tone turns apologetic. "I didn't mean anything by it. I'm fond of him, that's all."

"He likes you too." Elisabetta turns away, sitting back down in her solitary chair.

"Maybe it's nice for him to have a father figure."

"He has a father. Francesco and I aren't living together anymore, but he's still in Paris, and Giorgio sees him."

Bellino's hands clench at his sides. The firelight plays over his profile, casting shadows over his skin, darkening his eyes. "We aren't ever going to be together again, are we, Elisabetta?" His voice sounds brittle. Fragile.

I wish I could melt into the floor. I shouldn't be overhearing this, but I'm afraid to move in case they hear me.

Elisabetta tilts her face up to look at him, her expression bleak. "No."

Bellino's posture gains intensity, somehow reminiscent of something feline as he paces in front of the fireplace. "Because of the emperor? I don't give a damn about that. And that bastard Cavour had no business selling you to him. You're a free woman, you can do what you like—"

"I'm married. I am not free."

"I would have married you," he growls.

"We've spoken of that before—let's not bring it up again." Elisabetta stares at her hands, folded in her lap. "I'm sorry, Bellino, but the past is as it should be. We have no future together, at least not the one you want."

He turns violently, his arm catching on the vase of blood-red roses on the table, sending it crashing to the floor with a cacophony of shattered glass and cascading water droplets. He reaches for the crumpled flowers, then halts the motion, pressing his handkerchief to his finger. He must have cut himself; crimson unfurls along the white cloth.

I wonder, now, if I should interrupt. I could check his wound, though it is likely superficial. I doubt if I could successfully act as if I'd just arrived, though, a cheerful interruption into so much tension.

"I wish I could be free of you." Bellino's voice breaks like the crystal, and then he turns toward the door.

Breath held tight in my lungs, I take the opportunity to lurch backward, around a corner, my shoes thankfully quiet on the floor. Bellino doesn't see me as he storms out.

I wait a few moments, feeling ridiculous hiding in the shadows of Elisabetta's hallway, but I don't want her to know that I witnessed that scene. In some ways, I feel as though I have a greater comprehension of her relationship with Bellino now, of their closeness and the tension between them, and at the same time, I don't think I understand at all.

When I venture into the room, smiling and mentioning the salve, as if I've just come from Beatrice's room, Elisabetta beams, her eyes bright and teeth gleaming white. She tells me she knocked over the vase while practicing poses for a photograph, throwing her arms out wide.

"It's a miracle Giorgio didn't waken. Children sleep so deeply. I should call for his nurse to put him to bed now."

"I won't stay long." I note the flicker of relief washing over her face, but I understand. "I just wanted to let you know I left the salve."

When I see Bellino the next morning, he has a neat little bandage on his thumb, and he smiles and jokes as if nothing is amiss at all.

On the night of the opera, snowflakes swirl through the air, but my spirits fly with them. Caterina copies an elaborate hairstyle from a ladies' magazine, and manages to replicate it with my dark curls. "I'm rather proud of myself," she says. Braids frame the sides of my head, gathering into a low bun at the nape of my neck. "It looks almost exactly like, and now I'll slip in the butterfly hair comb at the back, just to add decoration."

"Thank you." The butterfly was a gift from my mother when I turned thirteen, and is still one of my most treasured items of jewelry. To finish it off, I also wear one of the family heirloom necklaces Niccolo gave me—a strand of pearls with a garnet pendant—choosing it specifically because he said he likes red. I hope it pleases him, for I like the new shift in our relationship. I survey my appearance critically, deciding it's a good thing voluminous gowns are in fashion because the extra fabric mostly hides the curve of my belly. I almost don't look pregnant in this new, dark blue gown.

"I wish you were coming with me," I tell Caterina. "I'm sure you'd enjoy a night at the opera too."

She shakes her head. "Another time, perhaps. I think it's just as well I'm not included tonight. You need to spend time with your husband. He should have taken you out before this, in fact."

"I was never interested before." I feel it isn't fair to fully blame him.

Caterina straightens one curl of hair so it lies along my cheek. "There. It's good to see you getting back to your old self. You don't need to hide."

"I suppose I've been overwhelmed."

She pats my hand. "There have been a lot of changes, but exciting ones, too, like tonight. Now go and have fun—if you linger in the bedroom any longer, I'll have to read your tarot cards." She laughs when her mocking threat encourages me toward the door.

At the opera house—not the Théâtre Impérial de l'Opéra, as it turns out, but the Salle Ventadour, where an Italian opera called *La Traviata* is performing—Elisabetta looks quite at home in the box, her skirt trailing over the edge of her seat in a way that somehow reminds me of a nymph, with a mysterious smile curling around her mouth and her golden hair twisted up like a crown. She and Bellino seem to be particularly close tonight, clinking their champagne glasses together and laughing. It's like their scene the other night never happened. I don't think Niccolo approves of their closeness; I suppose he's thinking of the emperor. Though he's very solicitous, offering me a drink and telling me the opera we're about to see is adapted from a novel called *The Lady of the Camellias* by Alexandre Dumas—which adds to my enthusiasm, since I've read it—I sense a sliver of his attention is always on the pair of them.

Once the music starts, I forget about the claustrophobic tensions of all these relationships, transported by the beautiful arias and the elaborate costumes. My spirits feel lighter than they have in months.

"Are you enjoying it?" asks Elisabetta during the intermission.

"Oh yes. It's wonderful."

Her eyes glint wickedly. "Didn't I promise we would gossip about everyone during the intermission? Look below, there's Comtesse Marianne Walewska, wife to the foreign minister. I can't believe I'm pointing her out to you. She's my rival, you know." Her voice drops further. "For the emperor. He sees her sometimes—too often for my liking. If she was as pretty as me, perhaps I shouldn't mind as much, but I think he only likes her because his uncle, Napoleon I, also had a mistress named Marie Walewska. Emulating his predecessor gives him a sense of grandeur."

Speared by a surge of defensive loyalty for Elisabetta, who has been a good friend to me, I peer down from the box in distaste. "Her gown is exactly the shade of a chicken pox pustule."

Elisabetta collapses into a peal of ringing laughter, arms wrapping around her waist and her head tilting back. "Livia! My dear, I think that may be the best insult I've ever heard about someone's gown. Perhaps I should seek some medical knowledge myself, to sharpen my tongue."

"I can tell you about plenty of unpleasant medical things," I assure her.

"Perhaps that shall be the topic of conversation for our next tea, then."

Bellino leans in, with a fresh glass of champagne. "What are you whispering about? The people below? You can see everything from up here; it's almost as entertaining as the opera." He swigs from his glass. "The emperor once watched fifteen men get arrested from the safe, voyeuristic height of a theatre box, you know. Sitting here now really gives one an appreciation for the excellent view he must have had. I imagine he must have felt a great deal of satisfaction." His gaze flicks to me. "They were trying to assassinate him, you know. Fifteen of them, all lurking in the audience below and armed with daggers. They were to have struck at him after the performance, but somehow he got wind of it in advance and the whole scheme was foiled."

"How fortunate." Elisabetta's voice sounds as sharp as one of those daggers.

"It likely wouldn't have succeeded anyway," says Bellino. "Fifteen conspirators is far too many, although I suppose it worked for Caesar. How many murderers did he have, again?" He looks to Niccolo, admittedly the most scholarly of the group and most likely to know this fact.

"Possibly as many as sixty men participated," he answers reluctantly. "Only three main conspirators, though."

Bellino blinks in surprise. "Heavens. Perhaps fifteen is a manageable number after all." He turns to me. "Did your father ever treat someone with a stab wound, Livia? Did you see it?"

I nod. "It wasn't pleasant. The man died of infection several days later. He was stabbed low in the stomach, and the knife pierced his bowels."

"What an awful way to die." Bellino clicks his tongue.

"Oh, stop it." Elisabetta takes his champagne glass from him, putting it down beside her. "This is an awful topic of conversation. I hope the intermission is nearly over. I want to see the rest of the story."

"I'm only talking about history," Bellino argues. "It happened, perhaps in this very theatre. I actually don't know that part. But they were Carbonari members, determined that a political death would help Italy go into revolution and then freedom. I believe it's called the 'theory of the dagger,' and it's our history, even if it's a dark piece of it."

Elisabetta's eyes narrow, turning dark and dangerous. I almost think she'll lift her champagne glass and toss it into Bellino's face. I'm uncomfortable myself with the detail he describes in front of Elisabetta when speaking of the emperor's brush with death. He must be more jealous than I thought.

"A small piece of history," says Niccolo firmly. "Very few Italian nationalists believe in using assassination as a weapon of revolution, and yet Italy is gaining a reputation for political violence because of those few. It isn't a credit to them; it's shameful."

"I didn't say it was a credit," responds Bellino coolly. "Just that it existed."

Elisabetta stares at the stage, thoroughly ignoring him, though she spared a brief nod of approval for Niccolo.

I straighten my necklace, settling back into my seat. Now that I've realized that Bellino and Elisabetta have a romantic past, his jealousy of the emperor shows in many small ways, and as much as my heart aches for him, I wish he'd be more tactful for Elisabetta's sake. The lighthearted fun of the evening has been snapped by the tension of politics, but at least the rest of the music should be beautiful. It's heartbreaking, too, though. Maybe the story of a tragic love was a poor choice for our group.

CHAPTER NINE

Paris, October to December 1856

Aconite poisoning primarily affects the heart, slowing it into eventual paralysis.
— Excerpt from Livia Valenti's book of herbal studies

My new arrangement with Niccolo changes our relationship, as I suppose it was meant to. As agreed, we meet every evening before bed and talk until we learn at least one new thing about each other. As the weeks pass, my nervousness around him eases, and I find myself looking forward to our private moments together.

We begin with simple facts. I discover he likes the scent of lemons, while my favorite is the clean smell of mint leaves. A few nights later, he admits to feeling nervous around snakes. I decline to share a fear, finding the topic too vulnerable, and instead tell him that I've never ridden a horse.

"When you've recovered from childbirth, and we've returned home to Turin, we can go together," he offers. "I have a very quiet gelding that would suit you. He has a black mane."

"What's his name?" I almost expect him to wrinkle his brow at my question, for in spite of his kindness, Niccolo doesn't give the impression of being sentimental enough to name all the horses in his stables.

"Amico. I named him myself, when I was twelve."

A smile springs to my face that Niccolo would name his horse as a friend. I like being proven wrong about his sentimentality.

"He was just a colt then, and I was convinced we would be best friends, that he'd carry me everywhere and be loyal as a dog." Niccolo grins too, and it lights up his face, making him look happy and handsome and full of vitality. My stomach does a little flip when he focuses that smile on me.

"Was he loyal?" I manage to keep my voice steady.

"Yes. I'm still very fond of him. He's about fifteen now, and stabled at the country house near Camillo's estate, Castello Grinzane."

Sometimes, in spite of the size and elegance of our house in Paris, I often forget that Niccolo's family is quite wealthy, and he's inherited everything since his parents have died. My family is not poor, and quite lucky to have the favor of the prime minister, Conte Cavour, but we only have one house.

"Amico will be the perfect horse for you to learn on," Niccolo continues. "He likes gentle walks around the stable, and you're so light he'll hardly notice you on his back."

I lace my fingers across the roundness of my belly, which seems to grow every day now. "At least I will be again someday, I hope."

Niccolo's eyes glimmer, as if he's amused at my ruefulness. "I have no doubt."

As our nightly meetings continue, we progress from sharing simple facts to telling stories. With some persuasion from me, since I feel Niccolo already knows more about my worst secrets than I do his, Niccolo tells me his most embarrassing memory.

"I have two, in fact. I can never decide which is the worst, even when the memories sometimes keep me awake, cringing, at night." He clears his throat as the tips of his ears redden. "The first happened a few years ago. Conte Cavour had invited me to a meeting with the king of Piedmont and some cabinet ministers, and I was even going to be allowed to make a small presentation.

I prepared for days, even practiced my speech. When the time came, I tripped over the chair leg and caught myself on the table."

"That's not so bad," I say, but my stomach churns with second-hand embarrassment that this happened in front of the king.

"I knocked over a pitcher of water as I caught myself," Niccolo continues doggedly. "Water swept across the table like a wave, destroying every paper in its path, and dousing the laps of everyone on that side of the table. We had to end the meeting early. Fortunately, the king found it amusing, since he didn't get wet."

"I don't know if I can bear to hear the other," I admit.

"You must—you asked, and now you shall suffer through the memory with me." He gives me a conspiratorial smile. "The other isn't quite as bad, because I never saw the people involved again. This happened when I was about seventeen, I think. I'd been out celebrating with some friends, and had rather too much to drink."

"You?" It seems impossible to imagine Niccolo slurring and stumbling with drink.

"I'm more abstemious now," he says, a bit primly. "In any case, I was on my way home, and I opened the wrong carriage door, immediately climbing inside."

"The carriage was not unoccupied, was it?"

He shakes his head in sorrow. "No. And its occupants were not pleased with my interruption." He coughs delicately. "They were otherwise engaged."

I understand at once. "Like Madame Bovary."

He gives me a questioning look.

"I've been reading it in the *Revue de Paris*. It's a novel that's currently being serialized. There's a scandalous carriage scene in that, too."

If he's surprised by my reading—the novel is already considered rather shocking—he hides it well. "Then you understand perfectly," he says. "The man threw me out into the mud." He sighs with what seems to be dramatic relief. "There—now you know the two most embarrassing things that have ever happened to me."

Another night, I tell him how, aged twelve, I illicitly borrowed one of my father's books about surgeries because I wanted to read it, and Caterina joined me, even though she had little interest in the subject matter and was drawn more to the secrecy of the reading. I was fascinated by the book, but the drawings of amputated limbs ruined her dreams for the next two nights.

"I miss having access to his library sometimes," I conclude, after Niccolo has smiled at my tale. His remark on its uniqueness makes me self-conscious, but I can't pretend away my interests in medicine and reading.

"Make a list of the books you need, and I'll find them for you." Niccolo leaps to his feet, fetching a piece of paper and a pen, pushing them toward me across the table. "I'd like to do that for you. I'd like you to feel more at home here."

He's offered once before, but I've never given him a list. Caution held me back. I didn't want to be disappointed in case he hadn't really meant it, but I'm learning he never makes promises he doesn't intend to keep.

"I'm starting to feel at home here," I tell him honestly. "It gets a little better every day."

Instead of waiting for him to take my hand for his habitual polite good night, I raise it for him. I might have imagined the quick flare of warmth in his eyes, but then his mouth brushes my skin softly, lingering for a heartbeat, and then I'm sure it was real.

Niccolo invites Roberto Rossi and his wife Angelica to dine with us the next night. Based on Angelica's quick glance around the parlor, and the elaborate style of her hair, braided with freshwater pearls, I suspect she hoped La Castiglione would be here. Niccolo did invite her, or rather, Bellino did, since he'd stopped by her residence again in the afternoon, but she declined.

"She says she wants a quiet night." He made a face. "Imagine, the most sought-after woman in Paris lying about on a sofa when she could be dazzling the world."

It must be quite exhausting to attend as many balls and social functions as she does, particularly since she seems to treat each of them like a performance, where she's a player on the stage or a feature of a painting. I wouldn't say it to Bellino, but I know she dedicates time to hair treatments to keep it smooth and fair, and anoints her skin with lotions to maintain her clear complexion. Being beautiful is hard work, as any woman knows.

As supper begins, I decide it's just as well Elisabetta isn't here. During the soup course, Angelica inquires of Niccolo if there's been any news regarding the emperor's sympathies toward the Italian cause, a question Elisabetta has told me she's heartily sick of answering.

I suspect Niccolo feels the same. "These things take time," he says vaguely, passing her a plate of fresh rolls. "The prime minister expects the emperor will likely throw his support behind Italy, sending troops to fight the Austrian rule, but he has his own country to govern. Its matters will naturally take precedence." He sounds so smooth and calm I understand why Conte Cavour chose Niccolo to help with diplomatic tasks.

Angelica seems less admiring, since Niccolo gave her no information at all. I can't blame her. I wish, too, that the emperor would hurry and make up his mind. I like to daydream that if he ordered the troops tomorrow, I could return to Turin before my baby is born, even though I know that's a false dream. It's one thing to return with a child of several months to a year, when people might wonder, but likely not comment. It's quite another to return home just in time to give birth, when my wedding is known to have been only five months before.

Roberto continues to bring up politics as the meal progresses. "Cavour may be clinging to false hope. If the emperor intended to support Italian independence, he would have done so already."

"Perhaps not," says Niccolo. "That's a rather grim outlook."

"I don't think so. Look at his history. He fought for the Carbonari in his youth. He was *there*, fighting, so if anyone understands the extent of corrupt Austrian rule, it should be him. He knows that even the Pope relied on Austrian soldiers to maintain rule in the Papal States—have you forgotten the summer of 1849?"

"Of course not." Niccolo's mild reply carries a trace of coolness.

I don't know my history as well as they do. The Papal States are far to the south of Turin, and I was only thirteen years old in 1849, spending the summer running around the garden with Caterina, our noses sunburnt. That was the year I stitched my first wound, under my father's supervision, when one of his friends sliced his arm on broken glass when a tree limb had snapped off in a storm and smashed the window of his house. I cared little for politics or far-off battles then. My expression must show I'm not quite clear, because Angelica tilts her head in my direction.

"The emperor—although he was only prince-president then, of course—sent French troops to the Papal States, and even briefly drove the Pope from Rome. It should have been a victory for the Carbonari, but instead he allowed the Pope to return. There's even a permanent garrison of French troops there now."

Roberto scowls. "See how much he has changed? His actions go against everything the Carbonari stood for. The emperor won't do anything to help Italy now. You'll see."

"A grim outlook for a grim reality," Bellino chimes in.

"Supporting Italian independence is not as simple as signing an agreement," says Niccolo. "It means going to war against Austria."

"He thought it well enough to fight battles for the Carbonari in his youth." Roberto's fork flashes through the air, candlelight gleaming on the tines as he punctuates his words, his plate of dessert forgotten.

Relieved for the safe distance of the table between us, I glance at Angelica, seated beside him, apparently unperturbed by his wild gestures. She listens with serene concentration, hands resting along the edge of the table. As his cutlery jabs again, like the sword of a musketeer in the Dumas novel I recently read, I think it's a good thing my father taught me how to stitch up and bandage a wound. Who knew politics would inspire such vehemence at the table?

Niccolo catches my eye, and the corner of his mouth twitches. I realize he's just as entertained by Roberto's antics as I am, and I must take a quick bite of my pear *galette* to stifle the laughter rising in my throat. I never expected to share silent jokes with Niccolo over the supper table, but my spirits sing. If our nightly routine of visiting is bringing us this much closer, then I consider it valuable time indeed.

"The emperor is more of an obstacle than a help for Italy," Robert continues, fork stabbing through the air again. "The Carbonari see him as a turncoat—why, I know a man who says—" His cutlery clinks against his water glass, cutting his tirade short.

"You might want to put down your fork." Niccolo's interruption warns Roberto to collect himself, though his tone remains mild. "Else my wife may have to stitch up someone's grievous dinner wound."

Warmth spreads along my skin, both for the fact that Niccolo really was thinking the same thing as me, and also that he called attention to my particular talents in front of everyone.

Roberto plunks the fork down, ducking his head with chagrin. "Sometimes my passion overtakes my manners. My apologies, signora."

"I understand," I tell him. The dinner conversation may have been on the tense side, but at least it was lively. It's just as well Elisabetta is absent, though.

*

The next night, shadows lurk under Niccolo's eyes, and though he smiles to see me, he looks tired.

"Are you well?" I ask.

"It's nothing. Just a headache."

"Where? Any other pains?" I thought my fear of poison had disappeared, that I'd reconciled myself to being mistaken about the berries, but now this quick jump of fear proves me wrong. All this talk of the theory of the dagger, and the emperor as an obstacle, has clearly kept suspicion whetted in my mind.

A sound of amusement rumbles from his throat. "I ought to have remembered a doctor's daughter would question for other symptoms. I'm well, *cara*. It's only a normal headache."

It's the first time he's used an endearment when speaking to me. The word glides over me like smoke, warm and lingering.

"I have an ointment made with peppermint, which might help. I'll fetch it." Turning on my heel, I go to fetch the jar of ointment before he can argue. It makes me feel useful.

He looks relieved when I return, and rises from his chair.

"No, sit down." It sounds more brusque than I meant. "I'll put a little of this on your temples."

He sits down obediently, tilting his head back slightly as I move behind him. His eyes fall closed as I use my fingertips to gently massage the peppermint oil into his temples. After a moment, he leans into my touch, seemingly out of reflex, almost like a cat arching into a petting hand.

"I'm not used to having someone care for me like this." His voice is a low rasp. "I think I could get used to it. Thank you, Livia."

"It's nothing," I say. I wonder if Carlotta ever tended his ills, and the question springs thoughtlessly to my lips. "Didn't your late wife soothe your headaches?"

His eyes remain closed, but the corner of his mouth tightens. "No. Ours was a marriage of convenience; our fathers were friends. My father wanted the alliance because her family was wealthy, and I think her father wanted to take advantage of my family's connections to Conte Cavour. I think she liked the idea that her son—although it turns out we never had any children—would inherit the country estate. We didn't spend much time together."

Still, she must have shared his bed at times, which is more than I'm currently doing. I don't say this aloud, though. Niccolo will still have a child to inherit his property, as the baby reminds me by shifting inside me.

"I know our marriage is unconventional," he continues softly. "But I like that it feels like we're having a courtship, even if it's late." When he glances up at me, his irises look fathomless and deep as a stormy sky. "If circumstances were different, Livia, I would have courted you first."

His tender words make a lump rise in my throat. Things might have been so different. I smooth the last of the ointment into his forehead and straighten. "Better late than never."

He rises as I turn away, wiping my fingertips on a handkerchief. "I hope so." Niccolo's gaze sweeps across my belly, impossible to hide now. No matter what dress I wear, it bells the skirt away from my feet. By the end of the day, the cumbersome weight of my pregnancy makes me grateful to curl up in bed. As the baby kicks, the dangling red ribbon decorating the waist of my gown sways and his eyes pinpoint on the movement, staring.

"Do you want to feel?" I see curiosity and longing etched all over his face, and don't need to wait for him to answer. I take his hand in mine and press it against the swell of my belly. The heat of his palm warms me even through the layers of cloth and the confines of my corset, a special one for supporting my belly, and the unexpected comfort of it makes me blink even as I press closer to his hand.

"It's so hard." His forehead wrinkles with interest. "I never imagined you'd feel like a pumpkin." The corners of his lips curl.

The baby hasn't kicked again yet. "Push a little," I tell him. "Usually the baby will push back."

He obeys, but so lightly I hardly feel it. "Like this." Hesitating for only a second, I lace my fingers with his and push so we're both prodding at my belly. When we're instantly rewarded with a kick, an awed, heart-lurching smile unfurls across his face.

"He's like a little mule. Or she." He pushes a little again, not quite as hard as I did. "You must grow weary of being kicked all the time."

"I do. My mother told me the last month is the most uncomfortable, because otherwise women would be too afraid to give birth. This way, we're eager to get it over with."

"I'd promise you the best doctors, but I suppose you know better than I about that. I should have thought of it earlier. Do you need help finding someone?"

"It's fine. Caterina and I already spoke to a local midwife who seems very experienced."

"Good." His voice drops to a lower note. "As the time draws near, I find myself worrying." Niccolo's hand still hovers over my belly, and now he strokes it gently. The baby lurches inside me, pressing against his palm again.

"All will be well," I say, with slightly more confidence than I feel, although I know my chances are good. I've had a normal, uncomplicated pregnancy. "I'm strong, and there haven't been any problems so far."

Niccolo reaches forward, slow and tentative, and tucks a loose strand of hair behind my ear. The soft gesture feels unbearably sweet. It sparks yearning all along my skin, a hollow loneliness under my ribs.

"You're very brave," he whispers.

"You're very kind."

His mouth tightens briefly, from impatience or frustration, I can't tell. "I'm not, at least not all the time. Not to everyone. I want you to be happy, Livia. I know our marriage was sudden, that it didn't begin how you would have liked, and I know you likely didn't want a child before it even began. I can't change all that, but I can try to make things better now."

"You are," I tell him, and it's the truth. I'm lucky he's solicitous, that he lets me have some measure of authority over the household. That he lets me follow my interests in medicine. "You are," I repeat, and squeeze his fingertips in mine for emphasis.

His lips part, and I sense he rocks toward me even though his feet don't move. His eyes gleam like moonlight on the sea.

Anxiety flares through me. "Good night, Niccolo." I turn away before he can say anything else. Before he can slide his arms around me, before his mouth can find mine. Before I risk stepping to a precipice where I must let him, or push him away. I'm not ready to make that choice. Taking my cowardice with me, I slink back to my own rooms.

CHAPTER TEN

Paris, December 1856

*"Poison is in everything, and no thing is without poison.
The dosage makes it either a poison or a remedy."*
— Quotation from Paracelsus,
noted in Livia Valenti's book of herbal studies

When Elisabetta's maid arrives at the door, pink-cheeked and breathless, I'm about to retire for the night, having just finished knitting a swaddling blanket. The days left until my labor dwindle; I'll need the blanket in a couple of weeks.

"You must come at once." Beatrice's voice trembles. "She's quite ill; she vomited in the salon, and I made her go to bed, but she looks dreadfully pale and she asked for you especially."

My mind casts feverishly back to the vision of the nightshade berries gathered prettily in that white bowl. Panic bolts through me like lightning. "What are her symptoms?"

Beatrice wrings her hands. "Weak and sick. She said the room was spinning and her skin tingled, like it was burning. I'm sorry, I came so quickly—she'll tell you everything when you arrive."

Beatrice's inability to provide further details is frustrating, because I don't know what medicines I should bring. Elisabetta could be deadly ill, or just suffering from a stomach upset. In the end, I tuck a few things for different types of soothing teas into my bag, including ginger for easing nausea. With the fear of poison in the forefront of my mind, I also pack powdered charcoal to help slow the absorption of any toxin she may have ingested.

In spite of the late hour, Niccolo and Bellino are both out, having gone to dine with some other diplomats in King Vittorio Emanuele's service who are stationed in Paris. I make sure Lorenzo knows where I've gone, and then Caterina and I hurry outside, walking as quickly as I can manage through the deep shadows of the street. Elisabetta's house is close enough that we'd be there by the time the horses were harnessed for the carriage, and I won't waste a moment.

Elisabetta reclines against a propped pillow, the blankets tangled around her legs. Her black nightdress gapes away from her throat, showing her collarbones are streaked with red scratches. She looks terrible, her complexion grayish and skin gleaming with sweat. Her eye sockets seem cavernous when she fastens her gaze on me, and her face splits into a skull's grin.

I cross to her bedside faster than I thought able, given the ever-growing bulk of my pregnant belly. "Don't move." My voice rings with command as she presses her palms against the mattress and attempts to push herself upright. "What's wrong? How do you feel?"

"You are here," she says in a wondering, hoarse voice. "The moon told me you'd come soon."

Is she delirious? My mouth feels dry. I squeeze her cold hands in mine. "What do you mean? Elisabetta—what do you mean?"

She blinks several times, eyelashes clumped into jagged points. "I counted the minutes through my breaths. I couldn't move, and time turned slippery, but still the moon told me time was passing as it slid through the window frame, and I knew you'd be here soon."

I don't like the nonsensical way she speaks, and press my hand to her forehead. She doesn't feel feverish; on the contrary, her skin sticks to mine, clammy and cool.

"Tell me how you feel." I squeeze my hand around hers.

"I ache all over, and my throat and stomach are burning."

"Have you vomited?"

Her mouth twists in disgust or embarrassment, I can't tell. "Yes. In the salon."

The burning in her throat could be from the acid emptying from her stomach, but I must know why she was vomiting at all. "What did you eat tonight?"

"Soup and bread, but hours ago." Her head lolls on the pillow, and then she squints up at me, hands twitching as she tries to reach for mine. "I drank some brandy. I don't even like it. Just one gulp, because I was worried the emperor canceled on me tonight."

"And were you sick right after?" Her strength wanes every time she speaks, and it takes me a few times to ascertain she drank the brandy, and threw up shortly after, when the symptoms began. I feel cold all over as all my dread of poison comes rushing back.

Her eyes meet mine, and they seem dark and fathomless under her dilated pupils. Her voice fades away, but I see the words on her lips. "I'm afraid, Livia."

"I'll help you," I promise. "But it won't be pleasant."

Her eyelids flicker, half-closed. I'm not sure if she even heard my warning. We're both in for a long night, but I'll do everything I can to help her.

As I slide my fingers along her cold throat, feeling for the delicate flutter of her pulse, I frantically catalogue her symptoms against my knowledge of different poisons. I wish I had a couple of my books for reference. First, though, I need to try to stop the poison's absorption. If the brandy was the culprit, she was poisoned about an hour ago, but there's still time to help her.

Even though she already vomited, I need to be sure she expels every trace of the substance from her stomach. I send Beatrice, hovering at the foot of the bed and twisting her fingers unhelpfully, to the kitchen to fetch a small cup of water I can mix the charcoal in, as well as an empty bowl. While she's gone, Elisabetta starts to panic, her fingernails digging into my hands, the white of her eyes showing as she stares straight into my soul.

"You're not dying," I insist, though I don't know for sure. "You're strong. Now breathe, slow and steady." I show her deep, calming breaths, and encourage her to continue breathing like that, although the movement of her chest rising is still too shallow.

"This will help." Infusing as much firmness into my tone as I can, I press my palm under her head. Caterina helps me raise her up, and as Beatrice returns and passes me the basin, I perch it under Elisabetta's chin. Some doctors force ingestion of a mustard infusion or salted water to stimulate vomiting, but my father always regarded these as a waste of time.

"Both will cause upheaval of the stomach," he'd explained, not quite keeping the disdain out of his voice. "But if it's important that a patient empties their stomach; there's no good in adding to the contents."

I would have preferred to have a feather, but the shakiness of her breath and the pallor of her skin leaves no spare time to find one. I shove my finger into her mouth, keeping it to the side of her cheek so I can reach past her teeth and trigger her gag response. She tries to bite me once, out of reflex, so I stop coaxing and bark commands at her instead, swiping with my finger. It feels cruel, but it must be done. Beside me, Caterina cringes. We barely manage to get the basin leveled under Elisabetta's head to catch the remnants of her stomach contents as she vomits repeatedly. Beatrice wails in dismay.

Caterina turns her face away, mouth curling with disgust. I inspect the contents of the bowl, though, looking for signs of the food she ate. There's nothing solid, only a small amount of liquid, possibly brandy or just bile. Not enough to tell me anything useful. Considering I don't know how much she had to drink, I worry it could mean most of the poison has already been digested.

Once Elisabetta has stopped throwing up, I hasten to give her the charcoal water, to bind any remaining poison and slow its absorption. She's too weak to protest this time, even when the charcoal water leaks past the edge of the cup and leaves a dark gray smear across her jaw.

Caterina spurs Beatrice into action, and they bring a soft cloth and a bowl of warm water and sponge Elisabetta's face and neck, as I consider different types of poison. I'm afraid to rush into treatment and make a mistake, but many poisons don't really have a treatment aside from inducing vomiting and administering charcoal, which I've already done. Elisabetta's eyes flutter closed, and she seems to fall asleep. Sending Beatrice for more blankets, mostly to get her out of the room, I keep my fingertip pressed to the pulse in Elisabetta's wrist as I discuss the possibilities with Caterina, pondering aloud the different poisons.

"All of her symptoms, from nausea to pain, but especially the difficulty breathing, can be accounted for by aconite—monks-hood—poisoning," I muse, using the Latin name instead of the plant one, because my mind has shifted to cataloguing poisons. "But it tastes quite bitter. It seems unlikely she would have will-ingly eaten enough to be ill.'

"Does brandy have a strong enough taste to disguise it? She drank some, didn't she?" Caterina reminds me.

I consider this. "I suppose it's possible... the root of aconite is poisonous and could have been powdered and dissolved into a liquid. Strong spirits like brandy might disguise the taste, especially if she drank it quickly. Good thinking, Caterina." We smile at each other briefly, but my grin fades when the dark truth of the situation casts its black shadow over me again. "But who would want to do such a thing? Who could be so determined to kill her, and why?"

Caterina shakes her head, her expression as somber as mine feels. "I don't know."

"Well, first I must treat her," I say, trying to focus on the most urgent matter first. "Her heart rate worries me." I glance down at Elisabetta again. Though her pulse flutters against my fingertip, she's clearly not conscious enough to hear us. "It's very slow." I drop my voice to a whisper. "I might have to give her a small dose of belladonna." I look to Caterina, anticipating her shock.

Her eyes widen. "That's deadly nightshade."

"I know." I chose the other name on purpose, as if it somehow made it less drastic and dangerous.

She gnaws on her lower lip. "You know more of these things than I do, of course."

"I'd need to make sure it was a very low dose." My heart flutters at the idea, and my fingertips tremble. I press them into my skirt. "Nightshade is the opposite to aconite. It has a compound that counteracts the effects. Nightshade can raise the heart rate and breathing. Foxglove, too. I know it's risky. Hopefully the charcoal was enough. If not…"

Caterina gives me a sideways look, her blue eyes glinting. She knows I wouldn't speculate about nightshade unless I had it to hand. She knows it's a real option. "You have nightshade."

I nod. My fingers feel cold as I reach into the hidden pocket sewn into my dress, extracting the ebony box containing the nightshade. "I do… And I brought it just in case, after hearing how weak she was."

Shame twists through me. It truly did occur to me the nightshade could be helpful for a dangerously weak pulse—but I'd been carrying it anyway. Keeping it tucked against my skin, with dark whispers of murder in my heart. Every time I hide it away in my trunk, I find myself dragging it out again, the ebony box's sharp corners poking at me just as hard as my loathing for Corbara, who I fear is here in Paris.

"I've shocked you, haven't I?" The question sounds small and broken, and I can't quite look at Caterina.

"You know all about poisons, and their remedies," she says gently. "The good side, too."

Her confidence in my knowledge is like a balm. I tell myself it doesn't matter right now why I have the nightshade; the important thing is that it may save Elisabetta's life.

When Beatrice returns to the room, her brows drawn together with worry, I try to reassure her. "I'm doing everything I can, I promise. If you could please fetch some water, that would be very helpful."

"What's that for?" Caterina asks curiously, after Beatrice departs.

"To get her out of here while I prepare the nightshade, to have it ready in case it's needed." I cautiously remove a small amount of the dried root from the ebony box, using a slender pair of tweezers from my medical kit. Nightshade can be toxic to the touch, though in a less severe fashion than ingesting it. When it's ground to powder, I measure it into a small glass of water, keeping it in my hand so no one else can accidentally drink from it. A small risk in a sickroom, but still not one I will take.

Elisabetta slumps against the pillows, pale and still, her hair limp and clinging to her cheek. Her breath hitches, and for a heart-stopping second, I think I'm looking at a corpse, until her eyelids flicker and she twitches her fingers against the coverlet. "Livia?" The whisper breaks in two.

"I'm here."

I know then she needs the nightshade, but my voice cracks as I comfort her. She trusts me. She could have called for any of the emperor's doctors, but she wanted me when she fell ill. She has trusted me ever since our first meeting, when I thought I saw poisonous berries mixed into her dish of currants. She's my friend, and I'm the only one who can help her now, but I'm afraid I hesitated too long. I'm afraid I could be wrong.

Carefully, I count the beats of her pulse. Her heart seems perilously slow. I massage her swollen hands and ankles to stimulate blood flow.

I expect my hands to shake as I lift the cup of nightshade to her lips, but instead I feel steady and calm. Elisabetta needs the nightshade to stimulate her heart. It's risky, but as I inhale a slow, calm breath, I feel certain in my knowledge. I've judged the risk; I've considered the reward. I've made my choice.

"This will taste bitter." I slip my hand underneath her head to support her neck.

Her lip curls after the first sip.

"It will help you. It's part of the antidote." I hate to encourage the idea of antidotes, even if this is the closest thing to one, but its persuasion is successful.

"I'll drink it all," she says, managing to convey a grim sort of resoluteness in spite of her weakness.

"Not yet," I tell her. "Let it have time to take effect." I monitor her condition as those two sips of nightshade soak into her stomach, slipping through her veins. There's no noticeable improvement after a few minutes, so I give her one more sip, and study her symptoms anew.

She slumps back against the pillow, eyes closing. Her skin looks stretched over her bones, dry as clay. "Dying?" she asks.

"Not if I can help it." The thread of her life might be in my hands, but it doesn't make me feel powerful. Not like I imagined the nightshade would, if Corbara ever cornered me. It only makes me determined to save her. And perhaps it's arrogant, but I still feel certain I made the right choice. As I check her pulse again, it grows steadier. "I'll stay with you, Elisabetta," I promise. "You have a friend and doctor here. You must rest and not worry too much."

Beatrice returns with a fresh pitcher of water, and I make Elisabetta drink a few sips of it, very slowly. She seems to rest easier for being less parched, and I promise she can guzzle a whole jug of water soon. I drape a lavender-scented cloth over her forehead and dab moisturizing salve, made with olive oil and calendula, onto the dry patches on her cheeks and her chapped lips. She drifts into unconsciousness, but her breathing is even, if shallow, and I count her pulse every few minutes, reassured by its constant rhythm, growing stronger.

"Should we leave her to sleep?" whispers Caterina.

"Not yet." Her improvement seems steady, but I won't risk leaving her unattended yet. "I'll stay with her longer."

"I'll go and reassure her staff," says Beatrice. "They're all very worried."

She seems so shaken that I nudge Caterina into accompanying her. It's quiet without them in the room, but with every passing moment, I gain confidence Elisabetta will recover. She sleeps now, and it seems natural and peaceful. Her skin feels warmer under my fingertips when I brush her hair away from her face.

The baby turns and kicks restlessly inside me, and my lower back twinges in the threat of a spasm. I've been sitting too long. I rise and dig my fingers into my hips, trying to stretch my spine. Elisabetta sleeps on, her cheek cradled by the pillow.

I turn and survey the room. I've been here for hours, and yet hardly noticed any of it. A massive wardrobe stands on one side of her room, and mirrors hang on three of the walls. A small roll-top desk stands in the corner opposite the wardrobe, which surprises me. She doesn't seem the sort to write letters in her bedroom. Since the top is lifted, I glance at the few papers lined up on the desk. One appears to be a bill from Monsieur Pierson, her photographer. No doubt she receives a lot of those, with the number of portraits she commissions. An envelope lies across the bottom, preventing me seeing the total, and I don't touch it. By its salutation, the next paper appears to be a letter. Unwilling to read her private correspondence, I'm about to turn away from the desk when the slant of the handwriting, the jagged shape of each letter, strikes a harsh chord of familiarity in my mind.

I've seen those crookedly crossed t's and the i's capped like knives, with a sharp line instead of a dot.

Corbara's writing looks just like that.

My sense of propriety vanishing, I lean closer, reading each line without touching the paper. It tells me little, being a formal request for a meeting with the contessa di Castiglione, to discuss important matters relating to Italy's future freedom and independence.

At the bottom, his signature swaggers across the page, the ink heavy and dark. I can't tear my eyes from it, hypnotized by utter surprise and confusion. I feared Corbara was in Paris—I knew, really—but now the proof stands in front of me. An ache in my fingertips makes me realize I clutch my bracelet, the metal shape of the lancet digging into my bones. I hoped to never see Corbara again, and now it seems horribly possible—maybe even unavoidable, if he knows Elisabetta.

*

Turin, April 1856 (eight months earlier)

The last time we visited Corbara and Ferrero at their inn, my father pronounced them both well enough. "Rest that ankle a few days longer," he advised Ferrero, before telling Corbara to protect the new skin growing under the scabs of his burn. "You'll both be fine."

As we were about to leave, Corbara's fingers brushed against my hand. In contrast to the shock of the warmth of his skin on mine, I felt the dry crackle of a small piece of paper as he pressed it into my hand.

I managed not to react outwardly, though my pulse fluttered and my cheeks must have been glowing with excitement. The walk home felt very long, and even a discussion with my father about an American doctor who used ether on his patient during a tooth extraction to reduce pain couldn't distract me from curiosity about Corbara's note.

At home, I read it many times, studying the shape of his handwriting, the way he wrote my name with an elegant, sloped L. He asked me to visit him again before they had to leave. *I can't leave you without saying goodbye.*

I managed to visit him later that afternoon, stopping by the inn after a quick visit to the gardens at Castello del Valentino. My concern for appearing overeager was drowned out by my greater worry that they'd leave tomorrow, and I'd never see him again at all.

His face lit up when he saw me, a slow burn of a smile that made me blush. "I'm so glad you came," he said. "Shall we walk together a little?"

I nodded. Our sleeves brushed together as we strolled down the street. A sugary smell wafted through the air from a nearby bakery, matching the sweetness filling my spirits.

"In another day or two, we'll continue our journey to Florence." He'd spoken of this to me before, and I knew he wanted to meet friends who were Italian nationalists. When he wasn't flirting, Corbara liked to talk about politics and his desire for Italy's independence. He could grow so impassioned that I hardly got a word in edgewise, not that I knew much about politics. "Ferrero's ready to walk again, and my arm is healing well. We were very lucky not to be laid up for a longer time."

"I'm glad to hear you weren't delayed too long." I'd always known they wouldn't stay in Turin, but a tinge of melancholy crept into my tone. I would miss chatting—and flirting—with Corbara. Around him, I felt like a different person: someone exciting and attractive, not just the studious and quiet doctor's daughter.

He laid his fingers across my wrist, very gently. "Thank you again for your care. I'm glad I met you, Livia."

My cheeks warmed, and I couldn't stop the smile springing to my face. "I'm just glad your burn is healing so well."

"I could come back." His fingertips continued to trace little swirls over the soft, bare skin of the inside of my wrist. "My business in Florence won't last forever."

Hope lurched in my heart. I wasn't ready for him to leave. It felt like I was just starting to know him, and sometimes when he made me laugh, I imagined the joy I might have in my life if he remained part of it. Sometimes I dreamt of him as my husband. I tried to sound lighthearted, lifting my chin and making a careless shrug. "You know where to find me." He gazed into my eyes, his own dark and probing. The brown spot in his iris shrank underneath the dilated pupil. "I'd like that," I added, more softly.

Corbara's fingers curled around my wrist, and he tugged me toward him. "Come here, Livia."

I followed him to the partial cover of a knotted olive tree, its shadow deep and almost purple in the soft dusky light. I felt like my blood had turned to Prosecco, airy and quick in my veins, lending an edge of reckless excitement to my steps and a dash of nervousness to my lungs.

He raised my hand to his chest, pressing the palm flat against his shirt. His chest felt hard and warm under my hand, almost shockingly solid. I'd never touched a man so intimately, for I didn't count tending to wounds, which gave me a feeling of distance. "Feel how my heart is hammering? That's what you do to me." He bent closer, and his mouth swooped over mine.

In the ephemeral, significant second before his lips touched mine, my stomach flipped with exhilaration and my breath caught in my throat. I'd never been kissed before, and the thrill of it happening now spun through my limbs, tingling all the way down to my toes.

Corbara kept my hand flat against his chest, fingers squeezing mine, and his body pressed me closer to the knobbly trunk of the tree. His lips dragged over mine again and again, parting them open, and then his tongue thrust into my mouth.

I couldn't breathe. A twig caught in my hair when I managed to turn my head aside, breaking the kiss. "It's too much." My voice quavered. "I'm sorry."

His breathing sounded ragged. "No, don't be. I'm a beast, falling on your like that, but you make me wild. Was it your first kiss?" He released my hand, finally, and touched his finger to my chin.

"Yes." The admission made me want to squirm. I felt inadequate and painfully shy.

"I'm a lucky man, then," said Corbara. "Let me make it up to you." His lips drifted across my temple, brushing feather-light kisses, trailing them slowly down my cheek to the corner of my mouth. I thought he'd kiss my lips again, then, but instead he followed the angle of my jaw to my ear. My body quivered. I hadn't realized how sensitive the skin there would be. As he continued down my throat, his kisses grew wetter, more lingering, as the tip of his tongue occasionally flickered against my skin. As his arms wrapped around my waist, and his mouth at last found mine again, very gently and sweetly, I melted against him.

"There, that's better." His mouth curled at the corners in a faintly smug smile. "That's how your first kiss should have been. If I'd restrained myself from the start, I would have kissed you like that first, so let's pretend it happened that way."

"All right." My senses still whirled.

Corbara laughed, and dropped a kiss in the hollow of my throat. "I'm proud to be the first one to kiss you like that."

As we continued walking, a couple of merchants approached down the street, talking loudly to each other about the price of wine. I smoothed my skirt and tried to seem as collected as Corbara, who sauntered alongside me, eyes gleaming with satisfaction.

At the corner, where I'd turn to head home, he squeezed my hand briefly. "I'll see you again before we leave, I hope. Tomorrow?" He gave me a roguish grin and my heart thumped.

The next morning, I brought some boneknit salve for Ferrero, and a little jar of the Pomatum No. 64 for Corbara's healing burn. I didn't see Corbara anywhere, but Ferrero paced along the street in front of the inn, moving with hardly a limp.

"Looks like your sprain is all healed."

He nodded grimly. Ferrero always looked stern to me, with his thin mouth and narrow blue eyes. "Is that for me?" He pointed toward the satchel I'd put the salves in.

"Yes. Corbara told me you'd be leaving soon, so I thought you might want to take some of the salves with you."

"I can't pay for them." He crossed his arms over his chest.

"I didn't mean—" I scuffed my heel against the ground, feeling awkward. "You don't have to."

"I understand." He strode closer, reaching for the satchel. "Corbara's charm is currency enough."

My chin lifted with the abrupt shift from embarrassment to outrage. "No, that's not why."

A rough laugh scraped Ferrero's throat, but he didn't look amused. "There's no need to pretend. You can call it Christian kindness, or generosity of spirit—you can even tell me that it hardly costs you anything to make those salves. I well know you wouldn't give it to me, alone, for free."

The satchel swung in his hand as he bent his head closer to mine. I wanted to take a step back, but a cart full of wool, left beside the inn, knocked on my heels.

"It isn't the first time," said Ferrero. "It won't be the last. Corbara gets himself into trouble with women."

"Not this time." I hated the timid sound of my voice. "This is just well-being for a patient."

"I know he kissed you."

Silent, I stared back, meeting Ferrero's invasive glare. I could see the tiny red veins in the corners of his eyes. His sour breath curled through the air. "He did," I admitted at last. "But I don't believe it's any of your business." I started to turn away.

His hand flew out, and he seized my upper arm, holding me in place. His fingers had a bruising grip. "Perhaps not. Maybe I don't give a damn if your heart gets broken. But I do get fucking tired of him leaving a mess in our wake." I must have blanched at his vulgar language, because he smirked. "Did I offend your sensibilities? Proof enough you ought to steer well away from men like us."

He released my arm, shoving me away, and I staggered back a step. "Don't touch me," I growled.

"Listen to my advice, little tigress. Forget Corbara. Go home and mix salves, or sew bandages or whatever it is you do." He tipped his hat to me, almost an afterthought, but the courtesy felt empty.

I stalked away, head held high, but my legs trembled and my skin burned. I couldn't believe he'd spoken to me so harshly, especially after all the help my father and I had given him. His meddling displayed his ignorance about my relationship with Corbara. I wasn't a fool; I didn't doubt Corbara had a romantic history. He was far too much of an incorrigible flirt for that, and he clearly had more experience than me when we kissed. But I remembered the softness in his eyes as he promised he'd come back for me, the yearning in his face as he wrapped his arms around me. Ferrero hadn't seen that. He didn't know Corbara was serious this time.

CHAPTER ELEVEN

Paris, December 1856

In Greek legend, the three-headed hound Cerberus was said to have saliva infused with wolfsbane poison, which is also called aconite or monkshood.
— Excerpt from Livia Valenti's book of herbal studies

Elisabetta shifts against her blankets, sighing in distress, and I hurry back to her side, shoving all thought of Corbara out of my mind for now.

"Are you all right?"

She gasps as if parched, so I help her drink a little more water—plain, as I don't dare give her more nightshade, and have poured the small remaining amount of that mixture into the vomit basin. She subsides back into sleep almost at once, and to my relief, it appears to be a natural, if exhausted, state of rest.

"I think it's safe to let her sleep," I murmur to Caterina. "I'm a bit reluctant to leave her alone, though, just in case. But I need to examine that brandy."

"I'll sit with her," promises Caterina. "Here, I brought you some water." She presses a cup into my hand, and I take a grateful mouthful. "Why don't you take the brandy home, and look at it tomorrow? You look like you need to rest."

I'm not sure I'd be able to sleep. My hips and back ache too much. "I want to get it done tonight. Thank you, Caterina."

"If her breathing slows or she seems uncomfortable, I'll come and fetch you. God willing, she'll be fine."

"In the morning, I'll give her an infusion with marshmallow root to soothe her stomach."

Caterina presses her hand to my elbow as she clears her throat lightly. It gives me warning enough not to look startled, at least, when I turn to see Niccolo lurking in the doorway.

"What's going on?" he asks. His speaks softly, but his shoulders hunch with worry and tension. "Is everything all right? They told me at home that I'd find you here, that there was an emergency."

I guide us into the hallway. "Elisabetta has been very ill. She asked for me, so I've treated her. She's recovering now."

Niccolo's gaze skates slowly along my body. Belatedly, I realize my dress is spattered with vomit, the sleeve stained gray with spilt charcoal water. Loose strands of hair straggle against my neck, and if my face looks as tired as I feel, my eyes probably have shadows like inked thumbprints under them.

"Livia saved her life," Caterina says loyally, her defense an extra proof of my weary appearance.

"I'm glad I was able to help her," I say, with as much dignity as I can muster under the circumstances.

Except for the faint surprise showing in the arch of his brows, and a hint of tension around the set of his mouth, Niccolo looks as unruffled as ever, his hair neatly combed and the collar of his white linen shirt straight and crisp. It makes me feel even more unkempt, especially when the baby kicks hard enough that I wrap my arms around my belly, wishing I could lie down.

At once, Niccolo moves to my side and tucks my arm under his, but he doesn't speak and his lips remain in a taut line. Rather against my will, I find myself grateful for the support of his strength against me. My feet ache almost as much as my back, and the baby shifts restlessly, nudging against my ribs. Just before

Niccolo helps me down the hallway, Caterina passes me the water glass, giving me a knowing look. I'll need it for testing the brandy.

Niccolo leads me toward the doorway, ready to take me home, but I pull my arm free of his grip. "I need to go to her parlor first."

He follows me, steps quick and impatient. "What for? Livia, you look like you're about to collapse, and it's practically dawn. You should get home and into bed."

"I will soon." Crossing the threshold into the darkness of Elisabetta's parlor, I set the water glass down and fumble along the mantelpiece for the box of matches. My fingertips tremble as I try to light the candle, and Niccolo is about to take it from me and light it himself when the wick catches fire. Armed with that glow of light, I look for the brandy decanter, and spot it on the sideboard across the room. "There's one last thing I must do first."

"Why are you here, treating Elisabetta, in any case?" Niccolo is steady as ever, but I detect a shadow of frustration darkening his tone.

It makes me defensive, and that flare of anger burns off some of my weariness. "You know I'm a doctor's daughter. When I heard she was ill, I knew how to treat her."

"She has access to the best doctors in France. The emperor would see to that."

"She asked for me particularly."

"That doesn't mean you had to spend most of the night here, exhausting yourself. What if the baby came early because you overstrained yourself?"

I'm too tired to dance politely around Niccolo tonight, and can barely stop my eyes rolling as I scoff. "I was sitting at a bedside and pouring medicines, not lifting bags of flour. Besides, the baby can't come early." I put my hands on my hips, turning sideways to show off the enormous thrust of my belly. Behind me, in the glow of the candlelight, my shadow looms, even rounder and blockier than I am. "The baby can come on time. And it will, soon."

His mouth softens. "Still, you didn't have to put her before yourself."

Some of my ire fades, washed under by exhaustion. My shoulders slump. "You knew I wasn't a spoiled, wealthy lady when you married me. I never pretended to be more than the daughter of a respected doctor—if you think I'm prioritizing Elisabetta's health over mine just because she's a contessa—"

"It isn't that." His voice becomes a fraction louder. "I'm trying to tell you I'm worried about you. I don't like seeing my wife covered in someone else's vomit, and looking like she hasn't slept in days. You're more important to me than she is, Livia."

The earnestness in his tone dissolves most of my irritation. I lift my head, leaning into the comfort of his words, and I decide to trust him with the truth about tonight. If someone has tried to murder Elisabetta, he needs to know. "I doubt anyone but me could have saved Elisabetta, because she was poisoned. And I do not know who did it."

The bright, shocked gleam of his eyes conveys his surprise even more than his movement as his hands rise into the air as if grasping for the truth. "Poison? Are you sure? It seems far-fetched."

"I'm certain. You know I've made a study of poisons and their remedies. Elisabetta was poisoned with aconite, I believe."

"Aconite?" Niccolo's brow furrows.

"It's a flower, sometimes called monkshood or wolfsbane. Tall stalks, with little purple flowers like bells. Bees like them, but the entire plant is poisonous, the roots in particular."

"I've seen it." His gaze pierces mine. "Livia, you must tell me everything."

Conscious of the pre-dawn hour, and that Niccolo and I lurk in the nearly dark salon, I keep my voice soft, and explain Elisabetta's summons, her symptoms, and my treatment—although I'm not quite brave enough to share the specifics of the nightshade. I can't think how to explain that I purposely poisoned Elisabetta, confident that it would counteract the first toxin. Still, methodically recapping the baffling events of the night, while Niccolo listens in concentrated silence, helps calm me.

I turn back toward the decanter of brandy. "Based on her description of the sequence of events, it seems most likely the brandy was poisoned. I need to examine it to be sure."

I lift the stopper from the crystal bottle, letting the sharp, caramel scent of the brandy waft under my nose. I can't detect anything from the scent, which seems normal enough, although I'm no expert on strong spirits. I lay the stopper aside, and reach for the water glass.

"How will you do that?" asks Niccolo.

The decanter is quite full, so I'm easily able to reach the surface of the coppery liquid with my fingertip. "I'll have to taste it, I'm afraid." Cautiously, I bring my finger close to my lips. I won't swallow, of course, but since its smell isn't telling me anything, I don't know what else to do. Aconite should be unmistakably bitter.

Niccolo snatches my wrist and yanks my hand toward him. Before I can say anything, his lips close around my fingertip. I feel the gentle scrape of his bottom teeth as he licks the brandy clean from my skin.

The heat of his mouth seems to flood over me, a panicky burn that squeezes the air in my lungs before I find my voice. "Don't swallow!"

He nods silently, mouth pinched at the corners.

"Does it taste bitter? Unusually so?"

He nods again. The whites of his eyes catch the candlelight, reflecting the same dread curling around my own heart.

I lift the water glass to his lips. "One sip—swish it around your mouth. Then spit." As he takes the cup obediently, I snatch one of the empty glasses near the decanter for him to spit into. I make him repeat the process several times.

He sighs with relief. "I was so determined not to swallow any of it that I hardly breathed, either. It was very bitter. Even an amateur brandy drinker would have been put off by the flavor."

"Elisabetta drank it quickly, she said. In one gulp."

"Well, that's something I'll never do again, with any beverage."

I reach for his hand, squeezing it hard. "I can't believe you tasted the brandy like that, without warning. Don't you think it was reckless?"

His lips quirk at my scolding tone. "We're a reckless pair, then, Livia. I wouldn't take the chance of letting you suffer any of its effects, not when I can take the risk on your behalf."

"I knew the procedure, though. I was prepared."

His gaze drops to the expanse of my belly, heavy against the dark green of my dress. "I'm in a better position than you to be reckless, right now."

My gratitude is a bit belated, but I speak it sincerely. "Thank you. You've been very helpful."

He nods once, and his eyes turn steely, more gray than blue. "But this affair isn't over yet."

"She'll still need treatment. I must return in the morning."

"An investigation will commence at once. I'll bring the brandy home with us, in case you need to inspect it further, but mostly to make sure no one naively samples it—or disposes of it. Is there anything else I should order to be left alone?"

"Wine, maybe, if the bottle is already open. Anything with a very strong taste. You know for yourself how bitter aconite is." If its taste was as obvious as Niccolo says, though, I'm beginning to wonder if the poisoner knew just how bitter it is. If Elisabetta hadn't gulped it, it's unlikely she would have consumed enough to cause such sickness. "Niccolo, can you give these orders?" I ask. Elisabetta outranks him with her title, even though he's high in Conte Cavour's favor.

"Yes, I believe so. While Elisabetta is bedridden, I speak with Conte Cavour's authority."

I didn't quite realize how much Cavour entrusts Niccolo with responsibilities, how highly he must regard him. It's a bit of a surprise to me to recognize that perhaps Niccolo is more powerful than I understood. And I wonder again why he decided to marry me. Plenty of babies have been born out of wedlock and under a thin veil of scandal; most men would have let me be another of those mothers.

That musing is for another time, though. I shift the conversation back to Elisabetta. "I want to help question her cook, and some of the servants." Seeing the slight narrowing of Niccolo's eyes, I forestall any argument. "I insist. And since I know more about poisons than you, I don't think you would be wise to attempt to prevent me."

The corners of his mouth twitch. "Are you threatening to poison me if I forbid you?"

"No, of course not." Belatedly, I hear the dry tone of his voice, see the unexpected glimmer of amusement in his eyes. "I meant I'd be able to question them more effectively on the technical aspects."

"In any case, I won't dare risk your wrath," he says. "I hope you'll let me help you as much as I can, Livia."

"We'll do this together," I promise. It feels good to be able to trust him.

"You must be ready to collapse into bed. If you're to treat her again when she wakes, you'd best get some rest now." He guides me toward the door, which makes me realize my fingers are still curled around his, grasping for support. Exhaustion swamps me, and I let him assist me into the carriage before sliding my hand free.

Later, fleetingly, I think of the brandy as my mind lulls on the edge of sleep. I bet Corbara could be easily persuaded to drink brandy, although unlike Elisabetta, he'd probably know it shouldn't taste so bitter.

Perhaps Corbara knows the brandy is poisoned already.

CHAPTER TWELVE

Paris, December 1856

Death cap mushrooms, which are sometimes mistaken for a safe variety, can cause maddening thirst. Symptoms, which include abdominal pain and upset, may not appear for up to a day after consumption.
— Excerpt from Livia Valenti's book of herbal studies

After I've slept, I hurry back to Elisabetta's. She turns her head toward me as I enter her bedroom, carrying a tray of medicines as well as a bowl of soup, which I brought from my own kitchen to make sure it is safe. Her maid must have combed her hair, twining its mass into the neat braid coiled across her pillow like a dark gold serpent. Her eyes look bright and clear, but she makes no move to sit up.

"I ache all over," she says in greeting. "My bones must be made of broken glass, my skin of sand. My stomach feels like a stallion kicked it."

Rather impressed by the drama of her descriptions, I put down the tray and brush my fingertips over her forehead, feeling for fever or that sick clamminess of the night before. She seems to be a normal temperature, and her complexion, while pale, has lost that ghastly grayish hue.

"Your stomach muscles are likely strained from vomiting. Do you think you can eat?"

Her mouth pouts into a grimace, but she props herself up on her elbows with obvious effort and glances at the tray. "Are you sure it's safe?"

"Yes," I reassure her. "I examined it all myself. First, the medicine—it will soothe your stomach."

I expect her to complain about the taste, but she drinks the mixture of marshmallow and barley water obediently, and then sniffs appreciatively at the peppermint tea.

"Any lingering nausea?"

"No, thankfully. Just a splitting headache. I don't suppose you've brought any laudanum?" Her brows arch hopefully.

"No." She doesn't need it. It might erase her lingering discomfort, but that will pass soon enough as she continues to heal. I don't dare give her any laudanum in any case; it could react badly with any aconite or nightshade still lingering in her body.

She sips the tea, then leans back against the pillows as I set it back on the tray.

"It was the brandy, wasn't it?"

I nod. "It seems so. Niccolo and I examined it."

Her eyelashes flick in surprise. "Niccolo, too? I've no memory of him being here yesterday."

"You were asleep, and he didn't come into the bedroom."

"What was in the brandy?"

"Aconite. Monkshood," I supply, seeing she doesn't recognize the Latin name. I explain it to her the same way I did to Niccolo. "I almost didn't believe it at first," I tell her. "I don't know why anyone would want to poison you."

Her teeth show as she curls her lip, and her cheekbones look stark. "Don't you? I'm not well-liked at court, you know. Many women envy me, including the empress and Comtesse Walewska. My husband lectures me about expenditures every time we meet, and can barely stand to discuss the emperor, though he's willing enough to use me as a stepping stone as long as I'm quiet about it.

Your husband lectures me about getting things done for Camillo, that I'm not accomplishing anything for the cause of Italian unity. Bellino baits me all the time, under the delusion I'm some kind of saint or angel, and random petitioners are always trying to meet with me to either ask for favors from the emperor, or to plead Italy's cause." As she speaks, her voice grows hoarse and piercing, and her fingers clutch at the coverlet, twisting it into a knot. Her eyes look wild, glinting as bright as if she does have a fever, after all. "I have more enemies than friends, I daresay. Perhaps you're my only friend, Livia."

I lay my hand over hers, squeezing it reassuringly when she untangles her fingers from the blanket. Her nails dig like claws against the back of my hand. "I'm sure that's not true. But I'm here for you."

Her breath shakes as she sighs, draining some of the tension from her body. The cords in her neck disappear again. "Is it any wonder I love my photography? It's my one peace." She clears her throat, and the painful scratch of it makes me wince in sympathy. "In any case, I have enemies enough, as you can see. But if it was the brandy that was poisoned, then I doubt I was the target. I rarely drink it. I only did so last night because I was piqued. I keep it for the emperor."

I can hardly comprehend who'd want to assassinate the emperor, because the list of potential suspects would be enormous, even from my own acquaintances. Roberto Rossi certainly seems fervent enough, although he's friends with Elisabetta and I can't imagine he would risk harming her. But all through Paris, the emperor has enemies. Just last year, an Italian patriot fired a pistol at him on the Champs-Élysées, and I heard once someone laid a bomb on the track of a train he was supposed to be traveling on. If Elisabetta is right, and he was the real target, I can't help but think it was a sloppy attempt, and I worry other items might have been tampered with, too. Perhaps the nightshade berries really were meant for the emperor, in light of this new development.

I think again of Corbara. I know he was in Paris, and I know he has corresponded with Elisabetta. He's an Italian nationalist. Could he have poisoned the brandy, trying to reach the emperor? It seems unlikely that he'd be alone in the room to tamper with it, though. Elisabetta doesn't invite casual acquaintances to her private parlor—only to the salon with the nymph painting. I need to think. Corbara is my enemy, but that doesn't mean he's Elisabetta's. I fear I'm irrationally projecting my loathing. Besides, the intimacy of this situation, when the brandy is stored away from most visitors, kept only for the emperor, suggests it must be someone close to her—or at least someone who knows her habits. My stomach twists with anxiety.

I go down to the kitchen, intending to question Marco first. After last night, it doesn't seem quite so accidental about the nightshade berries. As I cross into the cinnamon-scented warmth of the kitchen, I brush aside the curl of guilt that I didn't wait for Niccolo. He wants to be involved in my questions for Elisabetta's household staff, but there's no time to wait for him.

Marco's assistant, a youth with rosy cheeks and a shock of dark hair kicking up from his forehead, looks up from chopping beets. Purple juice gleams on the blade of his knife, staining his fingertips.

"Is Marco here?"

He shakes his head, tossing a beet peel aside with an abrupt swipe of his knife. "He hasn't been here since this morning. Went out to the butcher's, and hasn't been back since, leaving me with all this extra work. It's a good thing the contessa won't be too hungry today, but the rest of us must still eat."

"When will he be back?"

His shoulder twitches. "I don't know. He did this once before, when he placed a lucky bet and quadrupled his gamble. Came back drunk, that time." His brow creases. "It'd be a bit surprising today, though. He knew the contessa was sick last night. We were all very worried."

"She's recovering well," I reassure him. "May I look around?"

"Of course." His gaze lingers doubtfully on the bulk of my belly. Clearly he doesn't think I seem nimble enough to poke around the kitchen and storeroom. "You won't find anything in the food, though," he adds. "She dined at home last night."

"Did you make it yourself?"

"Marco did most of it. But we all ate it—myself, Marco, Beatrice, Davide… Some nights she hardly eats anything, and it'd be a shame to let that fine food go to waste."

I should be relieved after poking through the kitchen and cellar, inspecting still-corked wine bottles and rounds of cheese, but I can't shake a sense of unease. I can't find anything amiss, but things are terribly wrong since a poisoning occurred at all. Marco still hasn't returned, and from the way he glances at the door every five minutes, his assistant is worried.

Returning home, I go straight to Niccolo's study to tell him of Elisabetta's revelation that the brandy is hardly touched by anyone in the household and kept only for the emperor. Grim lines etch along Niccolo's face, from nose to mouth, and his shoulders turn taut.

"This may have been an attempt on the life of the emperor, you mean?"

I nod silently, cradling my arm around my belly. The baby has been kicking incessantly, and I feel bruised all over, drooping with exhaustion. I know the birth is near because my body has become too crowded for us both. Neither of us is ever comfortable anymore.

Niccolo must notice my dull complexion, or the dark circles under my eyes, because he pulls a chair close to me, hand hovering over my elbow until I let him help me heave myself into the seat.

"I thought Elisabetta was the target," he says. "I'm sure she has enemies. Many ambitious ladies might envy her closeness to the emperor, and Elisabetta can be quite cool at court functions. Sometimes she sits in the corner, hardly speaking to anyone until the emperor arrives."

"I don't think that's a reason to murder her," I point out.

He blinks. "No, of course not. I was thinking, for a person vying to take her place as the emperor's mistress, it might make it easier to think of her in an impersonal way. I was musing aloud, and poorly." He clears his throat. "I don't want anyone to be a poisoning target, but it would be easier to protect Elisabetta than the emperor. I was going to suggest to Conte Cavour that perhaps she should return to Italy, for her own safety."

"She won't want to go." I know this for certain. Elisabetta likes it in Paris, where she can go to Monsieur Pierson's studio whenever she wishes.

A few days later, Elisabetta has recovered most of her strength, and even seems pleased the ordeal has slimmed her already tiny waist. She complains it dried her skin, though, turning it powdery and pale as parchment, so I spend the morning making a batch of lotion with sweet meadowfoam to restore luster to her complexion. We both massage it into our cheeks, and then she insists I sit near her by the window so that we may read together. It's unusual for Elisabetta to be so tame and docile, and seeing her with a shawl tucked around her shoulders, one of her photo albums open in her lap—she grew bored of the latest ladies' magazine after only a few moments—makes me feel a surge of protectiveness for her. After poring over her album, we read aloud together from a book of mythology, considering ideas for her next portrait. It's a pleasant, golden afternoon, where the shadow of poison almost seems to burn away, but it's only a temporary lull.

Marco still hasn't returned.

"I've quite given up on him," says Elisabetta in a scathing tone. "His absence makes him seem quite guilty. If he comes back, I'll have him arrested."

Her ordeal has left her in an understandably foul mood. Beatrice confided to me she'd complained of joint aches all morning, and when she dragged herself out of bed with a dogged air of martyrdom, she spent several moments staring at her reflection in the mirror with an expression of dismay, making me glad I'd finished the lotion already. I can't disagree with her harsh statement in regard to Marco, though. His disappearance immediately after her poisoning seems suspicious, but it doesn't give me any inkling of why he would have wanted to poison either Elisabetta or the emperor. As the cook, he would have had much better opportunity than slipping aconite into a decanter of brandy that might remain untouched for weeks, especially if he was prepared to flee after the poison had taken effect.

Caterina and I have discussed the topic at length, but I want to talk to Niccolo, since we agreed to investigate together. He's not seated at the desk in his room, though Luce naps in a patch of sunlight. Finding out from Lorenzo that Niccolo has gone for a walk in the direction of the Pont de l'Alma, I decide to go and find him. The warm sparkle of sunshine on the Seine lures me.

I find Niccolo standing alone in the middle of the bridge. Some people would lean on the railing, staring into the water below, but he stands straight, palms resting gently along the smooth stone top. He looks almost as stiff as the statue below him, the figure of a man standing on a plinth. I'm told Parisians use it to measure the rising depth of the water when it rains a lot.

"You look deep in thought," I say, standing next to him.

He turns to me with some surprise, lips curling in a small smile that doesn't light up his eyes. "I am. I find it's peaceful here, particularly when my mind is troubled." He turns away from the sleek ripple of the river to face me, lifting one hand as if to grasp mine, and then shoves it into his coat pocket instead. "I shouldn't have made you walk so far. I'm sorry."

"You didn't know I'd come looking for you." It's not something I've ever done before, so he couldn't have expected it. "It's good for me to walk a little, even if waddling feels difficult. I wanted to speak with you about Marco's disappearance."

The shadows under his eyes seem to darken when he bends his head closer to mine. "Livia, I'm afraid I have bad news. Marco is dead."

Goosebumps rise along my arms, and I cradle my arms around my belly for comfort. "Dead? By what cause?" Surely nothing natural, not given the suspicious timing.

"I'm told he was pulled from the river late last night. I only just found out. I don't think Elisabetta knows yet—I'd put out my own search for him. It isn't clear yet if he drowned or not."

I squeeze my cold fingers together, warming the knuckles. "I shall need to examine the body." A wisp of horror curls through me at the idea, but I must know what happened. For my own peace of mind, and for Elisabetta, too.

Niccolo's jaw clenches. "Absolutely not."

"It's important," I argue. "There's cause to believe his death wasn't natural. He could have been murdered because he poisoned the brandy—or he knew who did. He could have even been bribed to do it." I tilt my head back to stare fiercely into his eyes. "We need to get to the bottom of this, Niccolo."

His voice softens, losing the splintering cadence of his earlier refusal. "I don't deny the importance of investigating his death, and I won't hide any details from you. But I'm not going to allow an immensely pregnant woman to traipse around, jabbing at corpses, particularly not when she's my wife."

I open my mouth to protest further, but a soft wheeze emerges instead, when the baby connects a particularly ferocious kick against my lowest rib. As I rub the aching spot, Niccolo looks smug.

"Very well," I agree. "But Caterina goes with you."

"She may not want to. Not everyone shares your eagerness for proximity to dead bodies."

I hesitate. Caterina has never balked at any sort of adventure before, but it's true neither of us has ever encountered anything so gruesome. Much as I trust her to be my eyes in a scene where I cannot go, perhaps I can't ask this of her.

"If she's willing, I'll allow her to accompany me. And if she's not, I hope you'll find some measure of trust in me." He draws in an audible breath, as if steeling himself, and then the words tumble from him, fast and raw. "I want only the best for you, Livia, and I hope resolving this matter will help prove it to you. I understand you felt you couldn't approach me when you first saw the nightshade berries in the kitchen, since we knew each other so little, and I regret it deeply. I intend to use my—not inconsiderable—resources and connections to put an end to this matter as soon as possible." Falling silent, he waits for my response, his gray eyes earnest, lips slightly parted.

"So you don't need my assistance." I appreciate his promise to put a stop to the danger circling Elisabetta's household, but hearing him declare he'll use all the power he holds as a respected diplomat, as the prime minister's closest advisor, and knowing I can't compete with that, gives me a hollow feeling. I'm overstepping, not fitting in again. I don't know how to belong in Paris, in his household.

He steps closer to me. "On the contrary, I have great need of you. This problem affects our home—it's *our* problem, and we shall solve it together." Faint humor threads through his voice. "It just doesn't extend to you examining corpses when you look ready to go into labor any day. They say life and death is a cycle, but I'm not sure that should extend to giving birth in a morgue. In any case, your expertise in medicines is something I cannot match."

Tension unwinds along my shoulders, and I feel a small smile lifting the corners of my mouth. "It means a lot to me to be included. I'm not sure most husbands are so accommodating to the whims of their wives. I think I'm very fortunate."

"You aren't the least driven by whims," says Niccolo. "You're one of the most practical, cleverest people I've known, and I'd be a fool to ignore that."

A glow of warmth sparks around my heart, spreading under my skin until I feel lit up like a candle. "Thank you, Niccolo."

His voice turns soft and warm. "I like hearing my name on your lips. You don't say it often."

I glance up, meeting his eyes. His gray irises gleam like mirrors, reflecting back all the longing and loneliness twisted up inside me, a silent desire to belong to someone, yet also a fear of it. A lurch of yearning lifts my arms to his waist, the hardness of my round belly pressing against him as I try to nestle my cheek against his chest. My heart thumps rapidly, but the warm comfort of the contact unleashes a flood of relief. I've been so lonely, locking myself away behind a shield. I want to be held, and since Niccolo won't touch me unless I ask, I have to make the first overture.

Niccolo responds immediately. His arms sweep around me, one palm tracing small, gentle circles on my back. I think his cheek is pressed to my hair. My nose skims against his throat, and I realize he smells like soap and lemons and leather, and that I like it.

We stand that way for a moment or two, hearts pressed close, arms tangled together. When I lift my head, drawing back slightly, he releases me at once, but I like the crooked, surprised smile that lingers on his face. He glances around, as if to verify we didn't cause a public scene, and that I made him forget his restraint for a moment warms me inside.

"I trust you to tell me everything about Marco's death," I say. "I won't ask Caterina to accompany you."

"Not everyone would consider this romantic talk. But I do. It makes me very happy to gain a measure of your trust."

I tell him a list of things to look for, which might help determine how Marco died, but the river will likely have ruined most signs. If he was poisoned, any traces of vomit will be gone, and any swelling could be caused by decomposition. Even some wounds might be mysterious, because the current of the river could have bumped the body into rocks. If Marco was murdered—and it seems likely, for if he'd killed himself out of guilt, he probably wouldn't have ended up in the river—his killer has rendered my poison expertise useless.

Niccolo returns to the house a few hours later, pausing only to wash and change his clothes before coming to see me, as evidenced by his damp hair and the wafting scent of rosemary soap. I'm sitting near the window, where I was half-heartedly sewing yet another swaddling blanket, but I've fallen into a doze. I startle upright, trying not to cringe at the ache in my neck, tossing the soft material aside.

"I'm sorry, did I wake you? Caterina sent me in. She said you were sewing."

"I was. And then I fell asleep." I brace my hands on the arms of the chair, about to rise, but Niccolo gestures for me to remain, pulling another chair near.

He doesn't waste time getting to the point he knows I want to hear. "It's as we feared. I do not think Marco's death was natural. His head was badly wounded. I can't say for sure if it was before his death, but I suspect so. It looks like a heavy object struck the back of his head."

"Once?"

Niccolo gives me a sharp look. "I don't know. It was hard to tell with the missing pieces of skull and the brain matter that had been scavenged by fish."

"A broken skull seems likely to be caused by several blows," I suggest. "Or one good strike with a very hard object."

"I should have known you wouldn't be put off by the description."

"Were there any other injuries?"

"A few scrapes. Looked like his arm was broken. Nothing as serious as the head wound."

We both fall silent. The primary injury of a crushed skull seems to point to murder to me. Dread frosts over my skin. I didn't know Marco well, but I remember the cheerful way he presided over his kitchen, his eager-to-please attitude when Elisabetta deigned to visit it. A wave of pity for him washes over me. He may not have been innocent, but he didn't deserve a lonely, water-logged grave.

Niccolo drags his chair closer to mine. His fingers squeeze its wooden arms, even the stump of his missing one, and his voice drops so low I instinctively lean closer to hear. "I promised you could trust me, and so now I must make a confession. I wrote a draft of a letter to the prime minister, in which I included many thoughts on the political situation as it pertains to Italy."

I nod. This isn't surprising. Niccolo must write a great many letters to Conte Cavour, his employer. Only Niccolo would write several drafts of a letter, but this warms a flare of affection in me.

"You know an Italian man shot at the emperor last year, on the Champs-Élysées? Camillo wanted to know if it's much talked about, if it seems to have left an impression on the emperor. I can't speak to the emperor's feelings, but I have heard rumors here, both from Italian nationalists and a few French politicians. There's a line of thinking that if the Carbonari managed to assassinate Emperor Napoleon, France would go into revolt, and the Italy could take advantage of the unrest to revolt against Austrian rule, too. That's likely why that Italian assassination attempt happened."

"I understand. Like the theory of the dagger Bellino has described."

Niccolo nods. "Yes, precisely. Of course, I recounted all of this for Camillo. I don't feel any guilt for that; it's part of my job here in Paris to keep him informed. I do regret my incautious phrasing. I believe it may have read as if I supported the idea."

"Do you?" The blunt question slips out of my mouth before it occurs to me to ask more delicately, but I'm curious to hear his answer.

He flinches slightly, but his gaze remains steady on my face. "In theory, it could be successful. I've tried to be optimistic, but I don't think the emperor has much intention of siding with Italy over Austria right now. Given his past association with the Carbonari, and how long Camillo has been trying to meet with him, I think he would have taken action by now if he had any intention of it. Do I think it's an idea to proceed with? Of course not. I can't condone murder."

"I didn't really think you would."

His mouth softens slightly from its tense line, but he doesn't quite smile. "There's an adage, 'the end justifies the means.' I believe it's from Machiavelli's *The Prince*, although it's not phrased quite like that." Seeing I'm unfamiliar with the contents of that particular book, he waves it off. "I understand the idea behind the saying, as I'm sure you do, too. Perhaps it's true—an extreme case where the death of one person would benefit the rest of the population might exist. But this isn't it. Piedmont could go to war with Austria alone. It would just be riskier than having French support, which it would not in any case receive if France was in an uprising. The only benefit the theory of the dagger could bring is that France likely wouldn't support Austria, either. It would focus on its own interests."

It's an interesting topic, and gives me insight into the logical processes of Niccolo's mind, but I try to bring it back around to the letter. "If I'm following correctly, then, you wrote down some thoughts about the Carbonari theory of the dagger belief that

the emperor's death would benefit the cause of Italian nationalism—and it could sound incriminating."

"Yes, but it's worse than that. I lost the letter."

It's so unlike Niccolo to be careless that my lips part in surprise.
He never misplaces anything. He folds his napkin into a perfect
square, lining it up with the corner of the table, every night after
dinner. He always remembers the page of the book he's been
reading without using a bookmark. Just yesterday, he reached
blindly but unerringly into his desk drawer for the envelope
Bellino needed while his brother rummaged fruitlessly through
a stack of papers.

"That's impossible. You never misplace anything."

He looks faintly pleased by my declaration. "I ought to have
chosen my wording better. It's more serious than that."

"You think someone took it?" Somehow, I've grown comfortable enough with him to interrupt.

"Yes, and I know who. It was Elisabetta."

"*She* took it?"

"Yes. We argued about it, you see. She saw it on the desk—Elisabetta has no compunctions about snooping through someone's
papers. Her boldness would be admirable if it wasn't so irritating."

I open my mouth to defend her. Elisabetta is like the queen
on a chessboard. Powerful and protected, but also only on the
board because of the hand of another. I feel sympathy for her
position. Niccolo sighs before I can speak, though.

"I suppose I don't blame her. I'd want to be as informed as I
could be if I was her, and I know she doesn't trust me very much.
I'd protect myself in her position, too. She thinks I'm here because
she isn't getting the job of persuading the emperor done."

"Aren't you?" I ask gently.

"Not entirely. Camillo hoped I'd be able to support her, but
it doesn't seem to be working that way." He smiles crookedly.

"You've been more of a help to her than me, and I'm grateful to you for that."

"Do you want me to ask her about the letter? Perhaps I can get it back. And put her at ease."

He shakes his head. "She's probably made a copy by now. I just wanted you to know. You trusted me with the truth about the poison, and I want to trust you with a secret of my own." The lightness of his expression dies away, and he closes his eyes briefly. "Though the letter isn't one I would wish others to read, it isn't as dangerous as the fact that someone poisoned Elisabetta, while the emperor was probably the true target. I only wish I'd written it in cipher. I always use a code for writing to the prime minister, but this was a draft to gather my thoughts, so I didn't bother. It would make it harder for her if I had used the code, though."

"It doesn't matter," I say, hoping it's true. I want to ask if he has a suspect in mind, wondering if I should mention Corbara, but I don't know that he's still in Paris, only that he wrote to Elisabetta, and he could have done that from anywhere. And I hate speaking of him… I hesitate as Niccolo curls forward, resting his elbow on his knee.

"I need to find a way to end this situation. To keep us all safe." Niccolo's voice sounds muffled against my sleeve, but when he sits up, his eyes glint like iron, full of determination. "I'd like us to go home to Turin, to properly start our lives together. Everything in Paris now feels like a distraction, and I want to put our family first."

"We'll sort it out," I promise.

We must.

CHAPTER THIRTEEN

Paris, January 1857

In certain doses, tea brewed of tansy may be useful for women's ailments. Its pungent scent also repels insects and mice.
— Excerpt from Livia Valenti's book of herbal studies

On my way down to supper, I notice there's a letter for me on the tray in the hallway. I just had a letter from my parents only yesterday, and don't expect another one from them for a week or so. My mother has been writing to me more often than usual, as my labor approaches. I'd hoped she could come to Paris for my child's birth, but she had a fall a couple of weeks ago and broke her ankle. She downplays it in her letters, saying it gives her more time to sit and focus on correspondence, but I can tell my father worries over her injury. He won't let her walk on it at all, and I understand, even if I'm disappointed, she can't travel until it's healed. I pick up the envelope with interest.

Niccolo receives the most correspondence. In comparison, Bellino and I rarely have letters, and Bellino isn't even here now. Near the end of December, he returned to Turin in order to take care of some business matters for the estate, taking less luggage than I expected, which hinted that he'd be back before too long.

The writing looks jagged, and its harshly pointed t's and i's stab at me like needles as I recognize Corbara's writing. Fingers trembling, I tear the envelope open, ripping it apart in my clumsy panic.

There's no letter inside, only a soft green ribbon.

It used to belong to me. I'd threaded it through my braid on the last day I saw him, and he took it from my hair right before he sauntered away. His discarded souvenir curls in my palm like a serpent, and I can hardly bear to touch it. A sour taste fills my mouth. I thought the ribbon very pretty, once.

I can't possibly sit at the table, facing Niccolo, pretending everything's fine. I hate thinking Corbara has won, making me too shaken to have supper with my family, but I don't have the composure to meet Niccolo's intent, worried gaze. As the baby's birth draws nearer, he watches me all the time, as if I'm a glass ornament teetering on the edge of a shelf. Tension pulls my shoulder blades painfully tight as I slip down the hall and back upstairs to my bedroom. I clench my fingers around the ribbon, as if I could disintegrate it with the pressure of my closed palm, while my memories cloud my thoughts and my scalp aches with the ghost of Corbara's fingers wound tightly through my hair.

*

Turin, April 1856 (nine months earlier)

Corbara came to visit me one last time before departing for Florence. "Thanks to your thorough care, Ferrero and I are back to full health. I'm grateful to you, Livia."

It stung that Corbara sounded so cheerful. I understood he had to leave, but I wanted him to be reluctant about it. Instead of his bright grin, gaze shifting to the horizon, I'd imagined tender words, his hand tucking my hair behind my ear.

"I hope you'll stay safe," I said stiffly.

The angle of his sidelong glance made his scarred eye seem entirely brown and dark, the other green and glinting as spring leaves. "I will. I always do. You ought to hope for adventure for me instead." His voice took on a lower, softer note. "Adventure and glory, and a quick return to your side." He reached for my hand. "Perhaps I'll make my fortune while I'm away, and won't you be surprised when I swagger back into Turin carrying a sack of gold?"

"What would you do with a sack of gold?" I asked, smiling despite my disappointment.

"Oh, lots of things." He waved his hand airily. "Buy quite a lot of wine, I daresay. A necklace for you. Maybe even a house."

"Those are backwards in order of importance."

He laughed at the primness of my tone. "You always tell me the truth, Livia. I like that; you're good for me." He stepped closer to me, bending his head near mine. "You'll kiss me farewell, won't you?"

My heartbeat quickened. I'd thought a lot about his kisses, and I wouldn't mind if he kissed me again, but not too much. I didn't want a repeat of the first, forceful one, but memories of the second one made my stomach clench in a pleasant way. "Not here," I said, glancing around. No one was in sight now, but that meant nothing when we stood so close to my house. I wouldn't want my parents to see me kissing Corbara in the street. We'd need to duck into a shadowed corner.

"I have an idea." He grabbed my hand. "The storage shed. It's nothing fancy, but I bet it'll do for saying a tender goodbye."

I hesitated in the doorway. We hung herbs to dry here, and stored jars of oils and salves that needed to stay cool. The pungent scent of mixed herbs hovered in the air, concentrated in the narrowness of the space. It really wasn't proper to be alone with Corbara like this, but it was the last time I'd see him for a long time. Ever, possibly, if he never came back.

He tugged me to follow him, whispering how much he wanted to hold me one last time before we were separated. "Just for a moment," he said. "I want to remember the feel of you in my arms, the smell of your hair."

I succumbed to his persuasion, and closed the door behind me.

His lips skimmed across my neck, those soft, open caresses lighting my skin on fire. My breath felt shaky and too fast. When I shivered lightly and pressed back against him, his warm breath exhaled across my skin, tickling, and his voice rumbled in my ear while one arm snaked across my stomach, winding around my waist and pulling me close to him.

"I remember you liked that," he said. "When I kissed your neck, you practically melted in my arms. I've been thinking about it ever since. I've been going mad, thinking of you."

I let him kiss my mouth then, this time relaxing into the startling intimacy. I liked the heat of it, and though the slide of his tongue against mine made me tense at first, the low, pleased groan he made in the back of his throat sped my heartbeat again. As he gathered me more firmly into his arms, I surrendered to the insistence of his kiss, and my blood swirled like smoke in my veins. I liked kissing, I discovered.

When his hand tugged at my bodice and his fingers dove into the opening between the fabric and my skin, I pulled away. I'd just recently had my first kiss—I wasn't ready for more. I didn't want him to undress me. "Stop it."

The fingers of his other hand tightened like a vise around my wrist. "You don't mean it. You'll feel the pleasure in a moment, just like you did when I kissed your neck. You protested that at first, too."

"No—stop touching me." My voice echoed, shrill and tight. It confused me that Corbara didn't seem to understand the difference between a kiss and the removal of clothing. The warm buzz from his kisses faded, souring to bile in my stomach.

His fingers moved to my hair instead, twining the strands around his fingers and tugging at my scalp. When he yanked on my hair, wrapped in his fist, my head smacked hard against the shelf beside me. Pain lit stars behind my eyes and I almost didn't hear his next words. "If you didn't want this, you wouldn't have come with me to the shed. You're so beautiful… Touching you is like a dream. I never want to stop."

Later, my memories of what happened felt vague and distant. In my mind, I shoved at his chest, stomped on his feet, jabbed at his eyes, and stormed out of the shed with my head held high and my pride intact. In reality, I froze. My limbs turned to wood and my pulse hammered so hard in my throat that my head felt dizzy and weightless. I couldn't breathe. He maneuvered my body as he wanted, and I felt like a corpse.

After, once he'd rearranged his clothing again, he stroked my hair carelessly. It felt knotted, pins askew. My green hair ribbon had become untied, and he dragged it free of my loose hair and pocketed it. "You might have a bruise on your head. It's a little swollen already. I'm sorry about that. It was so crowded in here— I'm surprised we didn't knock the whole shelf over." When he smiled, his teeth looked sharp and there was nothing charmingly roguish about it at all. "You probably have just the salve to fix it, though, don't you?" He paused in the doorway. "I'll see you again, Livia. I'll come back to Turin when I can. I promise."

It felt more like a threat, and I wanted to retch when he blew me a kiss. Instead I sank to the floor, huddled around the ache of pain inside me, burning between my legs, cracking my heart, spinning in my head. I'd sit here for a few minutes, I told myself, to gain some composure. Then I'd pretend this never happened.

Caterina found me after a while, still crumpled into a ball on the floor. Somehow she seemed to know what had happened as soon as I turned my bruised face toward her. She rocked me in her arms and hushed me, crooning like a mother with a fractious infant. I wanted to cry, but I felt too cold inside.

"We can hide this if you want," she said. "I'll say I saw you trip and hit your head, or we can hide the bruise with your hair.

You can take something—you know the right mixture to prevent a child? I'm sure it's in your father's books somewhere."

Dutifully, I brewed a disgusting syrup. It made me vomit, and gave me a piercing headache and pinching pains in my stomach. But it didn't matter. Two weeks later, my monthly course was absent.

"It might just be a few days late," soothed Caterina. "Just wait a little longer."

"Maybe," I said, but with no real optimism. A few more weeks passed and I had to admit there was no use pretending nothing had happened.

I was lucky, in a way. When I finally found the courage to confess everything, I had the full support of my parents and the benefit of my father's impressive connections as physician to Conte Camillo Cavour, the current prime minister. They talked of sending me to live with my elder brother, who'd recently moved to the city of Alba to take over the clientele of a late doctor, but another solution presented itself.

"I spoke to the *conte*," my father told me, in the tone he'd adopted for speaking of my pregnancy. I hated its mixture of gentle and matter-of-fact, though that wasn't his fault. He was doing his best. The idea that the prime minister of Piedmont knew about my humiliation made me squirm. I wanted to hide.

"Unfortunately, there has been no news of Corbara or his companion, Ferrero. Conte Cavour promised to quietly put word about to find him—but not the reason, don't worry. He may yet be punished." Father's voice softened. "In the meantime, one of Cavour's staff offered to marry you. He's a diplomat."

For a second, my heart leapt with hope. If one of Cavour's diplomats married me, I could stay close to home, and my child would appear to have a father. I wouldn't be ruined. Then I thought about marrying a stranger and my mood sank again. My cheeks scalded at the knowledge that both the prime minister and at least one of his companions knew what had happened to me.

"I think you've met him," my father continued. His voice was still too soft. "He said you'd spoken in the garden at the Castello del Valentino."

"Niccolo Valenti," I said, remembering. "I assumed he was already married."

"He was, but his wife passed away two years ago from pneumonia. They had no children. He assured me your child would be treated as legitimate, as his heir. I know it must seem overwhelming, Livia. I'm sorry, but I can't think of a better solution. Marriage to a well-connected diplomat, favored by the prime minister himself, is better than I ever expected for you. Not that you aren't good enough for one—any man would be lucky to have you as his wife—but it reaches higher than I expected my connections to allow." He didn't need to add that the circumstances had made a good marriage even less likely. "We're respectable, but not very wealthy."

"Cavour's patronage helps." My voice sounded thin and far away. I couldn't help but think that my illegitimate pregnancy helped too, if Niccolo Valenti was set on having an heir for his family fortunes. It made me feel like a brood mare.

"His offer secures your future," said Father. "He was straightforward with me—he must travel to Paris, for a year or so, and he'd take you with him. I wish it didn't take you away from Turin, but it's not forever. This will be a good match. There's no one more suitable, anyway."

He said the last gently, but it still stung. I knew I was nineteen and without any suitors. It was partly why I'd enjoyed Corbara's attentions so much. Before him, there hadn't been anyone who attracted me, and I think most of the young men thought I was odd because I spent so much time helping my father treat his patients. I didn't care much, since I liked assisting him with medicine, but Corbara had soared into my life like a comet, bright and full of promise. I'd allowed myself to dream he might be my husband. The thought made acid burn against the back of my throat now. I pressed my palm against my belly, as if that burgeoning hard lump would miraculously disappear.

"I will marry him," I said, without enthusiasm. I didn't have a choice, but accepting it out loud at least created the faint illusion of one.

My marriage to Niccolo Valenti, diplomat, wealthy gentleman, and trusted advisor to Conte Cavour, took place at the end of July. I was four months pregnant, just barely beginning to show, but I wore a high-waisted gown with a full skirt to disguise this anyway. Our wedding was held in the local church I was used to attending with my family. In contrast, Conte Cavour hosted the wedding banquet at Castello del Valentino, in a room with high, painted ceilings, tall windows, and a chandelier that caught the light and shattered it into thousands of sparks. Apparently, parts of the castle were in need of restoration, having been damaged by French troops during Napoleon I's time, but the rooms I saw seemed splendid and impersonal. Cavour's generosity even extended to letting us spend our wedding night in one of the *castello*'s enormous rooms, since the royal family was not currently in residence.

Niccolo and I sat beside each other at the head of the table. He wore an elegant tailcoat of dark blue cloth, which brought out the gold glints in his hair and the lightness of his eyes. He looked composed and intimidating. And while I usually would have appreciated its finery, I hardly noticed my own gown, which was new, although Caterina had assured me the soft green shade complemented my sun-bronzed skin and made my tawny eyes look almost golden.

"Like a lioness," she'd said, half teasing, but also trying to cheer me up.

I didn't feel brave like a lioness during the wedding banquet, perched in my chair beside Niccolo, quietly staring at my plate while my stomach clenched into a tight knot.

Cavour made a brief toast, mostly about Niccolo's trustworthiness and his cleverness. Partway through, he seemed to remember this was a wedding, and wished us many happy years together. I must have spoken to him at some point, for I remembered his round, genial face and shiny spectacles as he wished me many felicitations, but most of the evening passed in a blur of dread and I couldn't recall anything of our conversation.

"I enjoyed our meeting in the gardens in the spring." Niccolo offered me a tentative smile. His fingertips crept to the back of my hand, sliding toward my wrist in one soft stroke.

It was a light touch, and I didn't think he meant anything more than to punctuate his words, but I had to resist flinching away. I reminded myself he was my husband now, and could touch me whether I wanted it or not.

His hand drew away from my frozen one, but his voice remained calm and steady. "I hope we can build upon those pleasant moments." He looked down, masking his eyes. "Though I know we're almost strangers now, I believe we can be happy together."

My voice rang too loud, grating with forced brashness. "Of course we will." I reached for the wine cup, changed my mind, and let my hand fall in my lap. My ears seemed to whistle, making it hard to think, and I stared at the roast chicken on my plate, unable to look at anyone.

"We can walk together in Paris, and see the sights there," added Niccolo. "Perhaps we will discover another garden together—the Tuileries has a public one, I believe. I know it must seem a bit daunting to leave Italy for a while, especially so soon after our marriage, but I hope you will like it in Paris. It may seem like an adventure."

"Of course," I said again, a heartless echo. Relocating to Paris was just another disruption in the endless train of them that had crashed through the recent weeks of my life. I didn't want to leave Turin for Paris, even temporarily, and I dreaded leaving my family behind. I understood Niccolo's diplomatic role required him to go to Paris, though, and the implicit added benefit that it would be better for me to give birth abroad, where no one could question my July marriage against my child's January birth.

Niccolo offered me a sympathetic smile, and his shoulder moved as though he might reach for my hand again.

"I will miss helping my father with his patients," I said, words spewing fast and thoughtless. "I helped him with a lot of treatments. Even some that were not so delicate, perhaps a little unexpected for a lady to help with, but I was always interested, always wanted to be helpful."

He nodded politely.

I couldn't stop now. "Once we had to lance an infected abscess. The phlegm and pus inside was like a waterfall—it squirted clear across the room. It was green as spring grass."

His nostrils looked pinched. "You must have a strong stomach, signora."

And he didn't, it appeared. Good—hopefully that description cooled any amorous thoughts he might have. I knew I'd only postponed the inevitable, but any delay felt like a victory to my ragged nerves. I was afraid of being alone with him.

Thankfully, no one made a fuss about putting us to bed together. I retired to the bedchamber in advance of my new husband, and spent some time exploring the room. I'd lived near the *castello* all my life, but never before spent a night inside it. I delayed unbraiding my hair and putting on my nightgown until Caterina started to fret that Niccolo would arrive before I'd even taken off my shoes, and my mother took me by the shoulders and pressed a hard kiss to my forehead.

"This is a good marriage," she reminded me, something I already knew but did need to hear again. We both stood straighter, her words pouring steel into my spine. "I'm proud of you, my sweet. I know it isn't the way you wanted it to happen, but he seems like a good man, and it raises our family higher than I ever expected."

I thought of my great-grandmother, growing up on a sugar plantation in Saint-Domingue, and dying there too, paying for her violence with her life. My grandmother had been lucky to escape without being tainted by her mother's actions, and she had always said she preferred Europe to the heat of the tropics. I supposed she'd be proud my wedding night included the luxury of a *castello*.

Though my mother and Caterina tucked me under the blankets, I wasn't in bed when Niccolo quietly entered the room. I'd flung the constricting blankets away from my legs practically the moment the door closed, but then straightened the coverlet again, afraid an unkempt, mussed bed would appear to invite seductive languor. I stood at the window, which overlooked the garden where Niccolo and I had first met. The moonlight washed white and gray over the landscape, and I stared at a spear of pennyroyal while the hoot of an owl ricocheted mournfully from the treetops.

Niccolo laid his jacket over the back of a chair and came closer to me. "I thought you might be asleep."

"I couldn't sleep." I looked back to the window, but kept my body half turned, so I could watch him out of the corner of my eye.

He stopped about a foot away. His voice sounded as hesitant as his posture looked. "I understand. Are you nervous? I am."

My fingers twisted the fringe of the knitted shawl I'd wrapped tightly around myself. "You've been married before. You shouldn't be nervous."

His lips quirked, and he stepped closer. "It's not like tying a knot, or—lancing an abscess." Amusement glimmering in his eyes turned them almost silver. "It isn't something that can be learned once, and never forgotten. I've never been married to you before, Livia."

I shivered to hear my name fall from his lips, heavy and slow with longing. An ache built in my stomach, pushing up under my ribs. I began to think it would be best to just get this night over with. I flung the shawl to the floor, letting it crash into a white heap like broken wings. I didn't know if my nightgown was fully opaque and feared to dwell on that, so I lifted my head and inched one of my feet closer toward him. "We aren't married yet, not entirely. Not until it's consummated."

"It's between us now." His voice fell to a rough whisper. "We said our vows, and that's what matters."

My heart battered against my throat. I could hardly breathe, let alone shape my dry lips around the words to say that consummation was necessary, and I just wanted it done. Instead, I fumbled for his hands, and pressed them to my waist.

"Livia." As he said my name, his breath skimmed past my cheek, soft as a butterfly. He bent his head close to mine, softly inhaling the scent of my hair, his lips feathering along my cheekbone.

I turned my head to prevent him kissing my lips, offering my trembling throat instead. When he gathered the fabric of my nightgown in his hands, pulling me closer, and his mouth descended on the bared side of my neck, I closed my eyes. Limbs heavy and stiff, like Daphne of the classics, who turned to an unfeeling tree under Apollo's insistent embrace.

Upon my metamorphosis to a statue under his—admittedly gentle—kisses, Niccolo released his grip on my waist and rocked back. His brow furrowed with concern, and the sadness draining the light from his eyes made me want to curl up under the blankets and hide.

"I'm sorry," I said, turning my head away, throat tight. "It's fine—just go ahead. Just do it."

He took my hand and squeezed until I stopped looking at the floor and met his eyes. "No, Livia. I've no intention of taking an unwilling woman, and I would never hurt you. There's no need for us to rush—we can take time to get to know each other."

Tears pricked in the corners of my eyes, because I wanted Niccolo to take me to bed. I wanted to be able to choose him, to have his touch—not Corbara's—be the last one I'd had within me. I wanted to take back control and I couldn't. My breath snagged in my throat and I swallowed back panic and despair. As two tears slid down my cheeks and my throat clenched around suppressed sobs, I managed not to cry.

"I'm sorry," I said after a moment. "I thought I could. I want to be a good wife to you."

"You shall." He lightly squeezed my hand again for emphasis.

"You know what happened to me." It came out as a statement. I knew he did, but we had to talk about it.

He nodded once, his mouth tight. "Yes. I don't mind, Livia, only that I would see Corbara punished, and you happy. I just want you to be happy," he repeated. His eyes flared with sincerity.

"You know I'm already carrying a child."

"Yes, I know it all. I don't mind that, either—I'll raise him, or her, as my own. Our family will never want for anything, Livia, I'll take care of you. I just wish…" Seeing my mind was whirling so much I could hardly listen, nerves taut as harp strings, he trailed off. "There will be plenty of time for us to get to know each other," he said, a little more stiffly. "Go to bed now, and get some rest. Don't worry about me; I'll sit in that big chair and be comfortable enough. It has a pillow." He smiled crookedly.

After I'd reluctantly climbed into bed, half-sitting up against the pillows with the blankets clutched to my chin, he stood a few feet away, his silhouette dark against the flickering firelight.

"I just want you to know, Livia… I promise I'll never touch you again unless you ask me. I swear it."

I nodded, grateful but silent because it seemed like a strange thing to say thank you for. Except for when he quietly bade me good night before retiring to the chaise while I curled up, feigning sleep, we spent the rest of our wedding night in silence.

*

Present
January, 1857

I curl up on the bed, struggling to fathom why Corbara would send the ribbon to me. I'd known he was in Paris, since I'd glimpsed him outside Elisabetta's house, and later saw his letter on her desk, but I hadn't thought he knew I was here. I tell myself he made that discovery recently and decided to disconcert me, because he's a black-hearted liar. It's a cruel joke, not a message.

Caterina wanders in, clutching her tarot cards. "I know you'll take it with a grain of salt, but I pulled the Nine of Pentacles, and I think it suggests you'll have an easy labor. It shows a woman in a lush garden…" Seeing my face, she shoves the cards aside. "What's wrong?"

I open my palm, showing her the wrinkled hair ribbon. "He took it from me, that day. Corbara took it, and now he has mailed it to me."

Without needing to hear anything else, she crosses the room to my side at once, wrapping her arms around my shoulder, awkwardly because of my protruding belly.

"I knew he was in Paris, but I believed our paths wouldn't cross again. I can't believe I was so naïve. I feel like it's my fault, like I should have done something about it, instead of trying to pretend it didn't bother me. What if he's the one who hurt Elisabetta, and I could have prevented it?"

"You don't know that. And guilt is like sand." Caterina's hand pats my back soothingly. "It shows up in the oddest places, and it scrapes you raw. None of this is your fault, and I refuse to hear you say that ever again."

I fret at my lower lip with my teeth. "I'm frightened… I was thinking of searching for him, Caterina. I thought he could have been involved with the brandy poisoning, because of his letter at Elisabetta's house. But I never did—I didn't know how to begin, and maybe I was too afraid to look. It's like he knows anyway, and wants to warn me off. It's like he's in my head and will never depart…" My voice shakes, but I manage to steady it with a few slow breaths. "I just want to leave the past behind. I want this to be over."

I know recovering from a bad experience isn't as simple as that. Once, my father treated a man whose shoulder had been impaled with a broken branch after he was thrown from a horse. It wasn't a mortal wound, and he healed well, on the outside. Under his skin, though, the scar was hard and lumpen, and pained him for years afterward. I suppose emotional wounds can take just as much time, even if the scar isn't visible.

"Of course you do," Caterina murmurs. "Every day is a bit better, and they'll stretch onward like that until one day it'll be like a speck in the distance." It's hard to imagine right now, but I like her imagery. "You may feel anything you like about Corbara and his presence in Paris, but don't let guilt be one of them."

My gaze skates to the floor, but I don't let myself look away for long. Caterina knows me as well as I know her. She's the sister I never had. My brother and I were never close, due to our age difference. He's nearly a decade my elder. "I'd rather feel guilty than afraid."

"There's nothing to fear now, Livia. You're married to the man who's practically the right hand of the prime minister of Piedmont. You are friends with the contessa di Castiglione, who's also the mistress of the most powerful man in France. Corbara can't reach you, and that's why he has to content himself with petty acts like sending the ribbon."

My lip curls as I stare at the ribbon. "I can't keep it." I cross to the window, intending to open it to hurl the wretched thing to the damp, icy street below.

Caterina stops me. "Tomorrow, when it's light out, we can go to the Pont de l'Alma. Drop it in the water, and let it float away. Maybe it'll take some of the memories with it, giving you some space."

I can only hope, but I like the poetry of her idea. "All right." I lay it on the windowsill. "Tomorrow, then." The baby kicks quite forcefully, and my back aches just like my heart. I rub the swell of my belly, and I must look rather lost or forlorn because Caterina takes my arm again, guiding me to the bed. "Sit down. Rest those swollen feet," she says lightly, although they aren't too puffy today. Some afternoons I jokingly lament to her that I look like an elephant with my swollen ankles, though it's an exaggeration. I've only had minor swelling, common for many pregnant women. "I'll arrange for your supper to be brought to your room. You can have a quiet evening here with your books."

She knows that sounds like the perfect evening to me. "Thank you, Caterina, for cheering me up."

I waste little time in opening one of my new books, a gift from Niccolo, hoping that immersing my thoughts in the treatment of chronic stomach pains will drown out any lingering wisp of Corbara.

And that's how Niccolo finds me, when he quietly knocks and then enters the room without delaying long enough for me to answer. We've grown intimate enough that I don't even mind.

"Are you all right, *cara*?" he asks, coming to my side. "Caterina said you weren't well."

I nod, rising clumsily to my feet. "I'm only tired."

"There's no need to stand on my account."

"It feels awkward, with you hovering behind me."

His hand wraps around mine, lightly enough that I could withdraw if I wanted, and he gently steers us toward the chaise by the window, where we can sit side by side.

"You didn't need to delay your own meal because of me. I'm fine, really. It's just that my back always aches now." Realizing I'm babbling, I pinch my mouth shut. Niccolo's solicitousness, and the intensity of his blue-gray eyes, leaves me flustered. He sits near enough that I feel the heat of him along my arm, our bodies almost touching. It's disconcerting, but not in a frightening way.

"I found a torn envelope on the floor in the hallway… It had your name on it. I hope it isn't bad news." From his cautious tone, I can tell he's worried about my mother.

I hadn't thought I would tell him about the hair ribbon, since I didn't want to think about it any further, but the soft steadiness of his voice and his use of an endearment melts through my protective reserve. I point to the ribbon, lying on the windowsill. "I received it in the mail today. I was wearing it when—on the day—"

A shadow closes over Niccolo's face like a curtain. To anyone else, he might seem impassive, but I know him well enough now to see the flat anger in his eyes, the slight tension dragging at the corners of his mouth and along his brows.

"I understand." His gentle tone belies his stony expression. "Livia, you're safe here. I will never let Corbara cross the threshold of our house. I wasn't going to tell you yet, in case nothing comes of it, but I'm trying to have him arrested and sent back to Turin."

I blink in surprise. "What for?" Not for me, although sometimes I wish he'd be punished for that. It would be too shameful for me to try to prove, though, and deep down, I still believe it was partly my fault for going with him.

Niccolo's brief hesitation shows he must share my thoughts on the matter, but he doesn't mention it. "He's suspected of arson and robbery. Once I started making inquiries, his name came up a few times. I was certain he'd have more crimes in his past."

I pay little attention to the shade of self-assuredness in his last sentence, although it surprises me a little. Corbara seems too smooth and cunning to be caught in anything. The mention of arson seizes my attention like a wire tightening around my chest. I treated him for burns, and he told me he'd saved a child from a house fire. Was that a lie? I suppose it doesn't matter. It doesn't change anything for me now.

"Can you do that?" I ask. "Can you truly have him dragged back to Italy?"

He nods once, jaw stiff. "I'm not as powerful as I would wish, because then he could never be beyond my reach, wherever he went, and I would see him punished. If I could, I'd even change the past for you." He lays his hand over mine. "I can't do that, but I do have a letter from the prime minister stating he's wanted for questioning back in Turin. It's only a matter of finding him. I was starting to wonder if he'd left Paris, but your delivery today suggests not."

"Thank you, Niccolo."

"I'd do anything for you, Livia. For you and our—your—child." He stammers a bit, as if he fears I'll be offended, but the earnestness in his gaze swamps me.

"Ours," I say firmly. This child will never know anything of Corbara, but I wonder if he knows I'm pregnant. And if so, does he wonder about the baby? My fingers slide along the warm silver of my lancet bracelet, fidgeting with it out of habit born after Corbara's attack, when I began wearing it constantly. My fingers push my sleeve aside, exposing my wrist.

Niccolo's fingertip brushes across the back of my hand, snapping my attention back to him. He looks at my bracelet curiously. "What is this, Livia? A lancet?"

Warmth floods my cheeks. "Yes—no, don't touch it." Rather self-consciously, I confess its special properties, how the hot pepper oils the blade is steeped in would burn all around the wound, maybe even into the veins if it sliced anyone's skin, expecting Niccolo's brows to rise in confusion or for his mouth to scowl in disapproval.

Instead, he laughs, and the low, luxuriant sound unwinds all down my spine. Impossibly, it makes me relax a fraction. "I don't think I'll ever know what to expect with you. I shouldn't be surprised after you proved to be an expert on poisons."

"I'm sorry," I say humbly. "I know I'm not even close to an ideal wife."

He shakes his head, eyes glimmering. "No, don't apologize. I like that you're resourceful. I would never have thought of such a thing as the lancet."

"It made me feel safer." My words emerge in a whisper. "I've never used it."

He matches my low volume, and it makes me feel like we're sharing confidences, that we're co-conspirators instead of just me confessing my secrets to him. "If you've been carrying it for the entirety of our marriage, I confess to being especially glad I've promised not to touch you unless you ask."

"You've been endlessly patient with me." We're close enough that I see his eyelashes are tipped in gold, and the faint roughness of new stubble shadowing his jaw. I must have leaned closer to him, but I like the lack of space between us. "I wouldn't use the lancet on you, not now."

Niccolo's head tilts toward mine. His breath smells cool, like the mint leaves I grow in a pot by the window. "Good. I don't think I could stand more burning. My veins are already on fire when we're near each other."

Fancifully, I imagine I feel the vibration of his voice shivering along my skin when he speaks in this low, fervent voice. I close my eyes against the thrill sparking inside me.

He keeps talking, his usual steady tone taking on an urgent edge. "Livia, when you're this close to me, all I can think about is kissing you. It makes me yearn for your touch, so I'm going to turn away now, so I don't risk breaking my promise." He leans back a fraction, but I narrow that new distance between us, stretching closer to him.

"No, you're not." My lips almost touch his cheek as I speak. "You would never break your promise to me. I know that now—I know you." Both of us sit absolutely still, but taut somehow, as if the delicious tension might break one of us at any second. I can hardly bear it. "Please, Niccolo, kiss me."

He makes a small sound in the back of his throat, a quiet groan of surrender, and turns his face toward me. I expect his mouth to swoop over mine, and tense in anticipation for it, but he moves slowly. His fingertips rest against the side of my neck, thumb gently stroking my cheek, and he leans forward so his lips brush mine. The warmth of his touch lures me closer, and when I reach for his hand and kiss him back, soft and tentative, he slants his mouth over mine, fractionally deepening our kiss every moment I clutch at him instead of pulling away. At last, it's a deep, slick kiss that makes my heart pound and my limbs tremble as I revel in the heat of him, the ragged rhythm of our breathing.

Niccolo's eyes look dark and cloudy when he draws back slightly, fingertips tracing the edge of my earlobe. "Livia... I've wanted to do that for months."

"Perhaps waiting made it better."

"Undoubtedly." His puff of laughter sounds shaky, and he bends his head close to mine again. I turn my face up toward his eagerly, intoxicated by the rough purr of his voice, the melting sensation pouring through my veins. It pools low in my belly, clenching into a knot. A very tight knot, in fact, squeezing hard enough that pain makes me grit my teeth.

Niccolo hesitates when my breath catches in my throat and my eyes widen. "What's wrong, my love?" His hand seeks mine, where it presses against my belly.

"I think we waited too long," I say. "Or not long enough. I think the baby's coming now."

He lurches upright with almost comical speed, moving to the front of the sofa and kneeling in front of me. "Are you certain? Are you all right?"

"Yes," I reassure him, smoothing an errant strand of hair away from his forehead. Now that I've begun touching him, I don't want to stop, even for small, innocuous caresses. "It was only one contraction, and not a strong one yet. We'll have to wait and see if more follow, although it seems likely they will. The baby has to be born sometime." I sound a little more cavalier than I feel, and Niccolo must sense this, because he wraps his arms around my bulky waist and rests his cheek against my belly.

When the next pain eventually comes, he scatters tender kisses across my cheeks. "Everything will be fine," he whispers. "It will be over before you know it."

I'd laugh at his naiveté, if I wasn't so nervous. "I've seen babies born before, and I'm quite sure it will feel very long." I summon a smile for him, though.

"Caterina had better go and fetch the midwife," he says. "Shall I help you to bed?"

"Not yet. I'd rather stay here until the pains are closer together. Later, I expect I'll be in bed quite long enough."

He stays by my side until the midwife arrives, fretting more than I do over each contraction and ignoring Caterina's puzzled sideways glances. I can't blame her—it's rare for Niccolo to visit my rooms, and our new closeness feels surprising to me, too. I'm glad of it, though; every time he presses my knuckles to his lips, it gives me a sense of strength.

The midwife, a rather severe-looking woman with white streaks in her hair and angular shoulders, glances at him, and then the door. "Time for you to get out."

"I'll see you in a few hours," Niccolo says resolutely, as if promising the birth will be speedy and free of complications.

The midwife snorts. "Patience, monsieur. It'll more likely be tomorrow." She turns to me as Niccolo reluctantly backs through the doorway, his face pale. "You're not very far along yet, but sometimes first births can surprise you. This is your first, is it not?"

I nod. Nausea tugs at my throat as the next contraction creeps closer, and I don't dare open my mouth. I think I'm glad Niccolo's gone now. I appreciate his support, but I don't want him to see me like this, either.

"You'll do fine. You look strong and the baby doesn't seem too big," she says cheerfully, prodding my belly. I take her word on the size of the baby, because it feels enormous to me as it kicks near my ribs. "A bit early, is it?"

"I think so. Maybe two weeks."

As she shows me how to breathe, and the contractions begin to come as relentlessly as the ticking of a clock, I try not to whimper at the crest of each one. The pain of my body clenching like a fist worsens each time, but the truth of my situation stings too. As I remember the care and concern on Niccolo's face as he had to leave the room, I wish desperately that the baby was his.

CHAPTER FOURTEEN

Paris, January–February 1857

*Mandrake, a member of the nightshade family, is said to
have been used as a sedative in ancient Rome. Ingestion of
too much may cause a person never to wake again.*
– Excerpt from Livia Valenti's book of herbal studies

Caterina's even more pleased than I am that it was an easy birth.
"You have to admit the card was right," she says, but she can hardly
take her eyes off my red-faced and squashed-looking daughter.

"I should have believed you." Exhausted and aching, I nevertheless feel like I'm floating on a delirious tide of relief. It's over now,
and my daughter and I are both fine, and though I didn't enjoy
any of it, the midwife tells me my labor was remarkably quick for
a first baby. It seems like a blessing; even though my daughter's
conception is one of my worst memories, her entry into the world
was uncomplicated. I hope it heralds well for her future.

After the sheets have been changed, my body sponged clean,
and I've managed to nurse the baby, Niccolo comes to visit me.
Caterina gives him a sideways glance as she departs to leave us
alone, but I see the small smile quirking around her lips and know
she's pleased by how quickly he made an appearance. I suspect
he would have come in even sooner, if the midwife had let him.

As he approaches the bed, the brightness of his smile kicks my
heart into a flutter. "Are you well, *cara mia*? Have you rested? I

couldn't wait any longer to see you, but if you need to sleep, I'll go." His teeth fret at his lower lip, and he remains a few feet away from the bed. His gaze flicks between me and the baby, swaddled in the crook of my arm.

"No, I'm glad you're here. Come closer—you can hold her, if you like." I see the curiosity in his expression as he approaches, fingertips reaching toward the infant's slumbering form.

"I'm afraid to drop her." Niccolo sits on the edge of the bed instead, stroking the baby's downy head with delicate softness, as if any greater pressure would break her. "She looks like you."

I smile. She looks like a gnome more than anything, face as lumpy as a mandrake root, although I know of course it won't last. I've scanned her face anxiously for signs of Corbara, and so far found none. "Her hair is dark like mine, and probably her eyes too." They're shadowy now, blurred and unfocused in the way of all newborns. Hiding my hand under the blanket, I cross my fingers that they don't turn green as she grows.

"She's ours." Niccolo cradles one of my hands between both of his. "She's here and we'll adore her." His eyes meet mine earnestly, and I understand the rest of the message he doesn't verbalize. *How she came to be doesn't matter*, he's telling me. *We all belong together now.*

Tears prick at the corners of my eyes and I sniffle loudly.

Niccolo squeezes my hand harder. "Did I say something wrong?"

"Sorry. I'm happy—I don't know why I'm nearly crying. Exhaustion, I suppose."

He leans closer. "That's allowed. You've been through a lot—you brought a whole person into the world." His lips graze my cheekbone, and he drifts tender kisses all around that area. "I should be letting you sleep, instead of kissing your freckles." He straightens, and his eyes look soft and dark as dusk. "Another thing I'd wanted to do for a while."

My lips curl into a smile. If I wasn't so tired, I might have blushed a little. "I had no idea."

He rises, stroking the baby's cheek again. "If there's anything you need—anything you want—I'll make sure you get it. Only tell me. And tomorrow, after you've slept, maybe we can talk about names."

"I need coffee," I say. "But later, when I'm awake again." Already I feel my thoughts swirling to a haze. The baby curls into my side, and I love the idea of us falling asleep together, though I know Caterina will move her shortly to keep her safe from my blankets and the risk I could roll over.

When I first discovered I was pregnant, I feared I wouldn't love the baby. I worried she'd would always be a painful reminder that Corbara took me against my will. As my pregnancy progressed, and I felt the baby move, my anxiety faded somewhat, but now that she's here, my heart surges with affection and protectiveness. In my mind, I already call her Rosa. I hope Niccolo likes the name too, because I don't know if I could change it.

From the first, Niccolo dotes on Rosa, hovering over her crib and suggesting items we could purchase to decorate the nursery. One day he comes home with a porcelain doll she certainly won't play with for at least a year, but it takes up a prominent place on the shelf near her cradle.

He never holds her, though. "She's so fragile," he says. After a fortnight, when she's lost the wrinkled, waif look of a newborn, he still makes excuses. "I've just been brushing Luce since he's shedding. I'd better wash first," he might say, before hiding himself in the study for a while. Or, when faced with the possibility of having to hold her, he'll remember urgent letters he has to write and excuse himself.

I fret about it to Caterina, worried Niccolo isn't truly accepting Rosa as his daughter, in spite of all his assurances he would.

She shrugs. "A lot of men aren't very interested in babies. I'm sure he'll be more involved as she gets older."

I try to accept her advice. I stop offering to place Rosa in Niccolo's arms, and his silence on the matter seems to emphasize his relief.

About a month after Rosa's birth, the nursemaid, Marie, a quiet woman with perpetually ruddy cheeks, has the afternoon off, and I've come down with a piercing headache. Marie is meant to prevent me having to get up in the night with Rosa, but I like to nurse her myself and was up twice last night.

Rosa seems just as irritable as I am. Her eyes squinch closed as she opens her mouth in preparation for a mighty bellow, and her skin flushes red as a sunburn.

"I don't know what she wants." Caterina sounds a bit panicky. "She's clean and dry, and you just fed her. I've been rocking her but she just won't fall asleep." Seeing me wince as one of Rosa's shrieks hits a particularly painful note, she adds, "I wish the two of you would fall asleep together."

"Give her to me." My heartbeat pounds in my temples, punctuated with the extra pitch of discomfort from Rosa's cries, and it gives me an idea I probably wouldn't have considered in a better mood. Clutching her to my chest, I go straight to Niccolo's study.

"She seems a bit grumpy today." In spite of his mild tone, he cringes slightly as I bring her closer.

"I need you to watch her for an hour." Without ceremony, I put her into his lap, so he either has to cradle her in his arms or let her slide to the floor, which of course he would never do.

His eyes widen in alarm as he supports her on his lap. "Livia, I don't know what to do."

"Just hold her. Rock her. Talk to her. I'll be back in an hour, but I'm dizzy with the pain of my headache, and Marie's away this afternoon."

"Headache? Are you all right?"

"I will be, once I've had a chance to lie down. Thank you, Niccolo."

"I hope you feel better, but I'm not sure Rosa will be happy with me."

"She isn't happy with me right now, either. You'll be fine." Ignoring the desperation in his voice, I head for the door, not giving him a chance to argue more. "I'll be back in an hour."

Caterina hovers at the top of the stairs. A breathy, surprised laugh escapes her lips. "I didn't expect you to do that." We both look down to the study. Rosa's wails pass clearly though the closed door. "Should I go down in a few minutes?"

"Don't you dare take her until an hour has passed." Based on the way she blinks, I must sound more ferocious than I meant, but my head feels like it weighs twenty pounds and I'm desperate to lie down and pull the covers over my eyes.

"Yes, signora," says Caterina with exaggerated meekness.

As I nap, the scent of the lavender balm I rubbed into my temples hovers through my dreams, and when I wake, my headache has dulled to a shadow of its former monstrosity. I go downstairs cautiously, but Rosa's shrieks have stopped clawing through the house and it's quiet enough that I can hear the clatter of horses' hooves on the street outside, and the chirp of a bird in the garden.

The door of Niccolo's study is ajar, and he doesn't notice as I push it open wider.

He sits near the window, Rosa cradled in his arms, fast asleep. He's watching her with an almost reverent expression on his face, and he leans carefully forward to brush his lips over her soft forehead, lingering to inhale her sweet, distinctive infant scent. At least, I assume that's the reason, because I do it all the time myself.

Noticing me at last, a shy smile blooms across his face, an answer to my own grin. "Are you feeling better?"

"Yes. It looks like you managed very well after all."

"My hand's asleep and I think my shoulder is frozen at this angle, but I still don't want to put her down." His brows knit together in puzzlement.

"I know the feeling. Still, you'll be glad to move your arms again." I gently lift her from his lap, smiling as she snuffles and twitches her eyes, but doesn't quite wake. She stays asleep as I take her upstairs, and Niccolo surprises me by following. Even as I lay her down in her cradle, she doesn't stir, and I exhale with relief. It's awful when she wakes up unexpectedly; she's always furious then.

"Her lower lip is shaped exactly the same as yours," says Niccolo, as if it's a miracle. His low voice matches the ardent gleam in his eyes.

That look disconcerts me, but in a pleasant, fluttery way. "I didn't know you had its shape memorized."

"Oh yes." His fingertips caress my cheek as he bends his face close to mine. "I've spent quite a lot of time noticing your lips. Thinking about them, too." Hesitantly as always, giving me time to disengage or tell him to stop, he trails his fingers along my jaw, gently coaxing my lips apart.

I expect him to press a soft kiss to my mouth, but instead he tugs my bottom lip between his teeth. That edge of pressure makes everything tighten all through me, and a tiny sigh of enjoyment whispers from my throat. I'm almost embarrassed, but as Niccolo continues to trace tender, nibbling kisses along my lower lip, teasing me until I kiss him back, I discover there's no shame in enjoying his touch.

His eyes gleam with pure happiness, pupils slightly dilated, when he ends the kiss. "You see?" His breath is a little ragged. "I'm convinced of their perfection."

When I wrap my arms around his waist, resting my head on his chest, his rapid heartbeat drums in my ears, matching the rhythm of my own.

After that, Niccolo often asks to sit with Rosa for an hour, until it becomes a habit for the two of them to have precious time together each day. I never stop feeling a little thrill of warmth when I see them together and, after a few weeks pass, I realize I've started, quite naturally and without reminders, to think of Niccolo as her father.

Elisabetta gushes over Rosa as well, and sends too many extravagant gifts, including a rattle with jade inlaid into the handle.

"You didn't need to," I tell her, examining the green shine of the stone. "Rosa has no idea of the luxury; you should have saved that money for yourself."

She tosses her head carelessly. "It was nothing. In fact, I can't take full credit for this gift, much as I might like to. The emperor asked me to send his felicitations, and this present is partly from him."

It seems astonishing Emperor Napoleon III would know of my existence, let alone that I just gave birth to a daughter, and I stare blankly at Elisabetta. "You must be exaggerating."

"I'm not." She crosses her finger over her heart dramatically. "I suppose I must have mentioned you a few times, including that you had welcomed the most beautiful little girl into the family." Her smile takes on a hint of wickedness. "Perhaps he mentioned the gift as a small persuasion to have me cease on the subject; most men tend not to have much interest in the familial affairs of others. Then again, sometimes I think he wishes for another son."

"Does he only have the one?" I ask, still a bit floored. From what I recall, the emperor's heir is about the same as Elisabetta's son, Giorgio. "A two-year-old boy?"

"One legitimate," says Elisabetta. "Named Napoleon, of course. He'll be a year old next month."

I realize Elisabetta has been the emperor's mistress for longer than a year now, and that the empress must have been pregnant when their affair began. Based on the way Elisabetta lifts her chin, she knows I've pieced it together and dares me to comment.

I won't. Who am I to judge?

"Of course," I say. "Well, it's beautiful, and the most expensive and unique rattle I've ever seen. I'm very grateful, if still slightly in disbelief about the emperor's involvement."

"My dear, you're very welcome. I only wish Camillo was as appreciative of my efforts."

We're alone, but I lower my voice anyway. "There haven't been any more food incidents, I hope?"

"I like your euphemism. No, everything has been quiet. I'm very careful, and it seems nothing has been poisoned again. I've put it about a bit that the emperor doesn't dine at my house. He scarcely even drinks anything at my house anymore. I open a new bottle for him every time. It's very expensive."

I nod, relieved that there have been no more poison attempts. "And have you been receiving any more pleading letters from Italian nationalists?" She doesn't know I saw Corbara's letter on her desk, but she told me once about how many people want to meet with her, seeking the emperor's influence.

"Always." She rolls her eyes. "Between those letters, and the ones I get from Camillo, I get so weary of the topic of nationalism…" She changes the subject with an air of relief. "I'll bring some of Giorgio's old swaddling blankets, next time. I had so many—some even with the most exquisite lace, and they're hardly worn at all. And probably a little gown for her. Since you rarely wear red, perhaps your daughter will instead."

I smile. "You're too generous, Elisabetta."

She lifts one shoulder in a careless shrug, her gaze skating sideways. "It pleases me to buy things for her. There's no sign of another for me, and I like your daughter. I don't care much for other people's children, as a general rule, but yours is an exception."

Before I can react to her heartwarming comment, she rises to her feet, sweeping her skirt clear of the table leg. "I must fly, my dear—Bellino and I are going to a play tonight, and I haven't decided how to do my hair."

Bellino returned to Paris only a few days ago, and Elisabetta welcomed him home with a lavish supper party, the two of them staying up until nearly dawn, whispering and laughing. I'm happy to see him again, and Niccolo seems pleased, too. It amazes me, sometimes, how happy our family has become.

In February, Elisabetta's excitement over an upcoming costume ball hosted by Comte Alexandre Walewski, the minister of foreign affairs, is so great that she shows me sketches of her costume, which will transform her into the Queen of Hearts.

"I spent a fortune having it made," she admits. "Francesco wasn't happy, but he'd also complain if I was overshadowed at the ball. 'What good in being mistress to an emperor if you aren't the most memorable woman at the ball?'" she says in a strong impression of Francesco. I've only met him once, at one of her dinner parties, but she's caught his pompous undertone perfectly. "You're attending the ball, aren't you, Livia? Bellino told me you were all invited. Why don't you spend the afternoon with me? We can dress in our costumes, and make sure everything is perfect. I'll lend you some jewelry."

"That would be lovely." Her suggestion sparks some enthusiasm for the ball. I wasn't certain I'd attend. When Niccolo told me we'd been invited, I couldn't hide my surprise. I was used to Elisabetta's glamour being muted by our friendship, the fact that our visits are usually in the simple setting of our homes. I can hardly imagine being in a ballroom with her and other noblemen and women, let alone the emperor and empress.

"We're asked because it's a foreign affairs event," Niccolo explained. "It would be rude not to include other diplomats, so we're invited. Even though Conte Walewski is known to oppose any suggestion of France interfering with Italy, therefore putting us in opposition, he extended the invitation."

Since I was heavily pregnant in December when the invitation arrived, I delayed making a decision. If my labor dragged until late January, the ball would only be a fortnight from then. However, Rosa was born almost two weeks early, and I am strong enough to go to the ball. I won't dance too much, but having an excuse to limit my participation in that area pleases me, because my rudimentary experience with ballroom dancing leaves me feeling graceless anyway.

"Wonderful." Elisabetta clasps her hands. "Niccolo and Bellino will be astonished by our transformations."

I give her a sidelong glance. "And the emperor?" She mentioned Bellino and not him. Ever since he returned, they've seemed closer than ever.

"Of course. I always dress to please him, but I meant Bellino and Niccolo will share the carriage with us. I'll meet the emperor at the ball." She smiles blithely. "I warn you, Livia, I like to arrive fashionably late."

"I'll manage," I promise, though I feel sure Niccolo will let us retire early if I get too tired. I don't mind being a homebody when it means I can be with Rosa.

On the day of the ball, Caterina comes with me to Elisabetta's, to help dress my hair. I wish she was coming to the ball, too.

"I had hoped you would bring your tarot cards," Elisabetta says to Caterina. "It feels like an auspicious time for a reading."

"You look like a figure painted on a tarot card yourself," she replies. "I like your costume."

Elisabetta smooths the silvery-blue skirt of her dress, her smile—deservedly—bordering on smug. "This one might be my favorite costume yet."

Tonight, Elisabetta unmistakably becomes the Queen of Hearts, with a vast number of scarlet hearts decorating her dress. A border of gold-trimmed red hearts trace her shoulders, along the hem and train of her dress, and across her neckline, which is low enough to show her luminous skin—I feel I can take some small credit for that, because she's been using my lotions religiously.

"The emperor will hardly be able to take his eyes off you," Beatrice says proudly.

I nod in agreement. "You look just like the playing card, if the queen of hearts came to life and wanted to make all men fall in love with her."

Elisabetta's light laughter flickers through the room as she slips on her shoes, each with a heart on the toes. "Court events are a game, so perhaps this makes me well armed." She turns to Beatrice. "I'm ready for the headdress."

She sits, impatiently, while Beatrice fastens the headdress, and then rises again at once, restless as a storm wind. Mounted on a gold crescent, scarlet hearts frame the crown of her hair piled up on her head, with some of it left to trail enticingly over her shoulder. The accompanying veil flutters behind her with every step.

Apparently satisfied with the effect, she smiles at Beatrice. "I'll wear this again for a photograph. It might be one of my best ones yet… I still need the final touch." She reaches for a bouquet of roses. "I'll carry these, too. They can come in quite handy—I can lift them to my nose if I come across the *comte* who always sweats under his wool frock coats."

"Surely he'll wear something else tonight," I say.

Elisabetta giggles. "Yes, perhaps he'll be costumed as a fuller. You look ravishing, Livia, my dear. Niccolo will hardly be able to take his eyes off you, I'm sure. Most men, for that matter."

"Thank you." I blush, trying to ignore the discomfort crawling over my skin. I don't like to think of being ravishing. I don't want to inspire ravishment.

Elisabetta is right, though, that Niccolo seems to like my costume. His eyes widen slightly, sparkling with silver like the stars, which is fitting because I'm going to the ball as Night. My gown is black, cunningly highlighted at the waist and neckline with dark blue under black gauze, and sewn with silver and decorated with little stars, and belted with a loose sash decorated with a silver pendant like the crescent moon. Elisabetta lent me a silver and sapphire necklace to wind around my throat, and I've left my hair loose, falling in dark waves around my partly exposed shoulders. I'm reluctant about my loose hair, but Elisabetta and Beatrice exclaimed it looked very beautiful, and even Caterina agreed, trying to encourage me by weaving silver through a few strands. Checking the mirror, I hardly recognized the sophisticated lady looking back at me, and that made me feel bold. This glamorous lady in the mirror didn't have any bad memories haunting her steps and leaching her confidence, and maybe tonight I wouldn't either.

Niccolo is dressed all in scarlet, including a doublet and trunk hose, and a short cape over the top. Two scarlet feathers adorn his hat, giving him an unexpected jauntiness.

"I knew you like red, but this is a surprise," I say. He looks very well, if a little self-conscious. I suppose he isn't used to wearing such tight clothing. Certainly I'm not used to seeing him in it, but he looks handsome and I think we can rely on each other to ease any feelings of being ridiculous in costume. "What are you?"

"Mephistopheles."

My brow furrows. "From Faust? I like it. I'm just surprised. He's a demon, is he not?"

Elisabetta sweeps her heart-bedecked train aside. "Truly, Niccolo as the devil is rather incongruous." Her smile has a jagged edge. "You surprise me, sir."

I don't think Niccolo likes her joking. He weaves his arm through mine, voice lowering as he speaks only to me. "I didn't choose him because he may be considered a literary representation of the devil. I thought it fitting, since you're dressed as Night, and the name Mephistopheles can be translated from the Greek to mean 'not-light-loving.'"

It takes me a second to comprehend his meaning, but when I do, the earnestness of his expression warms me all the way through. Only Niccolo would choose an obscure literary reference as a message, and expect others to understand it. I lean forward and kiss his cheek, my hair swirling over his arm. He breathes in its lemon scent, which I've favored since learning he likes it, and closes his eyes.

"You'll stay with me, won't you?" I whisper. "I'm nervous."

"Of course, *cara*. And we'll dance as much as you like."

"Or as little?"

His lips curve. "Yes, that, too."

"Sorry I'm late," Bellino calls, entering the room. "It took me forever to get this damned hat fastened." Catching my stare, he grins sheepishly. "What is it, Livia? Don't you like my costume?"

"I do," I say with perfect truth. "I never would have thought of dressing as a champagne bottle." He wears all black, with a fabric replica champagne label pinned to the front of his shirt, which has a gold collar, and a gold hat trimmed with wire sits on his head. Bellino's insouciant charm saves it from being ridiculous and instead gives it whimsical appeal. His eyes look bluer than ever under the gleaming gold cap.

"I know. All three of you became fixated on metaphorical costumes, completely overlooking the potential for everyday, valuable objects." His gaze sidles briefly to Elisabetta. "Sometimes the things that grant happiness have been right there all along."

"That's often true," says Niccolo softly.

*

Niccolo stays by my side, as promised, introducing me to various court acquaintances, and offering to fetch me drinks. We dance together once, and the way he looks into my eyes while his hand rests on my waist makes my skin feel warm all over. I'm not a confident dancer, and Niccolo moves through each step so correctly as to be a bit stiff, but in his arms I feel safe. We're at the edge of the crowd, quiet and unobtrusive, and I like that no one pays much attention to us, instead commenting over the most elaborate costumes, like Elisabetta's Queen of Hearts, and fawning over the most high-ranking guests. In this crowded room, we're tucked into a pocket that belongs only to us.

"I never thought I'd dance with you."

He frowns slightly. "Why not? Didn't you want to dance with me?"

I'm about to explain that we'd always been too formal and awkward with each other, when I see the impish glint in his blue-gray eyes and squeeze his hand tighter instead, a gentle acknowledgment that he teases me. "I didn't think of it at all," I say honestly.

He rests his cheek against mine. It's a good thing we've drifted even further away from the dancers, because we've lost the rhythm of the music, and I don't mind one bit.

"I did. I've often thought of the many things I want to do with you."

Tension unfurls over my skin, slow and pleasant. "Such as?"

"Dancing, of course. Making you smile, or even better, laugh. Seeing your hair unbound and touching the softness of it." His fingertips stir the ends, where my hair falls past my shoulders, and that light touch darts pleasant tingles over my scalp. "Taking you to my favorite place back home in Turin, since you showed me yours in the garden at the Castello del Valentino." He stares at my lips. "Kissing you."

We stop dancing altogether when he bends his head close to mine, but the room seems to sway under my feet as his lips hover near mine in a tantalizing promise of a kiss.

It takes a breath or two to steady the liquid heat tangled through my limbs. "You've done most of those things now," I observe. "You'll have to tell me more of them."

"Whatever you wish," he promises.

"Where is your favorite place?"

"Under the archway of the Palatine Gate. It's like standing with Roman history all around you." His voice drops and his breath warms my ear. "And I tried to carve my initials into the stone there, as a boy."

I laugh in surprise at the idea of Niccolo as a would-be vandal, leaving his mark on the world. "What stopped you?"

"My father. He threatened me with a beating if I didn't behave." His expression turns a bit guarded. "He was rather a stern man." Niccolo tightens his hand on my waist. We aren't dancing at all anymore. "Do you want to return to the dance, Livia?"

I shake my head. I'm a bit tired, already. Elisabetta would laugh at the idea of departing the ball well before dawn, but she didn't give birth only a few weeks ago. Niccolo and I withdraw to a window seat, and watch the lines of people waiting to approach the emperor and empress, remarking to each other about the various costumes, and observing Bellino dance with a succession of lovely ladies, persistently avoiding Elisabetta.

After a moment, Niccolo becomes drawn into conversation with Conte Walewski, the two of them standing a few feet away from my seat on the comfortable alcove bench. I turn my attention to the beauty of the ballroom, gleaming with bright silk and jewels, the candlelight making everything soft and lovely, almost hypnotic as dancers sweep by and people gather in groups to chat. I spot Elisabetta crossing the room toward me, although her attention scans the other side of the room, perhaps looking for the emperor. I realize the empress stands not too far from me, and I carefully avoid looking at her, intimidated by her resplendent green silk, with emeralds and pearls wrapped around her throat and a delicate leaf-embroidered train swishing behind her. She looks like a tree-nymph, albeit a sedate one.

Elisabetta pauses near the enormous, polished harpsichord just on the other side of the pillar from my seat, and the empress approaches her.

"The Queen of Hearts?" the empress guesses. Her voice carries clearly across the short distance between us.

Elisabetta dips her chin in assent. "Yes, Your Imperial Majesty."

The empress's lip curls. "Your heart is a little low." She walks away.

I half rise to my feet, intending to go to Elisabetta's side, but a man in a knight's costume approaches, pressing one of the keys of the harpsichord, and the pure sound snaps through the air. Elisabetta gives him a bright smile, and as he returns it shyly, the tips of his ears reddening, I can see his smile is a balm to her confidence. Her head tilts in her usual bold, aristocratic fashion.

And when the emperor himself strides toward her, I can't help but feel relieved that I didn't move just yet. I watch as he lays his hand on Elisabetta's tightly cinched waist, drawing her onto the dance floor. His lips nearly brush her ear as he whispers to her, and she glows under his attention, her skin rosy, lips curling in a provocative smile.

Niccolo returns to my side, sitting beside me, close enough that our thighs press together. His arm slides around my waist, and it feels natural for me to tuck my head against his shoulder. The warmth of his body feels comforting and exciting all at once.

"I feel utterly at peace when I hold you," he murmurs into my hair. "Yet it also makes my heart beat faster until I feel nervous, and I'm not used to that."

I smile, reaching across his lap for his hand. He's been so open and honest with me tonight, and I adore it. I like breaking through his usual unruffled exterior. "I was just thinking something similar. It's a good feeling, isn't it?"

"Extremely."

I'm about to ask him if we might return home, dreaming of some quiet time with him away from the bustle of the ball, when to my astonishment, the emperor approaches us.

Niccolo bows deeply, and I follow suit in a curtsy, sweeping my skirt wide. My back aches with the unaccustomed effort, but luckily he waves us up with a jovial smile.

"This must be Madame Valenti." His voice is smooth and agreeable, perhaps more enticing to listen to because of his slightly Swiss-accented French. "It's about time you brought your wife to one of these events, monsieur. And what a fine costume—Midnight, I presume?" His smile erases any trace of sternness.

"Close enough, sire. Just Night."

"Perhaps you'll switch it to Midnight. It's the most bewitching time of day—on the cusp between one day and the next, when anything can happen." Combined with the lilt of his voice, and the way his eyes linger on the stars at my throat, his words become almost flirtatious. I can't help thinking of his reputation as a womanizer, and that he must enjoy bantering with Elisabetta. She'd give him a pert reply, no doubt, unlike me. I only agree with him, the safest course of action.

He shifts his attention to Niccolo, and they skirt around politics by remarking the costume ball is a festive evening and not a time to discuss business.

"We will meet again soon, Monsieur Valenti," Napoleon says in parting, then smiles at me, drifting back into the crowd where he is immediately swallowed by a group of courtiers.

"And that's why we never make any progress," Niccolo grumbles to me. "It's never a good time to talk politics."

"At least we had a lovely time together."

He smiles, comforted by my words. "We did, *cara*."

While Niccolo lets Bellino know that we're leaving—his brother likely won't come home until dawn—I seize the brief window of time when Elisabetta is alone, not surrounded by admirers, and wish her good night.

"Did you enjoy yourself?" she asks.

"Oh, yes." Thinking of the closeness Niccolo and I shared as we danced, murmuring confidences to each other, fills me with a glow of warmth as wholesome and comforting as sunshine. "More than I expected. And you?"

"It's another ball." She straightens a ribbon on her gown. "At least the empress seems to have departed early."

"I suppose it's strange to be in the same room as her."

"I'm not the first to catch him," Elisabetta says sharply. "I try not to look at her, to be honest. It would do no good to feel sympathy for her jealousy, pity for taking her place at his side. It wouldn't change anything. I have my orders; I know what's expected of me."

It's rare for her to speak so candidly of her role as the emperor's mistress as a task set to her. I believe sometimes she does enjoy his company, but this reminds me how complicated her life must be. I feel sympathy for both of them, myself.

"I'm not cruel," she adds. "Even with my low heart—that tawdry, empty thing. I'm merely practical." The corners of her eyes look pinched.

"Of course you're not." If we were alone, perhaps I'd squeeze her hand, but the Elisabetta of the ball is a different one than within our households, a grandiose, significant figure. Eyes are upon her, and she plays a role just like within one of her photographs. "Good night, Elisabetta."

CHAPTER FIFTEEN

Paris, April 1857

Historically, and foolishly, mandrake root was sometimes used in love potions.
— Excerpt from Livia Valenti's book of herbal studies

My evening routine with Niccolo has continued since Rosa's birth, entirely transformed from the days of his chaste kiss to my hand after supper. Lately, the length of our conversations has decreased, too. I nurse Rosa, four months old already, and then leave her, sleepy and sweet, with Marie in the nursery, and hurry to Niccolo's room with light steps, my pulse fluttering like a butterfly. This hour or so of private time together has turned into one of the most cherished parts of my day.

"Are you well?" he asks, reaching for my hands as I slip through the door.

I think he means for me to tell him if I'm worried about anything, if there's anything I need for Rosa, but I answer with a smile. He asks me that all the time, and all I need is him, his calm presence, his soft adoration warming me like a flower in spring sunshine.

He pours wine for us, and I follow him to the sofa. We used to perch in separate chairs, then opposite ends of the sofa, but now we sit side by side, our heads bent together, our thighs pressed close.

"Did Rosa go to sleep easily?"

I'm not sure how interested he truly is in the answer; his fingertips trace circles on the palm of my hand, and his eyes look dark. I wonder if he's thinking of last night, when I asked him to kiss me again, as I've done every night for the past week. We kissed until we were breathless, clinging together and shaking with desire. I let my fingertips roam over his shoulders, running down his chest, and as he cradled my cheeks in his hands, mouth moving over mine with tender, restrained hunger, I almost asked him to take me to bed. I am fully recovered from Rosa's birth, and I want to become Niccolo's wife in every way. The question hovered on the tip of my tongue, but in the end I kept it there, savoring the sweetness of wanting him. There isn't any rush—Niccolo has told me he doesn't mind our slow pace, and I like the sparks building between us. I didn't get to enjoy this delicious tension before, and the utter delight of it now makes my head spin as if I've had just the right amount of wine.

"Yes, but she'll wake in the middle of the night, no doubt." I twine my fingers with his, leaning closer. My heart kicks against my ribs when Niccolo's lips part and he goes still, holding himself back until he knows what I want. I no longer doubt the depth of his feeling for me, but as a wave of affection and longing swamps me, it's overwhelming to realize how much I care for him, too.

Usually we'd talk more first, about Rosa's daily-yet-miraculous changes, or Elisabetta's—lack of—progress with the emperor, but tonight I don't want any of that. I press my lips to Niccolo's, and as his arms slide around my waist and his mouth slants over mine, it feels so warm and thrilling that a sound of enjoyment slips from my throat.

Niccolo growls in response, a low, rough rumble that rolls down my spine, echoing in sparks over my skin. His grip tightens, drawing my body closer to his, and he kisses me harder, the new edge showing me how strongly desire simmers in his blood. My bones are melting, leaving me weak and willingly pressed into his chest, my fingers curling over the fabric of his shirt.

He stops abruptly, tearing his lips away from mine and lifting his head, although his arms stay wrapped around me like he can't bear to let go. "I'm sorry." He sounds breathless. "I didn't mean to get carried away."

Maybe he thought my grip on his shirt was to push him away, not tug him closer. I slide my fingertips up past his collar, feeling the heat of his skin along his throat and under his jaw. "I liked it." He presses a trail of kisses down my cheekbone, curving toward my mouth again. "I want you," I whisper against his lips. "Please take me to your bed."

I see the flare of desire in his eyes, darkening them to midnight as his pupils dilate. He kisses me with such passionate thoroughness that I almost forget to breathe, and then he slowly draws back, stroking behind my ear with a fingertip, his expression earnest.

"Are you sure, Livia?"

I nod. Nervousness skims over me, but it's exciting too, lighting my skin on fire, turning my blood to smoke.

"If it gets to be too much, if you change your mind, just tell me."

"Could you stop?" I ask, inhaling the scent of his skin near the pulse in his throat.

"Yes, I promise."

"Wouldn't it be cruel of me to ask you to?"

"I'd survive." His mouth lifts in a crooked smile.

It's reassuring to know I still have control, but I don't feel any of the taut, twisting sickness I associate with memories of Corbara. This is Niccolo, and my whole body sings under his touch. I rise to my feet, so we can move away from the sofa.

My skirt swirls around my ankles as he lifts me clear off the ground, licking the hollow of my throat as he strides over to the massive bed.

"It's all right if you can't go slow." I've made him wait so long, tested his patience and control so much already.

Niccolo's smile makes his eyes glow. "Oh, Livia. I've no intention of hurrying. I fell in love with you the moment we met in
the garden, and I've waited a year to have you in my bed. I want
to savor every moment of it."

The passion in his words uncurls over me, trailing like ribbons
of sunlight, and I can only nod mutely, lifting his hand and
pressing my lips hard against his knuckles.

True to his word, he doesn't hurry. He undresses me slowly,
lingering over each new expanse of bared skin until his grazing
kisses erase my trepidation and I can hardly wait to feel the silki-
ness of his sheets beneath my back. Even then, he takes his time,
stroking and exploring with gentle hands but feverish eyes. I clutch
at his hair when he murmurs endearments in my ear, nuzzling
and kissing while I arch under his hands, longing deepening like
a chasm until suddenly none of it's enough. I can't bear any more
of these feather-light touches and I beg him for more.

Still, he holds back, moving gently as if I'm fragile as glass. I
don't know if he feels as I do, weightless and lit up like lightning,
stars peeking in the corners of my eyes, but I want him to lose
himself, to follow me as I feel the last threads of restraint fraying
apart. When I say his name, twining my limbs around him as if
I could pull him even closer, letting my teeth scrape against his
shoulder, at last he groans, shifting our hips to a deeper angle,
burying his face in my neck as he shudders with pleasure.

As the sweat cools on our skin and I sink into the pillow,
boneless and drowsy, I breathe a little sigh of triumph. Some
might say I belong to Niccolo now that our marriage has at last
been consummated, but I feel like I've reclaimed myself, too.
I had the power to choose, and it burned off the last shadows
haunting me. My body is mine again. I'm not naïve enough to
think I'll never cringe at the memory of Corbara at times, but
it's firmly in the past now, where it belongs.

I imagine tucking the nightshade box into its old hiding place in my trunk, in the toe of a battered slipper, wrapped in a rarely worn shawl. Maybe I can leave it there again, giving up the comfort of its sharpness against my skin.

CHAPTER SIXTEEN

Paris, April 1857

*In spite of their cheerful yellow blossoms, narcissus plants
are toxic, the bulbs occasionally mistaken for onions and
causing stomach upset. Named after Narcissus of classical
mythology, who was cursed to love his own reflection after
the nymph Echo perished of unrequited love, the flowers
possess an association of lost love and sorrow.*
  — Excerpt from Livia Valenti's book of herbal studies

On my way to breakfast, I encounter Niccolo in the hallway
outside the dining room. I crept out of his bed sometime after
midnight, following my desire to check on Rosa after hearing her
whimper from her nursery down the hall. Unsure, I went back
to my own bed after that. I don't know how to proceed now, but
that lingering shadow of bashfulness vanishes when he turns to
me. The softness of his glance pours over me like sunshine after
rain, warming me through.

"Bellino isn't home," he says. "Shall we have breakfast in the
salon, just the two of us?"

"I'd like that."

The coffee tray perches on the table, and he reaches for two
cups and pours for both of us.

I take the opportunity to let my gaze roam over him. I admire
the breadth of his shoulders under the fabric of his white shirt,

the way his light brown hair lies against the smooth skin on the nape of his neck. When he shifts, bringing his face into better view, I can't stop staring at the arch of his cheekbones, the curve of his lip. Inwardly, I smirk at my new wanton reaction to his presence, but I much prefer this to our old awkwardness.

"Here you are, *cara*." He passes me some coffee. "How's Rosa? Is she awake?"

"Yes. Marie is giving her a bath. Where is Bellino, anyway?" I ask.

Niccolo shrugs. "He's never been one for keeping regular hours, but lately he's been out very late. I suspect he must have a mistress."

"Elisabetta?" My initial reaction translates to a spoken question, and Niccolo turns to me in surprise.

"You know their history?"

"Yes. They're both a bit obvious about it, but Elisabetta hinted of it."

"You two are quite close now, aren't you? Well, I doubt she'd dare. It's one thing for the emperor to have more than one lover, but it's quite another for one of his mistresses to follow suit. She knows that."

"Poor Bellino." I can't help feeling sorry for him, pining for Elisabetta, who seems content with his friendship. I like the idea he might have met someone else and found requited passion. I hope it's true. He deserves that happiness.

I set my coffee on the table as Niccolo prowls closer, eyes darkening until they look more gray than blue. "He isn't as lucky as I am, having such a beautiful, desirable wife." He lifts both my hands, pressing kisses to my knuckles. I rise to my feet, and his lips are so close to mine that my eyes fall half-closed and my mind drifts somewhere languorous. His voice sinks to a low murmur as he strokes the ends of my hair, which I only half-pinned up this morning, instead of taming it into its usual plait. "Is this all right?"

"Yes," I say breathlessly. I'm not sure if he has discerned the reason I generally prefer not to have my hair touched, but I like that he asks me if he can continue.

"Can I loosen your hair?"

I almost refuse, but his fingertips graze the back of my neck, unleashing a torrent of tingles, and I remember how gently he freed a honeybee from my hair on the day we first met. He won't yank on it, won't use it to hold me into submission. "Yes," I whisper.

He tugs the pins free, tracing soft kisses over my cheeks. "I've rarely seen you with your hair loose. Some night, I want to see it falling all around us like a silk curtain, or fanned out on the pillow beneath you."

My skin flares with heat. I like this wilder side of Niccolo, when he sheds his usual propriety to confess his desires to me. "All right."

"I missed you when I woke up," he growls.

"I worried I might disturb you by returning after I went to Rosa's nursery."

"Not at all. I want to stay with you all night, Livia. I want to sleep with the scent of you all around me, with you tucked into my arms."

The feel of his fingertips gently stirring the ends of my hair, the dark pleading in his voice—both flicker over my skin like lightning. I want the whole night, too.

"Tonight, then," I promise.

Though we try to restrain ourselves until then, forcing our attention to the breakfast, I can't stop myself gazing at him, brushing my hand over his shoulder or thigh. The newly awakened hunger reeling through my body surprises me, but Niccolo seems to match it. Reaching for the breakfast tray, I offer him a strawberry and it leads us into snatched, sweet kisses, each one growing longer and more desperate until he moves us over to the door, fumbles for the key and twists it in the lock, keeping his arm around my waist the whole time. I expect him to pin me beneath him on the sofa, but instead he sits down in his chair, lifts my skirts out of the way, pulling me across his lap so my thighs bracket his. Lust lurches low in my belly as my body sinks down, joining us, and we both gasp with the sharp pleasure. I like the way I can see the desire and wonder on his face, revel in the languorous way our lips move together. Though we began with feverish haste, now I want this intimacy to last forever.

Later, we devour the last of the strawberries and now-cold rolls, lingering with our coffee. My cheeks feel warm, probably matching the slight flush of Niccolo's face. His hair isn't quite as smoothly combed as usual and that gives me a strange sense of pride.

He laces his fingers through mine, brushing his lips over my fingertips. "Sometimes I thought we'd never find so much ease together. I'm so glad we have."

I like that we share the same buoyant happiness about our new relationship. I never thought I'd feel like this, either. "I used to be a little afraid of you. You were so solemn." I use my thumb to smooth away the little crease denting his forehead. "I couldn't understand why you wanted to marry me. We only met once, and not many men…" I lift my chin to stave off my faltering words. "I was pregnant with another man's child, after all."

Niccolo's hand squeezes mine, holding tight. "I know a lot of people would be skeptical about falling in love practically upon first sight, but it happened to me. I cherish the memory of our first meeting in the gardens at the Castello del Valentino—I remember everything quite vividly. I only wish I had been brave enough to say something then. When I heard what he—what Corbara"—the name comes out through gritted teeth, cold as a knife's edge—"did to you, I wished I could take it all away from you. The best I could do was offer the protection of my name and my household, and I offered that gladly."

I slide closer to him on the sofa, nestling my head under his chin. The thrum of his heartbeat reverberates in my ear, soothing and steady. "Some men might have wondered if I was telling the truth, you know. Trying to pawn off a bastard child onto a wealthier father by way of a sad story."

"I know. I thought of it, myself. I didn't believe it, though." His voice drops to a gentle note, soft as velvet. "Besides, there are a lot of cruel people in the world, ones who'd judge a woman for an out-of-wedlock pregnancy even when she had no choice. Only a fool would risk her reputation by making up a story like that to find a good marriage, and I'd met you; I knew you weren't a fool." His fingers lift my chin so I can see the affection and sincerity warming his expression, and his lips brush mine in a sweet, gentle kiss.

In the afternoon, Niccolo and I are reading together when Lorenzo knocks timidly on the door. "Signore, there are policemen here to see you."

Niccolo frowns. "Send them to the parlor. I'll be there shortly."

I brace against the pang of fear that something has happened to Bellino, or that Elisabetta is ill again. Then, with a lurch of hope, I wonder if Corbara has been found and arrested for his crimes of arson and theft. Then I'd truly be free.

"Come with me." Niccolo looks worried too, his face pale, mouth taut. "There are no secrets between us anymore, Livia. If you're willing, I'd like you by my side."

"Of course." I smooth my hair by reflex, glad it's still pinned up. Straightening the red ribbon decorating the front of my cream-colored gown, I follow Niccolo down the hall to the more formal setting of the parlor.

Two men in dark coats rise as we enter, nodding respectfully to me.

"Niccolo Valenti?" the taller one asks. He has a long mustache, and its drooping shape makes him look like a mournful hound.

"Yes, that's me."

"This must be Madame Valenti?"

I nod, fighting the urge to fidget with my lancet bracelet. Their lack of smiles proves this isn't a social call, and the suspense makes the air thick with tension. I must look nervous, for the shorter policeman's mouth twitches in a small, forced smile, but I can't bring myself to return it.

"Please, let's all be seated. I'm afraid something serious has occurred. Very early this morning, an attempt on Emperor Napoleon's life was made."

"He is well, I trust?" Niccolo's hands twist in his lap. "You said 'attempt,' so I hope he is unharmed."

"Indeed, the emperor is in no present danger. Three men attempted to waylay him as he entered his carriage, departing from the comtesse de Castiglione's house on avenue Montaigne."

"I'm relieved he's safe, but sorry to hear such an awful thing has happened," says Niccolo.

I am, too. I can easily imagine how distraught Elisabetta would be to know the emperor's life was endangered mere steps away from her residence. She's probably nervous about any repercussions it could have on their relationship, and worried Camillo will be angry, too. I'll take her a packet of calming tea as soon as I can.

"The emperor was lucky not to be injured," says the mournful policeman. "Unfortunately, others were not so lucky. Monsieur Valenti, I'm sorry to be the bearer of unhappy news, but in the scuffle, one of the men fell beneath the carriage wheels."

The lancet bracelet digs into my fingertips, bruising my flesh down to the bone. *Not Bellino*, I pray repeatedly in my mind. It's not unusual for him to be away for a day or two, and I've never worried for him before. Now I'm filled with terror.

"He's identified as an acquaintance of yours—Roberto Rossi."

My shoulders tremble with relief, and then I'm immediately pierced with guilt. I'm glad it isn't Bellino, but it's still dreadful news. I didn't personally care much for Roberto, but certainly never wanted him dead, and I feel sorry for Angelica, his widow, and their two young children.

Niccolo bows his head. "This is very grave news. I can hardly believe he'd do this… Are you certain there's no mistake?"

"He was at the scene. He'd be imprisoned at the Conciergerie now, if he hadn't succumbed to his injuries almost at once." The policeman tilts his head, staring like a stern headmaster who suspects rules have been broken. "*La comtesse* indicated he was known to make political speeches, and was a supporter of Italian nationalism. It wouldn't be the first time a man with such ideals targeted our emperor."

I wonder if Roberto was a member of the Carbonari. He never said so, but it's a secret organization, so I suppose he wouldn't. His ideals certainly matched, but I can hardly understand why he would have risked his life for this cause. Even if he survived the altercation, the punishment for attempted assassination is execution by guillotine. Did he really hope to escape, to get away with assassination of an emperor, and still take care of his family?

The policeman leans forward, eyes glinting eagerly. "Where were you last night, Monsieur Valenti?"

It can't be a good thing they're inquiring about his movements, and my breath hovers in my throat, trapped by nerves.

Niccolo's response sounds steady as ever, though the tension in his thigh shifts across the small space between us on the sofa. Both of us are taut as bowstrings, ready to snap. "I was here, at home, with my wife."

"Is this true, madame?" The other policeman looks to me.

"Yes, of course." My throat feels too tight, almost swallowing my words.

"And did you remain at home all night, monsieur?"

"Yes. I retired to bed about ten o'clock. I didn't leave my room again until about seven-thirty this morning."

The policeman's attention slides to me. "And you, madame? Did you keep similar hours?"

"Yes, we went to bed at ten, just as he said." The tips of my ears burn, remembering all we did last night, the way we scorched away the last shreds of reserve between us. We were so happy in our newly discovered passion, and it seems unfair that we don't get to enjoy the contentment now.

"Were you asleep between the hours of four and five? Can you confirm your husband was still in bed?"

My chest squeezes. *Lie*, I tell myself, *lie to protect him*, but it's too late. The pause has grown too long; they'd see the untruth hovering like smoke in the air. "Our daughter woke in the middle of the night, around one, I think. I went to soothe her, and to my own bedroom from there." I stare at the floor. I don't know why they're asking about his whereabouts, but I feel like I've betrayed him by speaking the truth.

"It's true," Niccolo says heavily. "I was alone in my bed during the second half of the night, but I doubt anyone can vouch for me. At four in the morning, our entire household would have been asleep. You're welcome to question them."

The policeman nods. His mustache makes him look grimmer. "The emperor and la comtesse de Castiglione have both verified they saw three men in the attack on the emperor's carriage. One was undoubtedly Roberto Rossi. You have been accused of being a co-conspirator in this affair, Monsieur Valenti, of being one of the three."

The policeman produces a paper. "This letter theorizes the emperor's death would spark a revolution to help Italy win in a war against Austria." He passes it to Niccolo. "Do you deny it's your writing?"

Niccolo reads it carefully, although I can tell from the way the blood has drained from his face he knows it's his letter. The one Elisabetta took from him. It's shocking and painful to think she's accused him. I'm cold, like I've been caught in a snowstorm and icy sleet prickles on my skin. My spine seizes under the threat of a shiver.

"I will not deny I wrote this, but I never sent it. It's an overview of different beliefs on the intense politics regarding Italy, but I decided it sounded too revolutionary, and I never sent it to the prime minister." Niccolo must be appalled by Elisabetta's shocking accusation, but he manages to rein in most of his emotion. He sits straight, but his voice carries the faintest tremor. "He will vouch for my character, as well as confirm he never received the letter."

"It's one person's word against another right now." The policeman shrugs, managing to convey a brisk sense of efficiency mixed with a faint note of apology. "I'm sure you understand an attempt on the emperor's life is very serious business. We'll need you to come for a stay in the Conciergerie while the investigation continues."

The casual phrasing makes panic flood my body at the mention of the Conciergerie. Niccolo can't go there—I can't fathom it. Dread frosts over my skin.

"He didn't do it." My voice squeaks breathlessly on the last word. "It's a lie."

"You can't know that, madame," says the policeman who'd smiled at me earlier. "You said yourself you can't confirm his whereabouts at that time." The gentle pity in his tone stings like a nettle rash.

"If I'm only under suspicion, why must I be imprisoned?" Niccolo asks reasonably, but his fists are clenched, knuckles white.

"We can't have you running back to Italy, can we?"

"I'd stay under house arrest, of course."

Yes, I think. *Please let him stay*. I imagine waking again tonight to check on Rosa, and seeing Niccolo's bed empty, knowing he's nowhere in the house. Knowing Rosa and I are isolated, unprotected and lonely, while Corbara still roams Paris. My heartbeat slams in my ears as I pray for them to agree.

The policeman smiles, showing a slightly chipped tooth. "I believe you would, I really do. You seem honorable. Almost too honorable, even… No, I'm afraid we have our orders. Come now, the Conciergerie isn't so bad. It's reserved for the most important prisoners; even the emperor was held there for a while in his youth, when he had no title at all but a connection to Napoleon Bonaparte. Funny, how far he's come."

I hardly realize I've seized Niccolo's hands, holding them bone-creakingly tight, until he pulls me gently to my feet.

"Perhaps it's better if I get a chance to speak with everyone in person. I don't know why Elisabetta has decided to spread such slander, but at least I can defend myself."

"Can I visit him?" I ask the policemen. I'll see Elisabetta myself, and then go to Niccolo at the Conciergerie. After that visit, we shall leave together, because he'll have been proven innocent. I hope. Goosebumps rise into a topography of dread along my arms.

The sad-looking policeman instructs me where to go as a visitor with more grace than I expected from him. "Mention my name, Alexandre Lafontaine," he says. "I'm the warden, and any messages you send will come to me directly."

I make sure to thank him, thinking it can't hurt to have a sympathetic person at the Conciergerie. I sound as tremulous as I feel, but that doesn't matter. Nothing matters right now except keeping my family whole.

I turn my face up to Niccolo's. "You'll be home soon." My whisper brushes close to his lips. "I'll talk to Elisabetta." I hope he understands I mean I'll demand the truth from her, one way or another. I won't sit idly by while the fragile peace we've finally found crumbles to dust.

"Everything will be fine. And since I won't get a chance to straighten it up now, I'm sorry I left the cigar box out," Niccolo says. "I know you don't like the smell." His fingertips squeeze mine hard, the pressure snapping me out from staring blankly at him.

"It's all right," I tell him, understanding it is a message. "You'll be home again soon enough." I hate the crease of doubt bridging his eyebrows and try to give him an encouraging smile. It doesn't work. My face feels crooked, like someone having an apoplexy. My mouth trembles as if I might burst into tears at any second. I dig my fingernails into my palm, using that sharp bite of pain to hold them back. I won't cry. It's hard enough for Niccolo to leave now without a flood of sorrow from me.

He brushes a kiss over my cheek, but his fingertips cling to mine until he must pass through the doorway, following the two policemen to their carriage. My heart feels sore, beating so fast it might break into two. I watch the carriage slide out of sight, taking deep, lung-heaving breaths to try to calm myself.

I go to Niccolo's study, looking for the cigar box. It isn't in his desk, though I open each of the drawers and peek inside. There's no need to pry through his papers; everything is kept with such tidiness I can see at a glance the cigar box is absent. I dash up the stairs to his bedroom, and find it tucked underneath a copy of Augustinian philosophy. The faint scent of tobacco wafts through the air as I open the lid, but paper is the only thing inside. I unfold the thick parchment, written on expensive cream-colored paper and laden with rich black ink, and see it's the letter Niccolo told me about, the one Conte Cavour wrote to demand Corbara be sent back to Italy to be tried for his crimes, if found. I suppose this is where he's been keeping it while he undertook his own quiet investigation. The fact that he wants me to have the letter is a grim reminder that he might not be home quickly, that I may need to use it to borrow his authority, and that makes me grit my teeth. I'll get him out—I will.

I don't dare leave the letter here. In theory, it should be safe enough, but since Niccolo was just dragged off to the Conciergerie because of another letter Elisabetta took, I refuse to take any risks, and slip the folded paper inside my dress, tucking it flat against my ribcage between my chemise and my gown. It's an unconventional place, but safe from pickpockets or prying eyes. I'm not carrying the nightshade box—I felt safe enough with Niccolo to go without it—but now I fetch it, feeling the familiar smoothness of the wood as I conceal it between my breasts, lacking a hidden pocket in the gown I'm currently wearing. I haven't sewn them into most of my post-pregnancy dresses. Everything has been so happy since Rosa's birth that I thought I was done with the nightshade. I wish it didn't comfort me so much now to feel its sharp edges against my skin.

Knowing Niccolo made sure I could find the letter, in case he can't come back for a long time, makes my chest ache, like when I fell once and knocked all the air from my lungs as my back collided with the ground. I don't realize I'm clutching my lancet bracelet until my thumb throbs, and I force myself to let go. All the lush contentment of the day has dried to a dead husk, like the nightshade root carried close to my heart. A distant sort of calm falls over me like a cloak, as if I've locked my emotions in the nightshade box too.

I'm ready to face Elisabetta.

News of Niccolo's arrest has already spread through the house. I tell Caterina everything, and stride toward the wardrobe. "Help me choose one of my best gowns, please, Caterina. I'll change in a moment; we're going to see Elisabetta, and it isn't a casual social call."

As I leave my room, dressed in a formal blue calling gown, my curls wrestled into a rather severe up-do, Marie waits for me at the bottom of the stairs. Her embroidered traveling case sits at her feet, her coat is buttoned to her throat and a smart black hat perches on her head.

"I'm sorry, madame. I regret not giving you my full notice, but I can't work in the household of a man who would see my sovereign dead."

"Monsieur Valenti is innocent." I didn't expect this kind of reaction from Marie, and my initial disbelief shifts to stark disappointment.

She shrugs in a sophisticated Parisian way that, in happier times, Caterina and I have tried and failed to imitate. "My family have supported the Bonapartes for generations. Even if you're right and your husband is wrongly accused"—this said with strong doubt—"I'd be ostracized by my father if I stayed. Our reputation could be damaged. I am sorry; you've been a kind lady to work for." She clears her throat. "Rosa is asleep. She's been fed and bathed, and you'll find the nursery is in good order."

"Thank you." Numb, I don't even think of sorting out her final pay until after she's gone, the door clicking shut behind her. I suppose she'll send a bill if there's anything outstanding; I'm not even sure of the details. Niccolo always handled that. It's time for me to increase my involvement, and become the true mistress of the household.

Caterina must have heard from the top of the stairs, because a moment after Marie's departure, she arrives next to me and makes a rude noise. "She could have at least stayed for another week, until things are sorted."

"I suppose you'll have to stay with Rosa while I talk to Elisabetta. Do you mind?"

"Not at all. I'll help however I can."

I squeeze her hand wordlessly. The world has tilted and everything is spinning out of control, but Caterina is here and I'm so grateful.

Rosa's indignant wail hovers through the air, ghostly and faint due to our distance from the nursery. It shifts to the ear-spiking pitch that means she's been awake for a few minutes and is now offended no one noticed.

"I'll take care of her," says Caterina. "You don't need to worry about anything here."

"I just want to hold her before I go to see Elisabetta." Together, Caterina and I go to the nursery.

Hearing the thud of our footsteps, Rosa subsides to a few whimpers. I bend over her cradle and she latches her hands onto my sleeves, eyes wide and luminous, her cheeks pink and damp, and her rosebud mouth opens in an enchanting, toothless smile. Miraculous, really, in the circumstances.

Cuddling her close to me, we breathe together. Rosa snuffles like a hedgehog, and her milky, sweet smell makes me feel calmer, as if every inch of my skin is fraught with purpose. After a few moments, I press her into Caterina's arms, square my shoulders, and go to call on Elisabetta.

CHAPTER SEVENTEEN

Paris, April 1857

Laudanum, made from opium poppies, should be used sparingly. Though it can suppress coughing and aid nervous disorders, overuse will lead to patients discovering reliance on the mixture has bound itself through their veins.
— Excerpt from Livia Valenti's book of herbal studies

Outside Elisabetta's house, there's no sign of anything amiss. Any smears of blood on the street have been swept away, a bird chirps somewhere nearby, and when Beatrice lets me into the salon, sunshine pools through the windows, casting everything in gold. I'm kept waiting longer than usual, and each tick of the clock ratchets my agitation higher. If Elisabetta doesn't come down soon, I'll push my way upstairs to the bedroom she almost died in once, if that's what it takes to speak to her.

Instead, she swoops into the room in a cloud of smoky lavender and a swirl of black silk, rushing straight to me and clasping my hands in hers.

"Isn't it awful? I can't rest for worry, and I've got such a headache. I've been rubbing lavender balm on my temples all morning."

The clasp of her fingers around mine is strangely comforting. Even though it's her fault Niccolo's implicated in the assassination attempt, I have to resist the urge to cling to her, spilling all my fears in one long, breathless gust. It feels good to be in the presence of a friend. If she still is. I might not be able to trust her, and that adds to my heartache. "I'm shocked," I tell her. "I never thought this could happen."

Elisabetta goes to stand near the harp perched in the corner of the room. I've never seen her play it, but she drums her fingers along the arched top of it, relentlessly. "I can't sit down—can't stay still. I hope you don't mind."

"No, I understand." My own tension makes it nearly impossible to remain seated on the edge of the striped loveseat, and I curl my toes inside my shoes in an ineffectual attempt to expel energy.

Elisabetta doesn't seem to notice, throwing her hands out dramatically. "I'm so relieved the emperor is safe, but it was such an appalling morning. I saw it all. I don't usually watch him depart, but I felt restless, and I wanted to see the moon—I was thinking of posing for a photograph as the goddess Diana, with a crescent headdress. I won't now. The idea will always remind me of seeing the figure of a man lurch out of the shadows, his arm sweeping as he waved for the emperor's attention. Livia, I didn't comprehend he held a knife until Louis flung the carriage door open, bashing it like a shield into the man's arm, and the glass of the carriage window cracked. The knife blade didn't gleam in the pre-dawn light, but the glass did. Doesn't that seem cruel? The moonlight ought to spear it, highlighting its danger, its significance. I feel dazed, remembering, but the rough shouts bursting through the air are still ringing in my mind, and the image of Louis halfway inside the carriage, kicking at the man, is imprinted vividly. The driver's whip snaked through the air, and as the horses leapt, a second man jumped clear of those deadly, striking hooves. One of them crumpled to the ground, his body a blur against the spinning wheels. Two others dashed into the shadows, and that's how I know for certain there were three assassins. The policemen questioned me all morning. I still feel so shaky, Livia. You have no idea."

"I do." My reply sounds sour, but perhaps that's a good thing, because Elisabetta blinks her lashes like a young fawn, and then comes to sit beside me.

She seems to have dropped the theatrical act, thank goodness. Another moment of that and I'd have tipped the harp over or screeched through clenched teeth. This is real life, not one of her photographs.

"You're right, and I'm sorry. Did you know Roberto well? I couldn't breathe when I saw him lying on the road, already gone." She twists her fingers together. "I can't believe he would do this. I know he doesn't approve of the emperor, but to resort to attempted murder…"

She trails off and I notice the purplish shadows under her eyes, the stark whiteness of her cheeks. She looks troubled and afraid, but it somehow adds a fragile appeal to her usual loveliness. I hate that she hasn't mentioned Niccolo yet and feel a sharp urge to seize her shoulders and shake the truth from her.

"Niccolo is at the Conciergerie," I say harshly. "He's been accused of being a co-conspirator in the affair."

Her eyes widen, mouth drooping as if her tears will flow within the next moment, and she reaches for my hand. "Livia, my dear, I'm so sorry. I've been going on about my shock about Roberto, but Niccolo's arrest must hurt you terribly."

"Yes, it hurts." She tries to slide her hand free of mine, but I squeeze brutally tight, almost without thinking, channeling all my fear and confusion into that gesture. "He's innocent, you see. He says he wasn't involved, and I believe him."

"Darling, he would say that." She speaks to me like she might to her son, Giorgio, with gentle but firm enunciation. "I wouldn't have believed it of Roberto, either. How many times have we dined together? Seeing him there, at the scene—it was like falling overboard into an icy sea. I understand how you feel, truly I do.

It isn't easy to learn you've been deceived. And I understand you must be worried about the future. God knows I am."

Elisabetta seems poised on the edge of a long speech in an attempt to be soothing, but I can't bear to listen to her pretenses anymore. I cut her off, trying not to sound too harsh. "I haven't been deceived by Niccolo, and I'm more than worried for the future—I'm terrified that Niccolo might be imprisoned, perhaps even executed, for something he did not do." My voice trembles as I speak of his possible death, but I force myself to say it out loud, acknowledging how precarious his situation has become overnight.

Wrenching her hand free and rising to her feet in a rapid sweep of skirts, Elisabetta paces across the room, avoiding eye contact as she impatiently fidgets with a candlestick. "Livia, I don't believe Niccolo is as innocent as you say. He has speculated regarding the emperor's death, he might be involved with the Carbonari…" She rakes her fingertips across the harp and the cascade of musical notes effectively cuts off her accusations. "I'm sorry, Livia. But it's all true, and it looks incriminating."

"I know about the letter."

She doesn't look up from the floor, her tone flat. "You do?"

"Yes, Niccolo told me its contents, and that you took it." I can see she didn't expect Niccolo and I would be so close, but I don't blame her. We weren't, for a long time. "He told me everything. The police were rather forthcoming, as well. The only damning evidence against him was the fact that someone declared they saw him at the scene, and provided an incriminating letter he'd written as evidence."

She sinks to the chair opposite, resting her head in her hands.

"Why would you do that, Elisabetta?" I've been so fierce and cold during our confrontation thus far that it shocks me to feel a flood of tears burning a path down my cheeks.

"Oh, Livia. Don't cry." Her lip trembles, and then she weeps too. "Please don't. I'll fix everything. Somehow, I will."

After a moment, I manage to find my handkerchief, dabbing my face dry. Elisabetta doesn't bother, leaving her tears to shine like dew on her reddened skin.

"I don't think I've ever explained to you what Bellino is to me," she says at last. Her voice sounds raw, more honest than I've ever heard it. "Not properly. I've told you we grew up together. He's been my brother, my best friend, my protector, my lover, my enemy. He's part of me, and even now I love him, though perhaps not in the way he wants." Her breath shakes, and the hunch of her shoulders, the flicker of her enormous eyes, make her seem more vulnerable than I've ever seen her, even when she was dying of aconite poisoning. "You know I had Niccolo's letter. I didn't think—I just spoke first. I had the means to protect Bellino, and I instinctively tried to. I saw three men, and he was one of them. I never saw Niccolo there, but if he took his brother's place, Bellino would escape. Bellino would have done it for me." Her voice cracks. "It's how we are. And I thought Niccolo made you miserable with his coldness, that perhaps you were forced to marry him because of Rosa. I thought you felt trapped with him."

The idea that she thought she was helping me is as startling as being splashed with cold water, but there's no time for that just now. My heart aches for us all. "Niccolo isn't like that. And Bellino hasn't been home for a few days. He doesn't even know about Niccolo yet."

A fresh tear slides down her cheek. "He's probably in hiding since the attempt. He won't stand for it, you know. He'll confess once he hears about Niccolo."

"I know." I don't need to point out that if he does, Elisabetta's attempt to protect him will have been in vain. Her reaction splintered our friendship, and it won't even save him. Knowing Bellino will tell the truth isn't a relief, not at all. My mind doesn't want to accept that cheerful, gregarious Bellino has done this, but I force myself to remember the dark passion in his actions the night he and Elisabetta argued, and he broke the vase of flowers.

Elisabetta is telling me the truth, at last, and it hurts me. Thinking of how much it will hurt Niccolo makes it even worse, tightening my throat until it feels like sandpaper, and my eyes burn.

Either my husband or my brother-in-law will face the consequences for these events, and they're both beloved to me. It's hard to comprehend Bellino tried to murder the emperor. I keep trying to think of another explanation, to find a way out of this tragedy, but I feel like I'm locked in a dark room, scrabbling for a nonexistent door.

Elisabetta's voice rises, edged with distress. "I can't believe Bellino would do this. I thought he was the one person who would never hurt me, and now I'm so humiliated and afraid—the emperor might blame me—I'm waiting for him to come and see me, but so far there's been no word, and yet through all this, I keep thinking of Bellino and wanting to keep him safe. He doesn't even deserve it." Her hands fidget relentlessly, as if searching for a ring to twist, but she hasn't adorned herself with any jewelry at all. She digs her nails into her skin instead.

"Are you absolutely certain it was Bellino?" I hear the desperation in my question, but I cling to the hope she was wrong, that somehow Niccolo and Bellino can both be saved.

"Yes. It was quite dark, and I didn't recognize their faces at first. Even Roberto Rossi, as he was swept under the carriage wheel… Bellino lingered, though. He was about to turn back and try to help him, but then he ran away, following the third man. I know it was him. I know everything about him. The set of his shoulders, the way he holds his head."

"Did you see the third man?" The muscles in my spine seize, tilting my back ramrod straight. My hands close into knots. "Do you know who it was?"

I think I do, and it makes dread skitter over my skin.

Her mouth purses uncertainly. "No. I didn't see him well. He was wearing a dark coat. He was fairly tall. He didn't look quite like Niccolo, though. He had a different kind of swaggering walk. But surely it doesn't matter if you know Niccolo was at home at the time of the assassination attempt." Her gaze skates away from mine, and I think she's ashamed of her decision.

When the policeman asked, I blushed, but not with Elisabetta. We've been through too much together. Our cheeks are still wet with tears, and I tell her the truth.

"It isn't surprising," she says in a hollow tone, staring unseeing toward the portrait of herself as a nun, hanging on the wall across the room. "Having a new baby is quite disruptive, especially when you're so involved. I relied on a wet nurse, myself. And Niccolo is so cold and reserved to begin with, I should have realized you two keep to your separate bedrooms. It isn't uncommon."

I bristle at her description of Niccolo. I don't agree, not anymore. I know just how unrestrained he can be when he lets go of his protective air of reserve. My blood heats to remember the rasping groan he made as he pressed his bare skin to mine, the way he whispered loving words into my ear, holding me close. And I saw the poignant despair in his eyes when he had to follow the policemen from the house.

Now that I know him, Niccolo isn't distant or cold at all. Elisabetta's impression of his reserve may have helped her feel distant enough from him as a person to accuse him to protect Bellino, but I don't accept it.

"What if it was him, after all?" she asks, with a tremulous quirk of her mouth. "I could be wrong. Maybe I didn't recognize him in the dark." I can tell she hopes it's true, for it would redeem her and put us both in the same painful position. Both of us betrayed by the men we love.

I shake my head. Dread makes my neck stiff, my body winding taut with nerves. "I know who the third man is."

Corbara came to Paris to assassinate the emperor. I'm a fool for not seeing it earlier. I knew Corbara was a revolutionary, I knew he was in Paris. I know the danger of his recklessness. And I pretended I could ignore his presence in Paris, that doing nothing but carrying a dose of poison would keep me safe.

"Who? Livia, tell me."

I'm only speculating, technically, but I feel certain nonetheless. Caterina would call it intuition, and my father would probably tell the story of the old man who'd insisted he was going to die before next Sunday, in spite of being in apparently good health, and did.

"I think he's one of your petitioners. I think you've had a letter from him." I have to coax each word out. It isn't easy to tell her the truth. "He's charming but dangerous, and probably a Carbonari member with radical beliefs. His name is Vittorio Corbara." The last part sticks in my throat most of all, but it's time to tell her. "And he's Rosa's father."

Elisabetta says nothing until I finish my halting, skeletal summary of my history with Corbara. Telling the story to her gives me a feeling of liberation, as if I'd been carrying a bucket of water to the garden and my arms float with relief after setting it down. But a little bolus of sick shame threatens to unfurl into nausea, a feverish reaction that makes me want to tell her it was all a lie and then go to bed, burying my face in the pillow. It isn't easy to share my secret and admit my weakness, my shame.

"So Niccolo married you at once," she says. "Protecting your reputation, legitimizing your child."

I nod silently.

Elisabetta gives me a sad, knowing smile. "I had no idea he could be so sentimental and unselfish. Though I can imagine Bellino doing something similar; I can't even count how many times he's protected me over the years. I thought it was Niccolo who hurt you. When we once spoke of the rumors surrounding me in regards to the king of Piedmont-Sardinia, you had such a troubled look on your face. I guessed some violence had happened to you, especially since Rosa was born so soon after your wedding, but I didn't want to pry. And it wouldn't be the first time a woman had to marry her rapist, but I should have known Niccolo isn't that kind of man. Oh, Livia… how the honorable and reckless Valenti brothers have twisted our lives up…"

In spite of our current predicament, Niccolo has certainly made my life better. I'd have said Bellino has too, with his warm acceptance of me, his happy attitude toward life, but he partly caused this dreadful situation. I still can't quite reconcile myself to the idea that he tried to assassinate the emperor, and I cling to a shred of hope that somehow it's all a trick and Corbara is the only one truly responsible. "It's our turn to protect them," I say instead, as if there's a way we can save them both.

"I can tell you have an idea," says Elisabetta. "You wouldn't spill your secrets for nothing. Can I help?"

"I need to see the emperor." I've been mulling over the idea ever since it popped into my head, right after I found the warrant letter for Corbara's arrest. "I have proof Corbara is wanted for crimes in Turin. Your cousin sent Niccolo an official letter."

"Camillo doesn't usually bother with things like that. Crimes are beneath his notice, unless they threaten the state." She straightens, hastening to clarify. "Not to downplay this villain— I'm disgusted that I had tea with him once. I only meant Niccolo must have called in a favor."

"And hopefully it will work in our favor now. I can't imagine the emperor wants to see Corbara recalled to Turin for mere arson and theft, not when he could face the consequences of attempted murder in Paris."

"There's little risk of that," says Elisabetta. "We'll tell Louis that Corbara is one of his would-be assassins, and within the hour resources will be devoted to finding him. He won't be able to hide for long."

"There's only one problem. If Bellino really is with him, they could both be arrested at the same time. We need to find a way to single out Corbara."

I can't quite read the look Elisabetta casts my way. Pitying, but somehow grateful, too. "I admire that you still think there's a chance Bellino wasn't involved. I wish I could feel that way, too."

"It was dark, and you only saw him for a second. There could be more to the story that we don't know." Even as I speak, I can't think of any plausible or acceptable reason for Bellino to be in the company of two other assassins. I sigh. "It's probably better that only one of us is hopelessly optimistic."

We fall into silence for a moment. "You'll have to go to the Tuileries and see the emperor yourself," Elisabetta says at last.

I lift my head in alarm. I don't want to do that at all. I'd envisioned him coming to Elisabetta's house. Possibly that she would do all the speaking.

"He won't come to me until the men are arrested. My home is the scene of the crime. It's where he brushed close to death but outran it. He's a brave man, but he's not a fool, and it can't be a coincidence that he hasn't sent me a personal note. He must believe there's a chance, however slim, that I was involved in the plot."

"We could send him a letter."

One of her golden curls tumbles free of its pin, falling across her face as she shakes her head. "Do you have any idea how many letters and papers cross his desk every day? No, this must be entrusted to a personal conversation." She forces a cheerful smile to her face. "Don't worry. It'll be easy. I'll put you in touch with Jean-François Mocquard, his private secretary."

"All right." I'm still nervous at the thought of walking through the vast hallways of the Tuileries Palace, straight to the emperor. It's one thing to hear Elisabetta's references to him, quite another to speak to him alone. Unlike her, I have no title. I'm unaccustomed to court etiquette, but I'll do anything for Niccolo.

"Mocquard has been known to procure for the emperor." She waits while the meaning of her sentence sinks in, and I turn to her in dismay.

"Procure?"

"Don't look so shocked. Plenty of women are willing enough to entertain him in exchange for appointments for their husbands, for favors, even just for the story. Doubtless, he'll be looking for distraction now. It should be easy to get Mocquard to take you to him—I'll help you dress in something eye-catching. Then, once you're in his presence, you can tell him all about Corbara. That'll shift his excitement," she reassures me. "Louis is quite fond of intrigue. He'll enjoy being involved in the plan to capture Corbara. Perhaps you'll even see the secret staircase in his study. I never have, but of course I've been told of it. *Le pas des biches*, it's called." There's something bitter about her smile. "How many doe-eyed courtly ladies have dragged their crinoline skirts up that staircase to his rooms above, I wonder. I hope you do get to see. I'm curious to know if they're full of salacious paintings, or gilded statues."

"I think I'd prefer to stay within the austerity of his public study," I say.

"Louis uses his papers as an excuse. If he tells you his papers are calling, it will mean he doesn't like the subject, or you're losing his interest. I can't imagine that will happen in this situation, but it's a useful trait for you to know."

I appreciate the warning. "Do you think Corbara would come here, if you invited him back for tea?"

"The hard part will be reaching him, although I do have his calling card. I doubt he's at that address now, but someone there must certainly be in touch with him." She pauses. "This will be the tricky part of the plan for me. I think I shall have to hint I'd like to be involved in a second, successful attempt. Otherwise he'll probably be suspicious of my invitation as a trap and ignore it."

I like seeing the plan stitch together, closing all the gaps like a wound held closed until it heals. But I'm still scared.

Elisabetta pats my shoulder, her expression shadowed and serious. "Thank you for trusting me with your story, Livia. I thought you'd hate me after what I did."

"So did I."

"Instead, I feel we're closer than before. And I'm sorry." She seizes me in an impulsive hug, holding tight. "I'm so sorry. You're stronger and braver than I am." Her breath shakes. "And I don't know if you feel like it is, but what happened with Corbara wasn't your fault. You wouldn't be the only woman to be taken advantage of by a man." I give her a questioning look, catching the hint of viciousness slicing through her tone and remembering those rumors of her and the king of Piedmont-Sardinia, but she doesn't elaborate, and I don't press. It's up to her to tell me, if she ever wants to, and there's too much else to do right now.

First thing the next morning, I visit Niccolo at the Conciergerie. Alexandre Lafontaine himself escorts me to Niccolo's room, which is private and comfortable enough, if small and plain. He even leaves us alone, though I'm careful to whisper my plan, interspersing it with louder conversation, so it can't be overheard.

"Be careful." Niccolo looks so worried and weary that I can't stop touching him in little comforting ways, stroking his cheek or smoothing his hair. "I've spoken with Monsieur Lafontaine at length, and I think he nearly believes me."

"He will for certain once Corbara is found," I promise.

Elisabetta must have a guaranteed way of getting in touch with the emperor's private secretary, because it proves to be a small obstacle to meet with him. He doesn't say much, but I notice he inspects my appearance. He must find it suitable, for he guides me to an office on the ground floor of the palace. Elisabetta chose my outfit and fussed over my hair, two things I can't think about right now, so I'm grateful for her critical eye. My heart pounds and my mouth feels dry, my hands shaky. I clench them into fists until my nails bite into my palms, and that helps calm me. I've met the emperor before, I remind myself. He was kind then, not harsh, so perhaps he'll be the same today. And this is for Niccolo. I'd face any terror for him. My breath steadies, and I lift my head higher as I follow Monsieur Mocquard.

Emperor Napoleon III rises to his feet as Monsieur Mocquard ushers me into the room, stepping around the enormous polished wood desk. His hands feel warm and slightly damp as he squeezes both of mine.

"Madame Valenti, it is an honor to have you call upon me. We've met before, yes? I could never forget those golden eyes."

"Yes, Your Imperial Majesty. I was fortunate enough to attend the costume ball at the Ministry of Foreign Affairs a couple of months ago." I want to pull my hands free of his, but I'm afraid to offend him. Behind me, the door clicks shut as Mocquard leaves us alone.

"Midnight," he remembers, to my surprise. "You were dressed as Midnight, dark and bewitching."

He speaks with such intensity, all his attention focused upon me, that my cheeks grow warm—and burn again when his languid gaze scrapes over the neckline of my dress. I silently curse Elisabetta for suggesting I wear something more daring and low-cut than normal. She argued I needed to appeal to his chivalric side, which meant looking alluring. Trusting her judgment, I obeyed her advice, but now I wonder if she was being euphemistic in referring to his chivalric side—it seems rather more lecherous at the moment.

"To what do I owe the pleasure of your visit, madame?" Mercifully, he lets my hands go, but he still stands close, eyes devouring me, and as the scent of sandalwood drifts through the air, and the gilt frames of the paintings glint in the soft golden light, I get a sense of the power the emperor wields. I think of Elisabetta and imagine how intoxicating it might be to hold his desire, but I also understand, with a chill, how difficult it would be to decline any request he might make. Can one refuse an emperor?

"We have a friend in common, Your Imperial Majesty."

He shakes his head, leaning forward. "Please, I'd prefer not to be so formal when it's only the two of us."

As if I need a reminder of our solitude. "Of course, sire. I'm a friend of the contessa di Castiglione."

A shadow falls over his face like a curtain, obscuring some of his interested warmth, but his attention doesn't waver, that pleasant smile still fixed in place.

"And you're one of her countrywomen, as I perceive from your accent." He switches to Italian. "I spent quite a lot of time in Italy in my youth, and am happy to speak this language if you prefer."

"Whatever you wish, sire."

"Did the contessa send you?" he asks. "You'll forgive me for rushing you, but if you don't mind getting straight to the point, I'd be obliged." He gestures wistfully toward the desk. "My papers are calling."

"She did," I say. His wary expression shifts to a frown, so I hasten to explain, glad of Elisabetta's warning. "I know what happened outside her house. She told me about the danger you were in, sire."

"There was no danger." He sounds sharp. "I was safe enough, not even scratched."

I've wounded his pride, and must remedy that. I gentle my voice. "Any small amount of threat is too much when it involves you, Your Majesty."

He softens. "How kind of you to say. I do wonder, though, that the contessa is going around talking about the incident. I didn't think she would be quite so indiscreet." His tone implies he did, in fact, expect a certain amount of gossip from Elisabetta.

"She isn't. She only told me because I'd been telling her about an Italian man—a very fervent, dangerous nationalist—who has been troubling my family. He's wanted for crimes back in Italy, but is known to be in Paris. I believe he may be one of the despicable assassins."

The brief hesitation I feel over my use of dramatic adjective fades when he lifts his head like a hound catching a scent. "Indeed?"

"Yes, sire." I produce the letter from Niccolo's cigar box and pass it to him. He opens it at once, reading with an expression of concentration. The four precise creases of the paper wrench my heart a little, knowing Niccolo made them when he folded the letter to fit in the cigar box, so he could keep it safe while he secretly tried to find Corbara for me.

Emperor Napoleon drops the letter on the desk, and stares at me. "There are crimes enough to warrant his arrest, but nothing of his nationalism, or the recent attempt upon my life. What makes you think he was involved?"

"I met him once, in Turin. Before I knew he was a thief and an arsonist, possibly a murderer. My father is a doctor, you see, and this man was one of his patients. He spoke quite openly about his zeal for overthrowing Austrian rule in Italy, and of his belief in the theory of the dagger."

Napoleon pales, mouth tightening into a grim line. "I've heard of it."

I nod with relief. My stomach was twisting in dread of having to explain that particular idea to the emperor, and now that I've been spared it, some of the nausea stops pressing at the back of my throat. "I believe he's a member of the Carbonari."

If this surprises the emperor, he hides it, merely nodding. I think of Elisabetta's hints that he was once a member himself, but I can't tell if it's true.

"I know he's in Paris, sire," I continue. "I've seen him here. It can't be a coincidence."

Napoleon straightens the pomaded ends of his mustache absently, blinking as if deep in thought. "Perhaps not." Clearing his throat, he fixes that piercing gaze on me again. "You've given me a lead, madame, for which I'm grateful."

"I hope to give you more than a lead." I can't hold back the tentative pitch creaking through my voice; his scrutiny makes me nervous, and we're rapidly approaching the most delicate part of my mission. "I hope to deliver him to you, sire, as long as you are willing to help me lay a trap for him."

As Elisabetta promised, his attention shifts to excitement at the prospect of a scheme. He straightens, crosses his arms over his chest. "I might be, madame."

My fingernails slash into my palm as I knot my fingers into a fist, hiding it in the skirt of my gown, trying to find strength enough to continue in that bite of pain. "I believe, if invited, he would call on me. Not only because of our past acquaintance, or our shared homeland, but…" My exhale trembles and I can't steady myself.

Napoleon moves forward and rests his hand on my elbow, bending his head encouragingly. "Yes?" he says.

"This Corbara is a cruel man, as you can guess. He will likely find this turn of events worth gloating over. You see, sire, my husband has been arrested as one of the assassins, and I know he is innocent."

I suppose I expected him to be silent, to hide his dismay over this new information. I was so caught up in my dread over confronting the emperor, fearing he might not listen to me, and I'd lose my only way of saving Niccolo, that I forgot he already knew. He knew my name when I entered his study; doubtless he knew the name of the only man so far arrested.

His fingertips nudge my cheek, forcing me to lift my eyes to his. "I know about your husband."

"And still you admitted me to your private study?"

Instead of dropping his hand, he cups the side of my face, sliding his thumb over the top of my cheekbone. My heartbeat pounds in my throat, but I manage not to flinch. I blink against the intensity of his stare.

"I was curious," he says, in a voice as dark and secretive as a shadow. "I remembered you, and I wondered what you would say to me. I will confess I didn't expect you to stand in front of me with your head bowed timidly. Most women who come here looking for favors for their husbands are rather more brazen." His hand drops from my cheek, thankfully, but he lets his fingertips graze the side of my neck, the soft silk of the shoulder of my gown.

It does little good to know my lancet is wrapped securely around my wrist. I could never use it on the emperor. I lift my head instead. "I love my husband. I have nothing to give you, sire, except loyalty to you as my sovereign in Paris, and that which you deserve as a good man."

His hand falls to his side, but slowly, and his eyes glimmer as he smiles at me. "And a trap to catch an assassin. That is no small gift. Sit down." He crooks his finger at me, and I sit at the opposite side of the desk from him. "We must discuss our plan."

"Ours, sire?" Hope lifts my heart.

"Yes, I think it has merit. I believe you, that this Corbara could be involved, and I'd like to catch him. You need me to send guards to the appointed place and time, once you've lured him?" He arches a brow, and I nod in confirmation.

"And my husband?" I ask. It's easier to be brave now I know he likes my candor.

"First, we must capture Corbara. You've successfully planted a seed of doubt in my mind, but I'd be a fool to let your husband go before we've caught the more likely suspect. Don't worry; he'll be safe enough in the Conciergerie." His teeth show in a sharp, wry grimace. "I've been there myself, you know."

After discussion, we agree I will invite Corbara to call on me two days hence, to give him enough time to receive the invitation. I doubt he's currently living at the address on the calling card he left for Elisabetta, but I'm also reasonably sure he'll have found a way to receive messages. Elisabetta is still a potentially valuable connection for him, and the emperor agrees with me.

It's a strangely heady thing, to scheme with an emperor and have him praise your ideas, building upon them with his own suggestions. It's more dizzying than the rich, strong wine he poured for both of us, and which I've hardly sipped. My pulse already flies, making my limbs as light as though I could somehow take flight myself.

"You need a way to send messages to me quickly," says Napoleon. His eyes glitter. I think he enjoys this sort of intrigue, plotting with me himself instead of including any advisors. "I'll send one of my rings with you. Mocquard will recognize it—include it with any message, saying it's urgent, and it will get to me."

I expect him to rummage through his desk, but he crosses to the paneled wall behind the desk, and unerringly finds an invisible latch, which triggers a secret door to swing open. Napoleon laughs at my open astonishment, and gestures to the shadowy, narrow staircase behind the wall. "It's cleverly made, isn't it? My private rooms are just upstairs. I shall return in a moment, with the ring." His eyes rove over me once more, in speculation. "Unless you'd like to accompany me?"

"Thank you, sire, but I shall wait here."

He smiles. I don't think he expected a different answer. The stairs creak slightly as he moves upstairs. I notice the letter condemning Corbara still lies on the desk, half folded, and reach for it. In case this plan fails, I might still need it for another purpose.

Returning, the emperor presses a plain gold ring, engraved with a bee, into my hand. "Guard it well, madame. As you do your honor."

"I shall, sire."

He lifts his wine glass, gesturing for me to do the same, and toasts our plan. "May it be successful." We both sip, and then he rings a bell on the desk, and Mocquard reappears at the study doorway, expression impassive, ready to escort me out.

I look back over my shoulder before following him out of the room. "I won't disappoint you, sire."

He nods slightly, casting a shadow over his face. His looks inscrutable again, and I realize, much as he's enjoying our little conspiracy, he wouldn't hesitate to remove his favor if he thought I deserved it.

Everything is up to me now.

CHAPTER EIGHTEEN

Paris, April 1857

Hemlock flowers resemble those of yarrow, which has useful properties as a tonic. However, hemlock stems are marred with small but distinctive purple blotches, like bruises.
— Excerpt from Livia Valenti's book of herbal studies

Shadows drape the gardens of the Tuileries, ominous now instead of lovely. I dart down the street, wishing Elisabetta's carriage could have met me closer to the palace, but I understand the need for the distance. It's one thing to attend a ball, and quite another to be seen hanging around waiting for the emperor, outside his wife's home too.

Just past a low fence draped with climbing roses, a hand clamps on my shoulder and a hoarse cry tears from my throat.

"I apologize. Did I frighten you, Livia?" He doesn't sound sorry at all, and the smooth cadence of his voice darts along my skin with sickening familiarity.

The image of his face sears into my mind even before I turn. Corbara's green eyes, one streaked with brown, pierce mine, and it feels like my heart stops. I'm turned to stone by an alchemy of dread.

His gaze flicks up and down my body in a tangible slide that makes the hair on the back of my neck prickle. My pulse kicks with the surging impulse to slap him, to dig my fingernails like claws into his cheeks, rending that smug expression out of existence. I want to fight him the way I've wished I did nearly every night since, when I lie in bed and the memory of his assault on my body makes me cringe with shame.

I'm afraid to touch him, though. Frozen again. Helpless even to breathe as my throat squeezes tight.

I knew I'd have to see him again. It is necessary for the trap I've just planned with the emperor. I just didn't think it would be so soon. I didn't think it would be like this, alone in the dark, with the heat of his hand permeating the fabric of my light cloak as if his touch could scald my flesh. I swore to myself that this time would be different, that I'd be strong and cold and calm when I faced him, and instead the acid burn of tears pricks the corners of my eyes.

"I must confess, you're the last person I thought to encounter scurrying through the dark outside the Tuileries." Humor makes his eyes dance, playing around the corners of his mouth, but it doesn't set me at ease, not at all. "At least, you should have been, but I've been aware of your presence in Paris for a while."

I think of Niccolo, locked in the Conciergerie. He needs me; I imagine the steady sound of his voice, picture the glow of warmth in his eyes, reserved only for me. I wrench my shoulder from Corbara's grasp, but the grip of his fingers is like a chain.

"We need to talk." He slides his fingers along my arm, gripping hard just above my elbow. "I can tell you're startled and thinking about screeching, but walk with me, and don't cause a scene. You're good at that, aren't you, *topolina*?"

Little mouse, he calls me. A wave of humiliation slams into me, burning my cheeks and bowing my head. I am a mouse where he's concerned, freezing and letting him do whatever he wants. "Let go of me." My voice breaks into a shrill tremble, not the angry cat's hiss I hoped for.

He ignores my pathetic command, and steers me toward the shadow of the next street. And I let him.

"Not exactly pleased to see me, are you? I'm hurt, Livia. Why are you in Paris? I suppose you didn't follow me here." We've marched around the corner of the street now, venturing into a deserted alley. My feeble footsteps trail after his.

"I live here with my husband." The words scrape against my throat, but once I've found them, they release my limbs too, and I can move again. I try to stomp on his foot, but he dodges with an agile step back, squeezing my arm brutally tight. A bruise will be blossoming along my skin, swelling over my muscles and making the bone ache underneath.

"Your husband? Allow me to express my felicitations upon your marriage, although I'll admit they aren't heartfelt." He bends his head closer to mine. "I feel rather jealous."

I spot a couple of men walking a few hundred yards ahead, and I try to angle us toward them, praying they're guards or police patrolling near the Tuileries. "Did you follow me here?"

"No. I haven't been back to Turin since we were together last. It never occurred to me you would have left." The strange cheerfulness of his response oozes to a low, menacing rumble as he realizes I'm steering us toward the guards. "Remember, don't cause a scene. I've got a pistol tucked under my coat—here, I'll show you." He yanks my body closer to his, enough so I can see the polished wooden handle of the pistol as he lifts the hem of his coat.

"I don't believe you'd shoot me. That would cause more of a scene than if I screamed."

His teeth glint in the haloed light of the nearest street lamp, his smile razor sharp. "Probably. But aside from those two men, there's no one else in sight right now. By the time an alarm was raised, we'd disappear into the nearest alley and its protective shadows. I know my way around here. But I don't intend to harm you. I need to talk to you, and then you can traipse along home to your husband."

He speaks with such reasonable composure that I slip to the edge of agreement. He sounds just like old times, when we walked around Turin together and he told me stories to make me laugh. The tautness of my body stops biting at my spine, but my legs still tremble, shudders still rippling over my skin. My lancet bracelet swings against my wrist, and that gives me courage. I know how to flick it open with the slightest twitch of my finger, and I know where to press it against his skin to cause the most damage. I'm not as helpless as last time. My lancet is no match against a pistol, but that's tucked away under his coat, and I have the element of surprise.

The men disappear, heading in the opposite direction. I'm alone with Corbara again.

"What do you want?" My question's sharp, but at least my voice doesn't shake. Niccolo needs me; I must persuade Corbara to meet with Elisabetta, to step into my trap. I'll pretend I'm Elisabetta in one of her photographs, bold and strong.

"I knew you'd be sensible," he says approvingly. "I like that about you, just as I appreciate your cleverness. It's not many women—or men either—who have such knowledge of medicines and plants. Even the poisonous ones."

"I'm not going to give you poison." Though he hasn't asked, I automatically assume the worst of him now. "You don't need me for that, in any case. Poisons are common enough. Almost every pretty flower bed contains a secret promise of death."

Corbara steers me into the shadowy nook around the corner from a bookshop. The wall presses against my back as he looms in front of me. "That's quite a way of putting it. I wasn't going to ask for poison. I was merely remarking upon the uniqueness of your knowledge. It's partly what drew me to you, Livia." Falling from his lips, my name pierces like a needle into the edge of a wound, and his breath settles in my hair. I feel tainted all over. "I liked making the serious girl smile. I liked trying to make you react." His hand lifts toward my face, and I twist away. My pulse flutters wildly, like a moth trapped in a corner, but he only trails his fingertip along the side of my neck, smiling when I shiver under that light touch. "I still like it."

"I'm not smiling now, and I'm not interested in reminiscing. Tell me what you want."

"I saw you leaving the Conciergerie earlier. I have a friend— well, actually he's a friend of one of my acquaintances. He got himself into a bit of trouble. He's a criminal, in fact. I might as well be blunt. But my friend is worried, because he's gone missing. When you were inside, did you happen to see Roberto Rossi?"

I expected him to ask about Bellino, or even Niccolo, who's truly within the prison's walls, and relief sweeps through me that I was wrong. "Why would I know? Do you suppose I toured the whole building, meeting each prisoner?"

Corbara's laugh sounds delighted and harmless. "You've become a good liar, darling. I don't think you could have bluffed me so well when we first met. I'm impressed, and quite intrigued by what else you may have learned since then." He seems disappointed when I don't rise to his bait, merely regarding him steadily and silently. "I know you're on good terms with La Castiglione. Don't bother denying it; I've seen you outside her house, including tonight when I followed you. Roberto Rossi knows her, too. I'd wager all the money in my pocket you've met him, too."

"Is Roberto Rossi the one who introduced you to her?" I savor the satisfaction of seeing his head tilt in astonishment. This isn't really a game, but it's the first time I've ever been able to be one step ahead of him, and it makes me feel stronger.

"Yes, he was." At least he has the grace to admit when he's caught.

"I know you've written to her. I saw your letter on her desk."

"I did more than write—I visited her once. She seemed friendly at first, but I was never invited back, even though she practically promised me a spot at her next dinner party."

"She told me about you."

Interest flares in Corbara's eyes, and he bends his head even closer to mine. The wall of the shop chills my back, and his breath is too warm on my neck.

"What did she say?"

My breath drags shallowly, but I don't dare pause to steady it. The hesitation may show him I'm lying. This is my chance, one I never expected to have, to strengthen my ruse. If he believes Elisabetta supports his cause, he's less likely to be suspicious of me, in case he finds out Niccolo is already imprisoned. He's already asking about the Conciergerie—it could happen. And if I invite him to her house instead of mine, I might be able to catch him alone, without Bellino. I can summon the emperor's men to her house as easily as my own, with the ring to prove the veracity of my message.

"She thought you were dangerous," I whisper, lingering on the last word. "Fascinating, but risky to know. She wanted to talk to you, maybe even work with you, but didn't dare risk the emperor finding out, in case you were a man of the Carbonari."

He stares at me with narrowed eyes. "Truly? She said this to you?"

"She trusts me. We're close friends now."

His hand slides up the back of my neck, tightening in my hair. My pulse ricochets with fear, but he doesn't seem to notice. "You wouldn't lie to me, would you, Livia?"

"No." When he hesitates, apparently still uncertain, I find a dried, dead husk of truth, buried deep inside, and force myself to speak it and to help my current lie grow. "Corbara, you were my first love."

"I was a lot of your firsts," he says gruffly. His lips graze mine in the barest touch, a frisson of body warmth more than a scraping of flesh, before I manage to tilt my head away in spite of his grip on my hair.

"I told her not to talk to you anymore," I say in a harder voice. I don't want him to kiss me. I need to convince him of Elisabetta's support for Italy, and that I am the only thing holding her back from contacting him. "I told her I didn't think you were trustworthy."

He draws back from our too-intimate tête-à-tête. The brown slash through his iris seems to darken, spreading like a shadow through his eye as his expression shifts to a scowl. "Why would you do that?"

"What have you ever done?" My voice rises in a taunt. "I've seen you lie about rescuing a child in a fire, and tell charming jokes, but never anything of substance. You run from one city to another, chasing promises of revolution, but you never actually do a damn thing about any of it. You don't think—you only hurt people and then you move on, not sparing a second thought at all—"

My calculated tirade shifts to something real just as it breaks through his bravado, and he lurches back a step, swinging his hand up as if he might strike me.

"Enough!" He doesn't shout, but the intensity of his voice is sharp and grating as a knife on a whetstone. His hand presses against my chest, just below my collarbone. "Look," he says, forcing me to glance down and see the new, jagged outline of the dagger inked on the back of his hand, its point jabbing between his thumb and forefinger. "You know I'm Carbonari. You know I want Italy to rule itself, and Emperor Napoleon stands in the way. Worse, he's sworn Carbonari himself, and he turned his back on that. *Do not* say I've done nothing—you have no fucking idea where I've been, or the lengths I'll go to."

His hand could slide easily up to my throat, and the tension in his arm leaves me in no doubt that he's strong enough to squeeze the air out of my windpipe forever. I try to slow my breathing, but it comes in quick pants, making his hand rise and fall so the tattooed dagger threatens to jab at my skin.

"I forgot how you can stare." He sighs. "Those eyes, long-lashed like a fawn's but penetrating as an eagle's. Damn it, Livia. I did rescue a child, you know. That part wasn't a lie."

I think I understand. He likely set the fire, only realizing after that a child was inside the building. That he chose to run back inside doesn't erase his destruction or remove his culpability, though.

"And I thought of you." His hand slips lower, hovering near my breast, the sketch of the dagger poised to plunge into my heart. "I thought about going back to find you, even though I didn't think I meant it when I said it." His mouth quirks in a twisted smile. "How do you like the truth?"

My mouth is so dry I have to swallow before I can summon my voice to more than a croak. "If you're truly committed to Italy, come to Elisabetta's house in two days, at five in the afternoon."

"Are you saying you'll help me? Why?"

"Not for you. For our country."

"You haven't said exactly what you'll help with. I'm not sure I trust you."

I push his hand away, and this time he lets it fall. "Roberto Rossi is dead. He died of his injuries, after the emperor's carriage wheel rolled over him outside La Castiglione's house, when three men tried to assassinate the emperor. That plan didn't go well; you'll need another."

"You surprise me, Livia."

"Come to her house, and you'll see just how surprising I can be."

His eyes flicker at my words, lips parting, and fear lends me strength as I'm terrified he'll try to kiss me again. I slip out of his grip, and down the road to meet Beatrice in Elisabetta's carriage.

Corbara doesn't follow me.

Elisabetta comes over the morning before Corbara's due to arrive at her house. We eat a listless lunch together, unable to talk of much besides the looming pressure of our plan to catch him. I still don't know how I'll extricate Bellino from this mess. If I can. If I should. After excusing myself, intending to nurse Rosa but finding her asleep, I slip back downstairs to where Elisabetta waits in the study. As I approach, Elisabetta's voice carries down the hall, her tone sharp. A man responds, and I recognize the sound of Bellino's voice.

"Bellino, what are you doing here? Have you seen Niccolo?"

Bellino's brows draw together in puzzlement. "No, isn't he here?" He takes my hand and pulls me into a quick, fraternal hug, fluttering a kiss near my cheek. He smells of candles and smoke. "It's good to see you, Livia. I brought a friend—I'm sorry, I should have introduced him at once." Standing so close to me, he's blocking my view of the other man in the room.

I force a stiff, polite smile to my face. I don't have time for making idle conversation with one of Bellino's acquaintances.

As Bellino moves, Corbara steps forward, giving me a knowing glance. The foundations of our plan crack, just like my composure.

He isn't supposed to show up early, at my house instead of Elisabetta's. And he's supposed to be alone, not with Bellino.

A tremor of dismay shivers across my skin. I was prepared to see him at Elisabetta's house at the appointed time. But now he's here, in my own home.

And Rosa's asleep upstairs.

Bellino's casual introduction indicates he doesn't know Corbara and I have met—and worse, that he doesn't know about Niccolo, either. He can't find out this way.

Focusing on the thought of Rosa helps to drain most of the dread from my limbs. If I could undo the past, she wouldn't be here, and I don't want that, and it makes it easier to face Corbara again. I give him a chilly nod and turn back to Bellino. My family is more important right now.

"Thank you for your hospitality," Corbara says. "After the wretchedness of the past few days, it's a delight to sit in the comfort of your parlor."

"Yes, we've been on the road, utterly without news," says Bellino, brushing off Corbara's elaborately well-mannered greeting. Since I know Corbara has been in Paris, I conclude this is a lie and it cracks my heart. "Are you saying Niccolo isn't here?"

"Yes. Sit down, Bellino, there's a lot you must catch up on." Ignoring Corbara, I steer Bellino toward the sofa across from Elisabetta's loveseat. She poses languorously, her arm bent, cheek resting against her hand. Except for a bright glare in her eyes, the hectic spots of color burning high on her cheekbones, she looks bored and impossibly glamorous.

Upon my invitation to be seated, Corbara moves quickly, taking the spot I meant for Bellino, who then shifts to the narrow space beside Elisabetta. The only open seat is beside Corbara, and I'd rather sit on the floor than join him on the green-striped sofa. Heat floods my cheeks, both anger and the promise of humiliation, for I'm not as composed as I'd like to be. I stand in front of the fireplace instead.

"Oh, for heaven's sake, Bellino." Elisabetta's scolding tone cuts through the tension in the room. "You've taken Livia's seat. Must you barge in here like some kind of ruffian? You're crushing my skirt."

The glance he slants at her is puzzled, tinged faintly with annoyance, but he offers a distracted apology, and moves to the open space beside Corbara. I don't sit down, however, choosing to remain standing by the fire.

"Is everything all right, Livia?" Bellino's usual insouciance crumbles to something tentative.

It's easier to avoid looking at Corbara when Bellino needs me. I keep my attention focused on him. "No. I'm afraid I have bad news. Niccolo has been arrested. He's at the Conciergerie."

Bellino's eyes widen in shock, and the color drains from his cheeks. His gaze shifts to the floor, and he seems to be struck speechless. By the time he looks up again, his jaw looks stiff, his stare too direct. His fingers clench together in his lap, the tension seeping through the air. My own nerves shudder as Bellino's voice breaks. "What happened?"

The effort not to glance at Corbara makes my neck ache with tension. I don't want to talk about my husband's problems with him near, listening too avidly. "He's innocent. It's just a matter of proving it. Look, Bellino, now isn't the best time to discuss it, not when we have company—"

"Damn that," says Bellino harshly. "I want to know what happened to my brother."

"It's quite all right." Corbara's calmness contrasts painfully against Bellino's rising sense of panic, and mine and Elisabetta's wariness. We all turn to look at him. "We all know about the assassination attempt upon Emperor Napoleon III. I don't mind if you speak freely." He clicks his tongue. "Such a shame only one perpetrator has been caught."

Somehow, he already knows it's Niccolo who has been arrested. I can't tell if his ironic tone is mocking me, or Bellino, who freezes in his seat. Perhaps Corbara taunts both of us. The heat of the fire collides along my back, unbearably strong, and I stumble to the loveseat, sinking down beside Elisabetta. Dimly, I register that she reaches for my hand, giving it a reassuring squeeze. Her skin feels much cooler than mine.

Bellino looks stricken, his cheeks flooding scarlet. He rakes his fingers through his hair.

"I think you're the one who should speak freely," I tell Corbara. Somehow my voice remains level, just as Niccolo's probably would. "None of us mentioned that incident yet."

"It's common knowledge." He leans back, crossing his arms over his chest, and his eyes glint with idle amusement. He likes our attention fixed upon him. "The news of the attempt upon the emperor's life isn't hard to discover. Most of Paris knows that would-be assassins tried to waylay him outside his mistress's house."

Elisabetta meets his lingering glance, her expression dagger-sharp.

"The assassins were probably Italian too; why else would they be outside *her* house? Unless they thought he'd be an easy target after spending the night in her bed. Even an emperor might stumble, sleepy and drained, after expending all his energies in lustful pursuits."

"That's enough." Bellino's voice sounds thick. He lifts his head from resting his elbows on his knees.

"I'm afraid Bellino doesn't enjoy telling this tale, as I do," Corbara says to me in a confiding tone.

Bellino lurches upright, glaring down at Corbara. "Shut your mouth—you know why. This isn't a goddamned joke." His broad shoulders heave, and he turns to face me, hands clenched into fists. "Livia, it's my fault Niccolo is at the Conciergerie. We know all about the assassination attempt because we were there. I was one of those three men, along with Corbara and Rossi. We escaped, but poor Roberto didn't. I had no idea they'd latch on to Niccolo instead of me."

Though I knew the truth already, Bellino's raw confession hurts like the sudden penetrating pressure of the splinter I once snagged deep under my fingernail. I can't think of anything to say to him. Bellino's head bows in shame, his eyes gleaming bright and his chest shaking with each breath. His emotional state doesn't detract from his usual angelic charm. It's almost impossible to imagine him attempting to commit murder. He seems incapable of anything so serious and sordid.

"I'll fix this." A pleading, desperate note winds through his voice. "Niccolo can't face the consequences for something I did. I'll tell them—I'll confess—"

Corbara stands too. "Don't be ridiculous. If you confess now, it'll never get accomplished."

Bellino whirls on him. "I don't care about that anymore! I don't believe his death will make a difference anyway. I've tried twice and both times failed. Give it up, Corbara. This is over."

"Twice?" The word slips through my dry lips. My tongue sticks to the roof of my mouth, but a sinking weight of dread courses through me as I realize now who poisoned Elisabetta. "You tried to poison the emperor with the brandy?"

Bellino looks at Elisabetta, gaze unflinching though his shoulders hunch as if he expects a rain of blows. "I'm so sorry," he whispers. "I never thought you'd drink it. You told me it was for the emperor, that only he drank it. I wasn't thinking clearly…"

Elisabetta rises from the loveseat, her movement sinuous as a cobra as she reaches for the heavy brass candlestick on the mantel. The candle falls to the floor with a crack, snapping in half, but she pays no attention to that. Firelight races along the burnished bronze of the metal as she lifts it high.

"You thought I wouldn't drink it, but I could take the blame when he died in my house?"

"I thought he'd get home before the illness set in. It was a spur-of-the-moment decision—I lost my head."

"You will, likely." Elisabetta sounds more sad than angry. The candlestick wavers at her side. "Bellino, how could you be so foolish?"

"I don't understand," I say. My legs tremble like a newborn foal's, and my throat is so tight it hurts to speak, but I feel like everything is cracking all around me, breaking into a painful mosaic of shattered illusions and ominous truths. "It was aconite, wasn't it, Bellino? How could you put that in the brandy on a whim? It isn't something a person just carries around."

He swallows hard, but answers in a ragged voice. "I got the idea from you, Livia, when you told me about the mistake with the nightshade berries, and how many everyday plants are poisonous. I'm sorry, but it's true. I discovered monkshood plants are deadly, and they're growing in plenty of gardens all about Paris. I dug up a bit of the root and ground it up. I carried it with me for weeks. I never actually thought I'd do it, but I liked knowing I could, if I chose to."

The last part of his confession makes my own skin burn guiltily. I feel the same about my deadly stash of nightshade.

"How could you?" Elisabetta repeats softly, shaking her head. Tears stream down her cheeks. "I don't know you at all."

"I'd been talking about Italian nationalism with Roberto Rossi," Bellino continues doggedly. "I knew he believed in the theory of the dagger—that it would be worth assassinating the emperor in order to perpetuate the cause. But I'd be lying to say that was my only motivation." His avoidance of looking at Elisabetta tells the rest of the story.

"Did Marco see you?" I speak without thinking, as the question leaps to my mind. Marco's death is still suspicious, but my stomach curdles at the thought that Bellino murdered him, too. Murdering a witness is so cold-blooded that I can't stand to think of Bellino doing it. I never believed he would, but I was wrong about the brandy, too.

His forehead furrows. "Marco? The cook?" He seems to remember the man was found in the river under suspicious circumstances. "No! I didn't hurt him. I don't know what happened to him."

Corbara clears his throat. "I can supply the answer to that mystery. On the day I first called upon the contessa"—he nods toward Elisabetta—"Marco was heading out to the butcher's shop just as I was departing. I asked him a few questions, as I was trying to discern the emperor's routine here, and I'm afraid I wasn't very subtle. Marco seemed suspicious, and ended the conversation."

"So you killed him?" I know there's darkness in Corbara, but this goes beyond my belief, and incredulity leaches into my words.

He gives me a severe look. "No. My God, Livia, do you know me so little?"

Bellino's gaze flicks sharply to Corbara's face upon hearing his familiar use of my name, his lips parting in surprise.

"I hardly know you at all," I say.

Corbara snorts with wry delight. "If you say so, *topolina*. Anyway, after the most upsetting incident of the contessa's poor health, when she was poisoned instead of the emperor, Marco suspected me. I'd left him my address in case he changed his mind about keeping the emperor's habits a secret. He appeared at my lodging and started shouting all sorts of accusing things, waving his fists around, making threats. Roberto Rossi was with me at the time—he had quite the temper, hadn't he? I think 'fisticuffs' is the best word to describe their interaction as the situation escalated. Roberto shoved Marco, who went down and smacked his head right on the corner of the table. It was purely an accident, but there was nothing to be done." He makes a sympathetic clicking sound that seems quite out of place in this tense room, and not sorry at all. "He was dead. We waited until night and then threw his body in the river. I'll admit it wasn't a very respectful grave for him, but we couldn't have the police poking around, asking questions." He looks to Bellino. "I never told you, but Roberto did you a favor, it seems."

"I wouldn't say that," says Bellino hoarsely.

Suspicion flits through my mind. Corbara's good at half-truths—like saving the child in the fire. I wonder if it really was Roberto who shoved Marco. After all, Roberto will never be able to refute the tale now.

Elisabetta's hands twist up in her inky black skirt, her skin pale and taut looking, stretched over her cheekbones as her lips press together to hold back tears or angry words. I squeeze her hand hard in mine.

The silence following Corbara's confession feels oppressive, and it magnifies the creak of the door as Caterina knocks and enters the parlor. Her eyes meet mine and, realizing Bellino and Corbara are there, she ducks out of sight, heading for the stairs. I saw Rosa tucked in her arms, though, her soft blanket trailing halfway to the floor. She probably needs to nurse now.

I look to Elisabetta, trying to silently question if she'll be all right if I excuse myself for a moment. Rosa will start screeching soon if she isn't fed, her cheeks going scarlet with infantile outrage, and I don't want Corbara's attention drawn to her.

Elisabetta responds with a minute nod and makes a visible effort to straighten in her seat, lifting her head so her neck looks long and elegant, like a swan's. I bet she's as dangerous as a swan right now, too: utterly fearless and stronger than she looks.

"Excuse me for a moment," I say to Bellino, because I don't want to speak to Corbara.

"I want to hear everything," Elisabetta tells him. "From the beginning, leaving nothing out. You owe me the truth, Bellino, every last, treacherous bit of it."

"I'm so ashamed Niccolo has taken the blame for my mistakes." He sounds broken. "And I'm more sorry for hurting you than I can ever say, but somehow it doesn't surprise me that I did. I ruin everything. We've always been tumultuous, haven't we? I thought it was a sign our passion would burn forever, but maybe we simply aren't good for each other. Niccolo, though… he's so much more honorable. My brother's a good man, and he deserves better than me. So do you."

The ragged despair in his voice chases me up the stairs, where Caterina has retreated to Rosa's nursery.

"I'm sorry." She shifts Rosa to my arms. "I didn't know *he* was here." She knows I encountered him on my way home from the Tuileries, of course. I told her everything about that, and she knows each detail of the plan with the emperor as well. She has the ring in her pocket, so she can send the message at the appointed time—which must change to now, I realize. "I wouldn't have come down if I'd known—I heard Bellino earlier and thought it was only him."

"It's all right. Hopefully Rosa will fall asleep soon." My baby reaches for my necklace, a locket my mother gave me. I snipped a little of Rosa's impossibly downy hair for one side, and a bit of Niccolo's for the other. Her chubby, clutching hand and brown eyes full of appeal make me suddenly desperate to have just a moment of quiet, breathing in her scent, pretending just for a second that Corbara isn't here, that Niccolo isn't locked in the Conciergerie, that my carefully laid plan has not been ruined.

"Caterina, I need you to slip out of the house and get a message to the emperor that Corbara is here."

"Shall I go to the Tuileries, and try to get an audience?"

"No, it'll take too long." Caterina's pretty enough to be admitted to his study, with its convenient chamber above, but it's the middle of the day and the emperor is probably otherwise engaged. "You won't need an audience. Just get a message to Monsieur Mocquard—the ring will get his attention quickly, and he'll know what to do. And please ask him to also send a message to Monsieur Lafontaine, the warden of the Conciergerie."

"And Bellino?" Fear weaves through her tone, matching mine.

"Unless I can somehow get him to sneak away while keeping Corbara here, I think it's up to Elisabetta to save him now." I can't summon much optimism. It still seems hard to believe Bellino has made so many dangerous, selfish decisions. I don't want to see him hurt, but his choices have unavoidable consequences.

"I'll hurry back," Caterina promises.

Rosa's initial enthusiasm for nursing soon shifts to soporific peace, as her eyes flutter shut and her breathing slows. She's tired, with faint purple smudges under her eyes, so at least I have hopes that she'll stay safely asleep in her cradle until the guards have come and gone from the house.

I hover over her cradle as she falls asleep, adjusting the night-shade box back into its place in the bodice of my gown. As long as Corbara's near, so too shall be my poison. My great-grandmother sparks alive in my mind.

I wonder if she felt comforted by the sturdy feel of her knife's handle in her palm.

I am, by the prick of the nightshade box's corners on my skin.

CHAPTER NINETEEN

Paris, April 1857

*The juice of rue does no harm to the skin until exposed to
sunlight, at which point painful blisters erupt, resembling
burns. It's poisonous to ingest as well, but tastes bitter enough
that consumption is a small risk.*
— Excerpt from Livia Valenti's book of herbal studies

Before I go back downstairs, I bend over Rosa's cradle, pressing
my lips to the fine strand of hair curling over her ear, breathing in
her sweet scent. She stretches under my touch, but doesn't waken.
Her mouth squinches up as if she devotes great concentration
to the task of sleeping, and I resist the urge to pick her up again
and clutch her close to my chest.

I turn to see Corbara leaning against the doorframe. I lurch
like a skittish jackrabbit, pulse racing.

He ignores my reaction. "I didn't know you were a mother.
I would have congratulated you. They say motherhood is a joy
like no other. She's a lovely child."

I wish I could retort that she resembles her father, but the truth
is that Rosa doesn't look like Niccolo at all. How could she? My
daughter resembles me most of all, with olive-tinted skin and
near-black hair and brown eyes. To my eternal, pure relief, there's
no obvious mirroring of Corbara's features. Nevertheless, I shift so
my body blocks his view of her. "How do you know she's a girl?"

My waspish reply seems not to bother him. He points to the watercolor of a shepherdess with a lamb, and lifts the edge of the pale purple blanket over the back of the chair. "I guessed. The room has a feminine touch, although of course that could be your motherly tastes."

Still in the doorway, Corbara blocks my escape route, but my feet feel rooted to the floor anyway. I won't leave Rosa's side, won't let him even try to touch her. He needs to leave the room first. My legs tremble, but my voice rings steadily. "We need to go back downstairs. Empire-changing plans don't make themselves."

He steps hesitantly closer, his gaze flicking past my shoulder to see her satin cheeks and downy hair. "That child is older than I expected. You weren't married when I knew you a year ago."

"She's big for her age. How would you even know?" Men, in general, tend not to know much about babies, but I didn't expect such knowledge from Corbara in particular.

"I have seven brothers and sisters altogether. Big family." With a visible effort, he shifts his stare from Rosa to me, lingering on my waist. Thanks to Elisabetta's endless insistence I lace my corset tighter than I originally wanted, and that I forced myself through the exercises she taught me, I've mostly regained my pre-pregnancy figure. It isn't helping my deception that Rosa is younger than four months.

"I met my husband very soon after you left Turin." I move slightly away from Rosa's cradle, trying to maneuver Corbara toward the door. And I lie, building a shield between him and Rosa with my words. The corner of the nightshade box jabs my skin with every taut inhaled breath. "It was like something out of a play; we fell in love at once, and were married within the month, and I considered myself blessed to conceive right away."

His fingers close around my wrist. "It could be true. It might not. Most hasty weddings aren't for love." His mouth twists, brow arching in sardonic amusement. "For the consequences of lovemaking, perhaps."

Bile burns the back of my throat. There was no love in the actions that brought Rosa into the world, but I'm determined she'll be surrounded by it nevertheless. "I see where your mind is going, and she is not yours."

His grip tightens as he stares into my eyes, as if he's searching for lies. I don't know why he cares—certainly he doesn't seem the fatherly type—but I must break his determination to find out. I need to get him away from Rosa, and back to the parlor where Elisabetta and Bellino are sitting. But the pressure of his scrutiny is too much, too invasive, and it sparks a visceral reaction in me.

Panic surges to rage.

"What do you want me to say?" I'm not faking at being calm anymore, nor am I afraid. Anger unravels inside me, blooming like evening primrose awakening under the heavy cloak of night. "You want me to tell you she was conceived before marriage? Are you hoping I'll tell you that you took my innocence, and then I wantonly leapt into bed with the next man who came along? Perhaps you take pleasure in imagining yourself to be a corrupting influence, because then it means that you've left your mark on the world, and on me. But in truth, you fail at everything." My lip curls. "Couldn't burn down a house without hurting yourself. Couldn't assassinate an emperor." Dimly, I see his eyes have gone flat, but I can't stop myself now. "Couldn't break me—couldn't make me remember you."

Both of his hands clutch painfully at my shoulders, and he shoves me up against the wall. "Shut up!"

Rosa whimpers, on the edge of waking up in spite of her exhaustion, and as his attention slices toward her, an edge of panic gives me strength. I kick him in the shin. My foot aches in complaint, but he recoils too, enough that I can wrench myself free and lunge toward the door, hoping he'll follow me away from her.

He catches my arm just above the elbow, yanking me so hard my shoulder strains in its socket, and my head whips back. I wonder why Elisabetta or Bellino aren't running to investigate before I dimly realize that his voice isn't loud. It's rough and so close to my ear that his words shudder across my skin while his body blocks mine against the wall.

"I'd say you remembered me. Had people looking for me, didn't you? I'm not a fool—I knew your husband was trying to have me arrested. Almost succeeded once, but I managed to convince that guard he had the wrong person." His voice vibrates along the side of my neck, and his free hand, the one not holding my arm, traces the dip of my waist, slowing sliding upward. "I knew who your husband was, too. Imagine my astonishment when Bellino mentioned his sister-in-law. I enjoyed that coincidence, though it was nothing to the delight of finding out your husband had been arrested for my crime."

"You knew the whole time?" I can't fathom why he pretended to believe I'd help him scheme with Elisabetta if he knew Niccolo had been wrongly accused, but the information is like a lead weight tied around my ankles, dragging my spirits as low as my hope for the future.

"I did."

"Why did you pretend not to? Weren't you angry?" As I question him, I make subtle movements with my fingertips, trying to nudge my lancet bracelet into a position where I can wield it.

His breath burns as he nuzzles my throat, whispering the words into my skin. "Yes, I was very angry that you tried to trick me. Angry, even, that you were married to another man. But I didn't expect to be so drawn to you again. Somehow you provoke me, just so, and it gets my blood up." He groans softly, pressing his body against mine. "Tell me you feel it too, this passion. I know you do…"

I press the tip of the lancet against the side of his arm, the first place I can reach, my fingertip poised to flick it open. At the same time, his hand roams over my breasts, fingers seeking my flesh under my bodice.

Instead, he finds the hard shape of the nightshade box.

And I flick the lancet open against his bicep.

Corbara yelps in shock and pain, leaping back as blood blossoms to a dark, rusted stain against the green of his jacket.

"Jesus bloody Christ! What in hell did you do?"

"I'll make you bleed more if you ever touch me again." I'm proud of how little my voice shakes.

His hand presses against the cut, and he grimaces when he sees the blood smeared across his palm, but to my dismay he doesn't seem to be feeling the agony of the hot pepper essence burning over his wound, slipping through his veins.

"Goddamn doctor bitch," he mutters, fishing a handkerchief out of his pocket and shoving it down his coat sleeve to keep it in place. "You liked my kisses well enough once."

"I stopped liking anything about you when you raped me."

"Such an ugly word from a tease of a girl who followed me willingly to a secluded shed."

Before I can do more than hiss with outrage, too furious to formulate a reply, he seems to remember the nightshade box, fallen to the floor in the struggle. He bends to pick it up, holding it up close to his face. "What's this?"

"It's poison. For you." I don't bother lying. All my loathing burns into those words, and there's a dark, fierce part of me that wants to shove all the nightshade down his throat. For everything he's done to me. For the blame he's let Niccolo take in his place. For everyone else he's hurt or killed.

He fiddles with the box, and manages to open it far more quickly than I expected. I suppose a scoundrel like him is familiar with such items of trickery.

"You brought this today? For the emperor?" His eyes look glossy and green as he stares at me, incredulous. "This wasn't all a trap?"

It takes a moment for me to comprehend his reaction. He still believes I'm trying to help the cause. If he believes that, perhaps the plan might still work after all. I match his stare with a steady one of my own, which he seems to take as confirmation.

He gusts with a sigh of relief. "I should have known you'd be too honest and honorable to lie. Livia, I swear I won't touch you again. We'll see this through, and then part ways forever."

There's no suitable response I can make to this, and I don't believe him anyway. I cross to Rosa, snuffling faintly from her cradle. Poor darling, she won't remember this, but I still blame myself this scene happened in her presence. Her eyes are half-open, and it seems like a minor miracle she isn't crying. I stroke her cheek, soothing us both.

"Livia?" Corbara's voice isn't loud, but urgency laces through his tone.

I ignore him. Rosa needs me, and he can't hurt me anymore. I've lost my fear of him, and besides, it would take only a shout to bring someone to my rescue. Rosa's eyes flicker shut again, and her little rosebud mouth falls open, as slack as her breathing.

"Livia, I can see you're busy proving you're fierce as a mother wolf, but I need to know what the hell you put on that blade of yours. My skin is itching and burning all around the wound." Sounding faintly panicked, he shuffles a step closer to me, but seems wary enough to keep some distance.

"It's not poison. It won't kill you. It just hurts."

He curses under his breath, patting the handkerchief into place. In truth, I'm disappointed the hot pepper oil hasn't had a greater effect. I'd hoped for it to seep into his veins, wracking agony all through his body, but I should have known the blood would just wash it away. It's been months since I doused the blade with the oil, too. It may have lost potency.

Since Rosa has subsided back into sleep, I turn to Corbara. "I'd like you to get away from my child now."

"I shan't dare risk your wrath again. God knows what you'd do to me next." Though he presses his makeshift bandage tighter in a rueful gesture, his green and brown eyes glimmer with a kind of possessive pride that skitters over my skin like spiders.

I make him go first, but as we return to the parlor, his arm blocks my path, and I stop, avoiding touching him.

"Listen." His lips shape the word, his breath scarcely making any noise.

"Are you very angry?" Bellino's voice is tremulous. I don't know if he means for the brandy, or the second assassination attempt on the emperor. Maybe both.

"Yes. No. I was, but now I'm too worried to hold on to my rage. It'll return later."

He exhales shakily. "This is the end, isn't it?"

"Perhaps I can smooth things over," says Elisabetta. A bold claim: the emperor won't be forgiving.

"Even Venus couldn't seduce her way out of this mess. Although you'd be the next best thing. How much does the emperor really care for you, do you think?"

Elisabetta doesn't answer.

Bellino pours wine for himself, glass clinking as he fumbles with the decanter. "Anything to take the edge off. I know it's my fault, but I've never been so damn scared."

I've heard enough. Corbara looks content—eager even—to keep listening, his head tilted slightly, eyes alert, but I push past him into the parlor. Corbara follows me, carefully closing the door behind us.

Elisabetta's gaze focuses on me, flicking once—with disdain— to Corbara. I move my head in an infinitesimal nod to let her know that I'm all right.

Bellino swigs the last mouthful of wine in his cup, desperately, as if it might numb him inside and out. He'd probably be grateful for a few drops of laudanum, although it isn't a good time to encourage escapism. Then again, if I could somehow persuade Corbara to take some too, it might keep him docile and tame until the emperor's men arrive.

"What happened to you?" Bellino points at the dark patch of blood staining Corbara's sleeve.

"I had an accident." A few drops of blood spatter to the floor.

Elisabetta's eyes widen as she glances at me, one brow arching in question.

"I think Corbara has learned to be careful." Now that I've thought of the laudanum idea, it seems like a good one. I don't trust Corbara to sit here scheming until the guards arrive, and Bellino's ashen skin suggests he might be sick at any moment. "We're all at the mercy of our nerves just now. Would anyone like a calming drink? I can make a nerve tonic."

Bellino straightens hopefully. "I wouldn't mind."

"No." Corbara blocks the parlor doorway, crossing his arms over his chest. "Livia isn't leaving the room. God knows what poison or trick she'll come back with."

"What are you talking about?" asks Bellino with rough irritation. "I'm the one who poisoned the brandy. I take full responsibility."

"The brandy, yes. But Livia ensured my wound is burning with the fire of a hundred nettles, and I don't trust her."

"Nettles?" Elisabetta sounds impressed.

I shake my head. "No. Oil infused with hot peppers." I turn to Corbara. Smugness makes my voice overly sweet, but it feels good to have this victory over him, and Elisabetta nearby. "I can help with that, you know. A poultice of milk would likely help."

His lip curls, probably from the idea of the blood from his still-leaking wound mingling with milk. It isn't pleasant, but I've seen far worse. "I'll manage." He crosses to the sideboard, sniffing the decanter of wine. "A drink will take the edge off. Shall I ask you to taste it, Livia?"

Bellino steps forward, eyes narrowing. "I drank some of that wine myself, a moment ago. Look here, Corbara, I think you've got some answers to give now. You told us about Marco, but if you're saying it's because of Livia that your arm is bleeding all over the place, I'm damn well certain to take her side. What have you done?"

Corbara finishes pouring wine for all of us, methodical and apparently calm, but when he turns around, his narrowed eyes dark, his mouth twisting, he doesn't look handsome at all. He hands cups of wine to Bellino and Elisabetta. "Nothing she didn't begin herself. Never fear, Bellino. I've learnt my place." He prowls forward, pressing a glass of wine into my hand.

His looming nearness sends shadows rippling over my skin. I swallow, trying to keep back a spur of the fear I thought I'd broken. I can't resist glancing down at the wine. Swirling in the glass, its ruby shade looks delectable. And possibly poisonous.

Catching my reaction, Corbara's wicked grin flashes and his fingertips brush mine. I search his eyes for signs of deception, just as he winks at me, malicious and mischievous all at once, and drinks from his own glass.

Lifting my wine to my nose, I inhale carefully, sniffing for any note reminiscent of herbs, but catch only the bouquet of oak and blackberries. Corbara is in possession of my nightshade, and I think he's reckless enough to use it. He wants it for the emperor, though. Just because I don't trust him doesn't mean he'll waver from his dedication to the theory of the dagger.

Corbara seems to guess my suspicious thoughts. He sighs, taking the glass back from me and switching it for his own. He sips from it too, proving them both safe, then clears his throat, addressing everyone. Bellino and Elisabetta stop whispering to each other and snap their attention back to him. "Perhaps we should toast our fervent nationalism? We're to be partners in the next phase of this plan for Italy's success, are we not?" He raises his glass to the group, but his eyes stay focused on me.

Bellino plunks his wine glass down on the table, advancing forward. "Partners?" His stare shifts from Corbara to me, clearly suspicious of our wretched familiarity.

"Didn't Livia tell you? She found me yesterday—she'd been hunting me down to propose a scheme to ensure the success of our next attempt. She'd do the Carbonari proud."

"I didn't. That's not true—Corbara found me. Scared the sense out of me, in fact."

"But the two of you have met before." Bellino doesn't seem pleased by this conclusion. He turns to me. "Does Niccolo know?"

"Yes," I reply.

"I bet there's a lot he doesn't know," Corbara says at the same time.

Elisabetta's voice rings out, loud as a bell, as commanding as a queen's. "Sit down, both of you."

I obey, although she seems to be directing her imperious attitude toward the men.

"We have our differences—a great many of them—but the one thing we all have in common is a desire to see Italy rule itself. That is our focus now, as well as shifting the blame from Niccolo." She glances at me for this last part, but seems to be speaking more directly to Bellino, who sits straight in his chair, staring with resolute intensity at the floor, presumably imagining his own glum future.

Corbara scoffs. "I can't believe you'd ever want to see the emperor dead," he says to Elisabetta.

"It isn't a matter of wanting anything, myself. It's about sorting out this mess."

"It isn't as much of a mess as it could have been," says Corbara. "The attempt failed, and Roberto Rossi died. A tragedy, to be sure, but that's one person who can't be harmed by the consequences anymore. Bellino, I understand you don't like seeing your brother take the blame, but you have to admit it's convenient—it shifts suspicion from us so we can try again, and perhaps be more successful. What's one person in comparison to the welfare of an entire nation? That whole philosophy is why we agreed the emperor's life was a reasonable forfeit for the outcome it would create."

"It depends rather a lot on the person, I've learned." Bellino's words manage to cut through the room like a knife, in spite of his quiet delivery of them. "Besides, it isn't just one person. If my brother takes the blame, it affects me, and Elisabetta, and Livia most of all. I won't accept that." He shifts in his seat as if a great mantle of weight has fallen on his shoulders, and the lines dragging from his nose to the corners of his mouth make him look older. "It was easy to pretend that wasn't the case for the emperor, but he has people close to him too. This isn't the right way to help Italy. The theory of the dagger is wrong."

Corbara rolls his eyes, lurching to his feet. "You aren't strong enough to see the end goal. Too cowardly, backing out now that a few things have gone wrong."

"Gone wrong?" Bellino echoes. "We've been caught."

"Not yet, we haven't. We need to stay calm and think this through."

My own thoughts swirl, as a horrible suspicion settles into my mind in a cold, sinking way that weights my bones with alarm.

Bellino's glass contains the deadly nightshade. Just as Corbara said earlier, it's convenient that Roberto Rossi is dead and Niccolo is arrested. If Bellino perished too, he'd make the third man in the attempt, and couldn't deny that Niccolo had been involved, leaving Corbara free to try again or flee Paris completely. This opportunity might just appeal to him more than saving the nightshade for the emperor, when everything has gone wrong with his plan so far. He might want to start over.

I suspect Elisabetta's wine is poisoned too, but she won't drink it. She hasn't touched her glass at all, and after her experience with the brandy, she'd never drink something poured by a person she didn't trust. I'm certain of that.

I could be wrong in my suspicion—but I don't think so. I know Corbara. I know his darkness, which echoes mine. I must switch my glass with Bellino's. That way, if his nerves get to the point that he sips his wine, he'll have my glass, proven untainted, and I'll keep his safe and untouched in my hand.

Elisabetta stands too, striding close to Corbara, tilting her head to glare straight into his soul. She looks as fierce as a warrior queen, one of the Amazons of ancient legend perhaps, or a pagan goddess of death. Her black skirt swirls around her legs like smoke. "You seem determined to make another attempt, and as soon as possible. But you forget to whom you speak—you have no connections, no title. No means. You won't be in charge of this plan, and frankly, you're the least needed."

Elisabetta's ferocity reminds me of my great-grandmother, who found enough anger in her heart to commit murder, risking her life and her soul. It makes me think of Livia, the so-called poisoner and Roman empress, who I'm named for. And it reminds me of myself, bitter and frightened enough to carry poison for months.

Taking my wine glass with me, I go to stand beside Bellino, with Elisabetta on his other side. Together we form a half moon of unity, facing down Corbara, who doesn't like this one bit. He scowls at me.

"She has a point," I tell Corbara. I don't care about his disapproval. Disagreeing with him delays him taking action, giving Caterina time. "You're quite eager to let Niccolo take the blame, but you forget there's another possible scapegoat." I lift my glass to him and take a deliberate swallow of wine.

"You're enjoying this little game, aren't you, Livia?" His breath sweeps across my cheek along with his low, taunting words. "You think you've got me trapped, with Bellino here to protect you. You've certainly got him curled in the palm of your hand—your husband too, I suppose. I'll admit it's pure luck he's arrested now and not me—he put a lot of effort into having me imprisoned. But tell me, do they know what a whore you are? Maybe they do—maybe that's how you control them."

Bellino's retort snaps like a whip. "Enough!" Spots of outrage burn on his cheeks, and his blue eyes blaze bright as lighting against a storm. "You can't speak to her like that."

My hands tremble, but Corbara and Bellino are focused entirely on each other, and this might be the only chance I'll get. Reaching behind me, I slide my fingers along the tabletop until I find Bellino's wine glass. Once I've lifted it, I put mine down instead.

Grim amusement bubbles from Corbara's throat, rolling like melted sugar just coming to a boil, dark and sultry. "I can. I know her better than you do."

"That's not true." My voice scrapes raw, but I won't let Corbara pretend he still knows me better, not after what he did to me, not when I've spent a year growing to love Niccolo and Bellino and Elisabetta.

Bellino's hand brushes against my shoulder, as gentle as his voice. "I know." He faces Corbara with his chin held high. "I won't stand by for another assassination attempt, nor will I let my brother be blamed for this one. I'm going to tell the truth."

Corbara sneers. "An honorable speech, but I don't think you have the courage to go through with any of it. It could mean the guillotine. Are you so ready to commit to honesty that you'd climb the steps to that whistling blade? You were hardly brave enough to go through with the plan the first time. You would have backed out if not for Roberto Rossi's timely lecture about Italy's future."

Unfazed by the accusation of cowardice, Bellino regards him steadily. "I shouldn't have let him persuade me again."

"I'm not even sure it was him. He could string together a fine sentence, but a certain royally gilded carriage rolled past just around that time, too. I noticed the matched black horses with their polished harnesses. I know you did, too. Changed your mind again, then." Corbara tilts his head toward Elisabetta and drops his voice to a confiding tone, as if they're old friends telling secrets. "He straightened his shoulders and gritted his teeth and swore he'd help stab the emperor right in the heart. It was very dramatic."

Elisabetta's bottom lip looks chapped and red, nearly bleeding from how much she's bitten it, and her skin appears fragile and dry as parchment against that rawness.

Bellino's throat works as he meets her eyes. "Not precisely in those words, but I did change my mind. I won't deny that." He seems to be speaking straight to Elisabetta, ignoring Corbara's expression of intent interest, almost as if he's watching a play. "I've been reckless and foolish. But no longer."

A sliver of resolve chimes through his words, growing strong and deep as the roots of a chicory plant. He won't change his mind this time.

I feel like a harp string, stretched too tight and about to snap, as all my nervous tension coils along my bones. Dread gathers in me like a storm. I've never felt so certain, or so afraid.

Corbara will never let Bellino turn him in.

Bellino won't back down from his new-found honor.

Unless the emperor's men crash through the door any minute, one of them will die.

"I'm going to tell them my brother is innocent. I'll admit my part. They know three men were involved, so you'll be implicated too. I can't help that, but I will give you a head start if you want to flee Paris."

Corbara shifts forward. "How much of a head start?" He sounds like a gambler calculating the odds on a horse race, eyes gleaming with opportunistic interest.

"Enough. A day." The corner of Bellino's mouth twists in dark irony. "A fresh start is tempting, isn't it? Not the coward's way, after all."

"A day isn't enough." Corbara's hand nudges at his pocket, near where his pistol must be tucked beneath his jacket, just as he showed me last night.

And I know I need to act.

Corbara's glass stands on the sideboard next to me. He pays no attention to me as I shift my weight closer, all his attention utterly focused on the negotiation. I put my wine glass—Bellino's wine glass—in its place, shifting Corbara's to my hand. My fingers, stiff and cold, should be clumsy, but I manage the swap with no clink of glass on polished wood.

Now I just need him to drink again.

"I need a week," says Corbara.

With a careless half-glance, he reaches for his wine as Bellino's voice rings out with finality. "Impossible." He looks hard at Corbara. "I won't leave my brother in the Conciergerie for that long. You get a day. I won't budge on this."

A shadow flickers across Corbara's face, marring his handsome features, as he tilts his head in the ghost of a shrug. His hand sweeps away from the wine, reaching inside his jacket. Before I can move, his arm lifts, and the sleek curve of a pistol appears in his hand. "I think I'll decline your offer."

I start forward, with no thought in my head but to rush to Corbara's side and tug his arm down. My feet barely skim the thick rug of the parlor floor before the shot blasts through the air like a clap of doomed thunder, ringing in my ears. Its sparks flare against my vision, briefly splashing everything with tiny white stars.

The wreck of a scream rips from Elisabetta's throat. We both lurch forward, neither of us quick enough to catch Bellino before he crumples to the floor, eyes wide with innocent surprise, his hand pressed to the sheen of blood leaking over his shirt.

CHAPTER TWENTY

Paris, April 1857

Deadly nightshade poisoning attacks both the mind and the body, causing rapid heartbeat, seizures, confusion, and hallucinations.
 — *Excerpt from Livia Valenti's book of herbal studies*

I fall to my knees at Bellino's side. There's so much blood, coating his skin and clothing in a sticky gloss of scarlet. It smothers the ragged edge of the hole where the pistol ball tore through his chest, but the darkest, wettest patch is thankfully a couple of inches lower than his heart. The metallic scent of his blood fills the air, but it doesn't make me retch. It isn't the first wound I've dealt with, although it's probably the worst. I can almost hear my father's voice in my ear, telling me to stop the bleeding.

"I need a compress." I grope around for any kind of cloth, and Elisabetta hands me a pristine white handkerchief, which soaks crimson as soon as it touches Bellino's chest. "Not enough." I grab the decorative pillow from the nearest chair, and press it to his wound. "Elisabetta—hold this here… yes, like that. Not too hard but not loose, either. I'll be right back with bandages." I have yards of clean white strips of linen in my medicine storeroom, but I'll need to hurry, running as though my feet were wings, in order to get back quickly enough for Bellino's life.

Elisabetta breathes in sharp, hoarse wheezes, but she kneels at Bellino's side, heedless of the blood staining her skirt, and holds the cushion in place. "Hurry, Livia." She bends close to Bellino's face. "Hold on, my dearest."

As I stagger to my feet, I nearly bump into Corbara, glowering down at Bellino with his lips parted as though he can hardly believe what he's done. The pistol, a dainty, one-shot thing that would nestle easily into the inside pocket of his jacket, dangles from his hand, and he lifts his wine glass from the sideboard with the other.

I could stop him. I could pry the glass from his fingers, cry out a warning.

But this is Corbara. Rosa's father, and a danger to her. The man who'd see my husband executed for a crime he didn't commit, who shot my brother-in-law in cold blood rather than face the consequences for his own actions. Corbara, the man who may have murdered Marco, and burned down a house with an innocent child inside it. Who tried to kill the emperor, and will attempt it again.

The glass hovers near his lips.

Corbara, who was my first love, and my first enemy. The words fall to the back of my throat, sinking beyond reach.

He gulps three times, breathing deeply afterward.

There's no time to monitor his reaction—to save Bellino's life, I need to move quickly. If I was wrong about the wine, if Corbara didn't poison it, then he'll be fine.

I dash to the door, heading for my medicine room. Corbara's hand squeezes like a vise around my arm. "Don't rush off now, Livia."

I pummel his chest. My knuckles ache from colliding with his ribs, and he catches my hand on my second punch, eyes glittering with excitement.

"I do like your fire. Have I got the wrist with your little blade? I hope so."

I wrench my arm free and stomp on his foot at the same time. The wine glass careens out of his hand, shattering on the floor, splashing the last meager drops of wine against the front of the sofa. "I'm going." My determination rings through my words and, miraculously, he lets me go. I feel sick as I run to fetch the bandages.

When I return to the parlor, Elisabetta straightens from leaning over Bellino, the relief washing over her face making her look vulnerable and raw. "Thank God you're back."

Corbara sprawls on the sofa, but doesn't say anything, so I ignore him, turning to Bellino.

He lies so still that my heart lurches into my throat with the fear that he's dead, but then I hear his breath shaking with pain, high and raspy.

Elisabetta seems frozen in place, so I nudge her to the side, giving me room to work. She wraps both her hands around one of Bellino's, whispering reassuring words to him. "Keep looking at me, *caro*."

"Wouldn't want… to stop," he croaks haltingly.

"Good. If you can still appeal to my vanity, I know there's strength in you. Focus on me, and don't you dare leave me."

Shoving my sleeves up to my elbows, I gingerly lift the cushion, dropping it on the floor with a wet smack. I want to see if he has an exit wound on his back, but can't risk turning him over, so I slide my fingertips beneath his shoulder. The back of his shirt is dry, his flesh unmarred. The pistol ball must still be inside his chest. Filled with dread, I blot the wound, soaking up as much blood as I can. In the brief window of time before fresh blood coats the wound while I replace the bandage, I catch a glimpse of a bone shard, and determine one of his ribs has been broken by the gunshot. There's no sign of the pistol ball; it must be behind his ribcage. My father has a narrow pair of forceps for such extractions, but I have nothing like that, and lack the experience to know how to locate that wretched bit of lead. I pray the emperor has a skilled surgeon among his staff, perhaps a man with experience in a field hospital treating soldiers. That would be ideal. I don't dare leave Bellino's side, but on my prodding, Elisabetta pokes her head out of the parlor door and shouts for a footman to run to fetch a doctor.

"Livia." Corbara calls for me with such insistence that I dimly realize he's done it more than once. "Livia, I feel sick—my heart is about to break through my chest."

I glance over my shoulder. His pupils are hugely dilated, turning his eyes almost black. He did poison Bellino's glass.

"Make yourself throw up," I tell him shortly. I can't—won't—help him, and Bellino needs me, but I'll give him that little advice. My father always said it was a doctor's duty to provide aid to any person who needed it.

God knows I've shattered that moral already.

"I need help." His voice rises to a desperate pitch. "Please, Livia."

"I have to stop this blood. You need to vomit, Corbara."

He stumbles out of the room, and I turn my attention back to Bellino. His eyes are half-open, and flicker from Elisabetta's face to mine. They look glassy already, with no trace of the usual vivid gleam of humor.

"Livia," he whispers. "Can you help me?"

"I'm doing my best." I squeeze his hand, meaning to be reassuring, but blood makes both our palms slick and instead fear stabs through me. "I promise I reserve my best efforts for my most beloved brother-in-law."

The corner of his mouth twitches in the ghost of a grin.

"I'm sorry if this hurts you. I need to staunch the bleeding."

He closes his eyes, but doesn't make a sound beyond his labored, wheezing breathing as I press the cloth tightly to his poor torn flesh, applying pressure and packing the wound with fresh bandages. "There. Worst part's over."

"If you say so." His lips hardly move, dry and cracked looking.

"Should we move him?" Elisabetta slides her hand under the nape of his neck, looking worriedly toward the sofa. "The floor is so hard."

I shake my head doubtfully. "We'd have to lift him without jostling the bandages or hurting his rib. Caterina went to fetch help. Once the police get here, perhaps they can help get him into bed."

Bellino sucks in a ragged breath. "I can help."

"You've lost a lot of blood," I tell him. The rug beneath him that soaked up the initial pool of it is soggy now. "You might be weaker than you feel."

He turns his head toward me. "I'm not going to die on the floor."

"You aren't going to die at all." Elisabetta squeezes his hand in hers.

He grunts in response, trying to heave himself up onto his elbows. His skin seems to go three shades paler from the effort, and my panic lends me strength as I slide my arms under his shoulders, carrying his weight as he forces himself upright and Elisabetta supports his waist. Somehow, we get him stretched out on the sofa, with a pillow propped under his head.

"I'm cold," he says, and Elisabetta spreads her soft, expensive cloak over him at once.

"Are your hands cold?" She rubs them between her own. Her gaze flicks to me. "What else can I do?"

"Just sit with him, and wait." I crane my head toward the front window. Where are the police? I realize I'm wringing my sticky, blood-caked hands as I wonder if Caterina has even spoken to Mocquard yet, or how long it will be before a doctor arrives. I have no idea how much time has passed.

The sound of a crash ricochets into the room from down the hall, and I lurch to my feet, fearful for Rosa. "I'll be right back." I find Corbara staggering along the corridor, thankfully nowhere near the stairs and Rosa's room. A framed painting of a pastoral scene lies broken on the floor behind him. "What are you doing?"

He squints at me. His pupils are huge, obliterating his brown stripe. "Livia," he says with relief. "I've been looking for you."

I wonder if he vomited. If he did, and if I gave him charcoal, perhaps he would have a slight chance. Nightshade doesn't have an antidote the way the aconite did, though. As he clutches my arm, my skin crawls, and I'd rather shove him off me than treat him.

"Be careful." He sidesteps, dragging me with him. "Watch out for that flame."

"Flame?"

"Yes. Didn't you see the fire? This is a dangerous place to be. We'd better get out quickly. I don't want to be burned again, even though you took good care of it last time."

He's hallucinating, a sign that he's fully in the grip of night-shade poisoning. Even if I treated him right now, I don't know if I'd be able to bring him back from this. I resent having to try, when I should be at Bellino's side. Bellino, whom I tried to save from being shot in the first place, and failed. But my father's words echo in my mind, and as Corbara staggers, blinking at me in fear, I know I can't just leave him alone.

"We'll walk carefully." There's no point in telling him the fire isn't real. He won't be able to comprehend in his current altered state of mind. He doesn't seem to notice the edge of bitterness in my tone, either.

He mutters a few times on the way to my medicine room, talking to someone I can't see, but after a moment I realize it's Ferrero.

"What happened to him?" I ask. I've never dealt with night-shade poisoning like this, but maybe if I can get him talking, it will help to clear his mind.

"He stayed in Florence. We met with some Carbonari members there." Corbara waves his hand, staring at the dagger tattoo on his hand. "It changed my way of thinking—showed me how I could help, so I came to Paris to meet with another nationalist. Roberto Rossi, you know him. Ferrero wasn't interested—he wasn't fervent enough. I knew he'd change his mind, though, and see how I was proven right?" He grins at the wall, presumably seeing Ferrero's face.

Although Corbara seems to remember the past well enough, his memory of the most recent events is less clear, and although he thinks he threw up outside, he isn't certain. I'm not about to go searching the garden for vomit, so once we've reached my medicine storeroom, I help him to empty his stomach, swiping the back of his throat with the soft end of a long feather. There's not much, but the little liquid he does expel is red like the wine. I hold a cup of charcoal water to his lips, but he coughs and turns his head away after only two swallows.

"I can't drink," he gasps. "It's too hard to breathe. I need to lie down." He slumps in a nearby chair, resting his head against the back of it.

I rest my fingertips against his throat, searching for his pulse. It flutters too fast, spiraling erratically as the nightshade rips through his body. "Try to drink it one sip at a time," I tell him, lifting the charcoal again. "Breathe in between."

He can't seem to manage it, though, and his chest heaves with effort for shallow breaths of air. "I'm dizzy." His eyes meet mine, momentarily lucid. "I suppose you think I deserve this. I can't work out how I mixed up the glasses."

"I switched yours for Bellino's when you weren't looking."

His teeth show. A skeleton's smile. "It isn't funny, but it is. You're too good to kill anyone outright, made me do it to myself... Livia, I didn't think it would be so fast."

"It was mostly the root. It's the most poisonous part."

"No one would eat the root," he says. His voice creaks softer with every word. "I see. It has to be mixed into something. I didn't poison yours. I couldn't do it to you. Not you." He twitches his head slightly, as if to point upstairs. "Besides, you need to take care of that child, just in case it is mine." He falls silent. When I look in the right place, I can see his pulse kicking against his throat in a fast, uneven rhythm.

There's no medicine I can give him now. No antidote. There's nothing to do but wait, either for him to recover, or die, or be taken away by the emperor's men. I want to go to Bellino's side. I could check on Corbara again in a few minutes. As I edge toward the door, he stiffens.

"Am I dying?" His voice sounds thin, threaded with dismay.

I lick my lips, but I can't find any comforting lies for him. "I think so."

He gropes for my hand, clutching hard. "You'll stay with me? You won't let me die alone?"

"Everyone dies alone," I say, but gently, and I don't pry his hand from mine. Death is a doorway the living can't cross through. "I'll stay with you."

It's strangely comforting to learn, after everything, I'm not cruel enough to leave him alone with his fear. It's the last thing anyone will ever do for him, and the last time he'll be part of my own life. I can manage this. Perhaps, if she knew, Rosa would want me to. Much as I want to go to him, Bellino is as stable as I can make him, and he has Elisabetta for comfort.

Corbara's sigh of relief trembles with the shaky movements of his chest. "I can't really see you anymore. I wish I could."

It doesn't take long for his breath to catch in his throat, eyes filling up with darkness before drifting closed. His fingers loosen around mine, making it easy to slide my hand free.

I stare at him for a moment before leaving the room. Months ago, if anyone told me I'd sit with Corbara, holding his hand while poison tainted his body from living to dead, I'd never have believed it. I can't pinpoint how I feel, wavering between relief that I'll never fear him again, guilt for that visceral surge of relief, and a bitter sort of regret that he's gone, dead in my own private sanctuary, but all of the problems he created still linger.

I close the door of the storeroom, and hurry back to Bellino.

Elisabetta hovers over his prone figure on the sofa, clutching his hands between hers. From the way she rubs her fingers against his, I think his skin must feel cold, and a knot of dread twists in my stomach. Hopefully it's from shock and not blood loss.

"We've made so many bets over the years." The gentleness in Elisabetta's words undercuts some of her optimism, and her features look pinched. "Remember when we wagered a kiss that the *Divine Comedy* was written by Dante, not Boccaccio?"

"That was years ago," whispers Bellino.

"I can't believe you thought it was Boccaccio. My point is, I'm often right. You're exaggerating because you're in understandable pain and fear, but you're wrong. You aren't going to die. I'll concede a thousand victories to you, with joy, but not this one." In spite of her bold words, I see her chest moving as she breathes too fast, and her eyes flicker uncertainly.

Bellino looks wan and pale, already a ghost. His lips are blood-less, grayish against his marbled skin, but Elisabetta brushes hers against them anyway.

"I love you." Warmth shines through, despite the broken rasp of Bellino's voice. "I think you know, but I need to say it."

"You don't need to say it," Elisabetta murmurs. "You've shown me, all our lives."

His shallow breath shakes in what might be an attempt at laughter. "All our lives… so like you, Elisabetta, to assume I've loved you forever."

"We are forever, Bellino." She squeezes his hands tighter. "I've never been able to give you up, in spite of everything."

"I think I needed you more than you did me." His head twitches in a tiny shake, forestalling Elisabetta's argument as she takes a breath to speak. "You'll be fine… I'll watch over you, if I can."

"You'll regret being so dramatic when you recover from this," she says. "If I say I love you, too, will you stay?"

He smiles, and though it's colorless and deathly, it's somehow beautiful, exuding all his usual charm.

I move closer then, seeing Bellino's eyes half-closing. I'm glad he and Elisabetta had a chance to exchange such tender, honest words, but I fear it was their goodbye. My eyes burn with tears.

I touch his shoulder, inspecting his horribly soaked bandages without touching them, and his eyes flicker open, meeting mine. I can see he wants to speak, but his strength is fading fast. His lips soundlessly shape Niccolo's name.

"We'll save him," I promise.

After his chest stills and the tautness of pain relaxes from his face, I gently close his eyes. Tears spill down my cheeks.

Elisabetta stares, her eyes bright and stricken, her body hardly moving at all.

"I think he was still bleeding, inside," I say. "Sometimes it happens, when there's too much damage." Talking about Bellino's wounds is the last thing either of us needs right now. I feel my face crumple with fresh tears.

"Where's Corbara?" The question scrapes from Elisabetta's throat.

"Dead."

Suddenly, loud footsteps rattle up the stairs to the front door, and the rumble of stern, manly voices echo through the walls. The emperor's men have arrived at last. Far too late. I shudder with the mockery of it all.

"Livia?"

I look up at that disbelieving, tremulous voice. Niccolo stands before me, the haggard shadows under his eyes deep and dark, his shoulders shaking as he stares from Bellino's lifeless body to the gloss of blood pooled on the floor, down my dress and Elisabetta's. I probably look as though I've bathed in it, with blood spattered on my arms, soaking down the front of my skirt. I feel it sticky and flecked over my cheekbone.

Niccolo starts forward. "Are you hurt?"

"No. I tried—Niccolo, I tried so hard to save him." My voice splinters, and I stagger straight to him.

CHAPTER TWENTY-ONE

Paris, April 1857

As well as flavoring sweet or savory foods, the scent of lemon balm is known to enhance moods and energize spirits. Probably due to its heart-shaped leaves, it has a reputation in folklore for healing broken hearts.
— Excerpt from Livia Valenti's book of herbal studies

Niccolo's sudden presence is a miracle to me, a beacon of comfort from the blood-drenched horror. I sink into his arms with relief, hardly able to hold myself up any longer. But that brief flash of comfort dies to something barren and still. He isn't holding me back, not properly, and the mechanical way he pats my back and asks if any of the blood is mine makes me shrivel inside.

Through all the awfulness of the last few hours, I never stopped to think Niccolo might blame me for Bellino's death. Now, it's so obvious. I cringe at my stupidity, my failure.

Barely able to breathe, voice quavering, I tell him the bare bones of what happened, explaining Corbara shot Bellino, and that I tried my best to stop the bleeding but my efforts weren't enough.

Elisabetta says nothing, bowed over her clasped hands. She looks like a statue in a graveyard.

"Where is Vittorio Corbara?" asks Alexandre Lafontaine.

I forgot he was there, and swing my head around to see him. He looks alert and capable, and I'm ready to let him take control of this wretched situation. "He's dead, in the storeroom near the kitchen."

Niccolo's eyes narrow at this, but he doesn't say anything, only pats my shoulder in a perfunctory way again. We both notice at the same time that I'm shaking uncontrollably, and he throws his coat over my shoulders, rubbing my arms in a vigorous way that isn't the least bit comforting.

"How did you get home?" My teeth chatter.

"When Lafontaine heard what was happening here, I persuaded him to let me come, too. I had to see that you were safe." He looks past my shoulder to Bellino, blinking in shock, still unsure that it's real.

I feel the same way.

"He'd just about convinced me of his innocence," says Lafontaine. "I don't think it'll be difficult to drop the charges, now that all three of the real perpetrators are dead." He sounds vaguely satisfied that the threat against the emperor has been tied up so thoroughly, and I swallow against a surge of nausea.

Caterina takes my other arm, easing me free of Niccolo's impersonal grasp. Fresh tears of relief well in the corners of my eyes. I'd be lost without her.

"She's in shock," Caterina says. "I've seen it before, with her and her father, ironically enough." She glances to Lafontaine. "Can I take her upstairs?"

"Yes, of course. No one should leave the house until everything is sorted out…" He trails off, and turns to Niccolo. "Monsieur, we will remove the bodies with the utmost respect."

"You need a bath," Caterina says to me. "We have to warm you up." Taking me upstairs, she tends to me with a strangely maternal efficiency, brisk and warm at the same time. Rosa wakes and begins to cry partway through, so Caterina brings her into the room and I clutch Rosa's little hand in mine over the edge of the tub as she happily squirms and kicks on a thick blanket on the floor beside us.

My thoughts yearn toward to the small phial of laudanum I keep with my other medicines. It would help me sleep, floating on a soft wave of induced serenity, but its side effects can be unpredictable, and I know it should be used sparingly.

I brew valerian and chamomile tea for everyone instead. I wish I could give some to Elisabetta too, but she returned home. My heart aches for her.

After I've fed and kissed an already-sleeping Rosa, I change into my nightgown and Caterina helps me comb out my hair, both of us leaden and silent. It's a relief to be with her. We understand the depth of each other's sorrow, sharing it without words. She doesn't mind that I can hardly speak.

Caterina lays the comb aside. "I'll sleep with Rosa tonight. There's a fresh bottle of milk in the kitchen, and the little bedroom in the nursery is empty since Marie left. I'll take care of her tonight."

"You don't have to."

"I don't mind. I don't much fancy being alone with my thoughts. Having Rosa nearby will be a comfort." She lays her hand on my shoulder. "Niccolo needs you. I'll take care of Rosa, so the two of you can be together."

I give her a doubtful look. I'm not sure Niccolo wants to be near me. Remembering the impersonal way he last spoke to me pains me like pressing on an aching bruise. The stiffness of his shoulders and jaw as he turned away betrayed just how much he wanted to get away. I'd tried to save Bellino and failed. I blame myself for not acting sooner, for not being better at treating him. And Niccolo blames me, too.

"Trust me," Caterina says. "He's hurting, just as you are."

After Caterina disappears to the nursery, I throw my shawl around my shoulders, wrapping it tight for comfort and ignoring the urge to straighten the pillows on the bed. There's no point delaying.

I open the door just as Niccolo hesitates in the hallway, hand half-lifted to knock. Since I expected him to be brooding in his own room, reluctant to see me, I twitch in surprise, but relief washes over his face and he curls his hand around mine.

"Can I sit with you for a while? I—I don't want to be alone."

"Of course." I lead him into the bedroom and close the door behind us. "Niccolo, I'm so sorry— " A tide of remorse splinters my voice as tears burn at the corners of my eyes. "I didn't want it to be like this." I'm trying to sound strong and calm, but my words tighten to a shrill, painful note.

His arms wrap around me, pulling me tight, arms squeezing almost too hard against my ribs but it feels good and comforting to lean against his solid warmth. His words muffle against the side of my neck. "I know." His breath shakes. "I can't speak, either. I've been in shock. Can I just hold you?"

We crawl into bed together. I've left my hair loose, and it spills around us in a tangle of lemon scent—I scrubbed every inch of my skin and hair to wash all the blood off. "Sorry," I mumble, trying to twist it into some semblance of being contained so it isn't in Niccolo's face, but he lays his hand on my wrist.

"I don't mind." He sweeps it aside, fingers trailing over my shoulder until I relax, my back pressed against his chest.

"I tried to save Bellino." It's easier to speak when Niccolo can't see my face, spilling my words into the safe, velvet darkness. "I wanted to somehow fix everything." I let the tears flow, turning the pillow into a damp sponge under my cheek. Niccolo makes gentle hushing noises, but his hand clings to my arm, exposing his tension. I'm seized by the desperate urge to make sure he knows everything. Taking deep breaths to soften the lump in my throat and steady my ragged voice, I tell him everything, from my plan with Elisabetta and the emperor, to Corbara cornering me in the nursery, and Bellino's bravery. "I saved him from the poison, but I didn't think Corbara would use the pistol, not so fast…"

"I didn't realize the poison was meant for my brother," he confesses in a low voice. "Nor that Corbara's death was an accident. It occurred to me that you'd poisoned Corbara for everything he'd done to you, and now to Bellino... I didn't want to ask."

"It wasn't." The whisper burns my throat. "I didn't put the nightshade in Bellino's glass, but I gave that wine glass to Corbara on purpose."

I'm afraid to tell him the truth, but I know I have to. It's a heavy secret. He should know how much I wanted to save Bellino. Niccolo deserves to know there's darkness in my heart.

I wonder if my great-grandmother regretted her actions as soon as the first river of coppery blood flowed to the ground on that sultry night, with the moon watching and mosquitoes whining.

And I reflect on my own choice. I don't regret it. Corbara will haunt me forever, but he won't hunt me.

Niccolo lies very still, silent. "You originally procured the poison, and you swapped the glasses. But you did not administer it. I think that makes a difference."

"I didn't act quickly enough," I tell him, brokenly. "If I had, maybe Bellino would be alive."

"Maybe, for a while. But for how long? He would have gone to the guillotine, and I couldn't have borne that." Niccolo drags my hair across the pillow, stroking his palm across its length, over and over. It sends pleasant tingles along my scalp, but the almost-frantic repetition of his action worries me.

"What are you doing?" I whisper. I half expected him to recoil from my confession, but he hasn't flinched at all. He still holds me close.

He slows, but doesn't stop. "I'm making your hair perfectly smooth. I'm concentrating on that so I can't think about anything else. I won't think about how my brother is dead, or how you were nearly hurt, or how I failed everyone. I was pacing uselessly in the Conciergerie while my family was in danger. You tried to save Bellino, but I was no help to anyone."

I roll over so our faces are close together. His skin feels slightly damp when I brush my lips over his cheeks, and then it's my turn to make comforting sounds and wrap my arms around him while he buries his face in the crook of my neck and shoulder and begins to weep, his shoulders shaking in silent sobs.

Later, exhausted and drained, having spent all our tears, we pour out our hearts, seeking reassurance and absolution for our mistakes. I don't hold any grudge against Niccolo; he's still the most honest, honorable man I know and I'm still in awe of him, and I tell him so. He whispers that I'm stronger and braver than he is, making it sound like I could overcome anything, and I almost believe him. Perhaps I'm not beyond redemption, after all.

In the morning, when I wake with my leg thrown over Niccolo's and his arm draped on my waist, opening my eyes to see his beloved face so close to mine, I feel a tiny spark of hope. The sorrow still crushes all around me, constricting and sharp, but I know that Niccolo and I will be all right.

It's several weeks before I see Elisabetta again, a period where I spend most of my time with Niccolo, making arrangements for Bellino's funeral and for our return to Turin. Elisabetta has cloistered herself inside her stately home, only seeing me for a few minutes the couple of times I stop by. I understand she needs time to mourn and to sort out her undoubtedly complex feelings over the messy tangle of the assassination attempt, and try not to be hurt. Indeed, my own feelings are capricious, and sometimes I don't think I could face seeing her, much as I worry.

Her invitation for lunch both lifts my spirits and casts a shadow of weariness over me. I miss my friend, but I don't see how things can ever be quite the same between us. Sometimes I wish Niccolo and I were already back in Turin, far away from her, and other times I fear I'll miss her blithe, witty remarks and brilliant smile.

She looks beautiful, dressed in a black gown with blood-red satin trimming the sleeves and waist, but there's a sharpness to her smile that I've never seen before. When she looks away from me, staring at the bouquet of roses on the table beside her, her eyes look hard and cold, reminding me of pieces of brilliant blue sea glass.

"The emperor has returned to me." Elisabetta plucks a loose petal from one of the roses. "Camillo can stop harassing me about it now."

"Are you relieved?"

"Yes. Now I can remain in Paris. Otherwise, I would have had to return to Italy with Francesco." Her nose wrinkles. "It was close, though. The emperor avoided me for weeks, but I couldn't seem bitter about that, so I told him I understood he couldn't risk returning to my home, to the scene, until he knew it was safe again, and there was nothing left to fear. I suppose that was a mistake. Men hate that word—fear." Her brows draw together in contemplation. "Then he said it was an ill-conceived, hapless attempt, and there wasn't much real danger, but he had to be cautious for the good of his country."

I sense Elisabetta must have made a sharp retort. In her sorrow and bitterness, she may have taken the remark on the attempt's incompetence as commentary on Bellino.

"I agreed, of course, and pointed out his son is only a year old. Who would rule, if the worst should happen? It's good he's prepared for caution, I said, because many of my countrymen believe the good of our country is dependent on him. He took it as a threat," she concludes succinctly. "The moment was a precipice for my future. But I told him I was afraid it would happen again, and everyone would blame me. That I was afraid he would too, and he wouldn't be able to bear being near me. He always did like it when I was vulnerable."

"It must happen so rarely," I say. It doesn't sound as complimentary as I wanted it to, but her words sting. She made me so painfully vulnerable when she tried to use Niccolo to save Bellino. I want to understand her choice, but I loved them both, in different ways, and there was no possible happy outcome for me in her decision, even knowing she misunderstood my history with my husband.

She gives me a sideways glance. "Yes. In any case, I'm quite glad to be staying in Paris."

"Near Monsieur Pierson's studio."

"I do have some ideas," she admits.

After lunch, she leads me to her writing desk, telling me she has something for me. I watch as she shuffles through the scatter of papers on that polished mahogany surface, noting some sketches.

She sees me looking. "I thought I might commission a portrait from Monsieur Pierson. Perhaps I'll pose as Juliet, with my hair falling around my shoulders, a dagger in my hand. I could wear a red sash, streaming down my bosom like blood."

"I don't know about the sash." I shudder to remember Bellino's blood all over both of us. "I like the dagger, though."

Beneath the sketches lies a letter, to a Signor Orsini. Another petitioner, probably. She casts it aside, and at last produces an envelope with my name scrawled across it.

"This is for you. I hope it will explain things… read it at home, though, won't you, Livia? I can't bear watching anyone read something I've penned."

"Of course."

"And Livia?"

I lift my gaze from the envelope.

"I'm… I hope you and Niccolo are very happy, forever. And I'm glad for your sake that you're returning to Turin. I'll miss you, but I know it's your home in a way that Paris never will be."

I suspect this is the closest to an apology I'll get from her now that the assassination attempt is in the past, and both of us are looking forward. Impulsively, I squeeze her hand.

She does look vulnerable now, her eyes soft and her lips curved in a sorrowful frown.

At home, I slice open the envelope in private, knowing Elisabetta has meant this for my eyes only. Her handwriting is crooked yet elegant, the ink smooth and rich.

Memory of summer 1849

In one of the long, echoing, half-forgotten rooms at Castello Grinzane, an enormous dark blue tapestry, sewn with silver and gold thread like stars, hung on the wall. It was old enough to fray at the edges, and it smelled of dust. As a young girl, perhaps twelve, it fascinated me. I thought of its midnight shade as the color of solitude because I always tried to look at it alone. When I realized the stars traced the shape of constellations, I wanted to see them better. Standing on a chair, I unhooked the tapestry from its hangers. Dust clouded around my head, powdering my skirt. I folded the tapestry over my arm and carried it to the open window, shaking it out. Afterward, I spread it on the floor, poring over the shapes of Pegasus and Callisto.

There wasn't much to do at the castello, *since that day wasn't a day for lessons. Bellino was there, but we'd argued over a game of chess and I wasn't speaking to him. I seized the excuse to entertain myself however I wished, and I'd wanted to include the tapestry in my fanciful imaginings for a while. It was foolish, I suppose. Unladylike and careless, but I liked pretending. Sometimes I wished to be an actress or an artist's muse.*

I wrapped it around my shoulders, throwing it out behind me like a swathe of water, pretending to be Diana, huntress goddess of the moon, wearing a piece of the night sky. I stood in the center of the tapestry, twirling slowly with my arms raised like a strega. *I lifted one of the candles from its sconce, lit it, and tried to imagine I could see my future in the flame, that a vision might unfold in the luminescence of the stars glinting in the cloth's velvety folds.*

I don't know how it caught fire. I thought I'd been very careful, holding the candle pinched straight between my index finger and thumb. The tapestry plumed with black smoke and the earthy smell of hot dust twined with the acrid scent of smoldering fabric. I almost stomped out that hungry little flame, but remembered the gossamer trail of the lace along the bottom of my skirt, and stopped myself. I threw the unburnt edge of the tapestry over the rest, crumpling it up until the last tiny ember sputtered to nothing. I hung the tapestry back on the wall, but the bottom section was marred by a ragged hole and a black scorch mark.

Someone noticed its ruin by the next morning. I was scolded first, for it was known I was fond of looking at the tapestry.

Bellino came to my rescue. We'd made up by then, of course. We were forever fighting and forgiving each other, a cycle as natural as the sunrise and sunset. "It was me," he said, unprompted. "I accidentally lit it on fire. I dropped a candle." When pressed for details or explanations, he only shrugged, his mouth curling into a beautiful sulk.

He had to miss supper that night, but I smuggled a piece of apple torta *and a pear to his room. We crept outside to the garden, wandering through the shadows and looking for bats.*

"You didn't have to," I said.

"I know," he told me.

I hold the paper in my hand, staring into the fire, for a long time after I've finished reading. It helps, a little, to understand Elisabetta and Bellino, and I'm glad Niccolo is safe. But my heart aches.

There's another paper in the envelope, a stiffer parchment. I slide it out, and gaze upon the photograph that Elisabetta and I posed for. My breath catches; I've never seen a portrait of myself, and it feels strange but somehow magical. I look serene and strong, a contrast to the nervousness I remember feeling in the moment. My fingers curl delicately around the foxglove stem, whereas Elisabetta clutches hers too tightly. I feel as if the photograph has caught my affinity for plants, and I like that. I'm staring at the camera, a half-smile on my lips, and Monsieur Pierson has colored the photograph to highlight the golden tints of my brown eyes. Elisabetta looks stunning, of course, her hair like sunshine and her eyes like the sea, skin as pale and lustrous as cream. With her head turned toward me, it looks as though she's whispering a secret into my ear.

My eyes flood with unexpected tears. We have so many secrets between us now, and I would have thought they'd bring us closer. Instead, the dreadful weight of them is pushing us apart. And perhaps that is for the best.

CHAPTER TWENTY-TWO

Turin, July 1858 (one year later)

Though the berries are poisonous and should be avoided, honeysuckle blossoms contain sweet nectar that can be sipped. The fragrant flowers can also be added to salads or teas.
— Excerpt from Livia Valenti's book of herbal studies

Rosa clenches her endearingly chubby fist around a stalk of thyme, humming as she wanders through the herb garden I planted outside our home in Turin.

Niccolo smiles to see her, and it lights up his face, making him look just as golden and bright as the summer afternoon. He slides his arm around my waist. "She loves being outside as much as you do."

"She could hardly help it, since I brought her with me so often while I tended to my herbs."

His lips graze my cheek in an affectionate kiss, and he lingers in our embrace long enough to catch the scent of my hair. I notice, because I can't help leaning close to his throat myself, tempted to nuzzle his skin. The days when we stumbled to find conversation topics and shied away from touching each other feel very distant now. Caterina likes to tease me that she was right, after all, with her Knight of Cups card, only her prediction took longer than was fair to come true.

"I like seeing you and Rosa outside, with the sunshine making you glow," he whispers.

"I can't stay in the garden today. I can hardly sit still for excitement to see Elisabetta again. I'm a little anxious too, though. I don't know why."

"You haven't seen her for a long time, and many things have changed since then." Niccolo pauses, and I know we're both thinking of that awful, endless afternoon when we lost Bellino. I saw Elisabetta only a few times after, before we left Paris. As a year passed, our letters grew less frequent too, and I haven't heard from her in three months. We confessed our darkest secrets to each other, and lived through our worst shared moments. It could have brought us closer, but I believe Bellino's death took too great of a toll on us.

Shortly after his name was cleared in the assassination attempt against the emperor, Niccolo and I returned to Turin. We were both eager to be home, wistfully hoping we might be able to leave some of our sorrow in Paris, but Conte Cavour also wanted Niccolo recalled. Though he hadn't done anything wrong, we all understood he could not continue as a diplomat in Paris when his brother had attempted to assassinate Emperor Napoleon III. Cavour sent another diplomat, a man called Constantino Nigra, as a replacement.

Niccolo didn't seem to mind. "Cavour has other work for me," he said. "I'm relieved to go home, in truth. We found some happiness in Paris before…" He trailed off and I nodded in understanding. I often found myself reluctant to speak of the deaths, too. Bellino's weighed my soul with sorrow, and thinking of Corbara's stained me with bitterness. "But it was never home, living in that rented house, and I'm looking forward to you and I making a real home together, at last."

During our last visit in Paris, Elisabetta responded to the news of our departure in a rather blasé manner. She carelessly pushed a plate of *cantuccini* toward me, avoiding my eyes. "I'll miss you very much, but Camillo wrote me already that he was sending Constantino Nigra instead. I've met him; he's a poet in his free time, and I think we shall get along very well."

"Better than you and Niccolo," I said.

She had the grace to blush. "Livia, darling, I really will miss you."

"And I you, Elisabetta."

Now, she's returning to Italy at last, but in somewhat of a disgrace, no longer the emperor's mistress, and as much as I want to see her, I've no idea how she feels about the shift in her fortunes.

Elisabetta comes to see me in the afternoon, arriving about an hour later than expected, which makes her exactly on time. I think it bodes well that I still know her habits, and hope it means our friendship can resume, at least a little. I don't think I want the intensity we used to have.

She sweeps into the room in a swirl of violet silk, the shade of which seems to match her changeable eyes perfectly, and that familiar lily perfume hovers in the air like a ghost of remembrance. We embrace with slight hesitation, but then she squeezes me tight. "It's so good to see a friendly face."

"You look well," I tell her. Indeed, she's more beautiful than ever. She seems thinner, which highlights her cheekbones and the delicate shape of her neck and arms, and her hair is glossy and golden.

"It's all a mask," she says with a trace of bitterness, flouncing her full skirt about her as she sits in the sunniest chair near the window. "Is that *cantuccini*? Livia, I'm so glad you remembered they're my favorite. What a comfort to have them!" In spite of this, she eats only a bite of the biscuit, discreetly leaving the rest on her tea saucer. "I know I ought to be happy to come home, but

I long to return to Paris. I went to London last year—of course, you know that. I wrote you."

"Yes. You told me their queen, Victoria, is astonishingly short."

She flashes that familiar smile. "Does that sound terribly catty? But she is. Anyhow, London was exciting, and Italy is beloved—my feet positively rooted when I stepped out of the train, I swear—but I'm not yet finished with Paris." She sighs. "Even if the emperor is finished with me."

"Paris is more than the emperor," I say gently. "There's Monsieur Pierson's studio, for one."

She leans forward, nodding her head in a grateful way. "Of course. You always understood my passion for photography, Livia." She picks up her tea, staring into it. "It seems silly to admit it now, but I was afraid to see you again. I thought—I don't know. Everything was so awful, and Niccolo hates me. Everything fell apart after you left."

It started crumbling before I left, which was not entirely her fault, and I tell her so. "Niccolo doesn't hate you. He understands how much you cared for Bellino."

"When the emperor took me back, after, I thought it meant I truly held his heart, that perhaps he'd finally support Piedmont against Austria, or maybe even put aside Comtesse Walewska and keep me as his sole mistress. But it didn't work. Even though he knew nothing of the complicated details of my relationship with Bellino, he came between us. I saw Bellino every time I looked at the emperor, and he never trusted me completely again. I believe he feared I could have Carbonari connections, and if I did not, its members would always be drawn to me to get at him. I ceased to be his mistress only a couple of months after you left."

I nod with sympathy, and inwardly I'm relieved she brought up Bellino first. I think we have to talk about him, lest he become a shadow lurking in the room between us. I already know of her separation with the emperor, partly because she briefly mentioned it in her earlier letters, and also because Cavour tells Niccolo a great deal, but I don't want her to feel gossiped about. "Perhaps you did succeed in persuading the emperor," I say instead. "After all, he and Conte Cavour are meeting in Plombières this month." This meeting is a victory for Cavour, who insisted on opening a bottle of Prosecco when he shared the news with Niccolo. Though this meeting takes place nearly a year after Elisabetta's relationship with the emperor ended, he still partially credits her influence.

"That was nothing to do with me." Her mouth pinches sourly. "I could have whispered to Louis all night, every night, about Italy and he would never have listened. He's only afraid that if he doesn't do something, one of these days an Italian nationalist will actually succeed in killing him. The last attempt in January was a great deal more dangerous than Bellino's."

This is true, for unlike the attempt made by Bellino and Corbara and Roberto Rossi, this last one involved explosives. The main perpetrator, a man called Felice Orsini, threw three bombs into the road in front of the emperor's carriage, as he and the empress travelled to the theatre. They were relatively unharmed, except perhaps a small cut or two from the broken carriage glass, but eight people were killed and close to a hundred and fifty were wounded when the bombs detonated on the busy street. Emperor Napoleon insisted on attending the opera, as planned, to show the attempt hadn't frightened him. I heard Empress Eugénie, her dress spattered with a few drops of blood, reassured everyone that it was their business to be shot at, as the sovereigns. I wouldn't tell Elisabetta, but I was proud of the empress's bravery in that moment.

"I was surprised he wanted to pardon Felice Orsini," I say. When I first heard the news, his name seemed familiar to me and I couldn't remember why, until one early dawn when the memory of Elisabetta's letter to him, mixed in with the portrait sketches she'd shown me, rushed into my mind. I know they corresponded. I think of Elisabetta's descriptive letter of her relationship with Bellino, and can see it would be like Elisabetta to take up his cause for him.

Elisabetta shakes her head. "He was Carbonari. I think he and Louis may have even fought together, long ago, when Louis was only in his twenties. I'm not surprised he could hardly bear to execute him. It turns out that was the last straw, however, for now there he is, discussing war tactics with Camillo in Plombières. Just as my cousin always wanted."

She seems restless, a little bitter, and I try to think of a way to comfort her. I desperately want to ask if her letter to Orsini was on behalf of the Carbonari, but I can't quite summon the courage to bring it up. "At least you're free now. You can do whatever you like."

Elisabetta smiles. "That's true. Francesco thought I'd live with him again now. It baffles me that he's surprised I've refused, when we've been separated for over a year already."

"I suppose he thought the emperor was the only reason for that."

"He wasn't. I'll never live with Francesco again." I wonder if Bellino's memory is a reason for this, but she doesn't elaborate. "I intend to go back to Paris. I don't know when, but I am quite determined."

"I miss it sometimes. I'd visit you there." As I speak, nausea clenches in my belly, and I change tactics, quickly putting down my teacup and lifting an almond biscuit to my lips instead. Sometimes having something dry helps to settle my stomach.

Elisabetta's eyes gleam knowingly. "Another baby, Livia?"

I blink at her unexpected perceptiveness, but there's no point in hiding the truth from her. "Yes, I think so. I'm only in my second month, and haven't told anyone yet, not even Caterina or my mother. How did you know?"

"I saw you nearly every day during the second half of your first pregnancy. I'm quite familiar with the expressions you make when you're nauseous, or when the baby kicks you in a particularly painful way. Does Niccolo know?"

I shake my head. "I haven't told him yet." I think he does know, though. I keep waking in the mornings with him curled around me, his palm resting protectively over my belly. I've delayed telling him, waiting to be absolutely sure. He'll be filled with joy at the prospect of another child, this one of his own blood, and I don't want to risk disappointment by telling him too soon.

Elisabetta offers her congratulations. "I can see you're delighted about it, and I'm glad. You should tell Niccolo now, I think. I ought to bring Giorgio with me next time; he can play with Rosa. It will be good for him to spend time with her. He's rather spoiled, being an only child. I've quite given up on having another."

"You may yet," I say, but try to sound neutral, because I'm not sure if Elisabetta even wants another.

"One never knows, but I had horrendous labor with Giorgio. The midwife warned me he might be the only one, and so far she seems to be correct. I never tried to prevent a child with the emperor, and yet it didn't matter."

"Giorgio is a sweet boy," I say. "Bring him anytime."

"Francesco wants me to send Giorgio to him more often. I usually refuse. It's such a comfort having him with me." She rises from her seat, smoothing her skirt straight. "I really ought to get going. I've a dressmaker's appointment this afternoon. It's been so lovely seeing you again, Livia."

"And you. I hope we can visit lots before you return to Paris."

"Of course." She bumps her cheek against mine in a careless kiss. "Take care, my dear."

Niccolo finds me after Elisabetta has departed, standing near the window and watching Rosa chase a pair of birds swooping along the cypress trees across the garden, while my mother strolls behind.

"Did you have a nice visit?"

I turn to him. A thrill still pulses through me every time he gazes at me with that intense, devoted expression, and I lace my fingers with his in response. "Yes. She didn't stay long, but we found our old candor." I don't need to explain my relief, knowing he understands. "She wants to go back to Paris."

"Nothing stops Elisabetta, once she sets her mind to it. I suppose we might not see her too often, after all."

"It's all right." I understand the bond between Elisabetta and me. It's dark, maybe a little scarred, but also strong. Wherever we live, and no matter how much time passes between our visits, we'll never lose that precious familiarity with each other. Today's visit has reassured me of that.

Her advice flickers through my thoughts, and I decide to follow it. Elisabetta's not nearly as cautious as me, but sometimes I think that's better. "I have something to tell you." I shift Niccolo's hand to my belly, pressing his palm flat and smiling at the way he stills, eyes blazing with bright hope.

"You're making all my dreams come true." His lips brush my cheek. "I've always wanted a big family, especially with you."

I lay my hand over his, pressing it tighter to my stomach. "I love our life together, Niccolo."

Later that night, Caterina and I open a trunk full of Rosa's baby things, sorting out which garments can be reused, and which ones will need to be mended first. The nightshade box, caught in a fold of soft knitted yarn, falls into my lap.

I stare at the polished ebony for a moment, afraid to touch it. I haven't seen it since Corbara took it from me, in spite of searching. I thought it had been lost, probably in his pocket when his body was taken away, and was content to have it gone. It feels smooth and cold against my skin.

Caterina sees my hesitation. "I found it on the floor of the parlor. I didn't know what to do with it, and we were in the middle of packing—I shoved it into my pocket. I suppose it must have fallen out when I was putting Rosa's swaddling blankets into the trunk." She plucks it from my pinched fingertips. "I'm sorry. I can see it bothers you."

"No, don't apologize." I take it back from her. "I'm glad you found it. I don't like the idea of it staying in the house. It's time to get rid of it."

Together, and heedless of the warm evening, we light a small fire in the fireplace. Once the tendrils of flame flick hungrily over the kindling, I drop the nightshade box into the heart of the fire, watching its black shape dissolve to embers and harmless smoke.

A LETTER FROM MEGHAN

Dear reader,

I want to say a huge thank you for choosing to read *The Paris Wife*. If you did enjoy it, and want to keep up to date with all my latest releases, just sign up at the following link. Your email address will never be shared and you can unsubscribe at any time.

www.bookouture.com/meghan-masterson

I hope you loved *The Paris Wife* and if you did I would be very grateful if you could write a review. I'd love to hear what you think, and it makes such a difference helping new readers to discover one of my books for the first time.

I love hearing from my readers—you can get in touch on my Facebook page, through Twitter, Goodreads or my website.

Thanks,
Meghan Masterson

meghanmastersonauthor

@MeghanMasterson

meghanmastersonauthor.com

@meghan_m_author

AUTHOR'S NOTE

Historians grant the Countess of Castiglione varying amounts of credit for her role in Italian unification. Sent to Paris at the behest of her cousin, the prime minister of Piedmont, she succeeded in becoming Napoleon III's mistress, but since their relationship ended before the emperor committed to sending troops to Italy, it's more likely he feared a continuation of Italian assassination attempts than it is that she exerted much political influence. There had already been three attempts, the last of which, orchestrated by Felice Orsini and involving bombs, was dangerous to the public as well. I've implied the countess may have aided Orsini, but there is no historical evidence for that except their shared interest in obtaining Napoleon III's support for Italy.

The attempt on his life outside her house did happen, but I've fictionalized all three of the perpetrators.

The Countess of Castiglione is best remembered now for her early contributions to photography. Her passion for being photographed seemed an odd vanity at the time, but is more easily understood in our modern times when cameras are readily available at our fingertips and photos can be shared online within moments. I think she would have loved Instagram.

Just as she desires at the end of this story, the Countess of Castiglione did indeed return to Paris in 1861, a couple of years after her affair with the emperor had ended. She also remained separated from her husband and refused to live with him again during the two years she lived in Italy before going back to France.

Her return to Paris marked the pinnacle of her collaboration with Monsieur Pierson, and many of her most famous photographs date from this time period, including one where she posed in the Queen of Hearts costume. In fact, Pierson exhibited this portrait of her in the French photography section of the Exposition Universelle in Paris in 1867. Some of the photographs from this period are also her most scandalous, including a series of her bare feet and legs, and one where she reclines under a blanket, possibly wearing nothing underneath. The countess and Pierson had a second period of collaboration in the 1890s, where the aging countess put on her finery and stared proudly into the lens again, though her decision was surprising, since she'd become increasingly reclusive and perhaps mentally unstable. In 1878, she moved into an apartment with black-painted walls and three entrance doors to keep the world outside at bay, a grim hideaway where mirrors were banned. She died in Paris in November of 1899, leaving instructions that her death was not to be mentioned in the papers—a directive which was entirely ignored.

Livia is a fictional character, as are Niccolo and Bellino. Niccolo is loosely based on Constantino Nigra, a real diplomat in the employ of Count Cavour, who accompanied the Countess of Castiglione to Paris and would have been present for most, if not all, of her time as the emperor's mistress. Nigra seems to have been better friends with the real countess than Niccolo is with my fictionalized version of her, and she gave him a photo album as a token of her friendship. Since Niccolo and Elisabetta are often at odds in the story, Livia has taken on the friendship aspect instead.

Livia's interest in poisons proved to be a fascinating topic for research, as I discovered the properties of many poisonous plants have been understood for much of history, mostly as folk remedies and herbal lore, long before the scientific properties were revealed. However, Livia's knowledge remains based in herbal lore, and all her accounts of poisons and remedies are not applicable to modern treatments. Poison Control is a much better resource than any of Livia's theories within this work of fiction.

ACKNOWLEDGMENTS

Writing the first draft is a pretty solitary activity, but bringing a book into the world is not. Thank you to my fantastic agent, Carrie Pestritto, for being so patient with me through the extremely varied first drafts, and believing I'd eventually pull this story together. And I did! I'm also very grateful to my wonderful editor Cara Chimirri—I'm so glad you loved Livia and Niccolo as much as I do. Many thanks to Sarah Hardy, Alexandra Holmes, Belinda Jones, Rhianna Louise, Becca Allen and the rest of the team at Bookouture for all of your help, enthusiasm, and support in sending this book out into the world. Thank you also to Lauren Applebaum and Tara Nieuwesteeg, the best first readers ever. Both of you gave me wonderful advice for cleaning up some loose ends and bringing the characters to life and I owe you drinks when we get to meet again.

I worked on edits for this book during a difficult time in my life, and I'm so grateful to my friends and family for all their support. Thank you to my parents, Patty and Randy Masterson, for proving that you're never too old to be coddled, and making it so easy for me to focus on revisions. My sister, Mandy—I'm so happy you always made me laugh with silly texts during the hard days, and the good ones, too. Thank you to Sindhu Srinivasan—you remind me of Livia in some ways because I don't think I would have gone to the hospital that day if you weren't so worried, and going probably saved my life. Thanks to Scott Thomson, expert in venison chefery (it's a word now, just like lawctor) and the Mississippi Delta Blues. You cooked the best last stomach meal I could ask for.

Last, but certainly not least, thank you to everyone who reads my books. I'm honored, and I hope I can keep them coming for you.

Printed in Great Britain
by Amazon